Gothictown

Gothictown

Emily Carpenter

KENSINGTON
PUBLISHING CORP.
kensingtonbooks.com

KENSINGTON BOOKS are published by

Kensington Publishing Corp.
900 Third Ave.
New York, NY 10022

All Kensington titles, imprints, and distributed lines are available at special quantity discounts for bulk purchases for sales promotion, premiums, fund-raising, educational, or institutional use. Special book excerpts or customized printings can also be created to fit specific needs. For details, write or phone the office of the Kensington Special Sales Manager: Attn. Special Sales Department. Kensington Publishing Corp., 900 Third Ave., New York, NY 10022. Phone: 1-800-221-2647.

KENSINGTON and the K with book logo Reg. U.S. Pat. & TM. Off.

Library of Congress Control Number: 2024949546

ISBN: 978-1-4967-5054-9
First Kensington Hardcover Edition: April 2025

ISBN: 978-1-4967-5056-3 (ebook)

10 9 8 7 6 5 4 3 2 1

Printed in the United States of America

For my friends at Fellows

1864
Juliana, Georgia

*T*he three elders of Juliana met on a late November night in the sanctuary of the white columned Baptist church on Minette Street. Brass candelabra glowed on the altar. Rain lashed at stained glass windows that depicted the baby Jesus in the manger, Joseph and Mary huddled on either side. A wooden cross loomed ominously behind them.

The three men, hoary-haired, hands trembling with age, sat in a row on the front wooden pew. Rain dripped off three hat brims and pooled on the worn wood floor. The men's faces were grim but still fat and flush with good food and whiskey. Minette, Cleburne, and Dalzell were their names. Three of the eight original founders of Juliana, these were the men who'd taken on the weighty mantel of leadership. The ones responsible for steering the fate of the town.

Each man had seen plenty of death in his lifetime. Tuberculosis, smallpox, and scarlet fever had done their duty as cullers of the herd. Childbirth and cancer had taken plenty, too. But this new death the three men were witnessing, this terrible death brought by war, was a different animal altogether. Sons and brothers, nephews and neighbors, had been taken by an enemy with a face, an enemy who should've been an ally. This war-death was an affront to all the people of Juliana held dear. And, if reports were to be believed, it was now about to encroach on their beloved town.

General William T. Sherman had entered the state of Georgia.

Thirty-two years prior, in 1832, in the height of the Georgia gold rush, the small town of Juliana had been established around a gold mine along the banks of the Etowah River. The mine lay two miles out of town and was worked by a crew of simple, strong, and straightforward men. It had been quite profitable for its owner, Mr. Alfred Minette, one of the three elders of the town. Indeed, it was he who'd won the parcel of land in the gold lottery and named the hamlet after his firstborn daughter, the lovely but frail Juliana who had died many years earlier in South Carolina.

The gold mine had not only made Minette rich, but also the men who ran the shops and restaurants in town, and who sold the lumber to build the gracious houses and churches that now lined Juliana's streets. The village had thrived, becoming a popular summer getaway for many planters down in Thomasville and Savannah when they wanted to escape the southern heat.

After his miners had joined the Confederate army and marched off to fight the Yankees, Mr. Alfred Minette had compelled their wives and children to take over the dark, dangerous work. Minette's method of persuasion may have involved carefully worded threats of cutting off these poor folks' credit at the mercantile or seeing they no longer had candles to burn or bacon to fry—but no one had witnessed these conversations, so who was to say? The women and children might not have been able to drill as efficiently as the men, but some work was getting done and what gold was found continued to be shipped off to the stamp mill in Allatoona.

Now the three town elders found themselves in a quandary. Rumor had it that on his path to Atlanta, General Sherman was hell-bent on crushing all Confederate industry along the way. The Yankee devil was not only burning cotton and woolen mills, he was also destroying mines—both gold and coal—and smashing equipment and transport rails.

Juliana lay directly in Sherman's path. Once he found the gold mine, he and his men would blow it to high heaven, taking away the town's one source of wealth. Then, they'd probably burn the town, just for spite. Surely Juliana would not be spared, Minette declared in an ominous voice to the other two men. They must hide the mine and those who worked in it.

"I prayed to my dear, sweet angel, Juliana. My daughter, who watches us from her heavenly abode," he said. "I beseeched her to have mercy on us. To look down from heaven and show us the way."

Then he told them his plan.

Sherman's men stayed in Juliana for five days—long enough to confiscate all the potatoes, rice, corn, salt pork, and livestock they could find and send scouts out for the best spot to cross the river. They did not find the mine nor what was hidden inside.

It had been daring, the plan proposed by Minette. Before the Yankees had gotten to Juliana, the women and children who worked the mine had been supplied with a small amount of water, matches, candles, and blankets, then herded through the entrance and down the deepest shaft. Two members of the Bartow County Home Guard—former miners who knew their way around a stick of dynamite—blew up the entrance of the mine, effectively sealing it shut. They spread the rubble with brush and vines, hiding the entrance from view. The townspeople were told that the women and children had been sent away via train, and were ordered not to speak of the mine or risk the pain of punishment.

Sherman's troops had not discovered the mine. They hadn't even taken notice of the deserted shacks that lined one muddy street just outside of town. In fact, the Yankees had seemed wholly uninterested in the lovely Juliana, proof being they didn't set fire to a single building, not even on the square. But they stayed longer than the elders expected. When they'd finally de-camped and the two members of the Home Guard tunneled back into the mine, a gruesome discovery was made. All the women and children were dead, drowned together in a pool at the bottom of a cavern. The elders ordered the bodies to be left to rot at the bottom of the pool and, making the two Home Guard workers vow their silence, had them barricade the en-trance to the mine once again.

Life in Juliana went on. At the close of the war, the town's young men returned home and learned that the devil Sherman had sent their wives and children far away on train cars to Ohio and Kentucky and Illinois. Alfred Minette reassured the stunned soldiers. Gold fever had moved out West. The real resources of Juliana, he told the men, were the acres and acres of longleaf pines surrounding the town. Minette was building a lumber mill and would give them work. They could earn money and set out to find their families. Or better yet, they could accept God's will, take new wives, and begin new families.

A few of the men left. Most stayed. The two men of the Home Guard were both drowned in the Etowah. An accident, it was said. A tragedy.

One year later, the three elders gathered again in the church. The sanctuary was quiet. The stained glass glowed in the light of the full moon. Jesus, Mary, and Joseph gazed down at the three elders as if to say, You see? All is well. All will be well. But the cross still loomed over them all.

Minette fixed the other two with a grave look. "I have seen the light. The true way."

Cleburne and Dalzell waited.

"We hid the mine, hid the workers, and our town was saved. Not only that, but while other towns around us have withered and died, our Juliana has prospered."

Cleburne and Dalzell nodded. The lumber mill had indeed saved the town.

"Do you see?" Minette continued. "We may not have intended their deaths, may not have wanted such a tragedy, but it happened, and now I realize what must've transpired. Psalm Fifty-four, verse six. 'I will freely sacrifice unto thee. I will praise thy name, O Lord, for it is good.'"

The two men looked at him with expectant eyes.

Minette grinned broadly. "We made a sacrifice. A sacrifice to Juliana, my dear, departed daughter, and she was pleased. Like Abraham did when the Lord required him to bind Isaac and make of him a burnt offering, we left those souls inside the mine for her, and Juliana accepted our offering and in turn has blessed us."

Cleburne and Dalzell considered this. Alfred Minette was a shrewd man. A rich man. Surely, a man who had made so much money knew best. Surely, they could trust that he knew what had brought their town health and prosperity.

"Amen," said Cleburne.

"Amen," said Dalzell.

"From now on," Minette declared, his eyes lit as if from a blue flame ignited within, "whenever there is trouble in our town, whenever storm or pestilence or plague threatens, we know what we must do. We must offer a sacrifice to my dear Juliana, and she will save us."

Cleburne and Dalzell exchanged looks.

"Gentle Juliana," said Minette. It sounded like a pledge. A pledge and a command.

So, "*Gentle Juliana,*" the two echoed.

"*Gentle Juliana,*" all three declared in unison, their voices sober and strong, flames now lit in all their eyes.

It was decided there would be a party. A roasted pig and music and dancing and fireworks for the whole town to celebrate Juliana's narrow escape from the devil's torch. And a day to celebrate this new understanding, at least for these three, of who controlled Juliana's fortunes and what she required.

But before that, the three men would take an oath. None would speak of what had been done to the miners' families, other than to anyone named Minette, Cleburne, or Dalzell. Only the elders possessed this secret knowledge about Juliana's watch over their town. And in the future, be it ten years or one hundred, when hard times befell their town, it would be a Minette, Cleburne, and Dalzell who would do what was necessary.

Chapter 1

The email sat two-thirds of the way down my depressingly sparse inbox. ENTREPRENEURS, REMOTE WORKERS, PROFESSIONALS, the subject line read, then farther down in the body, The Gentle South Beckons You . . .

I paused the Netflix documentary playing in the background, another pyramid-scheme-turned-cult series where the perpetrators of whatever scam were now sitting in a jail cell. It was my jam these days, two years after New York's pandemic lockdown, comfort-watching shows about appalling scammers with God complexes. They reassured me that sometimes the bad guys really did lose. That the people taken in by them, the victims who had suffered major professional and personal loss, could rise from the ashes.

I tossed the remote aside and focused on my laptop. The email was from someone named Bonnie St. John. Probably junk, but what the hell. My Lower East Side restaurant, Billie's, had been closed long enough that I wasn't even getting any emails related to the business anymore. And I certainly wasn't getting any from Mom. So yeah, even spam had started to look interesting. I opened it.

Dear Billie Hope,

Start your life today in a community that cares, courtesy of the Juliana Initiative. Founded in 1832, Juliana, Georgia, is an idyllic, historic, riverside mill town that offers every amenity you need to start your new business, continue your remote work, or set up your practice in a safe, secure, and vital environment.

We may be two hours northwest of bustling Atlanta, but we are a world away from city life. Juliana has always been its own town, and we are proud of it. The weather is warm here and so are the people . . . a perfect place to raise your family or start one at last. Purchase your dream home in Juliana for only $100 and receive a generous business grant from our town council. We welcome all races, genders, orientations, religions, and creeds to Georgia's gentle jewel. . . .

Below the text was a picture of a quaint town square. It was straight out of a storybook—courthouse, bronze statue surrounded by ancient oak trees, rows and rows of street lamps. Below that was a link. I clicked on it, and it took me to the home page of Juliana, Georgia. The site was clean, modern, and professionally laid out, showing more photos of the town. Wide sidewalks, cute shops, and window boxes bursting with flowers. Gorgeous Victorian houses, all crisply painted in pastel shades. American flags on every corner.

My heart did a little flip as I reread the paragraph. One hundred dollars for a house? That couldn't be right. Although I had just recently read an article in the *Times* about how several cities across the U.S. and Europe whose economies were suffering in the wake of the pandemic were luring people to move with offers like this. Topeka, Kansas, offering low-cost apartments to remote workers who wanted to relocate. A town up in South Dakota handing out grants to small business owners.

Even a medieval village in northern Italy giving away castles for free. Times were hard. People were getting creative. But this was beyond.

I clicked through the rest of the town's website. There was the elementary and high school, the river spanned by a picture-perfect bridge that looked like it was straight out of a movie set. A list of services in the county. The population of Juliana, Georgia, was predominantly white—no surprise there—but the numbers showed a fairly racially diverse community. Not only that but, included with the rainbow variety of Christian churches located within a fifteen-mile radius, there was a Jewish temple and a Unitarian church.

My heart beat faster, and every nerve pulsed beneath my skin. I couldn't believe what I was seeing. Replies were to be directed to a generic email address, *info@gentlejuliana.gov*. I hit the link and typed out one sentence.

Is this offer for real?

I sent it. Almost instantly a reply pinged back.

Hello! Thanks for your interest in the Juliana Initiative. Please provide your contact information, and someone will be happy to call and answer any questions you may have.

It was signed *Dixie Minette, Mayor.*

My heartbeat ratcheted up to a full-blown patter. I typed my cell number and hit send, the whooshing sound giving me another wave of goose bumps.

"Peter," I said over my shoulder.

"Hmm?" My husband was on his laptop over at the dining room table he used for his office.

I looked at him, then over at Meredith. She was sprawled out on the rug, my old *Joy of Cooking* open in front of her, finger on a page, mouthing words. She'd started reading early, at four, and showed little interest in typical picture books. Ramsey lay beside her, the entire length of his substantial, orange cat body in contact with hers.

The goose bumps were now covering me head to toe. This was the way I'd felt when I'd first gotten the idea for Billie's. When I'd first envisioned the menu, the atmosphere, the exact space I wanted in Alphabet City. I'd had this same hair-raising sense of *rightness*.

"Do you know anyone in Georgia?" I asked Peter.

"State or country?" He didn't look up from his laptop.

"State."

"I don't think so. Why?"

I carried the laptop over to the table and stood beside him. His reddish-brown hair was mussed, and his round tortoise-shell glasses had slid halfway down his freckled nose. He smelled like my guilty pleasure: the phosphate-packed laundry detergent I bought furtively at the CVS on Orchard, the one with the scent of a chemical version of a grassy meadow. His scent surrounding me, my heart going wild, and every cell in my body on full alert, I felt like I was about to blast off into space.

A small town. Our own house. A perfect childhood for Mere and . . .

Another restaurant for me.

Peter was grinning at me. "Billie. What?"

I pointed at my screen. He read the email.

"Huh."

I leaned over, clicking around the Juliana, Georgia, website for him. "I mean, look."

He took it in. "It's a pretty town. I'll give it that."

"Check this out." I navigated back to the ad, which they'd given the spot of honor right in the middle of the home page. I pointed to a row of adorable Victorian houses. "A hundred dollars, Peter. One hundred dollars."

He looked doubtful. "Not for one of these. No way."

"Yes, for any of these houses. And look. The river that runs through the middle of the town. There's canoeing, kayaking, fishing. A historic mill." I clicked tabs maniacally. "Here's the library. Medical center. Once-a-month farmers market." He was nodding. "And here"—I paused for effect—"is Juliana Elementary School."

He stared at the screen, brown eyes blinking over his glasses. The lenses were smudged. It had been a long day. Back-to-back clients. My husband worked incredibly hard. He saved lives. For the past two years, he had been making a difference in this traumatized world, while I poured all the energy I'd previously used at the café into helping Mere navigate her schooling. She'd gotten off to a rocky start. Her pre-K year had ended abruptly, the following year of kindergarten had been mostly remote, and for first grade, I'd decided to homeschool her.

She needed extracurriculars, but she didn't love organized gymnastics or soccer or dance. What she loved was being outdoors. It had been an exhausting two years of trying to keep my daughter physically as well as mentally engaged, and this spring hadn't made it easy. It had been a brutal few months, cold and rainy, with most of the inside playground options permanently shut down after the pandemic. On rare nice days we invariably ended up taking the long subway ride to the Brooklyn Botanic Garden.

She had no interest in the kids' Discovery Garden there, with the preplanned activities and simple crafts and workers who talked to her like she was a baby. No, my six-year-old wanted to explore every other space: the Rose Garden, the Shakespeare Garden, and the Cherry Esplanade. She didn't want anyone telling her anything about the trees or flowers. She only wanted to take off her boots or sandals and run away from me as fast as she could, weaving through the trees and smelling every plant, whether it bore blooms or not. She liked to create intricate fairy houses in the roots of trees with acorns and rocks. She liked to lie on her back on the grass and see if she could convince the ants that she was a fallen branch.

"She wants to connect with the earth," Peter said. "Which is actually the best thing anyone can do for their mental health." But eventually she was going to need more than the Botanic Garden, and I was afraid I couldn't provide that for her. I'd spent all my restaurant savings on buying a house for my mom, and now, while certainly not broke, I wasn't exactly flush with cash. The cost of connecting with the earth in New York was too high for us.

Interrupting my thoughts, Peter pushed his laptop aside and pulled mine closer, navigating around the site for himself. I glanced over at Mere. Ramsey had jumped up on the back of the sofa and was staring at me as if he knew that something monumental was happening.

"They're giving up to thirty thousand dollars to people who open a brick-and-mortar business in town." He showed me some fine print on one of the tabs. My heart started to race again. I'd been so excited about the hundred-dollar house thing that I hadn't even registered that detail. "Kind of hard to believe. Thirty K?"

"Cities spend a lot more than that to attract manufacturers. They campaign for Amazon warehouses and car plants. Why wouldn't they offer it to regular people?"

He looked unconvinced.

"Peter. Think about it. I could open another café. Just breakfast and lunch this time, so I could be home when Mere gets out of school." I was talking so fast, I was practically stumbling over my words. "We could own an actual house, free and clear. Think about it. No mortgage in our thirties."

"Except I'm forty," he said.

"Whoops." I sent him a wry grin. "So old, but still so sexy."

"We could get some land," he said. "For Mere."

"Have another baby," I said. "Or two. We could afford it down there, easy." Our eyes met. "Our kids would grow up with grass and trees and sky. A place to run. A place to grow old and have a family of their own one day."

As he looked up into my eyes, I could feel our synchronicity kicking in. We were both drawn to the idea of putting down roots in a place that was more affordable with more room to breathe. Peter's parents were gone, his mom from uterine cancer and his dad from a heart attack. Losing his parents in his late teens was the thing that had propelled him into psychology and then family counseling.

We'd always had the essential things in common—both raised in New York, both preferred to spend our money on travel—or a house for my mom, in my case—rather than clothing or jewelry or cars. What we'd never said out loud, but what I was now seeing so clearly was that both of us were still searching for our true home. A place to ground our family, hopefully for generations to come.

Peter bent over my computer again. "I'm just wondering how it'll go over with my clients—"

"You could still see them online, right? Most of them have gone remote anyway, and I know there are all sorts of waivers now for seeing out-of-state clients. And for getting licensed to practice in multiple states, if I'm not mistaken."

"Yeah, no. You're right." He seemed to be thinking about something else.

"What?"

He leaned back. Looked up at me with a thoughtful expression. "I don't know, it just . . . Doesn't it feel kind of suspicious? I mean, out of the blue, this random email pops up, offering a hell of a lot of money for us to relocate to this amazing town?"

"I mean, sure. Maybe. But I think it's legit."

He shook his head, something obviously bothering him.

I felt my face grow warm and folded my arms. "Just say what you want to say, Peter."

He shook his head. He wasn't about to tread on that particular land mine, so I said it for him.

"You think this is the same kind of thing Mom fell for."

He softened. "I'm not trying to be a jerk, here, Billie. Honestly."

I sighed. He had every reason to be skeptical. Mom's situation had started off the same way—a out-of-the-blue email soliciting her participation in *a new, exciting adventure!* And he and I both knew how it was going to end. The cult documentaries on Netflix left little room for doubt.

It had been annoying at first, the ancestry hobby she'd gotten into when I'd moved her out to the house in New Jersey, but I hadn't been seriously worried. My mother and I were close enough, as close as Sibyl Sheridan Lewis allowed anyone in her life, so I figured if there was a problem, I'd know.

I was an only child. When I was young, my parents worked a series of low-paying, grueling jobs and were exhausted most of the time. We never went out to eat. We rarely even gathered around a table. For us, meals were survival, not social occasions. Then Dad died my first year in college. After graduation, I moved back to the city and got a job serving at a popular Northern Italian bistro in Soho. And, strangely enough, that's when I found the key that unlocked my mother.

Mom would show up at the restaurant, usually unannounced, and eat whatever I put in front of her. If things were slow, I'd join her, and we'd talk. At last—in those stolen moments, both of us picking at a plate of osso buco or pumpkin risotto—my mother let me in. She told me everything. All about her hardscrabble childhood, the dreams she'd had then given up. Her love for my father, ground to dust by their never-ending financial hardship. Over a meal, I finally got to know my mother.

And so, the idea for Billie's was born.

She was delighted throughout the whole process of opening the restaurant, my number one cheerleader. And when the restaurant started doing real numbers, I wanted to make it up to her, give her the house my father could never afford. Now I realized it had been a bad idea. The pretty Dutch colonial cottage I bought for her out in New Jersey was just far enough away that she got lonely. Then at some point, when I wasn't looking, her harmless hobby took a turn.

Online she discovered she had Irish ancestors who'd settled in Maine in the 1850s and had started a religious sect. A Quaker offshoot they dubbed The Gathering. The church only lasted a decade or so, but apparently the small town the group had built, though now abandoned, was still standing in western Maine in a desolate corner of White Mountain National Forest.

A couple of days after the lockdown, along with other descendants connected to the original group who met online, Mom decided to sell her house. It went for almost double what I'd paid for it. She moved up to Maine, to a patch of land they'd all chipped in to buy so they could revive The Gathering. From what little she shared in her sporadic letters, the new commune members spent their time either growing their food, fixing up the decrepit buildings in the town, or tracing every twig of their family trees.

Members of The Gathering were only allowed use of phones in case of emergency and computers to send supervised emails. Predictably, they were encouraged to donate whatever spare cash they had to the guy in charge, a person called Uncle Jimbo. If I had wanted to argue her out of going there, the fight was over before it began. One day, she was in Jersey, the next she was gone. I had a few handwritten letters from her, a few generic emails that sounded like PR blurbs, but no phone calls. Me and Peter and Mere weren't enough for her. And there was nothing I could do but accept it and let her go.

Now I squared up to Peter and took a deep breath. "You think it's a scam."

He hesitated. My husband, always so careful with his words, wasn't going to allow this to escalate into an argument. It wasn't his style.

"I'm saying it sounds really, really good. I'm saying"—he broke into a grin—"maybe we sleep on it, do some checking around, make sure the reality matches up with the fantasy."

"And if it does, would you . . . will you actually consider it?"

His fingers brushed my arm, tugging me closer to him. I pivoted until he could pull me onto his lap. He nosed into my neck, inhaling my scent.

"I'll always consider anything you want me to."

"Thanks for not beating up on my mom." Even though I did just that, if only to myself, almost constantly these days.

He kissed my neck then looked into my eyes. "We're all just looking for home, Billie. Your mom. You and me and every person in this jam-packed disaster of a city. That's all any of us really want."

I was quiet, thinking for the first time that maybe I could forgive my mother. If she'd been searching for the feeling of home, I guess I could understand. Because that word—*home*—the way Peter said it, it lit a fire in me, too.

Chapter 2

One week later, after roughly two dozen phone calls and a hasty flight down to Georgia, we were running out of reasons not to move forward. At least, Peter was. I was already 100 percent on board.

Juliana was not the Deep South of moss-draped oaks and perpetual humidity; it was the temperate South, blue-skied and softened with a caressing breeze, thick with green trees and flowers and climbing vines. One of the first people we met was Bonnie St. John, the woman in the mayor's office who called both Peter and me "hon." She had informed us in her smokey voice that there were currently only two places to eat in town—a barbecue place called Pig Out that was only open on the weekends, and the Dairy Queen. If I chose to open a place like Billie's, my old restaurant, I would be the only breakfast and brunch game in town. If things went well and I decided to expand my hours and menu, I'd be the only upscale dinner spot as well.

Peter and I drove down a network of streets lined with picture-perfect Victorian houses. Several I recognized from the website, all offered with the same unbelievable $100 price tag. It had been pure luck finding the house outside of town, the one sitting on twelve acres. When I'd called Bonnie to ask about it, she told me that the house and acreage were the property of the town and weren't included in the hundred-dollar offer.

The scrappy New Yorker in me, unwilling to let anyone tell me what I could and could not do, kicked in. I explained how we'd always wanted land, how my daughter adored the outdoors. I told her I planned to plant vegetables and herbs we'd be using at the restaurant and how that would be an even bigger draw to the place. Bonnie told me she'd see what she could do.

Back at the hotel, we'd met with three couples who'd made the move, asking them every imaginable question we could think of. Peter stayed maddeningly quiet. I knew he wasn't trying to tamp down my enthusiasm. He was just in his head, weighing all the pros and cons, managing expectations. Allowing himself the room to make a fully informed decision. But I had made up my mind.

It had happened earlier that day during our tour of the town. I'd seen a bronze statue in the square and made Peter park so I could get a closer look. The statue was a little girl, the original Juliana, according to the plaque, the daughter of the founder of the town. She appeared to be about Mere's age, was barefoot and wearing an old-fashioned dress with pantaloons. Her right arm was outstretched, a butterfly resting on her finger as if it had just alighted there.

A little girl who loved nature. It felt like a sign.

Now, back in our apartment in New York, as Peter and I bumped around each other in our cramped kitchen clearing the dinner dishes, the silence between us weighed on me. The next words we spoke were going to change everything, I knew, no matter which way we decided to go.

I ran water into a cast iron skillet, feeling shaky with nervous energy. I was about to burst, sick to my stomach. Was Peter waiting for me to say something? Was he reluctant to break the bad news that he didn't want to move? Or was he still truly un-decided?

"The suspense is killing me," I finally said, as lightly as I could manage.

Peter wiped the last dish and put it in the cupboard. He turned and leaned against the counter. I could feel him watching me as I worked on the skillet.

"How long has it been?" he asked. "Since Billie's closed? Since your mom left?"

"Two years and one month."

I didn't even have to count. I'd closed the restaurant on March 15, 2020, the day before Mayor de Blasio shut down all the restaurants in the city except for takeout or delivery. Two days later, my mom had called with the news that she'd put the house on the market and was moving to Maine. The two events had happened so closely together, it was like they'd converged in my mind as one single, colossal disaster.

So, yes. Two years and one month to the day since I'd pulled the plug on my greatest career success, sending my employees home with boxes of food and admonishments to apply for un-employment ASAP. Two years and one month since I'd ceased to be Billie Hope, restauranteur, and had become Billie Hope who stayed home, made pancakes in a cramped kitchen for her daughter, and watched way too many lurid Netflix documen-taries. Two years and one month since I'd had an actual conver-sation on the phone with my own mother.

"What?" I asked him.

"I'm trying to figure out how to word this."

"Just say it." I let the pot clatter in the sink and faced him.

He sighed. "Okay. You can't just do this for yourself, Billie. You know that won't work."

"Who said this was just for me? I'm thinking about Mere, too. And you. This would be better for all of us." It was mostly the truth.

"It's not going to be the same, opening a restaurant in a small town. You're not going to have the critics and movie stars and ballplayers or whoever coming in and out every day."

I laughed. "I know that, Peter."

"I'm just . . ." He shook his head. "I'm worried it won't be the same for you."

"Look, I liked that part about Billie's—the glamour—I won't lie," I said. "But it's not the part I miss the most. It's not the part I truly loved about the place."

"You could always start another restaurant in New York."

"I could, with a slew of investors. And you could go on seeing people traumatized by living in shoeboxes for the past few years. And Mere could grow up playing kickball in the hallway outside our apartment door. But is that what we really want?" I cocked my head. "Is that what *you* want?"

He didn't miss a beat. "I want what's best for my family. I want my wife happy. My daughter safe."

"Ninety-six percent of Juliana High School's graduating class not only attend, but graduate from, a four-year college," I said. "And the crime rate is practically nonexistent."

He did that laugh-head shake thing he always did when he knew I'd won an argument. "Okay."

"Okay, what?"

"Okay, I think I'm up for it. I'm up for moving. As long as you know what you're getting into." He smiled at me, his clear brown eyes dancing through his glasses, freckles standing out against his flushed skin. I giggled somewhat nervously, and then he did, too. The next moment, we both burst into giddy laughter.

"Oh my God," I said. "What the hell did we just decide?"

"We're leaving New York."

"We're leaving New York," I repeated, the words really hitting me. "I mean, just saying it—"

"—feels right?" he supplied.

It did feel right, in a kind of heart-swallowing, don't-look-down way. Finally, after all the heartbreak and fear and grief we'd experienced in the past few years, something was going our way. We were being proactive. Bold. Taking steps to ensure our family had a future.

Just then, Mere, in rainbow cloud pajamas and wet, side-parted blond hair hanging over one eye, appeared in the doorway. "What are you guys laughing about?" Ramsey brushed past her, then leaped up onto the counter and surveyed us three. King of the Kitchen.

"Shoo!" I waved him off the counter, and he let out a crotchety meow, swan-dived through the opening onto the living room floor, and skidded out of sight.

Mere ran to Peter, hugging his legs ferociously. "What's so funny?"

I scooped her up, burying my nose in her wet blond hair. She smelled like vanilla and mint toothpaste.

"You remember when Daddy and I went on a trip the other day and you stayed with Jane?"

She nodded. "You went to Georgia."

"Right. Well, we were wondering if you'd like to move down there. There's a small town called Juliana that looks really nice, we thought. Like a good place for our family."

She frowned. "How small?"

"Way smaller than New York. It would be like living in a little village but also the country."

"Like the park, but everywhere?"

I nodded. "Yeah, it's like a big park. With fields, meadows. A river with a mill and a bridge. It's got woods, too. Forests."

She laughed at that. I laughed, too, because the description sounded almost too idyllic to be real. "Does that sound good, babe?"

"We can talk about it as much as you like," Peter said. "We can answer any question you have."

"I don't have any questions." Mere grinned. A few of her bottom teeth were missing, and for some reason, the sight made my heart twinge. "No questions!" she repeated louder. Now she was bouncing up and down in my arms. "I already know the answer is yes! I want to live in the country!"

"Makes decisions like her mother," Peter said wryly.

"With her exceptionally trustworthy gut," I said, then addressed Mere. "You promise you won't miss the subway rats and the cockroaches?"

"I won't miss them at all!" She leapt out of my arms, ran into the living room, and started bouncing around the furniture. This riled Ramsey up so much he started racing across the tops of the furniture like a motocross bike with orange fur. We followed Mere. Peter picked her up and tossed her in the air, and I turned on some music. The Stones' "Honky Tonk Women" blared even though I knew I'd catch hell later from at least two neighbors. I didn't care. We were all laughing and dancing, giddy with the idea of a completely new life, with the thought of the freedom of cutting ties to this grim, gray city.

From the mantel over the fireplace my phone trilled. I picked it up. Opened the email from bonnie@gentlejuliana.gov and read it.

"Peter," I said. "Peter, Peter, Peter!"

He and Mere both stopped dancing and looked at me.

I held up my phone. "Bonnie from the mayor's office wrote back. The town council members have decided to let us buy the twelve acres and the house. They've sent a contract."

His eyebrows shot up. Mere looked from him to me.

"We're really doing it," I said. "We're about to be the owners of our very own home. We're moving."

Chapter 3

Exactly two weeks later, on a perfect Friday afternoon, Peter, Mere, and I rolled into Juliana, Georgia.

Peter had driven the nine hundred miles from Manhattan to northwest Georgia in our newly purchased, gnat-encrusted Subaru Forester pulling the rented U-Haul behind it at approximately fifty miles an hour. Although my husband could navigate the MTA or hail a taxi with his eyes closed, behind the wheel he apparently turned into a ninety-year-old grandma, in no hurry at all. I didn't mind. Mere and Ramsey were cuddled in the back seat, Ramsey having declined his crate somewhere back in New Jersey. Peace permeated the car. We would arrive at our destination in exactly the right amount of time. Even the journey to our new home was heaven.

Juliana was only a couple of hours northwest of Atlanta, but it might as well have been a hundred, the way the town seemed totally separate, insulated and cut off from the sprawl of the big city. After exiting I-75, it took a good twenty minutes of winding, two-lane country roads past boiled peanut and tomato and peach stands to get to the square. But when we finally arrived, I was dumbstruck all over again, as if I was seeing the place for the first time.

Or maybe I was just seeing it through Mere's eyes. From the squeals of delight coming from the back seat, it would appear that to her, Juliana looked like something out of a fairy tale or a movie studio backlot. She kept calling out for me to look—at the small houses on the outskirts of town, at the Dairy Queen with the old-fashioned dip cone for a sign, the white clapboard church with a picket-fenced cemetery.

I rolled all four windows of the Forester down and let the soft April air flow over us. It was laden with the scent of flowers and cut grass and charcoal. A frisson of excitement passed through me as I hungrily took in the sights of the town. It was perfect. Puffy white clouds drifted over the horizon, slowing my blood pressure to match its rhythms. While the town wasn't exactly bustling, there were a handful of people out, walking up and down the wide, shady sidewalks. There were even a few golf carts buzzing around the square.

I wanted to laugh in anticipation, cry in relief, scream with joy. Like I'd written in the brief, one-page letter I mailed to Mom at the compound in Maine, I couldn't wait to start our new life. I hadn't gotten a reply to that letter yet, let alone an email or phone call, but it didn't matter. At the going-away dinner my friends from Billie's had thrown me, I'd been showered with plenty of love.

Peter cruised into the downtown area, with its neat square, red brick courthouse, and bronze statue of the eponymous Juliana with the butterfly on her finger. Around the pedestal of the monument, the black fountain shot out multiple sprays of water. I scanned the main streets that extended from the square, each of them neat as a pin and lined with the wrought-iron street lamps. Minette Street, Cleburne Street, Dalzell Avenue, and then a host of others that Bonnie St. John had told us were named after the other founding families.

Mere's nose was smashed against the window. "Look, there's a Street Road. Why they didn't just—"

"—call it Street Street?" Peter said.

I let out a short laugh. "Okay, stop it. No jokes. Seriously, *y'all*, we're officially Southerners now. Juliana is our town, and we will be proud of it. Got it?"

Peter glanced at me with warm eyes and that wry expression that never failed to make me feel protected and understood. I covered his hand with mine, and we squeezed at the same time. I leaned my head back and breathed out every bit of the pain of the last few years. Enough of grieving the past. It was time to focus on what lay ahead.

"Go around again, Daddy," Mere said, and he did.

I checked out the vacant storefronts that dotted the town square. Bonnie had told me there was no rush to choose one, but I didn't want to lose out on the perfect spot. And clearly, the decision wasn't going to be easy. The spaces all looked incredibly inviting, and lots of them were big enough for a restaurant. I'd have to do some serious reconnaissance in the next few days. As soon as I chose a spot, the new business grant, thirty thousand dollars, would be deposited in my bank account.

And then . . .

Then I'd be busy again. Then I could fill my mind with the chaos of starting a new restaurant. Stop obsessing over Mom. Focus on Mere and Peter. Restart my life.

I gazed out the window, allowing myself to be enraptured by every sight Juliana was offering me. Trees shaded every corner of the square. Gardenias and impatiens and ivy spilled out of pots clustered on the sidewalk. Rows of old, arched brick storefronts with tile thresholds flanked each street. There was an antique store, a lawyer's office, a florist, an insurance office. The small hotel, Juliana Inn, with three floors of lacy, wrought-iron balconies. A bar with a sign that read THE DREDGES. And on one corner a perfectly preserved, old-fashioned movie theater, proclaiming itself on a huge sign lined with lights, THE JULIANA. Its marquee showed a double bill of *Pleasantville* and *The Sandlot*. The only thing missing was a bookstore, a situation which undoubtedly would be rectified eventually.

When we passed a barbershop with a spinning barber pole out front, Mere piped up. "Mama, what's that thing for?"

"Good question," I said, and googled it on my phone. I swallowed when I read the origin of the helical poles: they indicated that bloodletting occurred at an establishment. The blue stood for the veins, the red for blood, and the white for the bandages applied to patients. I slipped my phone under my leg. "It just means that's where you can get a haircut."

Peter turned left onto Dalzell Avenue. We drove past a tiny brick post office and Laundromat, then two more blocks of quaint, gingerbread houses. American-made SUVs were parked in most driveways. American flags waved from the same porches. Bikes and scooters lay on front walks. I saw a handful of kids tossing a football.

I was already dreaming about the new café. What I was going to call it. Not Billie's. Billie's was the blue-tiled, hole in the wall in the East Village, with the stained-glass windows over the front and back doors. It had been a punk bar in the eighties, a dry cleaner in the nineties, a macaron shop in the aughts, and then a pet groomer's before I signed the lease. Billie's was my staff. Billie's was the regulars. For a couple of weeks, Billie's was Pacino's favorite place to sit with an espresso and crepe, and the place where Taylor Swift supposedly met up that one time with her secret boyfriend. I couldn't call another place by the same name.

Billie's had been my first love, my first heartbreak, the place I dreamed might make me a millionaire and a celebrity chef. Prepandemic, I was on my way to reaching that dream. We were fully booked with reservations from eight o'clock to ten at night. Walk-ins, ever hoping for a last-minute cancellation, typically waited on line for over two hours with no complaints. My applesauce hotcakes, sage sausage and egg frittata, and specialty cocktail, a fig-infused Paloma, got written up by every food critic in the tristate area.

I rolled out new dish after dish. There were wild seasonal coffees and cocktails, twists on breakfasts from every corner of the globe. Medialunas from Argentina, Middle Eastern Haleem, hagelslag on toast from the Netherlands. It seemed like I could do no wrong—breakfast, lunch, and dinner were always packed.

And then the goddamn virus. After a couple of weeks of struggling to transition to takeout, I made the decision. I prepared one last family meal for my staff, my friends, and while I was doing it, came the lockdown order, effective the next day. I closed up shop that night. Called it a furlough because that's what everyone was calling it, but I knew better. People were scared. People were sick, even dying, so I decided there was only one thing to do. Let Billie's die with them.

"Mere," Peter said, shaking me loose from the memories. "Hold on to Ramsey. We're almost there, and I don't want him lost in all the luggage."

Dalzell Avenue had turned into Route 140, which ran parallel to the river, the Etowah, a golden-brown ribbon of water bordered by mossy banks and overhanging trees. Three-quarters of a mile down the road, we caught sight of a bridge made of huge old beams and riveted steel that spanned the water. On the opposite side of the river, partially obscured behind a row of trees, sat the old mill, a deserted, shingle-and-stone building with a huge paddle wheel that turned steadily.

I noticed a sheriff's vehicle parked next to the old structure. A young man in uniform was rolling up yellow tape that appeared to have been strung out between a stand of trees and a stone building. I straightened, peering out the window, trying to get a better view between the trees. Had there been an accident? Some sort of crime? I started to say something but then stopped myself. Peter hadn't noticed it, nor had Mere. No reason to call attention to it.

Just past the mill, we turned left onto an unmarked dirt road. Peter slowed as the Subaru and U-Haul bumped over the road, and we wound around clumps of pines and rolling fields. There was a huge, twisted oak that spread its gnarled branches over the road, then the ground rose gently. At the top of the swell, the house finally came into view. Peter braked, letting the car idle, and we all stared.

The stately Italianate Victorian house, nestled between towering magnolias, rose up like a perfect wedding cake. White with black shutters and doors, high windows, and a wide porch, it appeared to have been freshly painted. They must've done that last week. Everywhere I looked, I saw triple-arched windows, stained glass mullions, intricate wooden corbels, sparkling in the sun. Someone had mown the grass out front and planted a simple bed of lantana and petunias on either side of the front steps.

It was even more beautiful than I remembered.

"Wow," Mere said, craning her neck and visoring one hand over her eyes to block the bright sunlight. "We live in a mansion."

I glanced over at Peter. He had an odd look on his face. "Peter? You okay?"

He shivered, like I'd startled him. "I guess I didn't remember it being so big."

"We're going to have to hire a house cleaner," I said. "A very energetic one."

Peter stepped on the gas, and the car lurched forward. In front of the house, he switched off the ignition and we all climbed out, stretching and taking in the sight of our new home. In every direction, green fields met forests. Wildflower-dotted hills rose in the distance, meeting the wide blue sky. The sun was warm, and the air smelled sweet, redolent with some kind of blooming flower I didn't recognize.

At that moment, Ramsey shot out of the car and streaked around the far side of the house, to the paradise beyond.

"Ramsey!" Mere took off after him.

"Mere, no!" I yelled, but Peter caught my arm.

"Let her go." He spread his arms wide, to the rolling fields and the woods beyond them. "She's safe."

I let out my breath. I'd have to get used to letting my daughter out of my sight. We were in the country now. It was safe. I looked around the left side of the house. An old black sedan was parked there, behind the one fantastically twisted oak tree that hunched among the magnolias. No one had mentioned there'd be someone to meet us. The key was supposed to be under the welcome mat.

After a few moments, Mere reappeared around the opposite corner of the house. She was still running, but now she was crying, too. I could see her red face as she got closer.

"Ramsey's gone!" she wailed and flung her little body at me.

I caught her. She smelled like sleep and cat and French fries. "He's not lost, baby. He's just exploring."

"But he's an inside cat."

"We're in Georgia now, so he can be an outside cat, too."

She turned her flushed, teary face up to me. "He doesn't know how to be an outside cat."

"Sure, he does. It's instinct, in all cats. He's out there right now, remembering everything he has to do to take care of himself." I smoothed her hair. "Why don't you run up there to the house and make sure you leave your scent everywhere, so Rams can find you when he's ready to come back?"

She gave me a doubtful look but turned and approached the steps. I watched her gingerly mount them then walk along the porch, her hand trailing over the rail. Her face looked grim, lips pressed together like she was trying not to cry. I turned to

Peter, but he was busy at the back of the U-Haul, unloading the boxes. It would be fine. Ramsey would come back. We'd all get used to the space. The freedom. The quiet.

I lifted my eyes to take in the massive house again, to let it sink in. It was built in 1870, after the war—that being the Civil War, the event which I'd come to realize was the date everyone down here kept time by—by the young town doctor, Silas Dalzell. He married one of the Minette girls, one of Juliana's younger sisters. Alfred Minette, the father, gave them the land and built the house as their wedding gift. Four bedrooms, four baths. All manner of drawing rooms and parlors and even a conservatory. There was a new roof, updated plumbing and electric, and the place was furnished, mostly from the original owner's pieces.

Bonnie had told me the house had belonged to either a Dalzell or Minette until the 1970s when it was abandoned, furniture and all, by Oxford Dalzell when he divorced his first wife and moved closer to town. After that it moldered gently, peacefully, until the mid-1980s when the most recent owner, an older widower named George Davenport, purchased it. Davenport spent quite a bit of money refurbishing the systems and patching up the foundation.

"What happened to Mr. Davenport?" I had asked, almost afraid to hear the answer. A house that beautiful had to have a catch.

"One of his great-grandchildren moved him to an assisted living place near them in Orlando. George Davenport was a sweet old man, healthy as a bull. But at the end, his mind wasn't right, and his family wanted to be closer to him." She added that he'd passed away a few years later.

On the porch, Mere was now rocking energetically down the line of chairs while Peter ferried our luggage up to the double, etched-glass front doors. I sensed movement above that, on one of the upper stories. I looked at a set of windows, triple arched, stained glass, right in the middle of the second story.

In the center arch stood a man with a head of woolly, white hair. He was dressed in a rumpled, beige-colored suit, complete with a lopsided, brown bow tie. He stood motionless in the window, staring down, it seemed, right at me. In his arms was Ramsey.

Chapter 4

The old man met us at the door. Ramsey slipped between his legs and straight into Mere's waiting arms. She snuggled him and regarded the man with steady eyes. That was my girl, tough New Yorker even at six years old.

"Hey there." The man ducked his head when he mumbled the words, but before that I'd seen kindness in his pale blue eyes—and a sort of innocence. Up close, I saw that his suit, the color of muddy river water, was frayed at the lapels and sleeves, and so wrinkled it gave the impression of having been run through the washer and dryer instead of dry cleaned. The shirt collar had a yellowish tinge to it and the buttons looked brittle. He'd dressed up for us, clearly, which wasn't something he regularly did. I liked him immediately.

"A warm welcome to our fair city," he said, as if he'd been coached. "I'm Major Minette, Dixie Minette's brother. Well, brother-in-law."

Dixie Minette, the mayor. Her picture on the Juliana website had shown an elegant, platinum blond woman in her seventies who wore a large gold and diamond broach in the shape of a

letter *J* on the lapel of her jacket. I hadn't spoken with her, only
Bonnie, but Mayor Dixie Minette had signed the official documents about the stipend and sent us a letter handwritten on her
elegant mayoral letterhead, welcoming us to Juliana.

"Major's not a military rank, it's just my name," Minette was
saying. "Although I did serve in Vietnam. But that was a long
time ago." He shook Peter's hand then mine, and I noticed his
hand trembled.

"Billie Hope," I said. "My husband, Peter. And this is our
daughter, Meredith."

He ducked his head at each one of us, and Mere nodded
back, studying him. She was used to eccentric people—the city
was full of them—but still she seemed on her guard.

"Mayor Dixie told me to open up the place for you," he said.
"She said it would need some airing out."

"Of course. We appreciate it," Peter said.

Minette noticed Ramsey struggling in Mere's thin arms. "So
what do you think about your new house, Meredith?"

"I've never lived in a mansion before."

I locked eyes with Peter. Our lips twisted in matched sup-
pressed amusement and maybe an admission that we probably
would've answered in the same way she did. We were all kids
here, giddy at our fortune. At the adventure that lay ahead
of us.

"It is a big old house," Minette said. "Not as big as mine,
though. I used to get lost in my house when I was little like
you." He looked over at the Subaru and U-Haul. "That all you
folks brought with you?"

I realized, for the first time, how small the U-Haul looked.
But it was all we needed. From the time we got married and
moved into the East Village apartment, Peter and I had only
ever had an apartment full of Ikea and whatever furniture I
thrifted. And most of that had seen better days. Knowing the
house in Juliana was fully furnished, we'd ending up setting out

most of our pieces on the sidewalk outside our building. We'd brought our clothes, the few pieces of art we had, and the sets of china and crystal and silverware that Peter had inherited from his Massachusetts grandmother, all monogrammed with a delicate *H*. Our life's possessions really didn't amount to much, I realized.

"We like to travel light," I said.

"Can I go inside?" Mere asked.

"Go on," I told her. "We'll be right behind you."

Mere slipped through the open door, Ramsey secured safely in her arms. Minette fished for the keys and handed them to me.

"Roofers finished up last week." Minette beckoned us to follow him, and we all entered the house. "Furnace and AC's been replaced. The floors could use a redo. Don't think they've been upgraded since old Silas built the place." He gestured around the wide, gracious, immaculately appointed hallway. "You could get rid of some of this dusty old furniture. There's a home goods–type place on the square that a Miss Coleman from Chicago just opened up. Got lots of pillows and cheese boards and dish towels with funny sayings on 'em. I bought Mayor Dixie one that says, YOU HAD ME AT MERLOT."

He chuckled. Peter and I smiled.

"'Course, there's always Cleburne Antiques," Major went on. "It's down on the square. Mrs. Cleburne used to run it, but the son does now. Jamie. Although you're chock-full of antiques here."

"What do you do, Mr. Minette?" I asked him, even though I was starting to feel antsy. I was longing to settle in, maybe shower, and explore our new house. But I should get things off on the right foot with this man. Show I was the neighborly type.

"Oh, this and that." His eyes slid away from mine. "I'm not married. Never found me the right girl. Always lived with

Mayor Dixie and them. Her son, Toby, and her husband, my brother Bobby. He was one of them lady doctors, even though he's long gone now. My brother Bobby, I mean. Bobby and Mayor Dixie's son, my nephew, Toby, does carpentry and some remodeling around town. He's single, too, but I guess you're out of the runnin', Mrs. Hope, being that you're already married."

I almost laughed from the sheer volume of convoluted information that I'd just received. Major Minette was clearly an odd fellow, but he was endearing.

"That's right." I winked at him and patted Peter's arm.

"Anyways, Toby likes me to look after Mayor Dixie's place, so she has more time for city business. I keep up with repairs, cut the lawn, trim the hedges, and look after her roses. She don't like to pay nobody to do that. She likes how I do it."

I nodded. "I appreciate you meeting us, Mr. Minette."

"Call me Major." He smiled shyly. "Mayor Dixie wanted to have everybody out here for you, waving flags and serving chicken salad and tea. Either that or she wanted a parade. She likes a to-do."

"That was nice of her," Peter said.

"Ox and James told her to hold off. Give you folks a minute to get settled in."

Ox must be Oxford Dalzell. And James was the Cleburne who owned the antique shop. It was going to be a challenge keeping all these families straight.

"Mayor Dixie sent me with a basket full of food to get you started. I set it in the kitchen. There's dinner for tonight and some of her preserves. Also, some staples she thought you might need."

"Thank you," I said, hoping this was the end of it.

But Major wasn't done. "Flour and sugar, ketchup and mustard, salt and pepper, what have you. Now, just so you've been warned . . . she's going to want to introduce you all around town soon as you're settled. To the old-timers and the new-comers, too. My sister-in-law loves this town, and she doesn't take lightly what kind of commitment you folks are making, uprooting your life in New York and moving down here. She's grateful. And I am, too. We hope you'll agree with us what a rare and special place Juliana truly is. Gentle Juliana . . ." His pink, mottled skin creased around his eyes and mouth, and for a moment I thought he was going to cry.

I took his hand. He clutched mine with his two big, withered bear paws. The skin was thin and dry, and I could feel the corded veins beneath. "Tell your sister-in-law thank you, Major, and I look forward to meeting everyone." I withdrew my hands. Waited for him to get the message.

He stared off into space, then snapped papery fingers. "There was something I didn't want to forget. Something Mayor Dixie said I ought to mention to you."

My throat tightened the slightest bit. "Is there a problem?"

"Oh no, no problem. It's just . . ." He rubbed his jaw and laughed nervously. "Lordy, why can't I remember anything these days . . . ?" He went silent for a moment, then suddenly brightened. "I got it. There's a well on the property, near the bluff on the property line. Not the well you get your water from, but another one."

Minette planted both hands on his wrinkly suit coat just where his hips should be and ambled down the length of the porch. Peter and I exchanged tight looks then followed. Minette gazed out over the western end of the property, over the rolling fields and the clumps of trees. The sun was setting now, putting on a glorious orange and pink and lavender show. He stretched a shaky hand out in the general direction of the setting sun, but I couldn't really tell what he was pointing at.

"I believe Old Silas Dalzell dug it when he dug the one for the house, probably for crops or livestock or something. It's way over yonder toward the bluff, before you get to the creek. When George Davenport moved into the place, he didn't have any cows or nothing so he didn't use the old well, but he never properly capped it either. You know, with a concrete slab so nobody would accidentally fall in."

I glanced over at Peter, my throat constricting. He looked back at me, and I could tell he knew what I was thinking. *Mere?* *Around an open well?* Had we put her in a compromising, dangerous position in our new home?

"No one mentioned anything about a well," I said. "I don't remember seeing anything about it in the contract."

Minette's face flushed, and he seemed at a loss for words. "Oh well. I don't much look at contracts. That's my sister's area."

"We'll be careful," said Peter, his tone gentle but firm. "In the meantime, we'd appreciate it if you'd send someone out in the next few days to get it taken care of."

Major looked dubious. "Well, I'd have to talk to Mayor Dixie."

Peter squinted his eyes, and I felt the slightest twinge of annoyance. And then annoyance at my own annoyance. Even if no one had mentioned the well, it wasn't the end of the world. We were getting this vast property for a pittance. We really had nothing to complain about. I needed to just downshift. This wasn't New York. It wouldn't help matters for me to come out swinging.

I smiled at Major. "It's just our daughter. We wouldn't want her accidentally happening upon it and, you know, falling in."

"Oh, dear me, no." Major frowned. "That would be . . . no. No, we wouldn't want that at all. Not at all."

"All right. Outstanding. You'll talk to Mayor Dixie and get somebody out here, right away. We'll all stay close to the house until it's repaired."

Peter glanced at me. I widened my eyes in response. *It's fine.* Minette was already hobbling down the front steps, tapping his fingers on the banister in an agitated manner.

"I'm fixing to go down there right now," he said. "Right to

Mayor Dixie's office and tell her she's got to find somebody who will take care of it."

I turned back to tell Peter it was fine, but he was already heading back inside, probably to check on Mere. To make sure our daughter hadn't wandered out the back door and in the direction of the mysterious, open well that nobody had told us about.

Chapter 5

That night in our newly set up bed, I nestled close to Peter. I breathed in the unfamiliar scents of our new house: old man, uncleared AC flues, stacks of old newspapers. And underneath all that, the faint whiff of some chemical I couldn't identify. I didn't mind the hint of mustiness: in fact, it was comforting. The smell of stability.

"Round of applause for not ripping into that poor guy about the well." Peter rested his hand on my right shoulder, finding that spot just beside my shoulder blade. That knot that was perpetually lodged in the middle of my trapezius, which had come from years of hunching over a stove. His thumb moved in small circles and I melted.

I sighed. "I mean, how can I be mad about a one-hundred-dollar estate?"

"In all fairness, they should've told us."

"Would that have changed anything, though? I mean, honestly, we were still going to get this place for nothing. We've just got to remember the bees with honey thing. Not that you have a problem with that. I'm more of a bees-with-a-bulldozer person."

He laughed and pulled me closer. "I've always liked that about you."

I smiled, relaxing into his rhythmic touch. I remembered the crime tape at the old mill. The police cruiser. Now was definitely not the time to bring that up. Another time. Or maybe not at all. It was so peaceful, lying here with him, blissing out under the pressure of his fingers.

I was asleep in minutes, my dreams full of splashing fountains, rushing brown rivers, and the plaintive sounds of fiddle music. I saw children, huddled together, crying. In the middle of it all, an old woman emerged in the darkness. She had a crown of gray braids and a silver cross around her neck. Her withered mouth opened, and I smelled something fetid.

Whaaat . . . have they taaakennn . . . from you? she drawled in her crone's creaking, rasping voice. *What have they stooolennn, Billieeeee . . . ?*

I woke with a strangled cry. It was morning and Peter's side of the bed was empty. I got up, showered, and gave Mere her breakfast. Peter didn't reappear until I'd already made my way through half the coffeepot. He looked exhausted and sweaty, covered in grass and streaks of mud. He'd woken at four, he told me, heart racing about the uncapped well, and set out to find the thing. He hadn't had any luck. I gave him coffee and watched him head for the stairs and a shower. I certainly wasn't going to mention the bizarre old lady from my dreams, but her strange voice still echoed in my ears.

The following week, this became our default routine. Peter would toss and turn each night, then every early morning, usually before I woke, he'd head out to hike over our twelve acres. The twelve acres, which, incidentally, had started to feel vaguely threatening.

It was a strange thing. Major's revelation about the well had shifted something inside me. I felt ill at ease, definitely annoyed that no one had bothered to mention the well until we'd already moved in. Peter was downright obsessed with it. Now, as I stood at the kitchen sink, watching Peter tromp back home across the green field for the seventh morning in a row, I felt like I was looking out over someone else's property.

Until he found the well, Peter insisted Mere stay in the front yard, only going as far as the towering magnolia that lay a hundred yards down the drive while either he or I sat on one of the porch rockers and kept an eye on her. Since he had appointments, that person usually ended up being me. This bugged me. Besides keeping me from my search for a space for the restaurant, I just thought it was overkill. Mere was six, a smart and generally reasonable kid, not one who pushed back on boundaries just for the hell of it. But Peter was adamant—the well was out there, uncovered and unsafe. We'd never forgive ourselves if she fell in.

The few times we had gone outside, as soon as Mere opened the front door, Ramsay would shoot off across the yard, disappearing within seconds across the fields to parts unknown. Her playmate's absence didn't seem to bother her, though. Mere was content to entertain herself, exploring every nook and cranny of the yard surrounding the house, searching for pretty rocks, peering down holes dug by some animal, or attempting to climb the towering magnolia. It was only after several days of this that she grew bored. She would return to the porch, glum and listless. I couldn't blame her. There was a whole world to explore, but she was chained to the house.

I suggested we organize the house together. Mere agreed, a bit unenthusiastically. So after Peter returned from his daily well hunt, showered, and shut himself in the front bedroom he'd made into his office, we began. We chose a playlist and turned the volume as high as we dared. We began downstairs, trying to keep quiet so we wouldn't disturb Peter, but constantly failing. We dropped boxes, thumped our old vacuum cleaner into furniture, inadvertently slammed pocket doors, smothering our giggles every time we kept accidentally bursting into song with "Hey Jude" or "Carolina in My Mind" or "You Are the Best Thing."

The downstairs of our new house consisted of a wide center hall flanked by two parlors on either side, a dining room, conservatory, and kitchen, along with a hodgepodge of closets and hallways and small storage rooms that seemed like strange architectural afterthoughts. The parlors were mirrors of one another, the one on the left done in pale greens and yellows with an intricate marble mantel over the fireplace and a piano, the one on the right, in shades of cobalt blue with a leather chesterfield sofa and walls of books.

Fine Regency and Victorian furniture filled each room, and silk and tasseled draperies hung on the floor-to-ceiling windows. The wide plank floors, though scarred from a century and a half of use, still glowed. This house, full of all these antiques, would have gone for well over five million in upstate New York. I couldn't believe our luck. Portraits—Dalzell and Minette ancestors, I guessed—framed in heavy gold, lined the walls. I thought of poor widowed George Davenport, alone in the house, his mind slowly deteriorating. How lonely and scared he must've been.

Mere spoke behind me. "It looks like there's a girl's room and a boy's."

"Yeah, they tended to do a lot of that in the old days," I said. "Separate everyone into groups."

She crinkled her nose and peered into the blue parlor. "The boy's room has all the books."

I looked over her shoulder. It did indeed. Books somebody would have to dust—me, no doubt. Even now, they were covered in a fine, white dust. The shelves were, however, the perfect place to stash my bag of Godiva chocolate squares, where Peter and Mere would never think to look. "You pick where we start."

After we finished the parlors, Mere and I moved on to the dining room, where we stacked Peter's grandmother's china in the glass-fronted cabinet. Behind the dining room, off a side hallway, there was a small glass conservatory, which had obviously been skipped by the cleaning crew. In the center, a dry concrete fountain, cracked in several places, boasted an intricate blue tile pattern. The room was full of dead potted plants, and everything was coated in white dust. We dumped the shriveled plants in the compost heap out back and dusted and mopped the whole room. I promised Mere we could start with a few hard-to-kill plants and see where that led.

Late in the afternoon, when the sun's low rays were shooting through the windows of the house, we went back to the kitchen, which I had already fully cleaned and set to order the first day we'd arrived. The large room ran the entire length of the back of the house and included a spacious butler's pantry lined with glass cabinets as well as a collection of hutches and wooden bread tables. I loved the whole 1930s aesthetic: the red tiled floors, red-and-white cherry-patterned wallpaper, and the centerpiece of the room, an enormous, scarred pine farm table surrounded by eight ladder-back chairs. The room made me feel like I'd stepped into a slower way of life, a place where I could leisurely bake a coconut cake and thaw a couple of steaks for dinner while the setting sun sent its golden beams to bless my work.

That first day, at the deep, cast-iron sink, I had run the faucet. At first it spurted, then had started to run a dark rusty red. After a few minutes, though, it began to clear up. I turned off the faucet, hoping we weren't going to have to call out more people to fix the new well. It was the last thing I needed. Fortunately, we hadn't had a problem with it since.

The next morning, as I watched Peter heading back to the house across the dew-drenched field after another obviously unfruitful hunt for the well, I decided to take Mere to town.

The house was spotless, I didn't want to hover as she played outside, and I really needed to find a space for the café. I kissed Peter when he came into the kitchen for coffee, then ran up-stairs. I showered, leaving my chin-length hair to air dry. With the thick Georgia humidity, there was no point in blowing it out. After checking the weather on my phone—a balmy seventy-eight degrees with not a cloud in the forecast—I pulled on a green sundress printed with light blue flowers, and sandals.

Peter had started his first session in his office upstairs. I could hear his voice drifting through the house, not necessarily the exact words, only the deep, comforting rumble of his voice. I paused, letting the sound wash over me. I loved his voice—the way he said my name, the way he told a joke, like he fully expected everyone within earshot to be as delighted by it as he was. But I'd been married to the man for eight years, and I'd never heard that particular brand of gentleness in his tone when he talked to me.

I had no one to blame but myself. Maybe he would speak to me that way if I was truthful with him, but I hadn't exactly been forthcoming about how much Mom's move to Maine still hurt. I wasn't sure why. Maybe it was because I couldn't stand to admit that I was so emotionally needy. I'd just worked through the pain. Acted like everything was the same.

How could I tell him that even though I seemed fine, I still felt like crawling into bed and hiding most days? He needed a wife and a partner, not another patient. Still, I couldn't help but wonder what would happen if I walked into his office right now, sat down, and told him the mortifying truth.

I opened the first Billie's to make my mother love me, and now I'm opening another restaurant because I could use an easy win. I need it . . . and that's the reason I wanted this move.

Moving to Juliana wasn't for Mere or you.

It was for me.

What if I said the ugly truth straight out like that? Would he use that same gentle tone he used with his clients? Or would he finally see what a fragile, needy person I was—a person who had moved her family hundreds of miles away so she could repair her precious, shattered ego—and be disgusted? When I let myself even edge around the truth, it sickened and shamed me. How would it not have the same effect on him?

"I'm ready," Mere said, standing before me in jeans, an orange-and-red striped shirt, and her tiny, patent leather Doc Martens. Her long blond hair hung like a wet curtain over her shoulders. She grinned at me, my little hipster kid, as Ramsay wove a figure eight around her legs. "Mama, I thought of a name for your new restaurant."

"Oh yeah?"

"The Lottery," she said.

I smoothed her hair back. "That's an interesting name. Like the scratch-off tickets we used to get at the bodega back home?"

"No," she said, "like another kind. An old kind. With old-timey people in covered wagons and everything."

I stopped. "Where did you hear about that?"

"I read it, in a book in the empty bedroom. L-O-T-T-E-R-Y."

"That's right. Good sounding out the word, babe."

"And there was a picture. It said 1832."

"When were you in the other bedroom?" I asked.

"The other night. I had a bad dream that woke me up."

"Why didn't you come get me, sweetie?"

She shrugged. "I wasn't really scared. I just wanted to go look in the room next to mine. The one with all the books."

"Okay. So you had a bad dream, and you went into the spare bedroom?"

"Yeah. There are books in there with old-timey pictures. That's when I saw the L-O-T-T-E-R-Y. That's what you should name your restaurant."

I brushed her hair back and gave her a little squeeze. "We'll put it on the list, okay? We'll put all our ideas on a list and then you, me, and Daddy'll vote. Ready to go?"

She nodded, and I caught her hand.

"What was your dream about, babe?" I asked.

"Just some children."

"Children?"

She nodded. "Children in the dark. They were scared of the dark. I'm not, but they were, so they sang a song. And there was a lady with them. An old lady with all of these"—she circled her hand around her head—"braids."

Chapter 6

Under the brilliant blue sky, the town square was ablaze with color. The smooth lawn of green, the burnished bronze statue, the foaming white spray of the fountain. Yellow and pink flags whipped on street lamps and proclaimed their reassuring message: *Gentle Juliana, Your Forever Home.*

I put Mere's dream about the old woman with braids out of my mind. It had to be one of those weird coincidences—us having the same dream—the result of the two of us being so connected emotionally. Things like this happened. The universe was a weird place.

We took our time, leisurely walking down each street that bordered the square, assessing every empty space we passed. Most of them were too small for what I envisioned. The former Billie's had been a cozy spot, intimate, small even for a Manhattan eatery, but it had worked. Here, there was no reason we couldn't double the space. I was the only game in town.

"Mama, look!" Mere had stopped and was pressing her face to the glass of one corner space with a robin's egg–blue door and a brown-and-white checkered tile entryway. In the center, blue tiles spelled out the name Minette. I leaned against the window, too, cupping my hands around my eyes to block out the light. At the sight, I let out a short, sharp gasp of delight.

Brick and lathe and plaster walls soared at least twenty feet to a stamped-tin ceiling. The floors were worn pine plank. Being on the corner, light flooded in from both sides of the building. I could see instantly in my head where the bar would go, the barista station, and the host stand. We could do at least fifteen tables, three of them for large parties, and maybe four to six outside on the wide sidewalk. I'd need to see in the back to confirm there was room for a decent-sized kitchen, cooler, and storage.

"It's perfect," Mere said. I glanced over at her, and a rush of love filled my heart, almost cramping it. What kind of six-year-old kid instinctively knew what space would work for a restaurant? My kid, that was who. My perfect, adorable, quirky little kid.

"Want to see inside?"

I turned to see a man standing a couple of feet away watching me and Mere, his hands on his hips. He wore wrinkled chinos stained with paint and a navy crewneck T-shirt. A small chocolate Lab at his side was wagging its tail furiously. The man was in his forties with dark blond hair only slightly receding at his temples, a trim beard, and a warm, welcoming smile. He was blindingly handsome. Disconcertingly so.

"I have the key if you're interested in taking a look. I can let you in. Show you around." He gestured behind him. "I own the antique store next door. Jamie Cleburne." He tilted his head to the dog. "This is Ever."

He offered his hand, and we shook. His grip was firm and warm.

"Billie Hope. And Meredith. We just moved here for the Initiative."

"We definitely want to see it," Mere said. "Can I pet your dog?"

"Have at it," he said.

"If you're not busy," I said.

He snorted. "Trust me, busy is not a thing anybody ever is around here. Just give me one second." He disappeared inside his store, then returned a few moments later, unlocked the door, and ushered us in. Ever the Lab followed behind.

The space was cool and smelled of wood shavings, motor oil, and a hundred past lives. I took in the details. The impossible height of the ceiling. The windows, trimmed with intricate molding, that stretched the full length of the walls. The way dust motes swirled around me, anointing me with a sort of welcoming benediction.

"It was a general store," Jamie Cleburne said. "A mercantile, back in 1832, when Juliana was first founded. Would've carried everything from flour and salt and sugar to dresses and farm implements." He cocked his head. "Okay, now I got it. You're the family who bought the Dalzell-Davenport house, aren't you?"

I nodded. "I plan to open a restaurant."

"Well, this would be a perfect spot," Jamie said. He narrowed his eyes. "I didn't realize the Dalzell-Davenport house was available to the Initiative folks. I would've bought it myself if I had known it was on the market."

"It wasn't, not exactly, but I really loved the place, so I might've gone full New Yorker on Bonnie over at the town council, and they made an exception. Sorry."

He laughed and our eyes met. "Remind me to hire you as my next real estate agent."

"Oh, I'm much better at pancakes."

"I believe you."

I felt it then, a low-level warning alarm reverberating through my whole body. The eye contact between us was going on for longer than was actually wise. I directed my attention back to the space.

"What are you going to call it?" he asked.

"Her other restaurant was called Billie's," Mere said, appearing out of the shadows where she'd been prowling.

"I know," he said. I met his gaze again. "I ate there once."

I lifted my eyebrows. "You did? When?"

"Right before the pandemic—2019, I think. I was on a buying trip for the shop up there. Vermont, New Hampshire, upstate New York. At the end of the trip, I traveled down to the city for a show, to meet a friend, and have some good food. I had a particularly delicious sage sausage, uh . . ."

"Frittata." God, his eyes, they were this green-blue concoction, really beautiful, with the dust-mote light hitting them from the side like that.

"It was definitely worth the two-hour wait it took to get them."

"Sorry about that. We do advise reservations."

"I tried," he said. "You were booked out for months. Popular place. You definitely make an impression, though, I have to say. I hope you can recreate the magic down here in Juliana."

"That's the plan."

"Love a woman with a plan." He smiled. I did, too. He seemed to be mulling over something, his face thoughtful, and then he nodded once and turned to Mere. "What kind of tables would you put in here?"

Mere put her hands on her tiny hips, all business. "We had round ones at the other restaurant."

"Unfortunately, I sold them after we closed," I said. "For practically nothing."

"You know," Jamie said. "I have all these incredible pieces, marble-topped coffee tables and side tables from the turn of the century, that you could modify. I could help you cut them down. I also have this really spectacular bar if you want to take a look at it."

"Yeah, I was thinking about a bar."

"And a coffee station," he said. "Like the one you had at

Billie's." He addressed Mere again. "You want to come over and see what I've got?"

She brightened. "Sure."

Jamie clapped his hands together and rubbed them. "There's this side door." He gestured toward the back. "The spaces are connected. You ladies can follow me."

I could tell Mere was charmed by Jamie and his dog. Not that I wasn't, but I was on my guard. Mainly because of that warm smile and those blue-green eyes, and whatever it was that was making the air between us electric. It wasn't something that happened often, me noticing a man in this way, and it unsettled me. And if I leased the space, he'd be next door, every single day.

Jamie unlocked the door, and we followed him and Ever into the gloom. We were in the back of his antique shop. The space was dimly lit, with soft light coming in from the windows in the front of the shop. Other than the clutter of furniture, the place was similar to next door, with high ceilings, stamped tin, and that smell of a century and a half of commerce.

"This way." Jamie wound his way around stacks of bureaus, chairs, dining and bedroom sets, and curio cabinets. The sheer amount of furniture was overwhelming, but the place didn't feel dusty or oppressive. It felt like an unfolding adventure. Like all these old lives had entrusted their keepsakes to someone who saw their worth and cared for their future.

"I was thinking these might work." Jamie was standing in front of a collection of pink-and-green marble-topped tables. "Put them on metal bases and they'd look fantastic." He pointed to more tables. "If you need a six- or eight-top, these could work. I also have chairs somewhere in here." He led us to another section of the shop where he pointed out the bar. It was a long stretch of zinc and wood and shelves of etched glass, dumped from some old pub up North.

He ran his fingers along the surface and examined the residue.

It was gray and grimy, not like the white dust that we'd scrubbed in the conservatory in my house. "Needs a good cleaning."

"It's stunning," I said. "As are the tables. It's just I don't know if I can afford it all. It's probably way over our budget."

"We can work something out."

I furrowed my brow. "Like . . ."

"Like I get a few months of free breakfast?"

I surveyed the bar again. "I'm pretty sure that bar's worth about a decade of free breakfasts."

"I'm okay with that."

I wasn't sure how to answer that.

"Don't worry," he said. "This is how we do things in Juliana. We help each other. Barter here and there a bit. Consider the pieces yours."

"Thanks," I said. "But I should probably wait to see if I can get the space."

"Oh, you'll get the space."

I furrowed my brow. "How do you know?"

"Haven't you figured it out yet? You can have anything you want." He said it outright, in the least guileless way. No apologies.

I felt a whisper of suspicion ripple through me. "Is that so?"

"It is."

"Well, in that case I'd like the first year free." I laughed at my own joke.

He didn't. He just looked self-conscious. "Everyone's just really glad you're here, Billie. You and your family . . . and everyone else who's accepting the Initiative. All of you are basically saving our town. I look forward to brunch at Billie's Two."

Mere spoke up. "Or The Lottery. We may call it the Lottery." She was winding her way back toward us through the dusty furniture, running her fingers lightly over the carved surfaces, Ever close on her heels.

"There's a book about the land lottery in one of the bedrooms at our house," I explained to him. "I didn't realize the land around here had been distributed that way."

He nodded. "Unfortunately. Our local history is checkered, like most of the South. The story goes, when they found gold up in Dahlonega, about an hour northeast of here, the federal government basically took all the Cherokees' land and parceled it out to white settlers. It's not something we're proud of, but we do what we can to address it. Land acknowledgments before city council meetings and school events, for whatever that's worth. Some residents donate to the Cherokee Nation."

"And nobody ever found gold here in Juliana?"

"No. But we had Minette's mill, and it was enough to establish the town, for a while anyway. Now, we need more. Restauranteurs, for example." He grinned and handed me the key to next door. "I'll speak to Mayor Dixie about the space, and she'll get you the paperwork. Anything else you need?"

His eyes were kind, and I felt like he was someone I could be frank with. "There was something." I lowered my voice so Mere wouldn't hear. "The day we moved in, there was a sheriff's car at the mill. An officer, or deputy, I guess, was rolling up crime tape. I was just concerned, you know. I didn't know . . ."

Jamie's brows lifted.

"Well, I was wondering if something happened there. If there was anything my husband and I should know about, for safety's sake."

He looked grave. "Yeah. I think there were some kids out there messing around. Nothing major, just drugs and stuff, probably. You know kids. The town likes to keep an eye on that kind of stuff. It can get out of hand pretty quickly."

"Makes sense."

"It's nothing to worry about."

"Okay. Well . . . good." I thought about mentioning the uncapped well, too, but decided to save that one for another day.

I didn't want to come off as all full of complaints after the guy had just gone above and beyond to help me.

Jamie touched my arm lightly. "Let's talk more about those tables in a few days, okay? I want to make sure we get you what you need."

I nodded. "Thanks again."

"My pleasure. Looking forward to my first breakfast."

"Mere?" I called, but she'd already disappeared into the gloom of the back of the shop with the dog.

Chapter 7

True to his word, Jamie Cleburne fabricated all the tables for the restaurant from his shop's inventory. He even found a handyman to install the bar while I was supervising the kitchen build-out. I was grateful as I had my hands full. In addition to overseeing the renovations, I had to finalize the menu and figure out what I was going to call the place. At the same time, I was fielding so much interest in line cook and server jobs, Peter offered to shuffle his appointments to help me with interviews. Even Mere pitched in, sweeping up, hauling debris, and making endless pots of coffee for everyone.

The only thing I missed was Mom being there to see it all come together. I would've given anything for her to see the transformation of the old mercantile. To have her pinch my ass and say with that cigarette-raspy, deadpan voice of hers like she did when she first saw the layout of the other Billie's, "Where you going to put the official Sibyl Sheridan Lewis table?"

Missing Mom was hard, but other than that, everything was easy in Juliana: dealing with contractors, local vendors, and the staff over at city hall. People here were always on time, perpetually cheerful, and anxious to help in whatever way they could. I discovered Jamie's way of bartering was a common practice. I got an extra fridge from the mayor, two sets of bistro chairs from the Childers family, and a commercial ice machine from the one and only Oxford Dalzell.

"Ox," as everyone, even his kids, called him, was a lawyer who wore a suit and tie every day, a pair of thick, black-rimmed reading glasses perched on his bald head. He had stopped by the day the bar was being installed and mentioned the ice machine had been in the house he and his second wife had shared before she passed away. I accepted his gift gratefully, but warily. The free breakfasts were adding up. And there was something about Ox I wasn't sure I liked. Maybe it was his blustery Southern way that made me think he didn't quite see women as his equals, but in the end, I told myself there was no harm in playing along. It might take some getting used to, but if this was what community meant—the giving and taking of favors— I was here for it.

Staffing turned out to be a breeze as well. In less than a week, I found a barista Susy, a Michelangelo with latte art; a server Libby, who seemed to know everyone in town and brought them along with her to apply for the job; Halie, a firecracker with a razor-sharp wit who was experienced at expo. Finally there was Cam, a baker who brought along his own sourdough starter and enough charisma to pull in customers for decades. I was surprised when Major Minette came in with his sister-in-law, Dixie, the mayor, to apply for a job bussing tables.

"I like to keep him busy," the mayor confided to me as her brother ambled through the restaurant, hands in the pockets of his rumpled suit pants, inspecting the tables, bar, and open kitchen. Dixie locked eyes with me. "Keep him out of trouble. He's a pussycat, bless his heart, but he does like to ramble . . . and plenty of times where he shouldn't. You just have to have a firm hand. Remind him that he has to stay until closing."

It appeared to be a given in Juliana—the mayor issued orders, and you did whatever it was she asked. And we did need a busser, it's just that I wasn't a huge fan of being told who to hire. Or being used as a babysitter.

Mayor Dixie leaned closer, clutching her pocketbook. "He's got a tiny little shoplifting habit, is the thing. Likes to slip away when I'm not watching, drive over to the Dollar General or Walmart and pick up a few things, if you know what I'm saying."

Perfect. I nodded. "Oh. Okay."

"He won't take anything from here though. As long as you don't have fishing lures or shotgun shells laying around." She tittered and patted my hand. Her hand trembled slightly, just like Major's.

"There's something you can do for me, too," I said. "If you don't mind."

Mayor Dixie's thin, penciled eyebrows rose. "Of course not. Happy to help out a new neighbor."

"Major told us about the old well on our property, about it not being capped properly, and I've got to be honest, it's driving Peter crazy. He's worried our daughter might find it by accident."

She looked thoughtful. "Gracious, yes. The well. I'd forgotten about that."

I smiled, hoping to hide my impatience. "He's been looking all over the property so, you know, he can assess how dangerous it really may be. . . ." I trailed off, but she only tilted her head. "I was wondering if the city could send out a well guy, or whoever handles that kind of thing."

She pursed her bright pink lips. "Unfortunately, I don't think that's an expense the city would be able to cover. But I'll be happy to direct you to the property plats at city hall, in the records department, so you can locate it."

"Would you know a well company that could cap it for us?" I asked.

"Oh. Let me see." She touched her lacquered platinum hair with pointed pink nails. "I'm on city water so I'm afraid I'm really not familiar with well companies. Maybe the Cleburnes can help you with that? I think Jamie had a well dug for his daddy out on their farm outside of town."

I pushed down my frustration. This inconvenience was just that, a small price to pay for what we'd been gifted. I didn't want to come off sounding entitled. "Okay. Thank you so much, Mayor Dixie."

She was all business again. "I'll tell Major to come in tomorrow at seven-thirty?"

"Eight's fine."

"Major," the woman snapped over her shoulder as she headed for the door. Her brother trotted behind her, waving at me. I waved back.

By the end of the third week of renovations, I had managed to land both a burgeoning chef who could manage the kitchen, and a front of house manager in the form of twenty-two-year-old twins, Falcon and Finch Street. The brother and sister twins had worked summers at the Dairy Queen, then gone to the University of North Georgia up in Dahlonega where they both majored in hospitality management. They'd been contemplating a move to Atlanta, but hadn't wanted to leave their family or hometown, so they were elated to land jobs that would allow them to stay in Juliana. Not half as elated as I was. It was like the restaurant gods were out in front of me, clearing the way for my success.

The twins put me in touch with the couple who'd just moved down from Massachusetts, the Brennans, who were in the process of opening a bakery on the opposite side of the square and agreed to provide fresh, home-baked pastries every day. The twins also brought in more candidates for front of house staff. In a week and a half, I had a deep bench of servers, baristas, line cooks, dishwashers, and hosts, and a public chomping at the bit for a table at Juliana's newest breakfast, brunch, and lunch spot.

One morning on the way to the restaurant, I noticed a FOR SALE sign on an olive-green, used Jeep Wrangler sitting in the driveway of a bungalow on Cleburne Street. A member of the extended Childers family named Lloyd—there seemed to be dozens of branches of Childers, just like many of the other founding families—sold it to me for a thousand dollars. I told Peter he could use the Subaru, and Mere and I proceeded to drive everywhere, top off, wind in our hair.

A few days later, I met Falcon and Finch's mother, an earthy woman named Lilah who wore her long gray hair loose and waved down her back and a variety of paint-speckled overalls. Even though we weren't officially open, she had started popping in for oat milk matcha lattes with a small, redheaded girl in tow. Temperance, six years old like Mere, was Lilah's granddaughter, and had been left in her care while her mother, Lilah's oldest daughter, Wren, "found her path," as Finch put it. Apparently, Wren struggled with substance abuse and was now out west working on a marijuana farm.

Lilah, Finch, Falcon, and Temperance lived just off the square, in an enormous Victorian that was painted three different shades of green. After school hours, Lilah and Temperance dug in Lilah's vegetable patch, tumbled rocks, and read. Mere and Temperance immediately hit it off, and since we'd finished up Mere's schooling for the year, on impulse I asked Lilah if she'd be willing to keep Mere on the days I worked. She agreed on the spot. Peter wasn't thrilled with the arrangement, maintaining that we really didn't know the woman, but I pointed out that we didn't know anyone. At this stage, everyone was a stranger to us in Juliana.

"We have to trust them eventually," I told him. "And besides, she's *grandmotherly*."

He relented. He wanted Mere to have a grandmother as much as I did.

I'd been so busy with the restaurant, so Peter had volunteered to get in touch with Jamie regarding a well company. I was happy to let him handle it. Unfortunately, Jamie hadn't returned his call yet, and Peter hadn't had the time to drop by the antique shop, which meant we were at a standstill. We agreed that we didn't want Mere stuck inside, or attempting to sneak out to roam while Peter was working, so we decided Lilah was the answer to our problem.

"Fucking well," Peter grumbled, but I knew he was looking forward to the luxury of having the house to himself for his appointments without having to constantly shush me and Mere.

The day of our grand opening, I arrived at the restaurant to find a fairyland bower of roses, hydrangea, and lilies arching over the window. Over the freshly painted front door hung a gorgeous, wooden sign, a name painted on it in light blue script.

BILLIE'S.

I turned to see Peter watching me with dancing eyes and Mere literally dancing around him.

"It was the right choice," Peter said.

I mustered a grin, wondering if he'd be so enthusiastic if he knew why I'd chosen to stick with the name Billie's. It wasn't the biggest deal, using the old name. If anything, it was simply a cop-out. The name carried a cachet that was enough to possibly get me national attention from food critics, maybe even the James Beard people. Part of that easy-win thing I was so invested in. Piggybacking on my old glory to boost my ego instead of articulating my feelings about Mom. Amazing how self-aware I could be about all my shit and still refuse to deal with it.

"Do you like the flowers, Mama?" Mere asked.

I hugged her. "I love them. Did you help Daddy pick them out?"

"Mrs. Tilton gave them to us for free."

Of course. One of the Tiltons ran the florist shop around the corner. I suddenly saw an endless line of free breakfasts in my future.

Peter slung an arm over my shoulder. "How are you feeling?"

I shivered a little. "Honestly? I think I'm more nervous about this opening than I was about the other one."

Peter gave me a squeeze. "You're going to be a hit, just like you were in New York."

I wanted to tell him how much I wish Mom was there, but once again, something held me back. It just felt easier to pretend she didn't exist. That the hurt didn't exist. All that existed was the three of us and my beautiful new restaurant in our perfect new hometown.

I leaned into his comforting embrace and shaded my eyes against the bright sunrise. He kissed my temple and I felt Mere's soft hand slip into mine. Why did I have to get so hung up on what I didn't have? Or what I thought I needed?

Even if Mom wasn't here, it didn't matter. If the café bombed, that didn't matter either. I'd figure out something else to do. Hell, I'd dip cones at the Dairy Queen if I had to, James Beard be damned. I already had everything I needed, right here, standing right beside me on this sidewalk.

Chapter 8

The first week Billie's was open was pure insanity, the second, only one degree less, and the third was only an average amount of bonkers. By the fourth week, things were going so smoothly that I started to feel suspicious. Could we really be hitting our stride so soon? The growing population of Juliana would seem to say yes, forming a line at our door even before opening each day and then again around lunchtime.

I worked hard to remember names and faces, particularly those belonging to the customers from Juliana's original families. There was Bonnie St. John, the woman who worked at city hall and had handled all our paperwork for the house and café. There were the Calhouns, Ray and Darlene, who owned the lumberyard outside of town. Dr. Belmont St. John, Bonnie's cousin and the local internist who treated every condition from the sniffles to heart disease. Doc Belmont always brought his dog with him, a brown-and-white English cocker named Birdie, who waited patiently for him outside while the doctor ate.

Ox Dalzell, of course, was always around, as well as Agnes Childers, a widow in her eighties who owned whatever commercial real estate the Minette family didn't and who, with her collection of headscarves and jeweled pins, gave off major Grey Gardens vibes. She always brought her own silver flask of some kind of herbal-infused gin. Toby Minette, Dixie's adult son, looked like an overgrown fraternity boy straight out of *The Official Preppy Handbook.*

I left the door that connected the restaurant kitchen with Jamie Cleburne's shop unlocked, and one morning, sometime during the second or third week, he appeared and claimed a stool at the bar. He ordered a flat white, toasted everything bagel with cream cheese, and a side of turkey bacon. To my surprise, he bowed his head before eating, saying a prayer. It was old-fashioned yet endearing in a certain way.

I watched him out of the corner of my eye. I really didn't have the mental space to deal with the well, but the issue wasn't going away, and somebody had to deal with it. Peter said Jamie had never gotten back to him, but for a host of reasons, the main one being the appreciative way Jamie always looked at me, I had a sneaking feeling that I might get a better response from him than my husband had.

When he was almost done with his meal, I took a deep breath and approached him. "Hey Jamie, I hate to bother you —"

He glanced up at me, those blue-green eyes knocking me off balance once again.

I hurried through the explanation. "You wouldn't know anything about a well at our place, would you? Not the one that the house is connected to. One that Silas Dalzell dug for crops or livestock that might not have been capped properly. They told me you or your dad might know a well company that could handle it for us."

"That's interesting." He shook his head. "But no, I've never heard of an uncapped well there."

I guess he hadn't gotten Peter's message.

"Major told us about it when we moved in. I wondered if he

was just repeating something Dixie told him to keep him from wandering."

His expression changed. "Oh. Well, maybe. Major does wander. But there could definitely be an additional well on any of these properties. On the other hand, old George Davenport might've dreamed it up and told Dixie. He was a little batty toward the end."

I furrowed my brow. "Yeah, I heard that. Just in case, you wouldn't happen to have the number of the company you used, would you?"

"Actually, my dad handled all that, but I could ask him."

"Thanks."

He slid off the stool and turned toward the door. Before leaving he looked over his shoulder. "Best breakfast I've had in years."

I beamed, probably warming to the compliment more than I should, then self-consciously erased the grin. This was a small town with a longtime hierarchy cemented in place. Jamie Cleburne might be able to get away with flirting with every woman in sight, but I most certainly could not.

He returned the next morning with the phone number for Childers Wells—"One of Agnes's grandsons," Jamie said. I called, but got a recording. I left a message that day and for three or four days after, then decided to let the matter rest. I was frustrated but reluctant to mention it to Jamie. I'd already asked for enough favors. I'd just find another company.

After that, Jamie came in every morning for his bagel, turkey bacon, and flat white. He always did the silent prayer, and after he finished his meal, he'd typically have another cup of coffee and chat with me whenever I worked the kitchen window. He told me all about his growing up in Juliana. He was forty-two years old and an only child. His mother had died a decade ago, but his father was still alive. As a result of a recent stroke, his father was in a wheelchair and had a full-time housekeeper who cooked, so Jamie said I shouldn't expect to see him much in the café.

Jamie had been the star quarterback at Juliana High School, he told me, then played at Auburn University. After graduation he'd taken over the family antique business. He'd traveled all over Europe, western and eastern, stocking the shop, but he'd never been tempted to move away from Juliana. He'd been married, once, briefly. A woman from the D.C. area who hadn't taken to small-town life. She hadn't taken to Jamie either, apparently. She'd moved home even before the divorce was finalized.

He built his own house on the Cleburne family property, which was just outside town, past the mill. Between the Cleburne house and Jamie's cabin lay a twenty-eight-acre lake of clear, spring-fed water—Jamie's father's pet project. The elder Cleburne had tended to it carefully over the past decade, planting native vegetation and carefully introducing the right species of fish until it was a fisherman's paradise. No one was allowed to fish there, except family and invited guests. There were numerous NO TRESPASSING signs around it, Jamie laughingly told me. Even the most brazen local poachers had spread the stories of old James Cleburne, sitting watch on his porch all night with binoculars and a twelve gauge for anyone who might dare to go night gigging.

One morning, after his premeal grace ritual, Jamie caught me watching him. I busied myself filling condiment bowls, but when I turned back to him, he sent me a wry grin.

"Force of habit," he said. "The prayer."

"I like it. It's nice. Everybody around here does it, don't they?" I'd noticed other customers, the locals, mouthing what looked like the same, silent words.

He nodded. "We all might attend a different church, but somewhere back in our history, the town elders decided we should all say the same grace. Keep that 'one for all and all for one' feeling alive, you know?"

"Yeah. Where do the Cleburnes attend services?" I asked.

"We don't, actually. Neither do Mayor Dixie or Ox Dalzell."

"Any reason?"

"Are you kidding me?" He laughed. "You're telling me you haven't noticed? We all worship Juliana around here. What's the point in going to church?"

I laughed ruefully. "I hear you. Sometimes I think I worship this place. I'm here enough."

He took a bite of his bagel. "You don't hear me complaining."

I smiled. "Can you teach me? The prayer?"

He looked incredulous, then touched. "Really?"

"Sure, why not?"

"Okay. Fold your hands."

I did.

"For food that stays our hunger . . ." he intoned. "For rest that brings us ease."

I repeated the words.

"For homes where memories linger, we give our thanks for these."

I looked up. He was studying me closely, his eyes soft. The expression on his face was unguarded and something I could only describe as tender. For a brief moment, I had the wild urge to touch his face, the line of his jaw. To stroke the silken blond beard with my fingertips. I shook it off.

"And then you always . . ." I grabbed the gold chain around my neck. I had noticed that everyone who said this grace in the restaurant always reached for their necks or wrists before or after.

He fingered the silver chain around his neck. "A lot of us have charms that stand for Juliana." He laughed. "Go ahead, you can say it. It's a little nutty."

"I don't think so. It's obviously very meaningful to you all."

"Did I just hear a *y'all* come out of your mouth?"

I laughed. "I don't think so. 'You all' is definitely not the same thing as y'all."

His smile was as seductive as they came. "If you say so, Ms. Hope. You're the boss."

I laughed again, blushing uncomfortably, then made a dumb excuse to head back into the kitchen. I told Falcon he was relieved for the time being and squared myself in front of the flaming stove. I needed the wall of searing heat to clear my head.

Occasionally, a blond woman named Alice who had delicate features and a gold hoop through her nose would join Jamie at the bar. She always ordered two lattes and a fruit plate. She was one of the Tiltons, I learned, one of the original families. Alice was a third-grade teacher at the elementary school and lived in a bungalow near the Methodist church. She and Jamie were dating—casually, I was told by a couple of the servers who seemed to be in the know. Still, every time she joined him at the café, I found myself, like some kind of insecure adolescent, dialing up my own charm to eleven.

All in all, business was good. The restaurant's numbers weren't at New York levels, but they were promising. Occasionally good enough that waiting customers started to block the entrance to Cleburne Antiques, and I heard that Jamie came out and asked them to relocate to the other end of the block. At the end of each day, I was bone-tired, reeked of smoked salmon and hickory bacon, the bluegrass-gospel mix we played all day earworming itself incessantly through my head. Still, I felt the kind of exhausted elation I hadn't felt in years. Every afternoon after I'd lock up, I'd retrieve Mere from Lilah's, and we'd drive back to the house while she described weeding the beet patch or polishing quartz rocks in rapturous detail, and I realized something. She was as happy as I was.

Peter was a different story. Getting his Georgia certification hadn't been a problem—the board had reviewed his credentials and awarded it immediately, also allowing him to keep his license to practice in New York—but he wasn't himself. In addition to his single-minded determination to find the well, he hadn't been sleeping. From our first day in Juliana, I'd been waking up all hours of the night to an empty bed. I'd found him more than a couple of times on the wraparound porch, staring out over the land, jaw tight and eyes wary.

I started finding him at various spots around the house at all hours of the day, curled up, fast asleep. Several times, when I'd come home from work, I found him on the porch, head thrown back, snoring softly on one of the rocking chairs. He fell asleep on the sofa before dinner and then after, in Mere's bed, a copy of *Ribsy* splayed facedown across his chest.

He told me not to worry, that he just needed to get in the rhythm of his new schedule. He was accustomed to the frenetic, horn-honking, exhaust-spewing energy of the city, he said, then joked that his body didn't know what to do with so much serenity and quiet and wide-open space. Still, I wondered if he shouldn't make an appointment with Dr. Belmont St. John, the old internist, so the man could run some tests. He said he'd look into it.

The last time I'd woken up alone in our bed, it was from a murky but disturbing dream that fled my memory the second I opened my eyes. The clock said two-thirty in the morning. I made some chamomile tea and brought it out to him on the front porch. I sat beside him and rubbed his back. The muscles in his back were tight and knotted, but he didn't lean into my touch. It was almost like I wasn't there.

"Can't sleep again?" I finally asked.

He just shook his head.

"You know, every time I lie down, this unbelievably maddening song from the playlist at Billie's plays over and over in my head. I was even dreaming about it, just now, I think."

Peter said nothing.

"It has this, like, insidious quality that just really drives me . . ." I attempted a smile in his direction. "Anyway, Finch and Libby and Susy absolutely swear the regulars love their old hymns, so in it stays, I guess."

"Where the fuck is it?" he said between clenched teeth, as if I hadn't said a word. "All I've found out there is trees and vines and that shitty creek running through the woods."

The tone of his voice made my stomach clench. The well. He was talking about the well again. I couldn't deny the feeling of dread that settled over me. Not because I was worried about Mere—at this point, I truly believed if there really was a well, it was so deeply hidden she'd never find it—but because Peter's obsession with it was starting to feel like a red flag I shouldn't ignore. Like he was really worried about something else and was sublimating.

"I know it's been frustrating—" I began.

"Have you heard from the well company Jamie recommended?" Peter let out a huff of frustration, raked his fingers through his hair.

"I left them a bunch of messages, but nobody's called me back yet."

"Ask him if there's another company."

I hesitated. "I don't want to bother him, Peter. He's already done so much for us." *For me.* "I was going to work on it myself. I've just been so busy, I haven't gotten around to it."

He was silent.

"What did you mean about the creek being shitty? Is something wrong with it?"

He stared out across the field. He looked so haggard, so empty. "The water looks dirty. Like rusty or something. I don't know. There aren't any fish in it."

"Huh. Maybe the water around here is bad. Jamie Cleburne's dad probably knows something about that. He's had to do all that work to get his lake right."

"So you and Jamie talk about his father's lake, but you don't want to tell him his well company won't return your calls?" His eyes looked hollow.

"He's a customer, Peter. I don't want to make it awkward."

"Does he understand how dangerous an uncapped well is?"

"Don't get mad at me," I said.

"I'm not mad at you. I'm just . . ." He looked annoyed, not an expression I was used to being on the other end of. He rose, moved to the edge of the porch. The wind had kicked up, whipping around the eaves of the house, whistling tunelessly, joining the buzz of cicadas.

"This is not even an argument worth having," I said. "There's probably no well, and all of this is for nothing."

"Why would they tell us there's a well if there isn't?" he asked.

"I don't know, Peter, but no one seems overly concerned that we've got some kind of deathtrap on our property, and if anything happens, we could sue them for negligence or not officially revealing its existence and location. So . . . honestly, I'm not that worried about it."

"It's like they don't want us on our own property," he mused, like he hadn't heard me. "Has Mayor Dixie said anything to you about moving? Like, suggested we look at other houses or anything?"

"No."

"Maybe the groundwater's contaminated. Maybe there's a chance it could get into our well, and they're afraid we'll sue about that."

I laughed. "Okay, now you're being paranoid."

"Don't fucking laugh at me," he snapped. "Something's not right here."

I blinked in surprise, sensing the change in temperature. The wind whooshed through the leaves of the old oak beside the house. It unnerved me. He picked at the flakes of paint on the column, letting them fall around his feet like snow. His jaw pulsed. It looked like he was grinding his teeth to dust.

"I'm sorry, Peter," I said stiffly. "You have a right to your feelings."

Now he laughed. "Spoken like a true therapist's spouse. Oh God, maybe I really am just being paranoid. It just doesn't make sense. And I can't sleep, which means I can't think. I don't know what's wrong with me. I'm just so fucking tired."

I wanted to mention Doc Belmont again, but I bit back the suggestion. Better to keep the peace. Let Peter come around to it himself.

"I'll call Jamie's father," he promised wearily. "Mr. Cleburne. About the water in his lake and another well company. You just focus on the restaurant."

"Peter—" I wanted to say something more, something that would bridge the gulf between us. That would make us a team again.

"Don't worry about me. I'll be fine. I just need to catch up on my sleep."

I nodded, but I wasn't okay. We hadn't settled anything. There was something between us, something I couldn't put a name to or fight or even understand. I thought about that yellow crime tape at the mill. The song I'd been dreaming about ran like a golden thread through my brain. And now I remembered part of the dream I'd had tonight, right before I'd woken. It had been like Mere's dream.

Children singing in the dark, led by the woman with gray braids.

I wrapped my arms around myself, feeling a sudden chill even in the warm night air.

Maybe there was something to Peter's unease, at least on some level. I'd been on such a high from the restaurant's success, I'd pushed everything that didn't fit into my perfect picture—the crime tape, the weird dreams—into some out-of-the-way closet in my brain and locked the door.

But right now, it felt oddly like the world around me was trying to send a message. The sound of the wind fluttering the leaves of the oak and the eaves, even the buzzing of the cicadas, seemed to send a warning:

Beware . . .

In the days that followed, neither of us mentioned the well or our fight. On the plus side, Peter no longer went out on his reconnaissance missions. Maybe he had been right—Dixie and Major Minette didn't want us exploring our own land—but it was clear we weren't going to get anywhere arguing about it. I resolved to talk to Jamie again, but this time bring it up in a roundabout way. I decided I could do it under the guise of discussing my customers crowding the entrance to his shop.

A few days later, as we were closing for the afternoon at Billie's, he appeared in the door that connected our spaces. I waved him over to sit at the bar, which I was wiping down.

"You're closed," he protested, looking around at the flurry of sweeping, rolling silver, and stacking clean dishes.

I poured him a water. "Not to valued neighbors." He sat, and I grabbed a loaded plate from the expo window. "Also, I never discuss a beef without French toast. And mixed berry compote."

"A beef?" He grinned. "I didn't realize that was what was happening between us."

Flirt.

I spooned a dollop of whipped cream on top of the berries. "I figured you're probably mad at me. My customers have been blocking your shop entrance while they wait for a table."

He shrugged and dug into the French toast. "True, but it's not like my shop is getting stampeded."

"Still. It's not right. I should try to direct traffic elsewhere. Maybe I can put some benches across the street, near the statue."

He snorted. "Good luck getting Mayor Dixie to agree to that. The town council thinks benches encourage vagrants."

I raised my eyebrows.

"Her words, not mine."

"I haven't seen any around."

"Well, we've had our share of people struggling with poverty. Addicts and other displaced people. But since Dixie's been mayor, she's really tried to discourage it."

"Sounds ominous."

He'd already made it halfway through the French toast. "There was a problem a couple years back. Lilah Street's oldest daughter, Wren."

I felt a prickle up the middle of my neck.

"I heard she had a substance abuse issue," I said carefully, "but nobody told me she was on the streets."

He lowered his voice. "Oxy. Lilah finally had to ask her to get out to protect Temperance. Wren and her buddies hung around the square during the day, slept in one of the church basements. At least until Dixie had the sheriff shoo them away. After that, I think she actually ended up at the Dalzell-Davenport place."

My hackles went up. *Our house?*

He must've seen my shock. "The house was empty after George's family took him back to Orlando. I think Wren and her friends squatted there."

"Oh." It was all I could think of to say. I wasn't about to tell Jamie the truth, that my husband was already feeling uneasy about our new home, so uneasy he couldn't sleep. And that he'd started to lash out at me because of it.

"Just for a while. After a couple of months, she went out to California. She got a job on a weed farm. And the others left, too."

I nodded. I had heard the basics of that part of the story from Finch and Falcon. I had no words. I couldn't imagine having to leave Mere like that. It was unfathomable. Poor Lilah. Poor Temperance. What a shitty situation.

He shrugged. "Everybody's got their struggles. I hope she's clean and making herself happy."

"It's just so sad. For Temperance."

He eyed me. "And a little disconcerting for you. That people were living in your house, I mean. On top of the situation with the well. You ever hear back from the well company?"

Relieved the conversation had finally headed this way, I perked up. "Actually, no. I left a few messages. I'm sure they're just busy. I did wonder if you knew of another company that could handle it. It's just that . . ." I realized he was looking at me intently, his gaze unwavering. "Peter's really worried about it. You know."

"Is he?" *Say more*, his eyes said.

But I wasn't going there. "Yeah."

"Sorry to hear that. I'll ask around for you. See if we can find somebody." He slid off the stool and turned toward the door. He waved at the staff still hard at work then looked back at me. "Meanwhile, I'll ask Mayor Dixie about those benches. Can't hurt to try."

"Thanks."

"And Billie?"

"Yeah?"

"Tell Peter not to give the well another thought. You don't either. You've brought life to this space, to this town, and we are going to make sure you don't regret it. Mere could not be in a safer place than right here in Juliana, I promise you that. You have my word." He held my gaze for a second or two, then turned and walked out the door.

1934
Juliana, Georgia

Alfred Minette III, grandson of the original Alfred Minette, founder of Juliana, sat at his large mahogany desk in his paneled office on the third floor of the courthouse. It was technically the office of the mayor which Little Al, as he was still called even at age twenty-seven, was not. The actual mayor, Hubert Dalzell, was an outdoorsman and did not care for offices, so he let his best friend, Little Al, use it free of charge.

Little Al conducted the business of his two sawmills from the spacious, well-appointed office. He not only owned the mills and a good many properties in Juliana, but with his family inheritance had purchased nearly one hundred thousand acres of longleaf pine timberland in Georgia, Alabama, Mississippi, and Louisiana. In spite of the rest of the country's suffering in the hard economic times, Little Al Minette had cleared practically every acre of forest he owned and was a very rich man.

But he was not going to stay that way by sleeping on opportunities. His father and grandpapa had taught him well: how much had been sacrificed to make Juliana the town it was and how that tradition must be upheld by taking advantage of every opportunity that presented itself. Like the one that was headed his way now in the form of one Mr. Lank Stetler.

Lank Stetler was foreman of the larger of his two mills, a hard worker, and an honest family man. He was smart. Too smart, Little Al thought from time to time. He'd heard rumblings that Stetler was a union man.

"Come on in, Stetler. Have a sit," Little Al boomed.

Stetler, dusty cap in hand, sawdust-matted hair plastered to his grimy forehead, was ushered into the office by Little Al's secretary, Dolores, whom Little Al told to head on home. After she closed the door, Little Al leaned back in his leather chair and surveyed Stetler.

"So let's hear it, this idea you have."

Stetler proceeded to tell Little Al that he'd thought of a new use for the sawdust leavings they mounded in piles all around the mills and which were a nuisance to dispose of. Stetler had devised a machine that pressed the sawdust, along with a bit of paraffin, into the shape of logs. Logs that would burn longer, cleaner, and cheaper than either cord wood or coal. Logs that could create a whole new business opportunity just as the timber supply was slowing down to a trickle.

As the man spoke, Little Al's heart thundered in excitement. He maintained a poker face, however. It wouldn't do to give away too much.

"And how many folks have you told about this idea of yours, Mr. Stetler?" he asked.

"Just the wife," Stetler replied. "Her and nobody else."

Little Al nodded. He'd seen young Mrs. Stetler around town. She was a lovely girl, still fresh as she hadn't had young'uns yet. She wouldn't be a problem, Al thought. After all was said and done, she might even let Little Al buy her a nice dinner and a glass of champagne in Atlanta. Maybe treat her to a show at the Fox Theater, too. Who knows? She might even let Al kiss her on the neck.

He couldn't help himself. In the excitement of Stetler's idea, his mind skipped far ahead, to the time when he'd have the blades and belts taken out of the mill by the river and replaced with this sawdust-pressing machine. Skipped ahead to the time when he'd be making money hand over fist and would finally have a moment to look for a wife.

But there were important details to handle before that. He would pay the young Widow Stetler a nice stipend, enough to provide for her, and he had to make sure she understood that her poor dead husband's idea had actually been Little Al's idea first. Maybe he'd send a bit of extra cash her way. Surely that would soften her heart toward him. Maybe so much that she would let him kiss her neck . . .

Good golly, he really had gotten ahead of himself, and now he had a stiff one, right now, right under his desk, even as Stetler sat on the other side of it, going on and on about discs and extruders and water vapor.

He willed the pesky appendage down. This was serious business, offering a sacrifice. His father and grandfather had drilled that into him since he was a boy of thirteen. The three families, the Minettes, Dalzells, and Cleburnes hadn't made a sacrifice since the original one over seventy years ago. But times were desperate. He'd cleared most of his timber. Soon, Minette Mills would have no lumber left to saw, and the town's main industry would be gone. A sacrifice had to be made. It would turn the town's luck around, sure as shooting. He had to be a man about this. And he had to do it quick before Stetler told anybody else.

As Stetler talked, Little Al made his plan. He would ask the man to walk with him down to the sawmill. Ask him to show Al where the machine would go. Precisely how it would make the logs. Then he would lure Stetler toward one of the great jagged saws, perhaps on some pretense of something amiss with the machinery. . . .

It would be a quick death, and Al would pay that stipend to the man's widow right after the funeral. He would offer her his strong shoulder to cry on and perhaps suggest an arrangement. Would she dare consider him, the richest man in town, as a husband? After all, she was alone and near penniless, and Little Al was in need of a son to carry on the Minette family name.

He had to approach things careful-like, he thought. But be strong and resolute. The fortune of Gentle Juliana depended on him.

Chapter 9

By mid-June, even though it had been only two months, I felt as if I'd lived in Juliana forever. That my bones had always been warmed by this southern sunshine, that the honeyed accent had always been my native tongue, and that the smell of jasmine and magnolia and gardenia was now as familiar to me as that of baking bread. I may not have preferred the twangy gospel songs that played incessantly on Billie's sound system—and that had taken to weaving themselves into the unusually vivid dreams I now regularly had—but I was making peace with them.

I loved our house, every odd angle and nook, every slightly off-kilter corner and intricately carved flourish. Mere and I had filled the conservatory with every kind of plant, and she did all the watering. I even took the occasional mouse or cockroach that skittered across the floors in stride. Funny how in New York they felt dirty. Here, they just seemed like a part of the natural world that deserved to live in peace. The only thing I couldn't quite get ahead of was the constant layer of fine, whitish dust that covered everything. Even hours after I'd gone over every surface with the Swiffer, I'd discover a fine layer of it had settled again.

Billie's was chugging along, seating over a hundred covers a day, collecting a solid group of regulars, and not just among the original families. A lot of the new citizens, a diverse group of folks from all over the country, were discovering us. I had loved running the New York Billie's, but the pace of that town was nothing but hustle and grind. Somehow the work here felt easier, the new team, like a family. I might've lived my whole life in New York, but now I was home.

Peter, on the other hand, was still struggling. The insomnia persisted, and in between appointments, he would nap. At least then, there was peace. When he was awake, he was on edge, losing his temper easily and frequently at both Mere and me. When he wasn't snapping at us, he was ominously quiet, a glowering, grumpy presence drifting through our home. I tried not to let it bother me. The guy wasn't Superman. He was just an ordinary person who carried a lot on a daily basis. The weight of other people's emotions was a heavier burden than most people knew; and I reminded myself, sometimes it made him overlook his own mental health.

One morning, however, he did surprise me by saying he had made an appointment for the following week with Dr. St. John— Doc Belmont, as everybody called him—about the insomnia. He promised to let him do whatever tests he thought were necessary to set my mind at ease. I kissed him and went to work, reassuring myself that everything was okay. That I wouldn't worry, not until there was something real to worry about. I had faith in Peter. He'd be fine. And he'd come around.

He'd have to. Because Mere loved it here.

The sparkle in her eye, the skip in her step, it was all the proof I needed. My daughter was as happy as "a pig in collards," as Finch Street liked to say. Mere loved Lilah's house and had taken to calling Temperance her "bestie." I started taking Tuesdays and Wednesdays off to play with her or go see one of the old films playing at The Juliana Theater and have Cokes and tea sandwiches afterward at the hotel. She spent Saturdays and Sundays, our busiest days at the café, at home with Peter, staying up late on those nights so after I got home, we could play Chutes and Ladders or read together.

After speaking briefly with James Cleburne Sr. on the phone, who said he'd put in a call to the guys who ran the well company himself, Peter kind of eased up on the whole issue. If the well was real, he couldn't even find it, so it was a good bet Mere wouldn't either. He agreed we should let her ramble around, as long as she kept the house in sight. And did she ramble. Before long, rows and rows of sparkling rocks she'd collected on her expeditions lined every porch railing, bookshelf, and windowsill in the house. She forbade me to move them, telling me Lilah was going to tumble them in her rock polishing machine, so she and Tempie could make them into matching friendship bracelets.

She still had the bad dreams, the ones about the children in the dark and the old woman with the crown of braids. Sometimes the children lit candles, she said, sometimes they sang songs, but they were always afraid. I comforted her when she woke, but more often than not, she never came to our room, instead tiptoeing into the empty bedroom next door to hers, sitting on the floor, and flipping through George Davenport's collection of old books. I never told her how eerily similar my dreams were to hers. I underplayed them to Peter, as well.

At any rate, Peter said we shouldn't worry too much about the nightmares, hers or mine. It was normal after all the change we'd both been through, and the fact that we were living in an old house that she wasn't used to. As for the similar scenarios, he chalked it up to the power of suggestion. And the fierce protectiveness I felt for my daughter. I tried to accept this explanation.

What really bothered me was the idea of Wren Street and her friends living in our house. Since Jamie had told me, I couldn't stop thinking about it. Had they been shooting up? Trading sex for drugs? *Meth heads, tweekers, junkies.* I couldn't get the images out of my mind, of some motley collection of individuals using my house for their own personal crack den. Maybe that was why Mayor Dixie wanted us out of the place. She was worried that we'd discover the town had allowed squatters.

I decided not to tell Peter. He didn't need another thing making him uneasy about Juliana. I resolved to go over the spare bedroom one more time in case Wren and her cronies had left behind any signs. The next Saturday, after Mere struck off on another rock-hunting expedition, I threw together a bucket of cleaning products and a mop and headed upstairs.

George Davenport's old room was snug, with its own little fireplace surrounded by a brick mantel. Sunshine poured in through the western-facing windows. White dust coated everything. I attacked the books first, the white iron bed frame, a skeletal thing since I'd thrown out the old mattress, and then the heavy walnut desk.

I checked the drawers of the desk. There were no drugs, but in the back of one drawer I found a heavy, faded, green linen bound book. It was a ledger of some sort, with columns of entries written in neat handwriting with faded ink, obviously extremely old, maybe even belonging to Silas Dalzell. The actual words were almost impossible to make out but seemed to be expenses, staples, and supplies needed on a farm. I flipped to the back of the book, to a page that had been torn out. On the following page, written in a blocky script and with pencil, was a new, obviously more modern, list.

Ax, hatchet, chainsaw, brush grubber, root grapple.
Okay.
Pool shocker, ammonium nitrate, Drano, nail polish remover, cold packs.

This list had to have been written by George Davenport. I blinked, staring at the page, not comprehending what I was seeing. Not until I typed the particular combination of items into the search bar of my phone and the alarming headline of an article flashed on the screen: *Homemade Explosive Device.*

Why would Davenport need an explosive device? Maybe for the infamous hidden well. He might have been trying to somehow get rid of it or make it safer. But why didn't he just cover it with a slab of concrete? Blowing the thing up made no sense. But Jamie had said the old man was senile toward the end. *Batty.*

I replaced the ledger in the drawer and set to cleaning the baseboards with the bucket of soapy water and scrub brush. On hands and knees, I made my way around the perimeter of the room, attacking the grimy baseboards and molding like it was Lady Macbeth's bloodstained hands. As I neared the old bookcase against the back wall, I came across a string of crude carvings in the board. I ran my fingers over the gashes in the wood, brushing away the dirty suds so I could make out what was written.

For the children, the markings read.

I sprang back, as if the letters had burned my fingers. My heart was leaping wildly in my chest, my breath gone shallow. I tentatively crawled back to get a closer look at the baseboard. There were more carvings after that—a string of letters. *MBEDWS.*

I peered at the nonsensical letters, my mind racing.

Calm down, Billie. They were obviously just initials. *WS* was Wren Street. Wren Street and whoever was squatting with her in the house were dedicating their activities in the house to some children, whatever that meant. Maybe conspiracy-type stuff, paranoia fueled by the drugs.

Or maybe . . .

I thought of the dreams Mere and I kept having. Children in the dark. Children scared and singing with the old woman. Did Wren have those dreams, too, when she stayed here? Could they somehow be connected to something that had happened in this house—or around it—and now there was some spiritual . . . *residue* in these rooms?

I looked around the space, the mental image flashing in my head: children huddled together in the dark, dirty skin streaked with tears. Fear filled the dank air, sharp and slightly sweet. The scent of desperation. The smell of death.

I banished the vision. My brain was just conflating the nightmares with these carvings and turning them into something meaningful. Humans were pattern-seeking beings, Peter always said it. We always gravitated to connected dots, whether they made sense or not. I just needed to calm down.

I looked around the room, thinking. Then, spotting the walnut desk, I dragged it over to the section of baseboard where the words were carved and pushed it up against the wall. It looked awkward there, and if you crouched, the carved letters were still visible, but it would have to do. I couldn't have Mere or Peter finding it and asking questions.

I heard a door open and slam, and I jumped. I hurried out into the hall to see Peter, dressed in jeans, a white button-down, and a charcoal blazer, heading down the stairs.

"Hey."

He turned toward me. His hair, still wet from the shower, curled at his temples. His clear eyes under reddish lashes and eyebrows locked into mine. I smiled, that open invitation that always existed between us.

He grinned back but gave me a warning shake of his head, reading my mind. "I can't. I've got that doctor's appointment."

"Doc Belmont sees patients on the weekends?"

"He was doing me a favor. I think he wants a couple of free sessions for his granddaughter."

"Sounds about right. There's literally nothing in this town that can't be bartered."

He gave me a charged once-over. "Looking hot with that mop bucket."

I shimmied seductively. "Got a maid fantasy, do you?"

"I've got an anything-that-involves-you fantasy. You know that." He was on me in an instant, his hands moving down my back, over my ass.

I did the same, feeling something in his back pocket. "Shit." I pulled out a small square of sea salt dark chocolate in a shiny blue wrapper. "You found my stash."

"Bookshelves. Too easy."

I laughed. "You're never going to find them again."

"Oh, I will. You're a terrible pirate. I always find your treasure." He kissed me and gently took the chocolate from me. "See you later, gorgeous."

I laughed and he was gone, down the staircase and out the front door.

After work, when I went to pick up Mere at Lilah's, she invited me in and went to pour us coffee. While Mere and Temperance raced through the house, screaming and giggling, I looked around the living room. It was a cluttered but cozy space, crammed with trailing plants in macrame hangers, polished rocks, and whimsical found-art sculptures.

I took note of a framed photograph on the mantel, a black-and-white senior class photo of a girl who had to be Wren. She wore a silky sundress and was leaning against a brick wall, arms and legs crossed. A pageboy cut of dark hair framed wide eyes and a frank expression.

Lilah returned as the girls thundered on the floor above us. "Do you want me to go get them?"

"No rush. I'm happy she's having fun."

"Can we sit?" Lilah's face turned serious. "I did want to mention something to you."

I sat in an armchair covered with a multicolored afghan. "About Mere? Is there a problem? I know she can get mouthy." I laughed nervously. "She gets it from me. You can take the girl out of New York—"

"Oh lord, no." Lilah laughed and waved a dismissive hand. "It's not anything like that. Mere's a perfect angel. It's just something she brought over. A rock she found on your property, she said." From her pocket, Lilah drew out a rock. It was about the size of a golf ball, a dull gold color and strange lumpy shape. "Mere wanted me to tumble it for a necklace, but I told her it might not be the best idea." Her voice was low, like she was afraid the girls might overhear. She handed it to me, and I noticed her hand trembled the slightest bit. "I know this sounds strange, Billie, but I think it might be gold."

I held the rock up. "No. It couldn't be."

"Actually, it is possible. Georgia had a gold rush back in the early 1800s, even before the California one. Most of the big mines were northeast of here in Dahlonega, but there's a possibility some could be down here."

I studied the rock. "You know, Jamie and I were talking about it the other day—the land lottery—and he said there wasn't any gold found here in Juliana."

Lilah was watching me closely. "How did you know about the land lottery?"

"Mere told me. She read about it the first night we were here. George Davenport left a bunch of books in his house about Georgia history."

Lilah tilted her head. "Such a shame how old George's family whisked him away so quickly and left behind his stuff."

"He must've been very sick."

She nodded. "Completely lost his memory. Started to hallucinate. They had to drag him out of the square one day. He was ranting and raving at the statue, like it was a real person." She grimaced.

"Ranting and raving? About what?"

Lilah waved a dismissive hand. "Oh, I don't know. Just a bunch of hooey about how Juliana Minette wasn't a little girl but some kind of monster or something. That she had horns sprouting out of her head. Wings. He threw a can of paint on her. It took them weeks to get it off. So sad."

I wasn't sure if she was referring to the defacement of the statue or George Davenport's decline.

"You said Mere was reading history books?" she asked me.

I blinked. "She's always been advanced, although I don't know that she understands everything that she reads. That night she had a nightmare. She couldn't sleep. She has them a lot." As soon as the words were out of my mouth, I regretted them. I liked Lilah, but I was wary of oversharing.

"What are the nightmares about?" Lilah asked.

"Oh"—I lifted a shoulder—"nothing specific."

Lilah looked doubtful. "That is an old house you live in."

I smiled. "Ha. Don't go there. You'll freak me out. I sleep in that house, too, you know."

"No, I'm serious. There's something to a house's history. Do you have the gift in your family? Second sight or psychic sensing? People around here call it the Holy Spirit's gift of prophecy."

"Um, no. I definitely do not have . . . whatever that is."

Her eyes twinkled. "Don't be so sure. More people have it than not. Women, mostly. Girls, before they learn from this hard, mean world how to ignore it. They feel it in their bones. They get headaches, tummy aches, cramps. They dream dreams. Have recurring nightmares," she said with a look of significance. "You know a lot of folks in this town are dreamers. I used to have these ones about monkeys—"

I smiled to cut her off. "I think Mere's dreams are just your basic, run-of-the-mill, kid nightmares."

"If you say so. If you want, I can send the rock off to get it verified," she said. "In case it does turn out to be gold. That would be exciting, right?"

"That's so sweet, but you don't have to. I mean, we both know it's probably pyrite."

"Well, a girl can always hope. And I don't know what your contract said," Lilah said with a smirk and a quirk of her eyebrow, "but if it is really gold, I bet Mayor Dixie and the rest of the town council will *definitely* have something to say about those one hundred smackers you and Peter paid for that property."

I handed it back to her. "Just polish it up for her. She'll think it's gold, and she'll love it."

"Sure thing." Lilah pocketed the rock. "It'll be our little secret."

Mere and I had chicken salad sandwiches for lunch then spent the afternoon baking a coconut cake. Billie Holiday played on the record player Mere had set up on the counter. While Mere was busy stirring the batter, I surreptitiously slipped out and re-hid my chocolate stash in the dry fountain in the conservatory. As I passed through the blue parlor, I stopped to do a quick search on my laptop. There was nothing about a mine in Juliana. The only mention of gold found in our county, Bartow, was at a site called the Allatoona Mine, which apparently had been quite small and quickly played out. And according to the map it would've been located over fifteen miles away from here. So much for that.

Back in the kitchen, I dipped a finger in the batter. "Where's Rams?" I asked Mere.

She was measuring flour. "Out."

I glanced at her. Her bare feet were dirty, and her golden hair was tangled around her pale face, making her look like a feral child. "Does that make you sad?"

It was the kind of question Peter liked to ask, but seeing as Peter was not around—not in the mental sense, at least—I guess it was up to me to keep Mere in touch with her emotions.

She shrugged. "Yes, but outside is where he likes to be now. And that's what Daddy says you do for people you love. Let them be where they want to be. It's called acceptance."

I smothered the laughter that wanted to erupt. My heart expanded in wild, out-of-control directions. God, my girl was a smart one.

I heard the back door screen creak and glanced over. Ramsey had pawed it open, slipped through, and was picking his way across the tile.

"Speak of the devil." I looked over at Mere. She hung back, pressed against the hutch, her hands crossed behind her. We watched Ramsey navigate the tile, like he was slightly disgusted at its smooth surface, being an evolved creature who now traveled fields and pine-needle-strewn forests and pebbly creeks. He walked to the middle of the room, making a serpentine path around the chair legs.

"Here, Ramsey. Come on. Come see me." He ignored me, which wasn't all that unusual. I grabbed a treat from the glass container on the counter and held it out. "What you been doing, Ramsey? What kind of adventures you been having?"

Ramsey prowled under the table, ignoring me and the treat. Clearly, he wasn't interested in divulging what he'd been up to while he was out in the wild beyond. And Mere was still pressed against the hutch.

"Sweetie, you okay?"

She kept her eyes trained on the cat. "He looks different."

"Who? Ramsey?"

She nodded.

I followed her gaze, studying his orangey stripes. "Different, how?"

She shrugged. "Just . . . different."

The cat had slipped out from the table and was now pacing in front of Mere. She made no move in his direction. I pocketed the treat, scooped him up, and tried to give him a once-over. He struggled in my arms, but I managed to flip him over, inspecting all the relevant orifices. He mewed angrily, and I held him out, legs dangling in midair, to her.

"He's fine. He's just gotten an attitude, running around outside. All he needs is a snuggle."

She didn't budge from her spot.

I waggled the cat a little. "Come on. He's fine." I caught her eyes. They shone with some sort of unspoken pain I'd missed. "Mere, honey. What is it?"

Mere looked at me, her eyes wide. "He's the Catawampus," she whispered.

"The what?"

"The Catawampus. Lilah told me and Temperance about it. Something's turned Ramsey into the Catawampus, and I don't want him anymore. I don't want him." She turned and fled the room. A few seconds later, I could hear her footsteps pounding up the stairs, then a door slam.

Just then, I felt a searing pain inside my wrist. Ramsey, clawing at me. "Shit!" I dropped him and he hit the floor like an Olympic gymnast. Then, with a snarl and hiss, he streaked through the swinging door and out of the room.

Chapter 10

Juliana did like itself a party. A *to-do*, as Mayor Dixie called them.

I was constantly fielding a barrage of invitations to luncheons, book clubs, hoedowns, crawfish boils, cookouts, cocktail hours, and Fourth-of-July block parties. Most of the invitations came by word-of-mouth or evites. Most, I declined. I needed to be at the restaurant as much as possible, at least in the early days. And Peter wasn't exactly in the party-going mood.

Mayor Dixie's dinner party invitation for the new citizens of Juliana came the old-fashioned way, through the mail, elegant print on heavy card stock in a creamy envelope. Our names and address were written in flawless calligraphy. After dinner Mere went off with my *Joy of Cooking* under her arm and Peter started on the dishes. I propped the invitation against the candle holder on the kitchen table.

He picked it up and scanned it, then putting it back down without saying a word, stacked his plate on top of mine and went back to the sink. He ran the water, so hot that steam billowed up around his shoulders.

I folded my napkin calmly. "I think we should go."

"Can't. I have appointments."

"It's at seven P.M. You don't have appointments that late."

"Sometimes I do."

This was news to me. "With who?"

He shut off the water. "I can't tell you."

Now he was just being difficult. But two could play that game. "Okay," I said, calmly, coolly. "Can you reschedule?"

"I'd rather not." He was going at one of the pots now, a dish towel flung over his shoulder.

"Just for one night."

"I'd rather not. The patient . . ." He leaned against the sink. "Consistency is an issue. I don't want to cancel on them."

"You know, people in this town are making an effort with us, Peter. With you. You've been asked to skeet shoots, quail hunts. A crappie—"

"It's *croppie*."

"It's *croppie*. As in *crap*. A crappie fishing weekend on the famous, uncontaminated, ecologically balanced Cleburne Lake, by Mr. James Cleburne himself. Which you turned down."

He turned suddenly, whipping off the dish towel. "You want me to go fishing with Jamie Cleburne? Seriously?"

"Why not? You could use some friends around here."

He seemed oddly amused by this.

"What?"

"I don't think it's me Jamie Cleburne wants to be friends with."

I laughed, which sounded guilty even to my ears. "That's ridiculous. I'm sure he wants to be friends with both of us."

His comment was out of character. Peter had an immensely reasonable view of relationships and marriage and the way normal human beings operated, and because of that, I'd never before felt any guilt over a random, biological pull toward another man. But now he was looking at me like he couldn't figure me out.

"Right," he said.

"What are you trying to say, Peter?"

He shook his head. "Why didn't you tell me about him? About Jamie?"

"What about him?"

"Why have you never mentioned that he comes into the café every morning?"

I shrugged. "A lot of people come in every day. We call them regulars." But I was covering. There was a reason I hadn't mentioned Jamie's presence at my bar every morning. It was because I was starting to depend on it. Starting to like it just a little too much. "You said it yourself. Jamie and I are friends. Just friends."

He turned back to the pots in the sink.

"I just want to go to a party with my husband, Peter. I just want to feel like we're both a part of this town. That's all."

He kept his back to me, scrubbing like his life depended on it.

The following week, one bright, hot morning after the breakfast rush, I asked Jamie if he knew anything about Lilah and the Catawampus story.

He rolled his eyes. "Ignore Lilah. She's into all that woo-woo stuff. Crystals, astrology, Native myths." He held up a hand, like he was testifying at church. "She told me she had a ghost in her house once."

I thought of old George Davenport, his mind disintegrating with dementia, throwing a can of paint at the statue of little Juliana Minette. Of Peter's insomnia. Mere's dreams and mine. *For the children,* Wren Street had carved in the baseboard. If any house was haunted in this town, it was mine. . . .

An image, horrible and grisly, flashed in my head. A young girl. I pushed it away.

Still, my scalp prickled painfully. I couldn't resist the pull of the macabre. And my house really did appear to be in the center of it.

"What happened to Juliana Minette? What did she die of?"

He shrugged. "I don't know. But she died long before the Minettes founded the town." He studied me. "What makes you ask that? Is something wrong?"

"Nothing," I said briskly. "Back in a second. I've got to run to the back and grab some to-go boxes." I ran into the kitchen, breathless, heart hammering, and flattened myself against the fridge.

I gulped and shut my eyes, trying to banish the image that had flashed before me seconds ago. Little, dead Juliana Minette; her rotted corpse, gray and glistening, with strips of sinew hanging loose and bright white bone shining through. Her fingernails were yellowed and flaking away. Her hair stringy and snarled. She bared her baby teeth, her jaw unhinging as if she yearned to consume something she saw.

Somehow, I knew. What she wanted was me.

The one invitation I definitely couldn't refuse but could handle without Peter was a meet-and-greet at Juliana Elementary School, held in the summer for the new members of the Initiative. That day, I left work an hour and a half after Billie's opened, ran home to shower and change into dark denim overalls over a lacey blouse and my requisite black Doc Martens. I headed over to Lilah's so the four of us could go together.

Lilah and Temperance walked with Mere and me the three blocks to the school, the girls chattering the whole way. Lilah was in a gossiping mood, going on about the staff drama at the home goods store where she'd started to sell her homemade jewelry.

I was distracted. Maybe it was the Catawampus issue. I'd told Peter that Jamie thought Lilah was harmless, but he hadn't been satisfied. Regardless, it wasn't going to help matters to bring it up now. Lilah might be a bit of a kook, but she was my friend, and I didn't want to jeopardize that.

Still, I felt antsy as we walked. A little like I was being watched. A couple of times, I looked over my shoulder, but there was no one there. I shook off the feeling. Little, dead Juliana Minette wasn't watching me nor were a pack of singing children led by a creepy old woman. This was just what it was like to live in a small town. People knew you. They watched you. You weren't just another one of the invisible ants like in New York. I just had to get used to it, that was all.

Juliana Elementary was just as storybook-quaint as the rest of the town. An old limestone building just a quarter of a mile from the square with an imposing scrolled façade and matching persimmon trees on either side of the front walk that led up to it. Inside, you could smell the mustiness, but the marble floors were polished, and the old, crank-out windows sparkled. The kindergarten, first, second, and third grades were located just down the first hall to the left of the main office. When we walked into the classroom with both Mere's and Temperance's names on the list by the door, I found myself looking into the face of Alice Tilton.

She wore a yellow dress, her blond hair pulled back in a clip. Mere raced right up to her, hugged her, then ran off to investigate the cozy, colorful room.

"I thought you were a third-grade teacher," I blurted, realizing belatedly that I probably sounded disappointed.

"I was," Alice said. "They moved me this year because one of the new Initiative residents also taught third."

"Oh." I pasted a smile on my face, hoping she hadn't picked up on my attitude.

"It's fine. I was ready for a change." She turned her gaze to watch Mere and Temperance who were digging in a wicker dress-up box. "I'm excited to have Meredith in my class."

"I'm glad to hear that." I nodded. "She does read really well. Above her grade level, actually."

"The principal filled me in. And I want to assure you I have experience in all sorts of challenges our kids face, even if it's the kind where they need more advanced material to keep them engaged."

Okay, I liked the way she said *our kids*. Against my will, I felt a small rush of warmth. "I just want her to love learning, that's all."

Alice met my gaze. "Oh, if there's anything I can promise you, it's that all my kids love school. At least the year of it they spend with me."

It was obvious to me that Mere already felt at home in Alice's classroom. She and Temperance had made their way from the play center to the math center to the reading rug where racks of books were arranged around a colorful circular rag rug. They'd both plucked books and were sprawled out reading.

"I am concerned about something else, though," Alice said in a low voice.

I turned to find her watching me, face tense.

"I think we might have a conflict of interest."

"About what?" My heart had gone into overdrive. Was she talking about my friendship with Jamie? Did she somehow feel that we were in competition?

"I'm seeing Peter," she said.

For one split second, I thought she was telling me that she was dating my husband, and I let out a bark of wildly inappropriate laughter. The next instant, I realized I had missed the point entirely. My face turned blood red, and I clapped my hand over my mouth.

"No, no, no," she said in a rush. "I mean he's my therapist. I just wasn't sure if that was okay. Me meeting with him and having his daughter—your daughter—in my class."

"Right." I thought fast. "Yeah, okay, I will admit, this is a new one for me."

Peter hadn't told me he'd begun meeting with locals. Not

that he was obligated to. In fact, quite the opposite was true. He wasn't allowed to divulge the identity of his clients, in order to protect their privacy. I knew this. I was accustomed to this. So why was I freaking out? Hadn't I expected this transition? Hoped for it, in fact? I wanted Peter to finally start to settle into Juliana. To love it as much as Mere and I did.

"It's fine," I said firmly. "It's his job. He's a therapist. And it's fine that he's your therapist—I mean, fine with me."

"We did talk about it," she said. "Meredith being in my class. He said it was probably not ideal, but that it didn't violate any standards."

"Okay."

"I just wanted to lay out all the cards." Her face had gone bright red, now matching mine, and a lock of blond hair had fallen across her forehead. She looked nervous. It was possible she was just being respectful, but something about it didn't sit well with me. Like there was something she was hiding from me. Something, possibly, that she felt guilty about.

I turned toward Mere and Temperance and tried not to think about the fact that one more aspect of living in this town had suddenly gotten weird. Add it to the ever-growing list, I thought, of the downsides of small-town life.

Chapter 11

That night, I made carnitas bowls from a pork shoulder that I'd put in the slow cooker before leaving for work. Peter and Mere cooked rice with black beans, chopped tomatoes, and onions and jalapenos, and grated mounds of Monterey Jack. I whipped up a pitcher of margaritas for Peter and me then went to work shredding the fragrant, tender meat.

At one point, Ramsey stalked into the kitchen, and Mere flinched, eyeing him fearfully and leaning away. Peter lifted an eyebrow at me, but I shook my head and shooed the cat out of the room without comment. For once, Peter wasn't physically or mentally MIA. He was here with the two of us, wide-awake, joking with Mere and touching me at every opportunity. I wasn't about to make a big deal over the cat and jinx this situation.

We sat around the long kitchen table, and I started to dig in when Mere insisted on saying the official Juliana grace. After she'd finished, she touched a spot on her wrist and then pressed her fingers against her lips.

I looked at Peter. His brow was furrowed, but I shook my head again. If our daughter wanted to say grace, what could it hurt? It wasn't a battle worth fighting. Thankfully, Peter let it go, and after dinner, Mere asked if she could paint. I rolled out butcher paper on the kitchen table and set out pots of poster paint. She went to work while Peter and I sat on the back porch and finished the pitcher of margaritas. I told him about the school meet-and-greet, omitting Alice's admission of being Peter's client.

"Mere's really excited about school," I said. "And Alice Tilton's got a whole bag of tricks for keeping her engaged." I hesitated. "I was feeling kind of down about not being able to talk to Mom about it, but it was really nice to have Lilah there, you know? Like, next best thing."

There was no answer.

I leaned forward. "Peter?" I put down my drink and peered at him. His chin had dropped to his chest, and I realized with disbelief that he'd actually fallen asleep. I stared at him for a few seconds, resisting the urge to panic. He looked agitated, his eyes moving beneath their lids, his breath coming out in labored, staccato puffs, like he was running. Beads of sweat dotted his temple and ran along his hairline. He let out a soft whimper.

I reached out to shake him, but before I could, he stiffened and let out a bloodcurdling scream. I sprang back, clapping a hand over my mouth. He was struggling now, twisting in the rocking chair, legs kicking out, arms thrashing. He looked like he was fighting for his life.

"*You fucker*," he spat out. "You demon fucker! Don't touch me with those wings. Those fucking wings . . . I hate 'em. The feathers . . . the feathers . . . *I said get the fuck back!*"

I eyed him with a horrified, transfixed fascination, my heart thudding against my chest.

"You *fucker!*" With a great jolt, he flung himself up and out of the rocking chair, launching himself in my direction. I screamed and jumped to the side as he charged past me and crashed into the railing. He woke up then, sprawled on the ground, sweating and breathless. I ran to him.

"Peter!"

He rolled to a sitting position, head in his hands. "Oh God. Oh my God . . ."

"You were dreaming. What was it?"

He blinked. Then let out a disbelieving laugh that sounded almost like a moan.

I put my hand on his chest. "Peter. Talk to me. You have to talk to me. I've never seen you like that. I've never seen anyone like that."

"I don't know. I don't know." He kept shaking his head, like he was trying to shake off the vestiges of the dream. Then he covered his face with both hands.

"Peter. Please. This is me. I'm here."

He breathed deeply. Reoriented himself. "There was this horse. It was white with spots, but just a lighter white, like a spray of sunspots or star . . ." He trailed off, at a loss. His eyes were huge, full of a pain I couldn't identify, and he couldn't seem to describe.

"You said something about wings," I prodded.

"The thing . . . it had feathers. Wings. And it was coming after me. It wanted to hurt me. To hurt us. It was a demon, Billie. Some kind of demon-horse."

I tilted my head. "A demon-horse."

"Yeah, you know . . ." He gazed off across the back fields to the west, to the orange setting sun. "It belonged here, to this place. Over there. Over by the bluff. But it was angry. It . . ." He turned to me.

"What?"

His eyes were pleading. "You've had them too, right? The dreams?"

"Yeah. No demon-horses. Just that song. Kids singing that hymn we play at the restaurant. An old woman sometimes."

"It's got to mean something, don't you think? Like we're all having bizarre dreams. We're all having trouble sleeping."

I wanted to say that I was having trouble sleeping mainly because he kept waking me up, but I didn't. "Want to take a walk?" I asked instead. "Just a short one? Mere will be okay."

"I don't think so. I'm tired."

I folded my arms, my mind clicking away. I was not going to let this night end with Peter turning in early, and me sitting by myself catching up on whatever reality show was trending on Netflix. I was going to make my husband talk to me, even if it killed the both of us.

I sat beside him on the wood planks of the porch. "Have you heard back from Doc Belmont yet?"

"No. He said he'd call when he got the lab results."

I touched his arm. "Come walk with me. You'll feel better."

"I don't want to walk, Billie. I don't feel like it."

I felt chastened, like a toddler who'd just gotten her hand smacked for some naughty deed. "Tell me about your day then."

He sighed. "It was just a day like any other day. I listened to clients talk about their shit. I don't know what you want me to say."

I went hot all over. It felt like he'd slapped me in the face.

He sighed. "Sorry. That was uncalled for. I'm just so tired of being tired." He stood. "I should go to bed before more dumbassery comes out of my mouth."

He helped me up and pressed a kiss to my hand, but it felt perfunctory. "I'm sorry, Billie. I really am."

I lifted my chin to meet his eyes, but he wasn't even looking at me. He was staring out across the damn field, that faraway look in his eye that was fast becoming his default expression.

I jerked my hand out of his. "What? What is it that you see out there, Peter? Is it a well without a cover? Is it a demon-horse covered in feathers? Whatever it is, I want to go out there with you and find it."

For a split second, there was a desperate look on his face. Then he composed himself. "It's not the well. It's something else. It's—"

I lifted my chin, glared at him. "Let's just go out there and find the fucking thing once and for all and be done with the whole damn issue. I'm tired of you pushing me away. That's not how we do things. It's not us."

His jaw worked. His eyes looked watery and unsure in the porch light.

I stepped closer to him. "I don't know why you're so obsessed with the well, but you are, and I have to accept that. I accept it—my husband is more interested in some well on our property than anything, anyone else in his life."

"Like the way my wife feels about a restaurant."

"Okay. Great. Finally. That's what you're upset about. So let's talk about it."

He was quiet for a moment, then spoke. "I know you don't get that same charge here at home as you do at Billie's. Over there everybody's dying for the owner to come talk to them. Everybody's looking at you. You're the star. Here, you're just Mom. Nobody's writing stories about you. No one's kissing your ass."

The nastiness of the comment took the wind out of me. Also, the small vein of truth that was buried within it.

"I'd suggest we start back on the date nights, but I can barely get you to leave the house," I said bitterly.

"I'm tired, Billie."

"You're absent—"

"You're not here either! You're always there! Always at the restaurant!"

The glass whizzed through the air so fast, smashing against the side of the house behind me, that I barely had time to register what was happening. But then I did. *He'd just thrown it.* My husband, my calm, reasonable, therapist husband had just thrown a glass, and it was now shattered in a million pieces on the porch. I stared down at the glistening shards around me, then looked up at him. Had he meant it to hit me?

"Don't you think I'm scared, Billie?" he yelled. "Don't you think I know something's wrong, that I shouldn't be falling asleep every goddamn second of the day? Don't you think I'm terrified that they're going to tell me I've got some kind of rare, auto-immune thing or a brain tumor or some kind of degenerative—"

"Maybe it's not physical, Peter!" I shouted. "Maybe you just hate being here, hate seeing me happy, hate it that you feel like you followed me—"

"Go ahead, Billie! Cut me open! Get up in here"—he jabbed a finger at his head—"and tell me everything that's wrong with me! It's not like I'm not beating myself up enough about all this."

"Who's got a brain tumor?" Mere's trembly voice floated across the porch. We both whirled to face our daughter, paint-brush dripping watery green poster paint on the worn boards, watching us. She glanced at the mess of broken glass on the porch floor.

"Daddy had an accident," I said. "He dropped his glass. And nobody's got a brain tumor. We were just talking." I glanced at Peter. His face was grim and gray, and he was running his fingers through his hair. His hands were trembling. "Peter?" *Say something.*

He sniffed and planted his hands on his hips. "Hey, Mere. How's the painting?"

Her eyes were still wide, taking in the whole scene. I was pretty sure we weren't fooling her. "Good."

"Ready for bed?" I asked.

"I'll take you." Peter hustled Mere inside before she could protest. I watched them go, wondering if she was going to ask more questions. Would he tell her we'd been fighting? That he wasn't feeling well? That he was scared?

I downed the rest of my margarita and stared morosely at the constellation of broken glass on the porch. I could try all I wanted, but it was clear Peter wasn't going to talk to me. I put the glass down and listened. Cicadas buzzing their unearthly, electric song. An owl hooting so loudly it seemed like it had been amplified by a megaphone. I clattered down the steps, walking out into the grassy area behind the house. It was full dark now, with only a sliver of moon lighting up the clouds. I still couldn't get over how dark it got out here at night, unlike the city that was constantly glowing, no matter what time it was. But I liked it. I felt safe. The darkness out here felt like protection.

I clicked on my phone's flashlight and walked over the uneven ground, taking care not to step in any holes that the burrowing animals might've left. I was headed in the direction of the woods, Peter's domain up until now. Whatever secrets this land held—whether it was a well or a demon-horse or just some nefarious corporate-sourced pollution—I was going to find it.

Entering the woods, I realized instantly the safe feeling I'd had was misplaced. I was not only not wearing the right shoes for hiking, but the denim cutoffs I'd thrown on after work left my legs vulnerable to scrapes, bug bites, possibly even a startled snake. Major Minette had said the well was near the western property line, right before the bluff. I concentrated on keeping my phone's light trained on the trees. There was a path, a faint one, that wound through them. It was covered with a thick blanket of leaves and crisscrossed with fallen, rotting branches, but I could follow it.

I forged on, periodically checking the compass on my phone, telling myself this was going to be like one of those situations where Peter stood for fifteen minutes in front of the open doors of the fridge, insisting we were out of mayo, only for me to march in and locate the jar on the shelf where it had been sitting in front of him the entire time. When I found this stupid, un-capped motherfucker of a well, I was going to rub his nose in it for as long as I deemed necessary.

After a few more minutes, I stopped, feeling slightly turned around. The forest closed in around me. I couldn't shake the feel-ing of dread and oppression as the trees loomed over me. It was muggy and warm, but I shivered in my shorts and thin T-shirt. I had started to feel dizzy as well, the woods spinning around me, gaining speed as I stood still at their center. I drew in a deep breath, but it only made the sensation worse. I'd lost sight of the moon; I only saw trees crowding around me. They were so close. Too close. I threw my arms out and closed my eyes tight, a tightrope walker trying to find her balance.

I suddenly felt that I was no longer in the woods, but as if I was someplace else, someplace cold and wet with the dank smell of some hidden, ancient place. A forbidden, dark place, but also sacred somehow. I was scared to open my eyes, scared of what I'd see if I did. Would Peter's winged demon-horse be standing before me, snorting, pawing the ground, preparing to trample me with vile, filthy hooves? Or maybe it would be Mere's Catawampus—Ramsey, transformed into a fanged pan-ther, sulfur-eyed and thirsting to sink its claws into my flesh. Or maybe the rabid, rotting Juliana Minette.

My skin rose in gooseflesh. I heard a sound. Not owls or ci-cadas, more like music. I strained my ears. A soft wail, like keening, was rising up from somewhere ahead of me, some-where beyond the edge of the bluff. What was it? It did sound a little like music. There was the twangy echo of a banjo's strings, the plaintive cry of the fiddle as a bow slides across it.

But no, it wasn't music. It couldn't be. It was some kind of animal, down there, howling. A baby searching for its mother. The sound reminded me of Mere's thin cries when we brought her home from the hospital. That first week, before her lungs really found their stride, her cries sounded like they were coming from a doll. I wished I could cry that way now, just let out my grief for Mom in that unfettered, animal way. But for some reason, no tears came.

I didn't cry now, like I hadn't cried then.

The memory flooded me. When Mom had told me she was selling the house I'd bought her and was moving to Maine, I'd calmly listened to her explain her decision—*it's not a cult, it's a co-op, Bills*—feeling more disoriented and hurt with every word that came out of her mouth. All these years I'd spent working my ass off, creating Billie's, I realized then, it had been for her. But I'd never come right out and told her, had I? I'd never said, *Mom, this is a place for us* or, more to the point, *Mom, I want to know you;* I'd just blindly assumed I could keep her close to me with the restaurant . . . and now she was proving me wrong. She was heading off into the sunset to spend the rest of her life with a bunch of strangers. She wanted them, not me.

After I had hung up the phone, I left the apartment without my purse or phone and walked around the city for hours. I wound up in some posh corner of the Upper East Side at dark with blisters on my heels and no cash or card for a cab home. I actually had to ask a stranger to borrow their phone so I could call Peter.

Fuck her, I said to Peter when he'd come for me. I wasn't going to chase her down. I wasn't going to beg her to love me anymore.

And I refused to cry.

In the dark, I suddenly tripped over a root or fallen branch and, letting out a cry, pitched forward, stumbling over a sort of ledge. At first my feet sped up like someone on a runaway treadmill, then finally unable to keep up, I fell headlong, crashing through branches, inhaling rotted leaves, desperately clawing for some hold on something, anything to slow me down.

I finally landed—at the bottom of the bluff, I assumed—and

lay there for a moment, waiting for some shooting pain in my ankle or knee or wrist. But there was nothing. Nothing other than a couple of scrapes and a spot on my hip that was probably going to be a nasty bruise tomorrow. I groaned and sat up, brushing twigs and leaves out of my hair.

My eyes, adjusted to the dark now, were finally able to make out my surroundings. I was on level land, in a sort of clearing. The steep wall of the bluff I'd just fallen down rose up behind me, covered by a curtain of thick vines and ivy and spindly trees, their roots half exposed. Ahead of me was the supposedly polluted creek Peter had found, making the most normal, cheery burbling sound. Sitting here, it all seemed so normal. So mundane and harmless.

But my head was pounding, and my leg burned where I'd slid over the rough ground. I'd also lost my phone. I looked around, still feeling disoriented. The forest around me was quiet. There were no sounds, just the excruciating sensation of my aching body and this pounding headache.

We shall meet but we shall miss him . . .

The words came unbidden to my mind. That earworm hymn from Billie's playlist.

We shall meet but we shall miss him . . .

I heard the music in my head, banjo and fiddle again, and now a young girl's thin but steady voice.

There will be one vacant chair . . .

The singing girl sounded like Mere, but not at the same time. And now it felt like the music was not just in my head but coming from the woods around me. I gripped my head in my hands, as the music seemed to grow louder. I had definitely hit my head when I fell. Jesus. I closed my eyes. What a fucking dirge. I was going to delete it from the playlist when I went in tomorrow.

We shall meet but we shall—

"Shut up!" I yelled, and the music stopped. The music in my

head, I reminded myself. *In my head.* Not actually playing out here in the woods. Because that would be crazy.

Now there was only silence. And that sound the stars made. That high-pitched keening. Cries from light-years away. Cries that crossed time and space . . .

Stop it, Billie. Stop. Stars don't make sounds.

I stood, brushing the rest of the leaves and dirt off me, attempting to reorient myself. A breeze kicked up, tickling my skin, and I twisted my hair into a ponytail holder I found in my pocket. I heard the branches of trees clacking against each other. Some kind of animal chittered a few feet from me. I should be getting back to the house. To Mere and Peter. It had been a bad idea to come out here. A terrible idea. I swayed, the pain at the front of my head intensifying. It had a beat now, pulsating in time with my heart.

The cold, damp enveloped me, sharpening the pain in my head. Goose bumps rose on my arms and legs. A shudder rippled through me. What was it Mom used to say when she had that sensation—that someone was walking across her grave?

I turned to look behind me, then in every other direction.

Panic filled me, a buzzing even louder than the cicadas. The trees were holding hands above me, the canopy, and beneath me, their roots joined in a way I couldn't see. Was that the way the dead held us? Above and below? Death was so strong here; it was all around me, in the rotting leaves and fallen trees and all the decaying corpses of squirrels and rabbits and God knows what else, hidden from sight. Death held me firmly in its grip, so I couldn't run. So it could warn me of something. But what?

The trees bent lower, whispering death's message through their branches.

What have they taken from you, Billie?
What will they take . . .

The same message of the old woman in my dreams.

I let out a desperate, gasping sob. I was drunk. Drunk off my ass with tequila, likely concussed after that fall, and now I was thinking that the trees were talking to me. I was a fool, coming out here. I should start back. Go home and get in bed and press my body close to my husband. I needed sleep. We both just needed sleep.

I started walking. It stood to reason that I was probably closer to the road, Route 140, the mill road, than I was to my house. I headed toward the creek, which didn't look red in the moonlight, just black and oily. I splashed clumsily through the water and continued tromping through the woods, hoping I was heading in the right direction.

"Hey there!" came a man's voice through the dark.

The voice was accompanied by a dark figure and the bright, reassuring twin beams of a car's headlights. I sped up, tripping over a rock as I reached a slight incline. It was Jamie Cleburne, standing by his truck, which was parked by the side of the road. The mill road, which it appeared I'd accidentally found.

"Oh, thank God," I breathed, stumbling toward him. "I'm so glad to see you."

Chapter 12

In the safe, dry cab of his truck, Jamie told me he'd been on his way home from a night of inventorying a shipment from Vermont when he thought he saw movement in our woods. I said I'd been on a walk but lost my way, and explanations made, we fell into an awkward silence.

"Should I run you home?" he asked.

Did he have an inkling that Peter and I had been fighting? Was he angling to spend a few minutes alone with me? Regardless of why he'd asked, I was grateful.

"Not yet, if you don't mind." I wasn't ready to face Peter—or, if he'd gone to bed, the quiet of our house. Now that I was out of the woods, I realized I must be at the head-hanging, muttering, bone-tired stage of drunk, and wanted some time to clear my head.

Jamie offered me a sip from the aluminum water bottle in the cup holder, and I gulped down what was left of his water. The truck smelled good—like spicy cologne and wool blankets. A little doggy, too. I asked if he'd take me to the restaurant. I would wash my hands, use a proper bathroom, and change into the spare set of sweats I kept there. Make a pot of coffee, get some carbs inside me, and sober up. He said that was fine and executed a U-turn, heading back toward town.

He parked in front of his shop and, since I didn't have my key, let us into the restaurant through the connecting door. I started a pot of coffee, and while he settled himself at the bar, I went to the bathroom to wash up. When I came out, he was back in the kitchen, standing over the stove, stirring eggs.

"It may not be a Billie-caliber omelet, but it'll do. Sit. I poured your coffee already."

Another warm rush of gratitude surged through me. The guy seemed to always intuit what I needed. I did as he instructed and a few moments later, he put a plate in front of me. The eggs were fluffy and buttery, the slice of sourdough he'd toasted and slathered with blackberry jam, perfection. I inhaled it all as he cleaned up. When I was finished, he sat beside me, a mug of coffee in his hand.

"Want to talk about it?" he asked.

I sighed. "Peter and I fought. It was dumb. I was walking it off and fell down the bluff. I'm not really the outdoorsy type."

"You don't say." He smiled.

I smiled back, feeling warm, feeling full, and with that, feeling my defenses slip. I had left out the part about Peter throwing a glass. Was I protecting him?

"My mother joined a cult," I said abruptly.

His eyebrows shot up. "Excuse me?"

I bent over what was left of my food. "At the beginning of the pandemic. I'd bought her a house in Jersey, but I think she was lonely. She really got into tracing her ancestry."

"No kidding."

I shrugged, chewing. "It seemed harmless enough at first. Just the monthly subscription to the website. But a few days into the lockdown, she calls me and says that she's not going to be stuck out in New Jersey so she's sold her house, the house I bought her, mind you, and is moving to Maine. Apparently, there was a whole group of them, descendants of this religious sect who found each other through the website, and they decided to revive the old cult or commune or whatever it was up in this godforsaken patch of land they used to own."

"Whoa."

I nodded. "She lives there now. My mother—the same woman who actually cried the day I told her she didn't have to work at her shitty job anymore, that I was paying all her bills—voluntarily handed over her phone and works in a vegetable garden all day." I laughed, a caustic, hollow-sounding thing.

"Did you ask her not to go?"

"Not in so many words. My mom doesn't really do direct, clear communication. Or difficult emotions. After my father died, she woke up the next morning and kept going like nothing had happened."

"I might be able to relate somewhat. My father's a bit on the stoic side."

I sighed. "It's just hard to wrap my head around. That she's gone."

"Maybe not for good. So maybe she couldn't talk about it, but it sounds like she was searching, like you were, before you came to Juliana."

Our eyes caught and held. "Maybe." I looked away. "The thing was, I had already lost the restaurant. Losing my mom on top of that just felt like a cruel joke. My family never could afford to go out to eat, so Mom really loved eating in nice restaurants. Especially when someone else was paying. I actually opened my first place for her, in a way. And probably this one, too, if I'm being honest." There it was, all wrapped up in a few sentences. The one truth I couldn't bring myself to admit to Peter.

"I hope she sees it," Jamie said.

"She won't."

"That's really tough." He was looking at me with clear eyes and an open expression. "What did Peter say?"

I looked away. "It was a hard time for him, too. He had a lot of clients losing family members. Losing jobs. Their health. It felt selfish to whine about my mom. About losing Billie's and feeling like a failure."

He looked incredulous. "You're kidding me. You, a failure? You understand the pandemic killed Brooks Brothers and Chuck E. Cheese, right?"

"I know."

"Tell me how it happened."

I took a deep breath, thinking back to those terrible days. "Every day, our numbers were lower. I was going to have to furlough most of the staff and cut the hours for the ones who stayed on. I had to find a third-party delivery system. There was talk of small business payments, but I knew it would be barely enough to cover our rent." I rubbed my arms. "So I decided to cut the cord. I told all my employees to apply for unemployment, took my tax money out of my savings account, and gave them their last paycheck, and then"—I fluttered my fingers—"the place became nothing but a memory."

"Shit."

"We had our last supper. All the staff were there. So many friends ordered for takeout, many of them from halfway across the country. Family, friends, former employees—it was beautiful. At the end of the night, we were all half-drunk when we heard the mayor order the lockdown on the news. So, after everybody left, that's what I did. I locked the place down. I put an ad to sell the equipment online, but my general manager handled the sale. I couldn't bring myself to go back. To see the place . . . my place . . ." I covered my mouth with my hand, as if to stop myself from saying more. I really didn't want to cry here, not in front of Jamie.

"And you didn't talk to Peter because you assumed the last thing he needed was a wife who couldn't hold down the fort."

I shrugged.

"What about what you needed?"

His gaze was steady, penetrating, and I had the sudden, acute impulse to let everything out. To share the fear and disappointment that had tinged every minute of the past two years of my life. The suffocating feeling of loss and grief. The fear that my marriage wasn't going through a rough patch because we'd moved or because Peter was fighting some kind of unknown illness, but because, at the heart of it, I was still just a lonely, needy child who desperately wanted her mother's love. A child who irrationally believed a restaurant could somehow magically bring her mother back to her.

"What I need isn't going to happen," I said simply.

"But you can't honestly believe you're a failure." His eyes were warm, trained on me with an intensity that made my stomach twist pleasantly. "You're still standing. Still making things happen. You're a survivor. Maybe Peter can't handle that."

I let my eyes slide away from Jamie's warm greenish-blue ones, as if he could read my thoughts even as they flickered through my brain.

"You're a lifesaver, too, Billie, if you want to know the truth."

I knit my brows and his eyes dropped to my lips. Then he glanced down at his coffee. I was quiet. It felt like we'd just stumbled over some line, crossing over into some territory that felt taboo.

I looked down at my mug. "It's the coffee," I said lightly. "That is a real shitty brew you guys have had to make do with over at Pig Out's. Your standard is incredibly low."

His face held the serious expression, his eyes on me. "It's not the coffee. It's you, Billie. You're the lifesaver."

I didn't look up. My chest felt tight.

"I know I shouldn't say that. I don't have any right. But it's there, it's real, and I can't deny it."

I could barely focus over the thundering of my heart. I met his gaze. "What's there?"

"Come on. You know. How I feel about you."

His hand moved to mine, removing it from the mug and turning it palm-up on the bar. He traced a finger from my wrist across the palm, down my center finger. I was sweating, thoughts swirling like a tornado in my head. When he finally spoke, his words sounded like he'd rehearsed them. Like he'd known this moment would come and had prepared for it.

"I really enjoy Alice Tilton. I think she's a great person, but I'm never going to fall in love with her. I know that you love your husband, that y'all have a beautiful, smart daughter and something real and solid, that you've built over the years. But I also know some other things."

I held my breath.

His finger moved over the lines of my palm. "I know that I want to see you every day. To see your face, talk to you, laugh with you. Hear every single thought you have. So, what does it all mean?" He shook his head. "I don't know, but I can tell you this. I'm tired of trying to figure it out. I just want to say it out loud and let it be whatever it is."

He leaned closer to me, so close that I could smell the coffee on his breath. His green-blue eyes twinkled. "I'm not trying to get you to sleep with me, Billie. I swear."

I gave him a small smile. "God, I'd hate to see you really try."

He sat back and laughed. I smiled, feeling some of the tension dissipate.

"But sex isn't just about the end result," he said.

I flushed, my throat constricting and my mouth going dry.

"It's about everything leading up to it." He gently brushed my hair off my shoulder. "Getting to know the feel of someone's hair." He ran a finger along my jaw. "The line of their face." The finger moved under my chin, then down. "The way their neck curves right into this place." He stopped it right at the hollow between my clavicle bones and lifted my hand, lacing our fingers. "Holding hands is vastly underrated as foreplay."

I looked down at our joined hands. His was trembling the slightest bit.

"See, I'm nervous," he said. "It's so intimate. Palm to palm. Fingers separating fingers, opening up to each other, entering then fitting together." His thumb rubbed right below mine. My body was inclined toward his. I suddenly realized that even though all the businesses in downtown Juliana were closed for the night, it wasn't all that late. There could still be the random pedestrian out for a stroll around the town square.

I extricated my hand from his. "I can't. I'm sorry."

He sat back. "No apology necessary. Your hand is not mine to hold."

I brushed my hands together, maybe trying to wipe off the feel of him. I avoided his gaze. "Help me with these dishes?"

We cleaned up, turned off the lights, and I reset the alarm. We left the way we'd come, through the door to Cleburne Antiques. Soft music played on invisible speakers. "So Into You" by the Atlanta Rhythm Section. Had Jamie put on the music when we came in? No. He probably left it running around the clock.

The old wardrobes, dining tables, and dressers gleamed. Shadows wrapped around every nook of the place. On the long counter a lone Tiffany lamp sent out a warm light, bathing the store in a soft glow, making it look like a magical emporium that offered spells and charms instead of old furniture. For the first time, I noticed the paintings hung on every wall. Austere portraits of aristocratic-looking men and women. A few landscapes and still lifes. A handful of nudes.

Jamie looped back between the furniture. "Just give me a minute. I need to grab a couple of files in the office."

"Sure." I watched him go, fidgeting with the hem of my shirt. At this point, the more distance between us the better. Where I stood, I could see boxes of old vinyl, prints, engravings, dusty letters. I moved closer to one, peering inside. On the top of a stack of papers, a photograph caught my eye. I picked it up. It was one of those old tintypes of my house, the Dalzell-Davenport house, with the old doctor, Silas Dalzell, trim in a dark suit, standing in the front yard. Behind that picture was another, this one with a dour-looking woman with her hair slicked back and wearing a black dress with a white lace collar. Mrs. Dalzell, I presumed.

More pictures of the house were behind it, featuring families I didn't recognize. Dalzells and Minettes, no doubt. But there were also newer pictures, definitely ones that George Davenport had taken. And there were some old gas and electric bills. I didn't understand what they were doing here in a dusty corner of Jamie's shop. Lilah had said that George Davenport's family had left some of his things behind when they moved him out. Maybe Jamie had been in charge of collecting these before we moved in.

I rifled toward the bottom of the box and pulled out two more pictures, both old, badly faded, and damaged by mold. One showed three mustachioed soldiers in uniform, sitting in front of a tent, legs crossed, around a table. There was a meal laid out before them. From the tent pole hung an American flag. Confederate soldiers, I guessed.

The other photograph showed a group of solemn women and children standing in front of a clapboard building. None were smiling. I moved closer to get a better look. One of the children, a scrawny boy in the front and center of the group. He held a small sign. I leaned closer, trying to make out the words printed on it.

NOVEMBER 11, 1864.

And that's when I saw her. In the back row, the old woman with a lean, drawn face and large, plain cross hanging on a chain around her thin neck. Her head was wreathed with a crown of braids. Her dark eyes, like two pieces of glittering jet, stared into the camera.

Stared at me.

I felt the slightest whisper of a breeze on my neck. Goose bumps rose and I shuddered, and I heard my mother's voice. *Someone walking over your grave . . .*

I flipped the photo over, catching a glimpse of faded, spidery handwriting. It was in pencil, almost indiscernible in the dim light. A woman's name and *UGA*. I held the picture closer, just as Jamie's hand grazed up my arm. I dropped the photo back in the box, and in one smooth motion, he turned me to face him. His eyes were burning.

"Billie." His voice sounded like a plea. "I'm sorry. You may not want to talk about it, but I have to know."

I could feel heat radiating off his body, enveloping me. His breath coming fast and hot. He hadn't seen me with the pictures. Something else was happening here. Something that was making my pulse race, too.

My heart beat hard, in time with his breath. "What?"

He tilted his head, studying me. "Did Peter get physical with you tonight? When you fought?"

I was quiet.

"You can tell me," he said.

"He threw a glass. Not at me . . . I don't think. But still, it scared me."

"God. Billie. Of course it did." He sounded angry. Frustrated. Like he wanted to do something to defend me but knew he couldn't. "You don't have to talk about it."

But I wanted to. I needed to. "I don't know who he is anymore. I don't know anything."

He touched my cheek and I flinched. "I'm sorry."

"It's okay," he said. "It's okay."

But it wasn't. He was still touching me. His hand was at my rib cage now, moving up, slowly, tentatively feeling my body. My stomach leapt and, to my dismay, I felt myself go wet between my legs. In one corner of my mind, the one small rational sliver of brain that still made good decisions, I knew this was just my body responding to the touch of a man I happened to find attractive. It was just a physiological response to the drive built into me. But the desire was overwhelming. Sharp and sweet and magnetic, in a way that felt irresistible.

Oh God, Billie, not this . . .

This isn't what you want . . .

"You don't have to say anything." He rubbed his cheek against mine, slowly, gently, over and over, first one side, then the other. I closed my eyes and tilted my face up, letting out a sound that was somewhere between a gasp and a moan.

His beard was soft, softer than I'd expected, and I felt myself being lulled into a kind of trance. Being pulled down, down, down to a dark place. A hidden place. And then his lips found mine and I let them be found, kissing him back, inhaling the scent of him and forgetting all about the pictures in the box behind me.

1975
Juliana, Georgia

The girl who entered Dr. Bobby Minette's office, which was situated between the pool hall and the five-and-dime on the square, signed in with the name Sugar Smith. The nurse, Holly-Ann, looked at the signature and sniffed in delicate disapproval.

"Payment up front, sweetheart," she told the girl. "Cash only."

The girl's name was obviously made up, but it was of no consequence. She was not a Minette, Dalzell, or Cleburne. Nor was she even a second-tier Street, St. John, Childers, Tilton, or Calhoun. She was not from Juliana at all; that much was clear. She was just one of those hippie drifters, flower children who floated around the country, taking dope and protesting the war and getting irresponsibly knocked up.

Holly-Ann instructed the girl to pee in a paper cup, then led her to the last exam room at the end of the hall, where she told her to undress and put on the flimsy cotton gown. When Dr. Bobby entered the room, he sent Holly-Ann out. Dr. Bobby told Sugar to lie back on the exam table and she did. She asked if he wasn't

supposed to take her blood pressure or temperature or some-
thing first, but Dr. Bobby just patted the girl's knee.

"No need," he said, looking down at her. "Now, are you sure
about this? There's no going back." He took the tone of a kindly
uncle, but his eyes were flat and expressionless. She was just a
piece of no-count trash who'd gotten herself into the kind of
trouble she couldn't fix without a shortcut. It was an epidemic
these days, the way this generation just tossed human life into
the dumpster.

"I'm sure," Sugar Smith said.

He instructed the girl to hold out her arm, and after two
failed attempts, inserted the IV needle into a nice, fat, blue vein.
He'd have to look into that slight hand tremor of his that had
started up. He hung a bag of clear liquid from the metal stand
and looked at the clock on the wall. She'd be groggy in less than
a minute.

About thirty seconds later, the door opened, and two men
slipped in. Sugar turned her head, strands of greasy brown hair
falling over her glazed eyes, and blinked at them. "Whoo're
youu . . . ?" she slurred.

"Just a few visitors," Dr. Bobby said briskly. "Nothing to
worry yourself about, honey." He nodded at the men. Ox Dal-
zell and James Cleburne, descendants of the original founders,
just like him.

Dr. Bobby had called them the minute he'd seen Sugar
Smith's obviously fake name in his appointment book, request-
ing the one service he didn't typically like to provide. But this
time he would say yes; the timing was just too good. The pressed
log business wasn't what it used to be and, worst of all, the hous-
ing market had slowed to a mere trickle, leaving lumber rotting
in piles of the one remaining Minette Mills yard. With the reces-
sion, the oil embargo, and inflation gone through the roof, well,
there was just no getting around the fact that Juliana's economy
really could use a boost.

He wasn't exactly thrilled about the task ahead. Truth be told, he had moments of doubt that Juliana Minette really looked down from heaven on the old guard and rewarded them for their devotion. But the previous solution he'd suggested (a spectacularly expensive stained glass window in the Baptist church inserting little Juliana into the Baby Jesus's manger scene) had not turned their fortunes around, and so James and Ox had finally convinced him that an offering had to be made.

It was long overdue, the men had said. Since the offering at the mill back in the thirties, there had only been a handful of sacrifices. Roughly one per decade, if you wanted to get specific. The one in the forties, a hunting accident involving the town drunk, had been a relatively tidy affair. The one in 1964, the unfortunate drowning in the Etowah of one of those teenage hooligans who raced his car through the square, was a bit trickier to navigate. This one should be a cinch. Easy peasy lemon squeezy.

Dr. Bobby inserted a syringe into Sugar's IV. She winced then widened her eyes. After a beat, she moaned softly. "Ohhh . . . right on, maaaan . . ."

Dr. Bobby rolled his eyes. On the other side of the exam room, Ox and James pursed their lips, sighed, and waited.

Sugar spoke again, this time with great difficulty. "Sshhuh I put my fee in the shtu . . . shtu . . ."

"Stirrups?" Dr. Bobby supplied. "If that would make you more comfortable, go right ahead."

A puzzled look flickered across her face, then she seemed to forget her question and made a grunting sound. Only one foot twitched and just the slightest bit. This was his sign. In quick succession, Dr. Bobby inserted two more vials into her IV and then, after waiting another minute and a half, he pressed his stethoscope to Sugar's chest. He listened for a moment, then nodded and stepped back, stripping his gloves and dropping them into the trash.

He put a hand over his heart. "Gentle Juliana," he said.

"Gentle Juliana," Ox and James repeated, then kissed the chains that hung around their necks.

The three shook hands and agreed to return later that night to bury the body, probably down at the abandoned mill. But they would have to be careful and quick. This would be the first sacrifice that couldn't be chalked up to an accident.

"Give our love to Dixie," James said to Dr. Bobby.

"She pregnant yet?" Ox asked.

"Only been married a month, fellas. Don't want to make her feel like a broodmare."

The three men laughed.

"My love to Margaret, too," Dr. Bobby said to James on their way out. He almost said to Ox, "And to Barbara," before he remembered that Ox's wife, still childless, had reportedly started acting like a loony—seeing winged horses and demonic creatures—and Ox had had to file for divorce.

Dr. Bobby glanced over his shoulder, one last look at Sugar. Her eyes were open, but she looked at peace. That was good. An acceptable sacrifice for Gentle Juliana—he didn't know why he'd even bothered with that damned stained glass window. Offerings were really not that difficult to make. He left the exam room, locking the door behind him, and went to tell Holly-Ann he was ready for the next patient.

Chapter 13

"She can watch a movie before bed," I said to Finch Street. "Nothing too scary. Disney, but no Marvel."

"Got it."

It was late in the sweltering Georgia July, and I was wearing my favorite New York thrift store find, a vintage, pink silk, Christian Lacroix dress. Finch had come to sit with Mere, as I'd finally convinced Peter we should attend Dixie Minette's dinner party, the one we'd argued over weeks ago.

The convincing had come at a price.

The day after our argument, I went back in the woods and managed to find my phone near the bluff where I'd fallen. I tucked it in my pocket and returned to the house with no comment. Peter and I were both acting like nothing had happened. Not the argument, nor me losing my phone. And certainly not what had happened between me and Jamie.

Peter's insomnia hadn't let up, and now his eyes looked perpetually red and hollowed out, a constant grim set to his jaw. The labs Doc Belmont had ordered seemed to be lost in the ether, and the man was flummoxed. He'd written a prescription for sleeping medication, and scheduled Peter for more tests down in Atlanta the following week. Regardless, this party was one thing I wasn't willing to let go. We needed to take part in the community, and I didn't think turning down the mayor's invite was smart, so one morning while we were getting ready for work, I had brought it up again.

"You can get in a nap that day," I said. "Mere and I will leave the house to you. The Minettes control everything in this town, and I really want to stay on the mayor's good side."

Peter muttered something under his breath about the "old Southern guard," and I replied that in my opinion the old Southern guard had done a pretty damn good job keeping this town alive. He retorted that they hadn't done *that* great a job as there was no bookstore, and what kind of pathetic excuse for a town didn't have a bookstore? I then suggested he open a fucking bookstore if he considered it so crucial, at which point he frisbeed his phone at the mirror above the sink. The glass had cracked but not shattered, and I had rounded on him, the full force of my anger erupting.

"You can't just throw stuff, Peter!" I yelled at him. "You're a grown man! A father and a therapist, for Chrissakes! It's not okay!"

Without a word he picked up his phone off the floor and gone downstairs. I listened as he stalked back through the kitchen, and then I looked out the window to see him take off across the field behind the house where I'd planted our vegetable garden. I watched as he strode across the field and disappeared over the hill in the direction of the woods.

Well, fuck him. He could set up camp in the woods, for all I cared. He wasn't the only one who'd ever gotten by on two to three hours of sleep a night. When Mere was born, and I was working every day at the restaurant, I'd been a zombie, but I'd dealt with it. Now I was running out of patience. I had a lot on my mind, too. Mere and her fear of her own cat. A cat who, in the past few weeks, had turned into a feral creature who'd taken to only showing his face whenever he hadn't been successful hunting for his dinner. It was getting harder and harder to talk Mere out of thinking he was the mythical demon-Catawampus-thing. And then there was that nasty little secret I was harboring: the kiss I'd shared with Jamie Cleburne. I felt guilty about it every day.

I blasted the blow dryer on my hair and tried not to think of the way Jamie's body had felt against mine. After that night, things between Jamie and me had continued as if nothing had happened: he kept showing up at my bar for breakfast every day, sometimes with Alice, sometimes alone. I kept making him food and making small talk. He joked and laughed like we were just friends. Like we hadn't explored each other's mouths with our tongues, each other's bodies with our hands, grinding desperately into each other in the gloom of his shop. *I dream of this all the time, Billie. It's all I can think about,* he had whispered between kisses. The whole thing had lasted only a second, maybe two, then I had pushed him away and run for the door.

On the way back to my house, I'd felt so guilty, so ashamed, that I thought I was going to be sick. Jamie had apologized, and I'd apologized, and then I'd told him, in no uncertain terms, it would never happen again. He said he understood. When he dropped me off at home, I scrambled out of the cab of his truck so fast, I nearly tripped and fell.

After a week and a half, Jamie obliterated any feeling of awkwardness with his breezy way, and it almost felt like it had never happened. Almost, but not entirely. The whole situation had been a mistake, a betrayal, one born of my frustration with Peter and my isolation and maybe some sort of fatal flaw in my character. But I was done with it. Whatever the cause of my behavior, it seemed like Jamie was determined to move past it. So I decided I would, too.

After the mirror-smashing incident, I was downstairs in the kitchen making Nutella crepes for Mere when Peter returned from his walk. He was red-faced, pouring sweat, and approached me with a sheepish look on face. He kissed me on the temple, gently, and I smelled salt and earth and his sweat.

"I'm sorry, Billie. What I did was totally uncalled for. I was wrong, and it won't happen again."

I stepped into the pantry, out of earshot from Mere, beckoning him to follow. "You can't do stuff like that anymore, Peter. It's scary. Not just to Mere but to me."

He looked down at the floor, ashamed.

"And it's not like you. I don't understand. What's really going on?"

"I can't sleep in this house, Billie." He shook his head. Gazed over my shoulder. "At least, not when I'm supposed to. I thought it was because of the well, but then I started sleeping all the time, everywhere. During family time. When I'm supposed to be watching Mere. Do you understand what I'm saying, Billie? I fell asleep during a fucking appointment. While my client was telling me about her physically abusive mother."

He rubbed his forehead with one hand. "I've started to think it's something in the air—the dust everywhere in this house, the white dust. Maybe there's asbestos in this place or some other kind of gas. Radon, or something, I don't know, Billie, I don't know what it is. I'm just telling you, whatever is getting to me, whatever is"—his voice broke—"tearing at my insides, it's something *here*, in this *place*."

I held up my hands. "We can find someone to come out and do some testing. See if it's something that can be fixed. Or, I don't know, we can move. Find another house altogether."

He wilted a bit. "I don't want to move. This house, the land, the privacy. It's everything we've always wanted. I don't want to give it up."

"But no house is worth all this . . . your health. Your peace of mind." I took both his hands in mine and squeezed. There was another option beyond the ones I'd just voiced—an option I knew neither one of us wanted to address. Still, the unspoken words seemed to hover in the air around us.

Go back.

We could go back to New York and leave all this behind.

The mess I'd made with the betrayal with Jamie, the house with the weird vibes, the cat we could never find. But there would be a price to pay. I'd have to abandon another restaurant. And I really didn't want that. I didn't want to have to start all over another time. I'd come so far. Worked so damn hard. I wasn't going to give up that easily. I'd given up without a fight once. I wasn't going to do it again.

I held his gaze. "Peter. I am in this thing with you. We handle this and everything together, do you hear me?"

He nodded but didn't look convinced.

"And if it's not radon or asbestos, if it's something else—"

I flashed to the image of little dead Juliana's yawning mouth. The old woman with the crown of braids.

If this house is haunted, like Lilah said . . .

I forced myself to continue. "—we'll figure it out. In the meantime, I really think it would be good if you got out and just . . . spent some time with people. People here in town want to know you. They know me and now they want to know you."

He hesitated the slightest bit before pulling his hands from mine. He ruffled his sweaty hair then wiped his hands on his shorts. "Sure, yeah."

I hugged him, willing myself to do it unreservedly. Willing myself not to believe that somehow, at the bottom of all this, my husband simply resented my success. My happiness. "I love you."

"Let's just get this over with" was all he said.

I watched him, his face flushed and handsome, that curl of cinnamon hair falling across his forehead. I loved this man, but there was so much between us now--a wall that we'd each been building so diligently that now I wondered if there was a chance of dismantling it.

Now, Finch cleared her throat, bringing me back to the present. "Anything else I need to know?" Mere was already pulling her by the hand in the direction of the stairs.

"Maybe just keep her up until we're home," I said, thinking of the nightmares. "We won't be late."

Chapter 14

Dixie Minette's house—an Italianate Victorian painted a shocking Pepto pink—was located halfway down (no surprise) Minette Street. The place was blazing with lights when we drew up. An enormous University of Georgia flag whipped from a pole beside the front steps. The wraparound porch was packed with people, and I could hear a bluegrass group's music floating from the backyard. We parked behind a row of golf carts.

As we mounted the front steps, I recognized a few of the new families. The Brennans, who owned the bakery that supplied Billie's pastries. The Undergroves—the vet and wedding planner—and a collection of faces I recognized from the restaurant. The old-timers—the Dalzells, Cleburnes, and Minettes—must have been inside.

Tilda Brennan grabbed my arm. "Billie. You've got to tell us how you managed to talk Mayor Dixie into selling you the Dalzell-Davenport house. Before you moved here, Ned and I made an offer on it. A real offer with six figures, okay?" She made eyes at the group. "And all we got was a flat no."

I blinked at her, then at Peter. "I don't know. I just asked."

"Please tell me you didn't get it for a hundred dollars. I swear I will die," Tilda said.

Everyone laughed. Ned, her husband, shushed her, but all eyes were on me.

"Sorry," I said.

Tilda clutched her chest in mock pain.

"No offense, but what makes you guys so special?" Dr. Undergrove said. "Why sell to you and not anyone else?"

"She's a celebrity," someone retorted. "A famous restauranteur."

"Oh God, no, I'm not," I protested.

"Did you have celebrities at your place in New York?" someone else asked. "Like celebrities we'd know?"

"Oh. Well, yeah. Occasionally."

Breathless silence.

"Pacino came in pretty regularly for a while. Taylor Swift, once, I'm told. I missed that auspicious occasion, just my luck." They all nodded appreciatively.

Tilda Brennan was assessing me closely now, with narrowed eyes. "They wouldn't even give us a tour of the house." She was really stuck on the subject.

"You might've dodged a bullet," Peter said wryly. "I can't sleep a wink in the place. We're starting to think it might be haunted."

This started a whole new conversation, this one about what establishments in town might be haunted. I made our excuses that we wanted to grab drinks and pulled Peter into the house.

The inside of Dixie Minette's home was rich, opulent, and thoroughly Southern—a manor fit for a gentry of long ago. Each room was done in brilliant jewel tones of blue and peach or gold and green. Every floor was either marble or inlaid wood. The rugs, though threadbare, appeared to be priceless, and there had to be a mint worth of heavy antique sterling silver crowding every surface. The heavily scrolled letter *M* was embroidered in gold thread on pillows, throws, and even a few curtains.

The kitchen was completely renovated with walnut cabinetry and the biggest black enameled and brass range I'd ever seen in my life. Outside, a bluegrass quartet had set up in one corner of the vast expanse of flagstone. I could see guests milling about, drinking, dancing, and laughing. At the rear of the yard, beside what appeared to be an outside kitchen house, people gathered around a stone firepit. A constellation of glowing cigarettes lit the darkness. I saw Jamie Cleburne standing next to Alice. He wore a rumpled button-down shirt, untucked, and shorts with leather slides. She wore a pale blue slip dress and had one languid hand draped on his bare arm.

I glanced over at Peter. "Want to go outside?"

"Sure."

After we made our way across the yard accompanied by a bluegrass rendition of Journey's "Faithfully," Peter surprised me by grabbing my hand and swinging me into his arms. We settled into each other with ease, feeling the music. He pressed a hand against my back, surrounding me with his embrace. I let a long breath out and rested my head against his. He smelled good, spicy and warm and like the man whose every shade and tone and mood I had always known intimately. The man I still wanted.

"I never thought I'd hear this particular version of this song," I said.

He laughed. As we danced, my heart settled into his heart's rhythm. After the third song, he released me, grabbed two bottles of beer from a washtub heaped with ice, and handed me one. He kissed me on the cheek just as Toby Minette, Dixie's son, hooted at me.

"Billie!" he called out. "My favorite restauranteur! I see you brought your better half."

Toby, in his early forties, was resplendent in a madras plaid pair of trousers and a pink polo shirt. He ambled up, his arm around a young Filipino woman wearing a simple black dress. He offered a hand to Peter. "Nice to finally make your acquaintance, and a formal welcome to Gentle Juliana. We do so love your wife around here. And her hotcakes." They shook and Toby squeezed the woman's shoulders. "This is Ronnie. She owns—"

"—the home goods store," I finished with him. "I've heard. Nice to meet you, Ronnie."

"Nice to meet you, too," Ronnie said.

Toby looked at her, eyes shining. "Can you believe my luck? The Initiative goes live in March, this girl moves down, and boom, four months later, she makes me the happiest man in the world. And just in time. For a while there, I was worried I was going to have to marry one of these Juliana girls. But you know what they say . . ."

Peter and I looked at him expectantly.

" 'Kissing cousins make damn scary babies.' " He burst into laughter, and Ronnie rolled her eyes.

"You two are getting married?" I asked.

Ronnie held up her hand. A huge diamond twinkled on her ring finger. It looked old and really expensive. Above it, on her wrist, dangled a delicate gold bracelet with two charms. The band lit into a bluegrass rendition of "Magic Carpet Ride." Peter and I exchanged glances.

Ronnie let out a little nervous giggle. "It happened really fast—" she began.

"Fast girls win trophies," Toby broke in. "That's all I'm saying." He snickered at his own joke.

"The ring is gorgeous," I said to Ronnie. "And so is that bracelet."

"Thank you. That was a gift from my future mother-in-law." She showed me the small charms hanging from a single link on the bracelet. "See, there's an *R* for Ronnie and a *J* for Juliana."

So this was one of the charms Jamie had mentioned. The ones they all pressed kisses to after saying the town grace. I didn't know why exactly, but at the sight of it, a ripple of foreboding shot through me. I wondered what qualified someone to receive one of those charms. Maybe marrying into one of the original families.

"Lovely," I said.

I glanced back up at the house. Dixie Minette, wearing a blood-red jumpsuit and gold heels and standing with Ox Dalzell and Jamie Cleburne, looked down at our little group with a calculating expression.

Toby followed my gaze. "Ah. The old guard, plotting their next move."

I raised my eyebrows in question.

"The three families who really run this place." Toby raised his bottle in a toast. "The old guard. So now you know who to go to if you need anything done quick."

Dixie had turned back to Ox and Jamie, who were now listening intently to the mayor. They all seemed very grave. I wondered what they were talking about.

Toby eyed Peter. "I haven't seen you around much. We were wondering if you were some kind of hermit or something. Mr. Billie Hope."

Peter smiled tightly. "I've been really busy with work. I'm a therapist."

"Well, we hope we see more of you at our get-togethers. You two are something on the dance floor. You know, there's dancing at the country club out Highway 86 every Thursday night. Live music, too. Sometimes bands from down in Atlanta or Savannah or even Nashville if we're lucky. There's a great golf course, too. If you're a golfing man, Peter, it might be worth applying for membership."

"Oh," Peter said. "I'm not sure we can afford a country club membership."

Toby flicked his fingers, sweeping away Peter's argument. "Sure you can. The membership committee's always open to a deal."

"I can't give away any more free meals," I said, not entirely joking.

Toby laughed. "How about some free sessions for me and Ronnie from the good doctor here, then? Premarital counseling?" Toby leaned closer to us. He smelled like whiskey and ocean-scented cologne. "Y'all know we dodged a bullet here in Juliana. Close call, before the town council came up with the Initiative."

"No kidding?" Peter asked. "What kind of bullet?"

Toby lifted his eyebrows. "They were gonna bring a car plant here." He looked at both of us with meaning. "And you know what that means. God-knows-who coming up from Atlanta to work at the factory. Moving in, eventually. Illegals. Folks who don't value education and work or bettering themselves."

Interesting logic, I thought. Thinking people who signed on to work a grueling full-time shift at a car plant didn't value hard work.

"I hate to say it," Toby went on, "but some people are trash, and that's what they'll always be no matter how many opportunities you give them. Those people don't want to work. They just want handouts."

I looked at Peter. He just lifted his eyebrows, his smile steady and closed-lipped.

The guy just wouldn't stop talking. "Anyway, when they rolled out the Initiative, everybody in town thought it was just a genius idea. It was the answer, you know? The way we were going to keep Juliana separate from that enormous, expanding monster-squid called Atlanta. The Initiative's going to keep us out of the path of urban sprawl. Keep us our own self-sufficient town. Because that's what it's all about, right? Making sure Juliana stays the way she always has. And that can't happen if we don't get the right kind of people here. Like you folks."

I felt suddenly sick to my stomach. I could feel the waves of tension rolling off Peter. The banjo music was really starting to grate on my nerves.

"That would've been a lot of money for the town," he said. "An automobile plant. Is there another company the town's pursuing instead?"

Toby fake punched my arm. "Well, we got Billie's raking in the dough over there on the corner of the square. That'll do us for a good little while, I guess, don't you?" Toby glanced up, suddenly noticing his mother glaring down at him from the back balcony. I saw him twitch uncomfortably under her gaze and hitch up his pants. "All right then, we'll skedaddle. Y'all enjoy the party." Toby clutched Ronnie's hand and whisked her away, into the darkness beyond the bonfire.

"Okay, you literally just met the worst guy in town," I said. "Everybody's better than him, I swear."

"Guy talked like the Initiative's some white supremacy, mail-order-bride operation." Peter curled his lip in distaste.

"He's just one guy," I said, grabbing his hand and shaking it. "I think we should give the club a try."

"I don't know."

"I'm sure they're some nice people there. And Mere could stand to improve her swimming skills, maybe learn tennis." What I didn't say was how inviting the idea of a weekly dance sounded—the only occasion I might be able to regularly feel my husband's warm, strong arms around me.

Chapter 15

When the band started to play Styx's "Renegade," Peter took my hand and pulled me toward the house. It was quiet inside, and we wandered for a bit, eventually finding ourselves in a library. It was an impressive room lined with walls of books that reached from the high ceiling to the floor. What looked like extremely old volumes of Dickens and Shakespeare, Fitzgerald, O'Connor, and Faulkner.

In the center of a thick and very old Persian rug, a long oak table held a huge Bible, opened on a stand. As Peter moved to examine one of the shelves and pull out an old book, I drew closer to the Bible. A passage, lit softly from above, was underlined in faded ink.

I will freely sacrifice unto thee. I will praise thy name, O Lord, for it is good . . .

I stared at the words, feeling a strange sort of fear rising in me. A fear that felt like a hand around my throat.

"Looks like you two found my favorite room." Lilah Street, dressed in matching pants and tunic of gray linen, drew the pocket doors half-closed behind her. Purple moccasins peeked out beneath. Her gray hair flowed over her shoulders and jet chandelier earrings dangled from her ears. She carried a glass of red wine.

She gestured at a portrait above the marble mantelpiece of an old, white-whiskered man seated on a carved chair that resembled a gothic throne. A young girl in a blue dress stood at his shoulder. "That's Alfred Minette, founder of the town."

"The guy who built the mill," I said.

"Mills," Lilah corrected. "Two lumber, one pulp, but the only one still standing is the one by the river. That's Juliana beside him, his first child."

I stared up at the little girl. Her brown curls lay against a white lace collar. One small pale hand rested lightly on her father's shoulder. Her pink lips curled in a cool smile, her eyes gazed out, flat and expressionless. The artist may have been unskilled at capturing life in his subjects, but still . . . the image of the monstrous, rotting corpse of little Juliana flashed before me, her open maw showing those needle-sharp baby teeth.

I turned away. It might be ridiculous, but even just looking at a likeness of the child made my skin crawl. Across the room, Peter glanced at the painting then at Lilah before returning his attention to the book he'd pulled from the shelf.

I smiled apologetically at her. "He doesn't love parties."

She sipped her wine judiciously. "The best ones never do."

"I'm trying to get him . . . you know." I gestured out to the sounds of laughter and clinking glasses. "Out more."

"Psh." Lilah sipped again. "Out is overrated. Give him time. He'll come to it on his own terms." She angled her body toward me. "Billie, I did hope we were friends. That you thought of me as a friend."

"I do. Is there a problem?"

"It's just that I understand you lost your mother recently," she said in a quiet voice. "And I was sorry you didn't feel like you could tell me about it."

"I didn't lose her. Not exactly—" I stopped short. I didn't want to cry, not here.

She set down her wineglass and opened her arms, and even though I didn't exactly consider myself a hugger, I let her enfold me into a warm, albeit bony embrace. "I know what happened," Lilah said. "Mere told me. She said she can't talk to her grandmother anymore because the church she's affiliated with doesn't allow it. She also said you were sad about it."

That stung. Mere had picked up on my pain without me saying anything about it. It made me wonder what else she had sensed. The discord between Peter and me, for instance.

"My father died when I was a freshman in college," I said. "My mom was really the reason I started my first restaurant." I didn't elaborate.

She looked into my eyes. "If you ever want to talk—"

"Thank you," I said briskly. "The situation hasn't been ideal, but I'm fine. These things happen. We all have to find our own way."

"We do." That was all she said. I wondered if she was thinking of Wren. "There is another thing," she said in a quiet voice. "Mere mentioned you were upset about the Catawampus."

I felt a little thrum of uneasiness. Peter didn't glance up from his book even though I knew he could hear our conversation. I could feel him listening.

"I wanted to explain," she said.

"It's fine, Lilah," I said. "The story just scared her a little bit. That's all."

"I only told her because it's an actual legend," Lilah said. "Part of Cherokee lore."

"It frightened her," Peter spoke up from across the room. He closed the book and replaced it on the shelf.

"My great-grandmother was Cherokee." Lilah addressed him archly. "I was only trying to share a bit of my heritage with the girls."

Peter eyed her with a bemused expression. "And she told you

those stories? Your great-grandmother? Around the campfire when you were a child?"

"Peter," I said.

Lilah was still. "I never meant to offend."

"You didn't offend us," I said.

Peter took a few steps closer. "No, you didn't offend us, Lilah. You scared my daughter, and you pissed me off. We moved to Juliana to give Meredith a good life. A life as free from fear and worry and death as possible. Where she doesn't have to hear ambulances all hours of the night. Where she doesn't have to see police on every street corner."

Lilah straightened. "It's not like I just made up the story. According to the Cherokee—"

"She's scared of her own *cat* now, Lilah," Peter said. "You should consider your actions. You are caring for our daughter, for your granddaughter. They are impressionable children. You should curb that imagination of yours."

"It's not my imagination, it's a real legend—" Lilah said in a level voice.

"—that I don't want my daughter hearing," Peter said with finality.

I cut in. "Honestly, guys, we don't have to get into it now."

"I will not have my daughter living her life based on superstition and fear," Peter said.

"Peter—"

He pointed a finger at the older woman. "You think you're going to scare me with your stories?" His face had grown red and was contorted. His voice had risen in volume.

"I'm not trying to scare you," Lilah said indignantly.

"I don't give a fuck what you were trying to do," he snapped. "And I don't give a fuck what nonsense went on in this town before we came here."

I held up my hands. "Whoa, Peter. Let's just lower the temperature here."

"I don't care about curses on the land or crimes your ancestors committed or any kind of Stephen King type of bullshit—" He was breathless now, squared up to Lilah, trembling with anger and sweating. I could see pinpricks of moisture on his temples. His eyes looked hard. Unrecognizable.

"Peter, please," I begged him.

"Let me tell you this . . ." He addressed Lilah in a low, threatening voice. "Major Minette said there was an additional well on our land, one Silas Dalzell dug and used for livestock or crops. But here's the thing. I've been all over that property. Checked the records at city hall and found out that no one has ever dug any other well on the property other than the original one Dalzell dug for the house."

I gave him a sharp look. This was news to me, Peter going to city hall to look into our property without telling me. Why in the world would he have kept this information to himself?

Peter took a step closer to Lilah. "So you tell me, Ms. Street, what's wrong with that house and that property—so wrong that the people in this town will lie to keep us from finding it out?"

"I have no idea what you're talking about," Lilah said. She looked fearful now.

"Is something wrong with the water?" Peter demanded. "That creek is as red as rust."

"I don't know. But whatever Major told you, you should take with a whole saltshaker full of salt—"

Peter loomed over her, his face red. "There's something wrong on that property, something wrong in this whole fucking town, and I want to know what it is!" he bellowed, and she shrank back.

I leaped forward and grabbed his arm, but he shook me off. He backed away, hands up, then bumped into a plaster bust on a pedestal. The bust teetered then fell, crashing to the floor and splitting into three pieces. He hesitated for one second, then stalked out of the room, slamming the door behind him.

For a moment the room sat silent, then I turned to see Lilah's ashen face. I sent her an apologetic look and started to stammer out some sort of an excuse. Before I could, the door creaked open again, slowly this time, and Jamie stepped into the room. "Everybody okay in here?" he asked mildly.

I raced to gather the pieces of the bust, not wanting him to see my stricken look.

He beat me to it, picking up the biggest pieces of plaster and depositing them in a pile on a nearby table. "Billie?"

Lilah made a gesture toward the door. "I should go."

I stood. "Lilah, stop. Please. I'm so sorry. I don't know what's gotten into him."

She put a wrinkled hand out. It was shaking, I noticed. "Billie, it's okay. I meant what I said. I am sorry I scared Mere, and I won't do it again. I hope you'll forgive me."

"Of course, Lilah. Of course, you're forgiven. Just give Peter some time."

"Don't worry about me, Billie. This isn't the first time I've been yelled at. I raised three children, remember?" She sent me a sympathetic look. "I was also married to a man who used anger like a hammer."

I felt nauseated. That wasn't Peter. At least, it didn't used to be.

"He's sick," I said to her. To Jamie. "He's never been like this. It's something . . . something with his sleeping. I'm getting him to the doctor." A pathetic excuse. One I could tell neither of them bought for a second.

Lilah patted my arm. "I'm here if there's anything I can do," she said, then glanced at Jamie and slipped out of the library. When she was gone, Jamie gave me a quick look.

"Killer dress," he said mildly.

I ignored the compliment. "How much did you hear?"

"All of it."

"Did anyone else?"

"I'm not sure. The door was open."

I fell silent. I was burning with humiliation. Jamie, hands in his pockets, watched me. Somehow, I didn't quite know how, I could tell Peter had left the house. I could feel it, that he'd walked down the street, gotten in the Subaru, and driven home without me. I could feel his absence right now. I was completely alone, and it opened up a chasm in me.

Jamie broke the silence. "Can I give you a ride home, Billie?"

I nodded. "Yes. I'd appreciate that."

And then something occurred to me. Peter had gone to city hall. He was doing research. Research that would prove the people had lied to us. Research that would give him a reason for us to leave Juliana. He hadn't told me because he wasn't ready. He was building his case.

Chapter 16

When Jamie's truck turned the last corner and onto our long drive, I noticed the windows of Mere's room were dark and Finch's car was gone. The only lights that remained on were coming from the side of the house. Peter's office. I wondered if he was at his desk, reviewing notes. Doing more research. Planning his strategy to get us back to New York.

"You okay?" Jamie asked.

I sighed. "I'm sure we set some tongues to wagging tonight. I kind of dread seeing everyone at the restaurant tomorrow."

"Gossip's part of the deal with Juliana. But trust me, in a few hours, somebody at Dixie's party will have drunk-driven their golf cart into their neighbor's mailbox, and there'll be something else for everybody to talk about."

I smiled. "I really appreciate the ride."

"Do you want me to walk you in?"

"I'm fine." But I didn't move. I could feel his eyes on me, and I liked it. I liked Jamie Cleburne watching me with his steady, piercing blue-green eyes. I liked the way he talked to me. I liked that he'd taken notice of what had happened back at the party and come to my rescue.

So what did that make me? A damsel in distress? Maybe just a woman looking outside her currently frustrating marriage for something that would give her a little hit of attention-dopamine. I loved Peter—I did—I just couldn't figure out how we were going to find our way back to each other. And Jamie was nothing but a distraction.

"Billie," Jamie said. He was staring at me, the way he'd looked at me that night in the restaurant. The way a man looks at a woman when he is not hiding what he wants. I held his gaze, playing this tense little game of chicken with him, until he finally looked away.

"I'm sorry." He propped his elbow on the open window.

"Are you?"

He laughed. "No. I'm not. I just said that because I don't want you to stay away from me. I want to keep seeing you. As much as I can."

I gave him a wry look.

"I didn't say it was right."

Everything inside the truck was quiet. The song had switched to a folk tune I didn't recognize, wistful and spare. There was a fiddle and a banjo, just like in that damn hymn from Billie's playlist. I felt a twinge of sadness and suddenly understood why I hated that song. Something about it—the melody or the plaintive voices or maybe the lyrics about death—filled me with a kind of haunting, indefinable kind of despair. That same way I'd felt death and despair envelop me back in New York after the pandemic. The way I felt now.

I guess it was the reality of life. There was no guarantee that Peter and I would stay together forever. I had always thought of our bond as unbreakable, but the last few months had proven that it was not. He was only human—and the perfect storm of circumstances could bring the whole life we'd built crashing to the ground.

"Peter and I have a good marriage," I said, more to myself than to Jamie. "But he's gone someplace out of reach."

"I understand," Jamie said. "I'm not going to get in the way of your marriage, Billie."

I sighed. "You already are."

Jamie was quiet for a moment, then he spoke. "Do you think he's seeing someone?"

I stared at him. I hadn't even considered the possibility of that.

"Billie?" Jamie asked.

"I'm just . . ." I shook my head. "That could be it, I guess."

"I mean, I hate to suggest this, but could it be one of his patients? I don't know what kind of oaths psychologists take, but I'm fairly certain that would be a breach of something pretty damn serious, wouldn't it?"

I gazed up at the dark house, the light spilling from Peter's office window. "He would lose his license."

"Maybe it's someone in town."

I shook my head. "He rarely leaves the house. It would have to be one of his clients."

"Are you serious?"

I couldn't help but picture the lovely Alice Tilton. The way she'd said *I'm seeing your husband* and then blushed so furiously. I had misinterpreted it, but maybe I hadn't been wrong. Maybe my intuition had been trying to tell me something.

"I don't know if I'm serious or not. I don't know anything." I reached for the door handle. I needed to get out of Jamie's truck. Needed to go in my house and find my husband and try to fix whatever was broken between us. I'd made mistakes and maybe he had, too, but that didn't mean I had to let those mistakes destroy us. I didn't have to sit by and watch our family disintegrate.

"Seriously," he said in an even tone. "I will come in with you." His meaning was all too clear. He was concerned that Peter might get physical with me again.

"No. I'll be fine." I heard the word in my head as I said it. *Fine. Fine.* I'd said it multiple times that night, but I wasn't fine, not even close. Even so, Jamie wasn't the one to help. This was something I had to do on my own. "Thanks for the ride." I slammed the door.

Inside, the house was quiet. Deathly quiet. It was an apt description. It felt like death inside my home. Death was in the air. I smelled it all around me. It seeped into my skin. Coursed through my veins, the same way it had that night in the woods.

I paused in the darkness, leaning against the console table. My eyes filled and I felt the tears choke my throat. It was too much. All this longing for things to be the way they used to be—all this regret for the ways I'd gone wrong—it was all going to break my heart.

My eyes adjusted somewhat to the darkness, and I brushed away the tears that had started to slide down my cheek. I could hear the ticking of the ancient fridge in the kitchen, the sighing of the wind around the old eaves, and the drone of the air conditioning. We were all safe inside this house. Mere, asleep upstairs in her bedroom. Peter, probably on the sofa in his office. And me, staring down this dark hall like a stranger in my own life.

I fumbled around, searching for the switch on the lamp, then checked all the downstairs rooms in case Ramsey had decided to grace us with his presence for the evening. The rooms were empty, so I locked the front door and mounted the stairs. I peeked into Mere's room. Everything was in order—nightlight on, window cracked. There was Ramsey, too, curled at the foot of her bed. Meredith's arms were flung wide, and her skin looked pink and dewy. I flipped on the rotary fan on her dresser and bent to kiss her, finding myself eye to eye with Rams.

"Catawampus," I whispered at him. He didn't blink, only flicked his orange tail. I wondered if he knew the word. If he did, he didn't let on. But that would be just like a cat. "You like that, don't you, everyone thinking you're a demon-monster?"

He lifted his back leg and began to bathe himself. I pulled

Mere's door closed and went back up the hall to Peter's office. Inside, only one lamp was on, and it cast a warm yellow glow in the room. Peter lay asleep, on his side, arms folded, knees drawn up, on the couch. It was the old brown corduroy sectional we'd thrifted in Queens when we'd first moved in together that neither of us wanted to let go of. One of the few pieces from our old life we'd brought with us.

He had two computers, one personal and one for work. The one open on his neat desk now was his work one. The screen was dark. Beside it lay a Ghirardelli chocolate square. *Of course.* He'd found my stash again. I shook my head, then checking to make sure he was truly asleep, crept toward his desk. Just as I did, the computer pinged and lit up. I froze, startled by the sound, but he didn't stir. I stared at the computer screen. The desktop was lined with neatly organized files labeled with last names against a violet-blue background. There were dozens of them, columns of ten each.

I moved closer, scanning the files. I recognized some of the names of his New York clients. Aylsworth, Bennett, Drake, Edward, Frank, Helvig, Ingram, Jones, Letts, Martino . . . I never pushed for information or asked him to reveal what he shouldn't have, but he wasn't perfect. Sometimes he'd let a patient's problem slip, tell me a story that shouldn't be told. It didn't matter. I kept it all to myself. I kept my husband's secrets safe.

But maybe he had other secrets, ones beside his patients' histories. Maybe he'd gotten himself into some kind of trouble, and it was eating away at him so he couldn't sleep. What if there were drugs or gambling debts or some other kind of hole he couldn't dig himself out of? Would he have any record of it here, on his computer?

I skimmed the neat columns of files. They were arranged alphabetically: Letts, Martino, Nance, Nicholas, Oscar, Settles, Tilton . . .

Tilton.

I touched the trackpad, positioning the arrow over Alice's file. I couldn't deny it, I wanted to open it. My finger was trembling the slightest bit and I held my breath. To hell with the laws and the rules. Jamie's suggestion had triggered something in me, and I had to know what was going on. The welfare of my family might be at stake. I tapped on the file and surveyed the contents. Instead of the word files I expected to see, though, I only saw row after row of MP4 files. My heart skittered in my chest.

Video files.

Peter had videotaped all their sessions. Which was not typical. Not at all. He didn't video his clients' sessions, or even record them on audio. He took notes. Handwritten notes on a legal pad that he transcribed later into Word documents.

Behind me on the couch, Peter stirred. I nearly jumped out of my skin, backing away from the computer. He opened his eyes. Rubbed them.

"Hey," I said in a soft voice, clasping my hands behind me.

He looked disoriented, groggy. "I fell asleep."

I quickly sat on the edge of the couch and brushed a lock of hair back. "You okay?"

He rubbed his eyes and winced. "Ugh. More nightmares."

"What about?"

"Doesn't matter." He swung his legs around, planting his feet on the floor and his elbows on his knees. "Sorry about tonight."

"It's okay."

"No, Billie. It was shitty of me. Really shitty." He stared morosely at his feet.

"Peter, it's fine. I just . . . Why didn't you tell me about what you found at city hall about the well?"

He mopped his face. "I wanted to get all my ducks in a row before I presented all the information to you."

I was right. He was building a case. "All what information?"

"All the reasons I think we should move back home."

I sat very still.

"I know you don't want to leave, Billie. But I just can't reconcile all this false information the people in this town have fed us. It doesn't make sense, and the truth is I don't think I even care to make it make sense. I just want to wash my hands of the whole place."

I said nothing. I had no words. I didn't even know how I felt. Was it empty? Utterly lost? I couldn't say.

"How did you get home?" he asked.

"Jamie Cleburne gave me a ride."

"Ah." He studied his hands thoughtfully. "Can I ask you a question?"

"Sure."

"How do you feel about him?"

"What do you mean?"

He looked at me. "I know you guys are friends. I know you kissed him. I would like to know how you feel about him."

"I . . ." My mind had gone blank, my heart hammering in my chest. "How do you know I kissed him?"

"That's not really the part that matters here, Billie."

For a moment, I considered countering his question with one of my own: *Why did you record your sessions with Alice Tilton? Was it really therapy she was coming to you for?*

I shut the thoughts down. I was just projecting, grasping for an excuse for my behavior. The fact was I'd gone too far with Jamie. Betrayed my husband and broken his trust. And now I had to face up to what it meant . . . for us both.

"I'm sorry, Peter. It was wrong. I was wrong."

He was quiet for a moment. "Do you want to be with him?"

"No." I hesitated. "I'm just . . . I was lonely. Sad about you."

He crossed and uncrossed his thumbs over each other. "So it's my fault."

"That's not what I'm saying. I'm responsible for my actions."

"But maybe it was not all that unexpected. I know I've been hard to live with lately."

"I just want you to get some answers, Peter. Some help for whatever is going on with you." I moved toward him. "It was a terrible thing to do, and I regret it. All I can do is tell you it will never happen again."

He seemed to turn this over in his mind. "I just never expected . . ." He didn't finish the sentence. "We came here for our family, Billie."

"We did, but—"

"But what?"

"Something's not right here. And I'm not talking about the well. It's you. You're not yourself."

"I'm not the one who kissed someone else."

"Peter—"

"In sickness and in health, Billie."

Shame flooded me. "I know. I said I was wrong. I meant it, and I'm sorry."

"I'm to blame, too, I know." He sounded so defeated, I wanted to take him in my arms, but I didn't dare. "I just don't know why I . . ." He went silent, shaking his head.

"Peter, I love you. I do." I wanted him to look at me the way he used to, with that warm, wry expression that told me it was him and me, that we were a team no matter what. But his face was a blank. His eyes devoid of any sort of connectedness. I felt like a part of my soul had been ripped away.

"I know you love me. I love you, too. I have a headache and it's late. We should go to bed." He paused. "I'm not crazy, Billie. I don't care what it looks like or what anybody is telling you—"

I opened my mouth to object.

"—I'm *not* crazy."

"I know." I cleared my throat. "Can I ask . . ."

"What?"

"Why are you videotaping your sessions with Alice Tilton?"

"I can't tell you. You know that."

"Are you sleeping with her?"

He gave me a warning look, a glance that told me in no uncertain terms that I was treading on dangerous ground. "Don't go there, Billie. Not tonight."

My heart felt like it was being squeezed. "Just tell me. Give me some explanation that will make sense."

His laugh was harsh. "I can't violate her privacy, Billie."

"But—"

"Why can't you trust me, Billie? You trust him, a stranger."

"That's not fair, Peter. This has been really difficult."

"And you're not making it any easier."

I felt so overcome with sadness, I couldn't speak.

He stood. "I think I should say good night now. Go to bed."

He patted me on the knee, and then he was gone.

Chapter 17

I dreamed about the singing children again.

I was somewhere dark and damp, but the voices propelled me forward. I stumbled, blind and groping, toward some destination I couldn't name but knew I had to reach. And then I saw her face—the old woman's—and knew. It shone in the dark like a withered moon, and I froze in terror. She hissed in my ear, her message from before.

Whaaat . . . have they taaakennn . . . from youuu . . .

I woke bathed in sweat, heart pounding wildly. The curtains hung still. It was purple-gray outside, the sun hadn't even fully risen, but Peter's side of the bed was cool. I got up and checked the bathroom. His toothbrush and razor were gone, as well as his deodorant, shaving cream, and hairbrush. I threw open the door of his closet. A third of his clothes were gone.

I spotted the note, a piece of yellow lined paper torn from one of his legal pads, on my nightstand. In something like a trance, I walked over and picked it up. For a moment, I held the folded note, time standing still. The note couldn't hurt me if I didn't open it, if I never read the words written inside. If I never opened it, I could still find Peter, beg for his forgiveness, ask him to erase what I'd done. Erase this whole part of our lives . . .

I unfolded the paper.

I love you, Billie, but so much has happened, I need to find some clarity. The time apart will be good for both of us, I think. P.

Tears burned in my eyes, and I started to tremble. I grabbed my phone from my nightstand and pulled up my messages. **Peter, I'm begging you, please call me. I want to talk. I want to fix this.**

Clutching my phone, I tiptoed down the hall to Peter's office. I pushed open the door, careful not to let it creak and wake Mere. My gaze swept the place. Everything was still in place, except his computer was gone as well as its charger. I composed another text.

Peter, you have to tell me where you are—if not for me then for Mere. Please.

The seconds ticked by.

Nothing . . .

Nothing . . .

. . . then three dots.

A wave of relief crashed over me. I would do whatever he wanted, shut down the restaurant, never speak to Jamie Cleburne again, even move back to the city. I'd move anywhere he wanted, just as long as our family stayed together.

I'm at the airport. Flight booked to New York. Please give me the space I'm asking for, Billie. It's the least you can do.

I stared uncomprehendingly at the words. He was going back to New York? Without us? A sob worked its way from my chest and up my throat, but I jammed the back of my hand against my mouth before it could escape. I couldn't let Mere hear me. I slipped out of the office and shut the door behind me, turning to lean against the door and jumped, startled.

Ramsey was sitting in the middle of the hallway, watching me. His eyes were wide, unblinking, and I noticed the line of fur bristling along his spine. There was something behind him, a small lump on the floor. An animal, lifeless. Ramsey pulled back his mouth to reveal a row of sharp white teeth and hissed at me, daring me to take his prize.

Like baby teeth, bared in a little girl's mouth . . .

Mere's door swung open. "Rams!" she cried.

I threw out my hand "Stop, Mere! Don't move."

She saw the dead rodent and her face fell. "Oh no, Mama. He killed it."

"It's okay, baby. It's what cats do. Just go back in your room and get changed for Lilah's, and I'll take care of it." She obeyed, her eyes swimming in tears, and after she shut the door, I could hear her crying.

"See what you did," I hissed back at the cat and then charged him. He twisted around, leaping on his kill, jaws snapping protectively over it. With one last baleful glance at me, he streaked past me and down the stairs, holing up somewhere safe and hidden in the big house.

At the restaurant, the breakfast rush dragged, the hands of the kitchen wall clock ticking at half speed as I scrambled eggs, fried bacon, and flipped hotcakes. I felt smothered by my own desperation. I needed to get out of that kitchen, breathe some fresh air.

I needed to cry. Scream. Beg Peter—again—to communicate with me.

Everything that could go wrong, did. We ran out of avocado, which was in practically every dish. The espresso machine malfunctioned. Tilda Brennan dropped by to say, with a smirk, that she'd accidentally sent our delivery of croissants down to a restaurant in Atlanta. To top it off, I discovered Major Minette had brought a flask of moonshine to work and had been nipping on it all through his shift. He ended up breaking a bunch of our more expensive cocktail glasses, then banging around the kitchen storage area after which I confiscated the flask and sent him home.

Jamie kept trying to catch my eye every time I bustled past, but I kept my head down, focusing on putting out the next fire. When he'd finished his breakfast and thrown down his usual twenty-dollar tip, he poked his head into the kitchen.

"Billie?" he said.

I looked up, face flushed from more than just the heat of the stove.

"You okay?"

I wiped my forehead with my arm. "Yep."

He looked puzzled. "Well, alright then. Good to see you."

"Always." I vanished back into the line and tried to jump into the flow at the griddle. But I couldn't concentrate and ended up scorching the sourdough toast and overcooking the poached eggs. I was useless here. I needed to go.

I called Lilah and asked if she'd be willing to keep Mere overnight. Temperance had invited her to sleep over on previous occasions, but Peter had always said he thought she was too young. She might be, but everything was different now. In leaving me and his daughter, Peter had forfeited his parental vote.

I paused, hands on hips, surveying the restaurant. In spite of the day's rocky start, everything seemed to be running smoothly now. Falcon could handle the kitchen. I could call Cam to come fill in as manager, and tomorrow was Saturday, which was my day off.

I was free to go. To point the Jeep in a direction, any direction, and drive until I found someplace to drown out this misery. Someplace far enough away that no one recognized me.

Certainly not at The Dredges, the dingy little pool hall several blocks down from the square. I needed to be anonymous. To sit in silence and drink until my out-of-control mind quit spiraling in every imaginable direction. It wasn't the healthiest coping mechanism, but I'd do healthy another day. Right now, I was desperate.

After I promised him a few precious days off in the next weeks, Cam agreed to come in. In the hot kitchen, I pulled Falcon aside. "A minute? I'm going to need the rest of the day, if that's all right with you. Cam's on his way over."

"Sure, boss. Everything okay?"

"It will be. Thanks, Falcon."

I hung my apron on a hook and went back to the office to grab my purse. I shut the door of the office, pulled Major's contraband flask off a high shelf, and reached for a mug from one of the shelves above the computer. After wiping it out with the bottom of my T-shirt, I poured a slug and knocked it back, wincing. Then I repeated the action. I breathed out, low and slow, feeling the burn in my chest. And an instant calm. I tucked the flask in my purse, zipped it closed, and slung it over my shoulder.

Outside, I let the humidity and heat envelop me like a comforting hug. I turned toward my car, which was parked in the alleyway behind the restaurant, and nearly ran into a young man in a sheriff's uniform and hat. He was Black, tall, and broad shouldered, but carried his size awkwardly. He looked fresh out of the police academy or wherever sheriff's deputies went.

"Whoops, pardon me." I stepped back then blinked in recognition. He was the deputy I'd seen that first day in Juliana, at the mill, rolling up the yellow crime tape.

"Ms. Hope?" he asked. I was definitely staring.

I tightened my grip on my purse and the contraband moonshine inside. "Yes?"

He handed me a business card. "Deputy Isaac Inman with the Bartow County Sheriff's Department. I wondered if you'd mind answering a few questions for me." He said it like a book report he'd memorized for English Lit.

"Sure. Can I ask about what?" I asked.

"Your property. The Dalzell-Davenport place." He shifted his weight from foot to foot. "I wondered if you'd seen anything out of the ordinary there since you've moved in. Around the place . . . or inside."

I had the impulse to burst out laughing. *Strange, you say?* Oh my God, where to begin? The dreams and nightmares and sleepless nights? The feral cat? Or what about the cryptic carvings in the baseboards? *For the children . . .*

"Ms. Hope?" He was watching me closely. I wondered if he could tell I was tipsy.

"I'm sorry. You know, funny you should mention it, there have been a few strange things about the place. The day we moved in, we were told that there was an old well, different from the one that supplies water to the house now, that had not been properly capped. We were warned not to let our daughter wander the property in case she might fall in it. My husband searched all over, but he never found it. And he couldn't find any record of it in the plat at city hall."

"Interesting."

"It was really getting to him for a while there. He was obsessing over finding it. Worrying about our daughter. He's been having trouble sleeping and then sleeping all the time. He had nightmares, these really intense and realistic dreams about all these fantastical creatures—"

He was staring at me, eyes narrowed, and I shut my mouth. It occurred to me that I was talking way too much and possibly sounded utterly insane. The thing was, I didn't care. I was tired of it all—the situation with Peter. The questions about this town. I was ready for some answers.

"Go on," he said.

"He went to see a doctor, Dr. Belmont St. John, here in town, but we haven't gotten any test results back yet. He's thinking about getting a second opinion."

"What do you think it is?"

"I honestly have no idea, but the lack of sleep can't help. I don't think he's happy here. He actually—" I sent him a tired look. "He left earlier today. Left me, that is."

"I'm sorry."

I let out a caustic laugh. "But that's not what you wanted to know about."

"It's fine."

"Are you investigating the kids who were doing drugs at the mill?"

He furrowed his brow.

I leaned forward and lowered my voice. "I actually saw you there, the day we got into town, back in April. You were rolling up the yellow tape. Although I thought yellow tape was only used for when they find a body."

Deputy Inman looked stricken. His mouth opened then closed, but no words came out. I cocked my head, the pieces falling into place.

"Wait. *Did* you find a body there?" I asked.

The guy looked like he wished the earth could swallow him whole.

"Because Jamie Cleburne definitely told me it was just kids messing around with drugs."

His eyes shifted from right to left. "I can't really—"

"What the hell is going on, Deputy? We live right down the road. I think I deserve to know what's going on."

"I can't—"

"You can." I stepped closer to him. He straightened but didn't back away. "Please, Deputy Inman. You can trust me."

He clenched his jaw then seemed to relent. "This stays between you and me, all right?" he said in a low voice. His face held an expression I couldn't read.

"No problem. Whatever you say."

"It was actually the same day you and your family moved in," he said. "It was bones, some clothing, and jewelry. I was the one who found them. Purely by accident. I was fishing on the river on my day off."

Bones. I swallowed. "Who is it? Was it?"

He shook his head. "Don't know, and I didn't have much time to find out. As soon as I reported it to Sheriff Childers, he took over the case. Told me to go back, get rid of the tape I'd rolled, and leave it to him."

"Okay."

"I think it was probably one of that group that used to hang out with Wren Street—"

"The ones who were squatting in my house?"

He looked surprised I knew about this but nodded. "—but he didn't agree. And then he said I was no longer needed on the case. He said that he would handle it."

I considered this. "So, Wren Street's friends . . ."

"People called them trustafarians. Trust fund babies who live the life of neo-hippies. Pretending they don't have money. Doing drugs. Panhandling. Then drawing a thousand out of the bank to fund a trip to Paris."

"Marie Antoinette pretending to be a milkmaid."

He nodded. "Exactly. People around here weren't too happy about them hanging around town. They were dirty, you know. Looked strange with the dreadlocks and the no-bathing thing. Folks thought it sent the wrong message. A welcome sign to more bad elements to come to Juliana."

"And you think one of them died at the mill?"

"Or at your house and they moved the body. But it has to be. Or someone passing through. Nobody around here's been reported missing."

I absorbed this. "My God. Do you think it was an accident? An overdose?"

"I don't know." Deputy Inman was regarding me closely. So closely, I started to feel uncomfortable. "But it doesn't matter because I'm not on the case. Technically."

"But you're here questioning me. And it's been . . . what, almost four months? Seems like you're not confident the sheriff's doing his job."

He said nothing, and we stared at each other, each of us trying to assess the other's trustworthiness. I couldn't seem to figure out what exactly this man was after. Or whose side he was on.

"I'm just trying to do the right thing," he finally said, "by whoever it was."

I nodded. "The squatters, the trustafarians, left carvings around the baseboards of one of the bedrooms. *For the children.* I don't know what it means. There were initials, too. *MBEDWS.*"

"The *WS* is definitely Wren Street. Emmaline Dalzell might be the *ED.* I don't know the other one."

"That's all I've got. Sorry."

He clicked his pen. Jotted some notes. "I appreciate it."

"Are you from Juliana?" I asked. "I don't remember meeting any Inmans yet."

"You wouldn't have," he said. "My family's from Cooper Creek. A little west of here." He clicked the pen and returned it to his shirt pocket, never averting his eyes from mine. Discomfort rippled through me. "Ms. Hope, I don't mean to . . ." He trailed off.

"What?"

"Is there a chance you've been drinking?"

I stared at him, unable to formulate an adequate lie. I found myself touched, in some odd way, at his concern. "What if I have? Could you blame me?"

Now he smiled at me. A kind smile that held an edge of humor. "No, I wouldn't blame you. I just want you to get home safe.

Sometimes the safest place to be when you've had a hard day is
at home."

"I thank you, and I really appreciate you confiding in me."
He looked a bit regretful.

"I'll be careful. And . . . I hope we can talk again. If you learn
anything interesting about . . . anything."

He pursed his lips. Nodded, all business again. "Yes, ma'am.
You have my number."

Chapter 18

I didn't go home. Instead, after watching Deputy Inman drive off, I walked across the street to city hall. After some alcohol-influenced wandering through the deserted halls, I finally found myself in the basement, location of the records department.

The basement was a cramped, dank, fluorescent-lit space that smelled of mildew, old paper, and something sharp and disgusting that I decided must be rat piss. The nameplate on the desk read NELSON ST. JOHN. I introduced myself to the man sitting behind an ancient desktop computer then asked for the plat of the Dalzell-Davenport property.

"Okey-doke," the guy said in an affable voice. He moseyed back, disappearing into the rows of metal file cabinets.

I picked at my fingernails, watching the minutes tick by on the clock on the wall. I glanced around the walls, checking for cameras, then pulled Major's flask out of my purse and took a couple of fortifying swigs. I found a metal folding chair and plopped down, scrolling the news on my phone.

Fifteen minutes later, the guy returned empty-handed. "I'm sorry, Mrs. Hope, I wasn't able to locate that plat in our files."

I stood. "That's incorrect. You actually do have a copy of it here." I tried to keep the New York edge out of my voice. "My husband said he saw it recently."

He just shrugged. "Sorry."

"We just bought the place back in April."

"Then it should be in your information," the guy said. "Or check your email to see if it was sent electronically."

I hesitated. We'd closed virtually, and I'd only really paid attention to the contract, the photos of the house, and the insurance documents. I did seem to remember a map of the property, but it had been more of a surveyor's sketch, not an official plat. A trickle of dread moved through me.

"Well, please call me if it turns up, Mr. St. John."

"Oh, I'm not Mr. St. John. I'm the temp, Jack. Just moved into town from Houston."

"The Initiative?"

"That's right. I freaking love this place. Got a freaking four-bedroom house built in 1910, in perfect condition, with a huge backyard and a fountain for one hundred goddamn dollars, pardon my French. It's freaking wild."

"Totally wild," I agreed.

"I'm just filling in down here, starting today. This place is a wreck, boxes and boxes of stuff back there, piled up to the ceiling, and half of it is water damaged. If they asked me to Marie Kondo this place, I can tell you the God's honest truth, I'd throw everything out. Anyway, I'm going to be gone in a month, opening a Tex-Mex restaurant." He leaned closer. "The mayor even set me up with someone. One of the Dalzell girls. One of the original families."

"Huh." I thought of Peter's comment—that the Initiative was like a mail-order bride service for the old families. *The old guard.*

"Super-hot, too. The Dalzell girl." Jack was nodding dreamily.

"Well, good luck," I told him and left.

In the stairwell, I sipped once more from the flask then set off in search of Mayor Dixie's office. I finally found it on the second floor—a set of spacious offices with high ceilings, dark wood paneling, and plush forest-green carpet. Feeling good and toasty from Major's moonshine, I breezed past my old friend Bonnie St. John at the reception desk out front and headed toward the back.

" 'Scuse me, hon," Bonnie called after me, which I only took as encouragement to walk faster.

Mayor Dixie's door was wide open, and I could see that she was on the phone. I entered her office and availed myself of one of the matched pink wingback chairs set in front of her massive mahogany and leather desk.

She held up a finger, a crease appearing between her brows. "Yes, thank you so much. We are so excited to hear that."

I nodded agreeably and crossed my legs.

Her frown deepened. "No, no, we do not have a chiropractor in town, but I can tell you we've got plenty of old spines that could do with one, including mine." She let out a chuckle.

I waited, smiling patiently.

Now she was glaring at me. "I apologize, Mr. Hollister. I'm going to have to call you back later. I look forward to telling you more about our Initiative. Okay, then. Bye-bye." She listened for a moment and then hung up.

She gently inclined her head, her forehead free of lines now. "Billie Hope," she said in a creamy voice. "To what do I owe the pleasure?"

To Major's moonshine . . .

"Sorry to barge in this way," I said. "I was just going to pick up that plat of the property—the Dalzell-Davenport property— like you suggested, but the guy in Records told me it wasn't in the file."

"Gracious. How strange."

I templed my fingers. "Yes, indeed. I thought so, too. Especially since my husband said he saw it recently."

"Odd." She narrowed her eyes at me. "You're still worried about the well, I take it?"

"Among other things, yes."

"Well, I'm sorry to hear the plat's been misplaced, but I don't think I'm going to be much help. Perhaps in a few weeks when our permanent Records Director Nelson St. John comes back from vacation—"

"Is it real?"

"Is what real?"

"The well. Or did you just make it up so Major—or other people—wouldn't wander around the property?" I stared at her, her face doubling for a second. God, I really was sloshed, wasn't I?

She laughed. "You think I would lie about a well on your property?" She seemed deeply amused by this. "Mrs. Hope, you're a regular riot, aren't you? I think you're the first Juliana citizen to come into this office and accuse me of lying."

"I'm not accusing you of anything, Mayor, I'm just asking."

"I don't know anything about a well on your property. I'm sorry if Major got confused, and I hope you resolve the issue. I don't mean to be rude, Mrs. Hope, but is there anything else? I have work to do."

I noticed the delicate gold bracelet peeking out of her jacket sleeve. It had two little charms, a script *D* and *J*. It was just like Ronnie Coleman's bracelet, the one she'd said had been a gift from Dixie. Jamie said they all had them. I wondered when the old guard would allow me to join their secret society club? Or would I always be an outsider here?

"Are you feeling all right, Mrs. Hope?"

"No," I said in a thoughtful voice. "I don't think I am. But thank you for asking."

She hesitated. "Can I help in any way with . . . whatever it is?"

I sighed and trailed my fingers along the pink taffeta arm of the chair. "Please, call me Billie."

"Okay, Billie." Her expression softened, and she leaned back against her cushy leather chair and regarded me. "I was a young widow. Did you know that?"

I shook my head.

"My husband, Bobby, Major's younger brother, was a doctor. Big man, tall. Like Major, but handsome. Whew, let me tell you. Looked like Troy Donahue. He got all the brains of the family, too."

"Poor Major."

She waved a hand at me. "Oh, don't you worry about Major. He has his own talents. What I want to tell you is this. Your happiness is your husband's happiness. If you're miserable, then he will do anything to make it better."

I stared at her, not understanding.

"You're not happy, Billie, are you?"

I let out a sigh. I had been happy. For the most part. Peter was the one who was refusing to make the effort. Harping on the negatives. Pulling against me at every opportunity.

"What is it?" she asked. "Does it concern the restaurant? Your daughter?"

"No—"

"Would you like to move out of the Dalzell-Davenport house, Billie? Because I can arrange that, if you do. We have several houses left that we're offering with the Initiative. They're not quite the caliber of your house. They don't have the acreage, but they're plenty big enough for you and your family—"

She paused, and I wondered if she had heard about Peter leaving me. Word traveled fast around here. Somebody had obviously told him about Jamie and me kissing. Somebody could've seen him filling the Subaru at a gas station on his way down to Atlanta to the airport.

"—and all of them are historically recognized and in excellent condition." She was shuffling through the papers on her desk now. "I'm thinking of one in particular, a little Craftsman bungalow over on Dalzell that I think you'd love. It's got a nice, deep porch, several built-ins. And the stained glass transoms are to die f—"

"I don't want a new house," I interrupted. "I want to know where the uncapped well on my property is so I can cap it and my daughter can play safely in her own backyard."

Mayor Dixie's pale blue eyes were steady. "Well, if you'll just take a look at—"

"I do not want a new house!" I shouted, springing up. I wobbled a bit as I did and grabbed the side of the chair for support. "I want that plat!"

"Billie," she said in a low, steady voice, "have you been drinking?"

I said nothing.

"If you have, I'm going to have to ask you to leave. There is no alcohol on the premises. We're a government building."

"Yes," I said. "I've been drinking."

She sat back in her chair, and it creaked loudly. She regarded me for a few uncomfortable moments. "Whatever it is, Billie, I want you to know, we are here for you. All of us."

I nodded. I was starting to get the feeling that I'd messed up in a bigger way than I knew.

She sighed. "If I have the time, I'll go downstairs and try to find the plat for you. Okay?"

"Okay. Thank you. I really appreciate it." I turned toward the door.

"And Billie . . ."

I stopped.

"If you plan on driving home, do be careful."

I drove home slowly, hands at two and ten. New plan: I wouldn't be getting hammered at some middle-of-nowhere dive bar. With warnings from both a sheriff's deputy and the mayor of my town, I was stuck in my palatial Italianate mansion, chock-full of priceless antiques and crystal chandeliers and possibly a band of creepy ghosts, where I would have to settle for a party of two . . . me and Major Minette's flask of moonshine.

I changed out of my work clothes, showered, and put on the oldest, stretchiest yoga pants I could find. Forgoing a bra, I pulled on a bright pink tank top. Feet bare, hair pulled up into a topknot, I slathered my face with a green mask, one of the outrageously expensive items included in the going-away gift basket my friends had given me.

In a cabinet in the green-and-yellow parlor, I found a set of adorable little footed, crystal whiskey tumblers, and after washing one out, poured myself a proper drink of the home brew. On my phone, I found a classic seventies rock mix, one that reminded me of my mother, back when I was a girl. She'd always put on music when we cleaned our little nondescript Garment District apartment and turned it up so loud the neighbors— above, below, and beside—all pounded on the walls. But here . . . here in this house on the knoll, in the middle of nowhere Georgia, I could play the music as loudly as I wanted.

And I wanted.

Now the Rolling Stones, Lynyrd Skynyrd, and the Allman Brothers blasted from the wireless speakers. I'd set them up when we first moved in, for some nonexistent party I planned to throw. Or for when, after we'd put Meredith to bed, Peter spontaneously swept me into his arms and danced me across the spacious room. But I hadn't gotten around to throwing a party, and Peter and I had never danced alone in this room, not even once.

I checked my phone. No missed calls from Peter. No texts, nothing. Presumably, his plane had landed by now and he'd cabbed or Ubered from JFK to whatever hotel or friend's apartment where he was staying while he contemplated what was left of our marriage. I just didn't understand why he hadn't contacted me. The man was a communicator by nature; it's what he did for a living. And I'd lost count of the times he refused to let me clam up during an argument, cajoling me into dealing with the issue, no matter how much I wanted to isolate. This wasn't like him at all. Even if he was furious with me, he'd still want to know what was going on with his daughter. I was the only way he could contact her.

Or was I?

He could've gone around me. Called Lilah to check in, to talk to Mere. The idea of it infuriated me, that he may already be cutting me out, going behind my back to create a new line of communication with our daughter. I poured myself another drink and sipped it, more slowly now that my head was already buzzing. Would he actually do something like that? Cut me out of the equation that way? I couldn't fathom it.

Had I really done so much damage to our marriage with my one stupid act? It didn't seem possible. But maybe I was just letting myself off the hook. Brushing the crime away because I didn't want to hold myself accountable. Maybe I'd really torched my life for good.

I closed my eyes, let the music move me through the rooms of the house. Parlor to parlor, library to smoking room, conservatory to dining room, I drifted through the spaces. Funny how these days people always knocked down walls for the ubiquitous "open concept." What made us think all that openness was better? Maybe the old-timers knew what we didn't. That we all needed our own little compartments so we could keep our meanness and our tendencies to hurt each other barricaded away.

I'd certainly done that. Hurt Peter and in doing so hurt Mere and myself. I'd tried to engineer the perfect family in the perfect, idyllic setting, but it had backfired. I'd been arrogant and overconfident. In trying to control every aspect of my life, I'd lost everything.

No, not everything. Not Mere, not the restaurant, not this

beautiful, enormous house. I still had the house. Owned it, free and clear. Which was, to borrow the words of Jack the Temp from the records department, pretty goddamn freaking wild.

I laughed and spun around, holding the crystal tumbler aloft and singing along with the music. It felt good, to dance in this big, glorious house. This house that was all mine. Because if Peter was really going to leave me, he was going to leave this house as well. This was where he couldn't sleep, where he obsessed over that stupid, nonexistent well. Where he hallucinated feathery, winged, demon-horses . . .

I blinked and looked around, realizing I had danced myself into the kitchen. I also realized I was hungry, starving actually. I put down my drink and set to work. I mixed up some dough and fresh marinara and rolled out pizza crust. In the fridge, I found some leftover broccoli and artichoke hearts. I sliced an early tomato and handful of basil from my garden and tossed it on. A few black olives, some jalapeno, and a sprinkling of fresh mozzarella, and the pizzas were ready for the oven. I found a bottle of Montepulciano and uncorked it as the smell of crisping dough wafted through the room.

"Go fuck yourself, Peter," I said to my silent phone.

I texted my New York friends: Gigi, Annika, Devon, and Jane. The women I'd worked with at the original Billie's. No one responded, but that was fine. It was still early in the evening. They were probably still working. Or busy with family.

I was the one alone on a Friday night, drunk off my tits and making pizzas in my Italianate mansion. I was the one who had cheated on my husband. Forced him to take a break from me. From our family. I was the one who'd blown up her life. And maybe . . . maybe I'd done such a shitty job of keeping in touch since I'd moved down here, my old friends had given up on me, just like Peter.

I smelled something burning. I raced to the oven, reaching in with only a dish towel. I pulled the pizzas out, one by one, yipping as the dripping cheese burned me through the fabric. I dropped them on the farm table and ran cool water over my fingers, then grabbed a knife and slammed it down through one. Then again, once, twice, three times, and then the second one. I started to take a bite, then paused.

I stilled myself. Bowed my head and said the words Jamie had taught me.

"For food that stays our hunger, for rest that brings us ease, for homes where memories linger—" I stopped, lifted my head, and looked around the empty kitchen. It was just me. No one else. I was alone now.

"—we give our . . ." My voice trailed off again.

Who am I thanking anyway? God? This town? Who exactly could I assign responsibility to for the place I'd found myself?

"Fuck it." I took a bite of the steaming pizza, barely noticing how it seared the roof of my mouth. It didn't matter. The pizza was excellent, and I ate slice after slice of each fragrant, piping-hot wedge of perfection.

I drank almost all of the wine, too, keeping a constant eye on my phone. Not one of my friends returned my texts, and I was starting to feel hurt. Could none of them spare a brief minute for a check-in for an old friend? Had I ceased to exist just because I didn't live in New York anymore?

Well, fuck them.

Fuck them right into the sun with a cannon, thank you very much.

I took the bottle of wine back into the parlor to switch the playlist to something sexier. A little late nineties, early 2000s Mariah, perhaps. I tapped on my phone and the bubblegum pop beat poured out. Peter hated this music. So it was perfect. Absolutely perfect.

I worked my way through the rest of the wine, twirling through the rooms of my house, everything growing hazier and softer and lighter by the minute. At one point, in the front hall,

I believe I knocked over a lamp, but I left it lying on the floor. Who even cared? Not me. I had dancing to do . . . in my freaking wild house. The golden sun had dipped in the sky, on the western side of our land and, for a moment, the house glowed. Every piece of furniture, every lamp, every framed portrait seemed to shine with a gilt wash. I blew a thin layer of white dust off a pair of candlesticks and lit the candles. I watched the flames lengthen and flicker, mesmerized by the light and life. Even in this light, the dust looked magical.

"Welcome, spirits." I stretched out my arms to the big, empty room. "Welcome, you creepy, singing children of the darkness and you, too, weird lady with the braids." I shivered, as if I'd just invoked something bigger and more powerful than I knew. Suddenly, I realized the house was doused in shadows. The candles were the only source of light.

I closed my eyes, and I thought about Mere's and my dreams—the children trapped in darkness with the old woman, singing songs to bring them comfort. It was never clear, though, why the children were afraid. Did Peter's dream have anything to do with it? Had the children seen the winged demon-horses that had terrified him? Nothing fit together. But it had to. Wren and her trustafarian friends had carved those words—*for the children*—when they were living here in the house. Maybe they'd had the dreams, too. Or understood something I still didn't. Some terrifying piece of the puzzle that eluded me.

An old secret, I suddenly thought.

A buried evil.

I opened my eyes. I was drunk and scaring the hell out of myself.

But . . .

What if mine and Peter's and Mere's nightmares actually *were* linked? What if Major Minette had told us there was an open well because there really *was* something evil on this property that they didn't want us disturbing? What if there really was some kind of curse on the land or even the house?

I lifted my arms, hands held open to the shadows. "Children!" I called out into the darkness. "Are you here? If you are, speak to me! Tell me what happened to you!"

I listened to the quietness — or rather the sounds of the fridge and mantel clock ticking — and then I really did hear something. Like the whirring, fluttering sound of wings beating against the air. I whirled, searching the dark corners of the room, but all I could see were the shapes of the furniture and the moonlight spilling in from the windows.

Billie, stop.

You're losing it.

Shaken, I grabbed my phone, shut off the music, sank down on the silk taffeta sofa, and FaceTimed my mother.

Chapter 19

Unexpectedly, Mom picked up. She was in a dark room. Only a quarter of her face showed on the screen. "This is forbidden," she whispered at the screen.

I caught my breath, rapidly blinking back the tears that had risen in my eyes and swallowing the lump that had done the same in my throat. She'd picked up. The woman had actually picked up. Seeing the curve of her wrinkled cheek, hearing her raspy, no-nonsense New York accent made me want to reach out and touch my phone's screen.

I composed myself as best I could. "Hi, Mom. Good to see you, too," I said in a light voice. "And what's forbidden? Me calling you, or you having a phone?"

She snorted in disgust. "You're drunk."

I leaned closer to the screen. She looked good. A little thinner, but healthy. "Seriously? How did you know? Are you psychic? Do you have the second sight? The Holy Spirit gift of prophecy?"

"What the hell kind of nonsense are you talking about? You know you're not supposed to call, and you only break rules when you've been drinking. Also, you just said, 'procephy.'"

I pointed at the phone. "Twelve points to Slytherin."

"Rah-rah, Smarty-Pants, I'm Hufflepuff."

I propped my phone on the coffee table, then covered my mouth with my hand to hide the grin that was spreading. Even though we'd immediately fallen into our pattern of joking around, sarcasm skimming over the surface of things, I already felt better.

"How are you, Mom? How's the Manson Family Compound?"

"It's called The Gathering." But she was snorting and coughing and wheezing into her hand, her brand of laughing.

"And what if they find out you have a phone?" I asked. "Does the prophet, or whatever he's called, punish you?"

"Uncle Jimbo. And he's not a prophet, he's just a leader. He's very attractive, Billie. Green eyes and this very nice, full mustache—"

"Oh my God, Mom. Ugh. Isn't he your cousin?"

"Distant cousin. We're all family up here. That's the point. But don't you worry about me. I can take care of myself."

I had bristled at the word *family*. "How is it there, anyway? Fun?"

"It's not about fun, Bills."

"My mistake," I said in a caustic tone. "And what about the religious part?"

She sighed.

"I knew it. It's getting on your nerves."

She hesitated. "I do miss my Candy Crush. Which is why I snuck into the main office and got my phone back." She let out an evil little *tee-hee*, like a recalcitrant child.

I kind of loved that—my perpetually cranky mom defying her cult leader. Again my eyes brimmed with tears, and I brushed them away.

"How's your new setup?" she asked. "Small-town living treating you right?"

"It's interesting," I managed. "Okay."

"Sorry I didn't write you back yet. I've been really busy. They go batshit overboard about a coupla weeds in the garden." I heard a lighter flick somewhere offscreen. Then a sharp suck. So along with her phone, she must've swiped some cigarettes.

The sound broke something in me. I wanted to tell her how much I missed her. Bawl like a baby, tell her everything that had happened in the past three months, and beg her to catch the first flight out of Portland. But that would send her running. I had to keep myself in check.

"I'm glad you're happy," I said in a measured voice.

"You've got a southern accent now," she said.

"I do not."

"You do. You sound like goddamn Scarlett O'Hara." She savored the cigarette. Let out a satisfied sigh.

I picked at a thumbnail. "So, Mom. I was hoping we could talk."

She made a sound, something between a sigh and a groan.

"Mom."

"So talk."

I puffed out my breath, determined to get it out. "I actually . . . I cheated on Peter."

She was quiet for a moment, then, "Well, that was dumb," she said in a clipped and matter-of-fact voice.

"I didn't actually sleep with the guy. I just . . . well, we just—"

"I don't need the gory details, Bills."

"No, Mom, I—"

"It's none of my business."

Now, like some faulty pipe had burst inside me, the tears finally sprang out of my eyes. As quickly as they came, I wiped them away. "Seriously, Mom, just listen. I know it's not your business, but I don't have anybody else I can talk to. I don't know anyone here. I want to tell you. I . . . *need* to tell you this."

"Okay, calm down. You don't need to get all bent out of shape. Just say what you gotta say."

I gathered myself. "So, yeah, I kissed this man. Jamie Cleburne. One night after Peter and I had a really big fight. I don't know why I did it. Maybe I needed the attention. More attention than Peter gives me because I'm . . . too needy. Or, I don't know, broken somehow. Maybe I did it because I'm just some sort of human black hole of need."

She snorted.

"Let's face it, I'm the person who named not one but two restaurants after herself."

"Jesus wept, Bills. You're really overthinking this. Sometimes these things just happen."

"No, Mom. It didn't just happen. I've been feeling lost. Lost and scared and . . . so strange, somehow. Peter doesn't . . . He isn't doing well here. For a long time, he wasn't sleeping, then he was sleeping all the time. We're fighting all the time. And there's something weird about this place, about this house."

"What, is it haunted or something?"

I swallowed. *No comment.*

"So tell me this . . . is Big Pete messing around, too?"

I shook my head. "I don't know."

"What do you mean, you don't know?" she snapped. "He's your husband. You make it your business to know."

"I'm trying, I really am. I just don't know what to do. Mom, if you could just get away. Even for a little while. Come down here for a week, or even a weekend. I could show you the new restaurant. You could see how things are—"

She was already shaking her head. "Bills, you know I can't do that. There's too much to do up here. And anyway, I can't be holding your hand. You have to take care of yourself."

"I am taking care of myself!" I spit out. "And Peter and Meredith *and* the restaurant!"

"Jesus—"

"No, Mom. Seriously, tell me. When have I ever not taken

care of myself? When did I not get myself up for school, wash and iron my school uniform, make my own breakfast, and pack my own lunch? When have I ever once asked you for *anything*, Mom? Huh? I just want my mother to act like a mother for once. Just for once, talk to me about something real."

She was quiet, but I could tell by the set of her mouth that I'd gone too far. I sat in regretful silence.

"Look," she finally said, "if Peter's screwing around, you gotta get the facts. Especially if you're headed for court. You've got Mere to think about."

My stomach clenched. I hadn't even thought that far, but she was right. This could be my future—Peter and I pulling Mere in opposite directions in a custody battle. I suddenly felt the weight of the world pressing down on me, smothering me.

"Is he . . . was he acting strange?" she asked. "Other than not sleeping?"

"There was this one thing. He has a new client, a woman who lives here. I saw her file, and he videotaped all their sessions."

She tsked. "Videotapes? Have you watched 'em?"

"That would be a violation of HIPAA, of boundaries and rules and . . . I don't know, all kinds of professional parameters, I'm pretty sure."

"Well, I'm sorry, but screw HIPAA. You're gonna have to watch them," she declared, like she hadn't listened to a word I'd said. "Whoops, here they come. Gotta run, Bills. And listen . . ."

"What?"

I could've sworn her face softened just the slightest bit. "You call again, Bills. You hear? Anytime."

I nodded. "Okay. I will."

The screen went black. I let the phone fall onto the sofa and sat very still. Then, with two hands I wiped under my eyes, expelling all the air out of my lungs. She'd asked me to call her. That was something. And she'd made a good point, in her

unique, crackpot Mom way. I had to watch those recordings
Peter had made with Alice Tilton.

Peter had taken his computer, but he did have an iPad he
rarely used somewhere in his office. If it was connected to his
files, by the cloud or some other hard drive, maybe I could un-
lock it. I checked my phone again—still no texts—then poured
myself the last of the Montepulciano and headed upstairs. I
opened the door to Peter's office and surveyed the messy room.
It was just as I had left it that morning; the unopened square of
chocolate was even still there. I went to one of the windows,
unlatched it, and pushed it up. Warm, sweet-smelling air rushed
in, and I breathed deeply, sitting in Peter's desk chair.

Okay, I could do this. I was going to do this.

I found the iPad at the bottom of a stack of files in the cre-
denza. It took me a while to find the right charger to get it
going, but once I did, after a short wait, it powered up. None of
Peter's files showed up on the desktop, like on his computer, so
I typed Alice Tilton's name into the top search field. Nothing
resulted, other than the few social media hits, which I pulled
up. They revealed little, other than the fact that Alice Tilton
didn't give a shit about keeping up with her social media.

Fuck. Did it matter if I managed to download a treasure
trove of files that proved that my husband and Alice Tilton had
an inappropriate relationship? Even if I could watch each and
every one—it wouldn't change what I had done. It wouldn't
somehow magically give Peter and me a better chance; it might
only make things worse.

I let the iPad drop to the desk, rose, and walked to the door.
When I opened it, a rush of air hit me. Cold air that smelled of
water and moss and something chemical in nature that I couldn't
identify. I felt my body rock back in the wave, but my eyes remain closed. Jesus. I was drunker than I thought.

I waited, letting my body adjust to being upright. Letting all
my senses settle in the strange smells that enveloped me. It wasn't

that I had the spins, it was more like a gentle rocking, pulling me into . . .

No, toward something I couldn't identify.

We shall meet, but we shall miss him . . .

The banjo and the fiddle played softly. It was coming from somewhere in my house. No, that couldn't be. Not in my house. In my head. The music, the song, filled my head. It surrounded me. I gripped my head with both hands. Was I really hearing it or was it just my imagination? How drunk did you have to be to hear phantom music playing?

There will be one vacant chair . . .

"What the FUCK!" I yelled into the empty house. "What is your deal? What do you want from me?"

I turned back to Peter's desk and stared balefully at the iPad. And then I laughed. A long, loud, full-throated cackle. The music was coming from the iPad. I rushed to the desk and jabbed at the screen. It lit up. "The Vacant Chair." That same damn song was actually playing.

I hit pause then dropped the device and backed away like the thing was possessed. What was this song doing in Peter's library? He didn't like gospel. He liked nineties music, punk, and rock and roll. Maybe he'd been playing a more folky list of songs and the music app must've just suggested it. Yes. That must've been what happened.

I slipped out into the darkened hall. The floorboards creaked beneath my feet. I tried the light switch, but nothing happened. The bulb must've burned out. I should take care of that in the . . .

I let out a scream. Ramsey, the cat, sat in the same spot I'd found him this morning, that same supercilious look on his face. It took me a full minute to recover. A full minute during which he remained motionless.

"What is it, Rams?" I asked him.

He meowed. Turned and walked away from me a few steps.

I stepped closer. "What, Rams? You got something you want to show me?"

He meowed again. Took a few more steps down the hall. Now I realized he was sitting right in front of the spare room. George Davenport's room.

He turned and pushing the door open, disappeared into the room. I hesitated at the door that was barely cracked open.

We shall linger to caress him,
while we breathe our evening prayer . . .

I shook my head as if I could stop the words of the song. "I'm coming in, Catawampus," I warned him. And then I walked into the room.

Chapter 20

There were no curtains on the windows, but the room was still doused in inky blackness. The moon must be obscured by clouds. I peered into the darkness, trying to manifest the runaway cat.

"Ramsey, get your butt out here." I was trying to sound strong, but even the cat could probably tell I was freaked out. "What have you hidden in here? A mouse? A mole? Mayor Dixie Minette?"

I pushed the door open and stepped into the room. The dark surrounded me, thick and suffocating. I stopped, inhaling deeply, orienting myself. There were no lamps in this room and no overhead light. I should bring a lamp in here tomorrow.

Yeowww . . .

The sound was soft but unmistakable, and I spun to the corner, between the bed and the window.

"Where are you, Rams?" I called out.

I closed my eyes and felt myself sway. The room seemed to expand, to grow beyond its walls, allowing the stars from the sky to flow in through the window. And now I felt I was standing, suspended in a vast expanse of space. A universal amphitheater that was about to put on some show. A great show. The show of my life, starring a bloodthirsty cat and a group of ghostly children singing a ghostly song. Or maybe I was just drunk.

I should've brought some chicken or tuna, I thought. Something to lure him. I moved deeper into the room. I couldn't see a damn thing, but I could hear a light scratching around the cast iron grate in the small fireplace. I heard another yowl and the sound of tiny paws scrabbling for purchase. He was on the mantel.

I headed toward the fireplace, arms sweeping, hands outstretched. I heard a growl. I was getting closer. "What is it, Rams?" I said sweetly. "What've you got back here?"

Suddenly my hands felt fur, bristling fur, and then a hail of sharp claws. I yelped and tried to hang on as he struggled in my arms, yowling and slashing at me. He took one particularly vicious swipe at my face, and I flinched, stumbling back. It was just the opportunity he needed, and he jumped out of my arms, clawed up the bricks onto the mantel, and then, in a flying leap, jumped onto the rolltop desk.

Something fell off the wall, hitting my knee and landing on my toe. "Ow!" I yelled, grabbing my foot and hopping in a circle. "You absolute dick." Ramsay leaped down and streaked out of the room. The pain was subsiding now, and either the moon had come out or my eyes had adjusted to the dark, because I could see the fireplace now. The three bricks had fallen out of place as a result of Ramsey's berserk mountain climbing adventure.

The hole they'd left was small, about as big as a tennis ball. I moved closer, close enough to put my hand inside until my fingers touched something. Some sort of fabric. Velvet. I grasped it and pulled, drawing out a small, purple drawstring pouch. A Crown Royal bag. Maybe hidden by George Davenport? I opened the bag and shook out the contents into my hand. Rocks. I hurried out of the room and back to Peter's office. I dumped them onto the desk and peered closer, sifting through them with a finger. They glinted in the light, giving off a soft sheen, like the rock Mere had found. It looked suspiciously like . . .

Gold.

I straightened. With everything going on, I hadn't had a chance to follow up with Lilah about that rock—if it was pyrite or not—but honestly it hadn't seemed that\ important. If George Davenport had found actual gold on his property, there's no way he wouldn't have told someone or pursued setting up his own mine. He wouldn't have squirreled away the evidence in a Crown Royal bag behind a couple of loose bricks in his house.

Unless he was afraid of the truth getting out.

My phone buzzed, and I jumped. Mom, FaceTiming me. I hit the screen. "Mom? Is everything okay?"

The screen was dark, the fuzzy shadow of her right cheek pressed close. "I got somebody here who can help you," she said in an urgent whisper.

My mind was blank. "Help me? With what?"

"With the cloud thing. You know, on Peter's computer."

"iPad. He took his computer with him."

"Whatever." There was a rustling, and another wedge of a face came into view. "This is Edge."

"Like from U2?" I asked.

"I don't know what you're talking about," Mom said. "He works with me in the vegetable patch and sometimes in the laundry, but he used to work IT for Amazon."

"Oh, okay, cool. Hi, Edge. I guess we're cousins."

Edge tilted his head, and I could make out a beard and a pair of wire-framed glasses accented by long frizzy hair. "What's up?"

I smiled nervously. "Oh, just trying to hack into my husband's iPad."

"He's cheating on her," Mom said helpfully.

"Possibly," I interjected.

"What happened to your face?" Mom asked. "Did he hit you, Billie?"

I touched the oozing scratch. "No, Mom. It was me. I was chasing the cat . . ."

Because he wanted to show me a hidden stash of gold nuggets . . .

". . . because he killed a mole."

"Ramsey did not kill a mole. That cat is one hundred percent chickenshit."

"Yeah, well, not anymore." *He's a goddamn Catawampus.*

"We better get this show on the road, ladies," Edge said. "It's almost vespers."

"I'm ready," I said.

Edge held the phone close to his bearded face. "Can you hear me?"

"Loud and clear."

"Okay, here's what you're gonna do. . . ."

An obnoxious beam of sunlight, lasering in through the window and directly through my left eyelid, roused me. I was facedown, drooling, on the lumpy silk Duncan Fyfe sofa in the yellow parlor. The girl's parlor.

I eased myself up and did a quick inventory. My mouth tasted like cat litter, my head throbbed, and my neck felt stiff. The topknot wobbled on my head and there was a mysterious stain on my pink tank top. On the cocktail table, Peter's iPad was propped open in its case, but the screen was dark. I groaned and lay back down, this time on my back.

Water. I needed water.

I felt around for my phone, finding it in the crack between the sofa cushions where it had apparently slipped before I'd passed out. Six-forty-one A.M. Of course, no matter that I'd polished off almost half a flask of moonshine as well as a bottle of wine last night. I still couldn't sleep past the crack of dawn. If all seven circles of hell were a person, it would be me.

Had I even cracked the code on Peter's files? I searched my

memory, dredging up the image, sharper than it should be, of my mother's face. I should've regretted drunk-dialing her, but I didn't. It had been so nice to hear her voice. So nice telling her everything I'd done.

And that guy with her. Her friend. Now I remembered him, too, fuzzily. A bearded, bespectacled man, patient, if a tad bit condescending, walking me through the steps to sync it with the house cloud account. I reached over and touched the screen of the iPad, and it glowed to life.

Or, I should say, Alice Tilton glowed to life.

Apparently, I had accessed the files, but only had gotten as far as the first one, where after opening it, and widening it to full screen, I had hit pause. Alice smiled shyly out at me—or rather, at Peter—from the iPad. She was dressed in a white, silky button-down shirt, and her hair was down, long and pushed back over her shoulders. Her face was free of makeup, her skin lumines-cent, and the nose ring glinted adorably. I'd always thought when I saw her at the restaurant with Jamie that she was pretty, but now I realized with a terrible sinking feeling down low, in the deepest recesses of my gut, that she was, in fact, beautiful.

My husband had surely noticed it, too. There he was, in a lit-tle box in the lower right corner of the screen. He was dressed in a crisp blue shirt, but there were dark circles under his eyes and his mouth was set in a grim line. Of course he'd seen how beautiful Alice was, and I'm sure she'd discovered how kind and gentle and giving he was.

Clearly, last night when I'd pulled up the file, when I'd real-ized I was about to violate the privacy of one of my husband's patients and risk more of his fury, I'd lost my nerve and hadn't pushed play on the video. Instead, I suddenly remembered I'd tried once again to get Peter to answer my texts. Dreading what surprise awaited me, I clicked on my messages and scanned the one-way conversation.

Peter, please. I love you. Can't we talk?

The silent treatment, really?

We've been through so much together. Please don't let it end this way.

Peter, I'm begging you.

Where is your heart, Peter? Nobody deserves this, no matter what they might have done.

Might have done.

Even when I was drunk-texting, I was still spinning things my way. I had done something, all right. I'd made out with Jamie Cleburne. There was no getting around it. Whatever Peter felt like he had to do to deal with his feelings, it was his choice. Not mine. My job was to wait until he was ready to talk. Until he had made up his mind about what he wanted to do. And last night, what he wanted to do was not speak to me.

I glanced at the iPad once more. I still wasn't ready to watch their sessions. Instead, I dialed Lilah, and when she picked up, asked if she'd be willing to keep Mere for a few more hours. She said it was fine, that the girls were happy, but she was obviously curious about my plans. I didn't expound; just thanked her and hung up.

Exhausted by that short interaction, I lay back, staring at the ceiling, letting the phone slip out of my hand. I began to cry, sobbing until, finally spent, I fell asleep again. I woke hours later to the sound of someone pounding at my front door. I started, then bolted upright, wildly looking around.

More pounding and a voice, muffled, calling my name. I held my throbbing head in my hands. "Hold on, I'm coming." I hauled myself off the sofa, checked myself in the mirror, as I hurried through the front hall. I opened the door to find Jamie Cleburne standing on my front porch. He held Ramsey, who'd somehow gotten out. The cat was purring docilely and looked like a limp noodle in Jamie's arms.

I stared in wonder. "You found my cat?"

Jamie set him down and Ramsey stalked past me into the

house. "He was on the porch. I came up the steps and he just sort of jumped right into my arms."

"What are you—"

"I heard Peter left," Jamie said unceremoniously. "I'm sorry."

I blinked, then nodded. Might as well let it all out. I would have to eventually.

"How—"

"People are talking."

I rolled my eyes, but even that was excruciating. "You're kidding me. This town . . ."

"I know. People pay attention."

"Too much attention. Are they saying why?" I gave him a meaningful look.

"Well, Tilda Brennan, who I saw at their bakery, seemed to think he couldn't"—he rubbed at his jaw—"deal with small-town life. That he was too New York."

"Tilda Brennan." I rolled my eyes. "She's still mad about me getting this house."

He was giving me a thorough once-over. I was suddenly acutely aware of my state: crazy hair, raccoon eyes, no bra. He glanced past me farther into the hall, to the lamp on the floor, a dirty glass, plate, and some random wadded-up paper towels. "You have a party last night?"

"I wish. Then feeling this way might actually be worth it."

He dropped his hands into his pockets. "I have the cure, if you're interested." He raised his hands. "Just as friends, I promise. I even brought a chaperone this time." I glanced past him, at the truck. Ever, the chocolate Lab, watched me from the open passenger window.

I nodded. "Okay." At this point, I could use a friend. "Let me get the cat carrier. I want to drop Ramsey at the vet on the way."

Chapter 21

I showered, dressed, and brushed away every trace of alcohol from my teeth, then found the cat carrier in the basement, which Ramsey trotted right into with an agreeable little meow. Jamie drove us to the new animal clinic, located across the river just past the mill, that Dr. Undergrove had opened. As we crossed the bridge and the old stone building with its huge water wheel, I remembered what Inman had told me.

The human remains he'd found.

And Sheriff Childers had taken the case from him.

I wondered if the remains were Wren Street's. If one of her friends, one of the people living in our house, had killed her and she wasn't really living on some weed farm in California. And then I put the thought out of my mind. I was going to a dark place. Torturing myself, imagining horror-movie scenarios in my head because I was sad about Peter. But I couldn't allow that. I needed to stay positive. Keep it together for Mere.

Dr. Undergrove—Michael, as he told me to call him—was a cheerful, balding man in his early thirties. He and his wife Becca had moved to Juliana for the Initiative right after Peter and I had. They were from San Diego and loved their new life in Georgia.

Michael ruffled the fur under Ramsey's chin, listened to my recounting of his strange behavior. "You know cats are closer to their wild predecessors than we like to think," he said when I concluded. "Maybe he's decided to be an outdoor cat."

"Just run the tests," I said. "I'll pay for whatever you think is necessary."

Outside the clinic, I climbed back in Jamie's truck.

"Okay," he said, throwing it in reverse. "Jamie's Juliana, Georgia's platinum hangover treatment, coming right up."

We drove away from town, past a Dollar General, a bait shop, and something called a Sparkle Mart, out into the countryside. There was the occasional house or trailer, with above-ground pools in the front yard or firepits encircled by mismatched lawn chairs, some with metal sheds covering trucks or four-wheelers, but mostly it was mile after mile of rolling fields dotted with trees and cows. Jamie had some sports talk radio station on—two guys and a woman talking about the Braves—and I lay my head back on the seat and slept.

I woke up to the dinging of Jamie's door. He shut it and leaned in through the open window. "Rise and shine," he said. "Course number one awaits."

We were parked on the side of the road next to a produce stand, a shed made of plywood with a corrugated green plastic roof with two folding tables set up under it. The tables were filled with wooden crates of fat red tomatoes, yellow squash and zucchini, cucumbers and melons. Mounds of green beans and some sort of purplish beans overflowed others. The sign said LINDA LOU'S FARM FRESH, but it was a man with a potbelly stretching out a pair of worn overalls and a grimy John Deere cap who handed Jamie a wet, mysteriously bulging paper bag and a glass bottle of Coke.

Jamie handed them to me, and we returned to the truck.

"Just tear open the bag." I did as he instructed, revealing a pile of wet peanuts still in their shells. "Boiled peanuts. Have at it. And the Coke, too. You'll feel better in a sec."

The peanuts were mushy and warm and tasted like earthy beans. I demolished them, as well as the frosty Coke, in a few minutes. By the time we had turned off the main road, we were at our second destination, which was apparently a tiny, concrete block structure, painted a mint green, sitting in the middle of a small gravel lot. The vintage sign out front simply read EATS, but there were no other cars around and the small building looked deserted. We didn't get out of the car.

"What are we waiting for?" I asked.

"To see if it's open." He sent me a bemused look. "The owner, Garnet, is a hay farmer. Has a big place a couple of miles south of here. This is just his side hustle so there are no regular hours. But the man can cook, so the deal is, if you're hungry, you just show up and hope for the best."

"Ah." I sat back, trying not to fidget. Trying not to think about the last time I'd ridden in this truck. The night Jamie had picked me up on the mill road. Ever pressed against me, sniffing for any stray peanuts that I may have dropped. I stroked her silky neck. The silence between us weighed on me. I thought of Jamie's lips on mine, the pressure of his body in the back of his shop.

Talk, Billie. Talk about anything other than that night.

"You know, when we were in your shop that night"—I smiled nervously and he did, too—"I saw a stack of old photos of the Dalzell-Davenport house. And I've been thinking about them."

If he was surprised or even perturbed that I'd looked at the pictures, he didn't show it. "What about?"

I shrugged. "I was just wondering why you had them, I guess. What they were doing back there in that dusty box. I would've thought George Davenport's family would've taken them."

He sat back and draped his hands over the steering wheel. "Yeah, it was weird how that happened. When George's family decided to move him down to Florida, they got in contact with me and asked me to collect some of his personal belongings. There was some business stuff, bank statements, tax information, stuff like that, too, as well as the photos. I was going to mail them to his new address, but his great-grandkids never got back to me."

"You would think they would've wanted his financial information after he died."

"Oh, they were just odds and ends. I'm sure they had what they needed when it came to the estate. Old George was a pretty wily character."

I nodded, thinking about what Lilah had told me about George's last days in Juliana—ranting in front of the statue of the little Minette girl, throwing paint on it. And the Crown Royal bag I'd found last night, full of what looked like gold nuggets. If George Davenport had struck gold on his property, I couldn't understand why he hadn't told anyone. Maybe it was something connected to that list in the ledger and the explosives. Or the page that had been torn out. Or maybe he was just what he sounded like—a quirky old man with a handful of odd obsessions and a case of dementia.

"Pretty cool that he had a picture of the Confederate soldiers," I said.

He nodded vigorously. "That one's really cool, right? My best guess is that it's the soldiers from Juliana's regiment. Quite a few men in town signed up to fight. Most of them were lost."

"How sad."

"Well, to be fair, they were fighting on the wrong side."

"It's just . . ." My mind started to connect a few dots. "Those guys in the picture I saw wouldn't be Confederate soldiers because there was an American flag behind them. Wouldn't they have the other flag, the Confederate flag?"

Jamie shook his head. "Well, the original Confederate flag looked almost identical to the Union flag, so that's probably what you saw. They changed it later. You know, if you're interested, there's a plaque with the names of the men who died in the war over at the courthouse. It's in some glass case, in the courthouse, part of the history tour."

"Ah." I looked out the window. I'd heard Alice Tilton led the history tours, on the weekends and summers when she wasn't teaching.

"We're not dating anymore," he said, reading my mind. "Alice and me. In case you were wondering."

"I wasn't."

He looked out the window, hiding a grin. "Okay."

"Actually, I've been wondering if she was seeing my husband."

His head swiveled back toward me. "For therapy?"

"And possibly other things."

He looked doubtful. "You think they're having an affair?"

I shook my head. "I don't know. I found files on his computer. Not his regular documents he keeps for patients, but video files from each session."

I could tell my words had stunned him. That he was turning them over in his mind, weighing the possibility. "I don't know about that, but I do know that she was struggling with some things when we were seeing each other."

"What kind of things?"

He hesitated.

"This is my marriage, Jamie. You said you were my friend. One of my friends, my *true* friends, would absolutely, one hundred percent tell me what they knew."

"Oh man. Throwing down the friendship gauntlet." He laughed, turning away from me and shaking his head.

"Just tell me," I said. "Please."

"She was upset about us," he admitted. "She took our break-up hard."

"And Peter was right there."

He inhaled deeply. "It's possible."

"He's never videotaped a patient before. Why would he do that unless he"—I huffed out air—"wanted to look at it later."

"Don't watch them," Jamie said. "Don't watch the tapes."

I blinked at him, confused. "Why?"

"When Peter calls you, which he will, see what he says. Give him room to admit a relationship with Alice, if that's what's going on. Or let him hang himself with his own rope."

"Wow. That's some high-level relationship chess right there."

"Well, this ain't my first rodeo." He sighed. I did, too, and then we went quiet, staring at the mint-green building. Suddenly a light flicked on, and Jamie straightened. He clapped his hands and rubbed them together. "We're on! Let's go!"

We were indeed on, to the tune of fried catfish sandwiches, fried okra, tomato pie, and a peach cobbler that I swore I was too full to eat but went down like it was borne on gossamer angel wings. Everything was chased with sweet tea with mint and lemon in it. Ever, who we'd left out on the front stoop with a bowl of water and a pork chop bone, wandered in sometime during the conversation, but no one seemed to notice or care. By the end of the meal, as Jamie and Garnet and one other guy discussed the merits of the many catfish holes along the river, my hangover truly had vanished.

When the conversation turned to college football, I excused myself to find the bathroom. On my way, I caught glimpse of the kitchen, a hodgepodge of ancient-looking commercial appliances and shelves crammed with boxes of food, Styrofoam cups, and God knows what else. A young woman, mid-twenties, stood at the sink, her back to me. She was dressed in a short batik-printed skirt and gray T-shirt, a muslin apron tied behind her back. Her blond hair was long and in dreadlocks that were held back by a scrunchie. She was scrubbing dishes and swaying to reggae music coming from a speaker on the shelf above her.

I stopped, remembering what Deputy Inman had called Wren Street's friends who squatted in my house. Trustafarians. Rich kids who adopted the trappings and style of the Rastafarian religion and social movement. Was this girl one of them?

The girl must've sensed my eyes on her because she twisted around. "Can I help you?" She was pretty, with a peachy complexion, freckles, and a toothy smile.

"Just looking for the bathroom."

"You're headed in the right direction. Just to your left."

"Thanks." I hesitated, thinking fast. "I'm Billie Hope, one of the new residents of Juliana. We moved down from New York in April, my husband and I."

She seemed slightly taken aback that I was talking to her. "Oh, okay. Right on."

"I opened a breakfast and brunch place on the square, next door to Cleburne's Antiques."

"Yeah, I've seen it."

I smiled. "You should come by. I'll comp you a mimosa."

"Oh, I don't drink. I just . . ." She pinched thumb and forefinger together and touched her lips.

"Anyway. Come by. Anytime."

"Sure thing. Thanks."

I tilted my head. "What was your name?"

"Oh. Emmaline. Emmaline Dalzell."

ED. The initials along with Wren Street's that I found carved into the baseboard in the guest room. Emmaline was one of the squatters.

"Great," I said. "Fantastic. Nice to meet you, Emmaline. The catfish was fabulous. The cobbler, no words."

"I'll let Garnet know. I actually just wash the dishes."

"The most important job." I was dying to ask her about

Wren, about the carvings in George Davenport's room, but I really didn't want to freak her out, so I continued on to the bathroom. Maybe she would show up at Billie's, and I could get more out of her. Like what exactly they'd been doing in my house. Like if they were aware of any gold on the property. Or any legends about children. And if Wren really had gone to California . . . or had somehow wound up dead and buried by the river at the mill.

On the way back to my house, Jamie and I were both quiet. I was grateful that he'd come to check on me and load me full of greasy carbs. And in spite of the distraction of possible gold strikes, murder, and all manner of creepy small-town secrets, I knew it probably amounted to a bunch of nothing. A bunch of nothing that I was trying to make into something so I wouldn't have to deal with Peter. I checked my phone one last time. Two of my New York friends, Jane and Annika, had finally texted me back. Jane, as usual, was fiercely loyal.

What the fuck? Peter walked OUT on you? Has he lost his mind? Would you like me to do murder on your behalf? I'm prepared, willing, and able, as soon as I get these kids in bed. XX

I smiled. Annika was a little more to the point.

I know the best divorce lawyer in Manhattan who will know someone in Atlanta. Call me.

Peter had texted me back, too, but I didn't want to open it. I didn't think I could bear any bad news. Not right now. Not while I was full of fried catfish and sweet tea and the sun was shining on my face. Not while I was in Jamie Cleburne's truck. I turned the phone facedown.

"What is it?" Jamie said. Ever was sprawled out between us, her head in Jamie's lap. He was absently scratching behind one ear.

"Nothing," I said. "Just a couple of old friends looking out for me. Vowing to do murder on my behalf." I gave him a rueful grin.

He lifted his eyebrows. "Good. I'm glad. You deserve it."

"I really appreciate all this. What you did today." I looked out the window, watching the green fields, but my fingers were scrolling to Peter's text. I couldn't avoid it forever. And maybe it was better to read it here, in Jamie's truck.

I opened my phone, clicked on my messages, and read what my husband had written.

I can't talk to you. Not yet. Tell Mere I'm traveling for work, and please don't contact me again. I want a divorce.

Chapter 22

I invited Jamie in, and he excused himself to go the bathroom. I dropped my purse on the console and tried to gather my thoughts.

I still didn't know what I was going to tell Mere about Peter's absence. Fighting an onslaught of guilt, I slipped into the blue parlor and called Lilah to see if she could sleep over one more night. Evidently, Lilah had heard the same rumor Jamie had, because she asked no questions and refused my offer of free meals in perpetuity. She put Mere on the line, who assured me she was having fun and she'd see me tomorrow. I asked, as casually as I could manage, if Peter had called her. He hadn't. I told her I loved her, but it felt like it was someone else saying the words.

Another woman in another life.

Ever padded down the hallway toward the kitchen. She probably smelled the pizza I'd left out last night. I turned in a circle, sensing something in the house was off. Not bad; *off*. The house felt different. Doused in the painterly late-afternoon light and eerily still, I watched the motes of white dust swirl through the air. In the hours I'd been gone, I realized the house had lost our smell: my CVS detergent, Peter's ground coffee beans from South Carolina, the bubble bath I used in Mere's nightly bath.

The house smelled of George Davenport again, the way it had that first day. Old man, uncleared AC flues, stacks of old newspapers. And, as always, the faint whiff of something chemical. Uncanny, how that underlying smell never seemed to go away no matter how much I cleaned. Even after months of us living here. It was as if the house was sending me a message: *I am not yours. I will never be yours.*

I still had the headache, which wasn't much of a surprise, after what I'd done to myself last night, but this was something different. This was a full-body, all-encompassing ache. Like I was standing here in this house, feet on the worn wood boards of the floor, but also floating outside of myself through all the rooms of the house.

I was numb. Dead inside.

My life was over.

Peter was leaving me.

And then, I had the oddest sensation. Intense pain, mine and . . . others—the pain of all the souls who'd lived in this house. Silas Dalzell and his family. And not just their pain but their emotions, too. I was feeling the generations of laughter, their tears. Their peace as they slept and dreamed, their fear when they had a nightmare. I felt the joy of them going picnicking, tromping off to fish in the rust-red creek. I was living inside the memory of this house, and it was a *present* thing. A living breathing, ongoing *now*.

Wren and her band of merry, dreadlocked, homeless friends, they were playing house here now, at this very moment, taking their hallucinogens and doing whatever it was they did here. I'd never experimented, but I could imagine how it felt. I was feeling that way now—the way your whole perception expanded.

The way you seemed to separate, mind flying from body, the two experiencing different realities at the exact same time.

I felt the spirit world, the world beyond the veil, but I also felt this world in a magnified way. The humming of the window unit I'd forgotten to turn off in my bathroom. I heard the *plop-plop-plop* of the leaky faucet in Mere's bathroom. The *tick-tick-tick* of the ancient refrigerator. The *buzzzz* of a fly trapped somewhere inside the house. He was banging against a window, flinging himself against the glass, desperate to escape.

Let me out of here, he buzzed. *Let me out of here.*

I closed my eyes. Visions assaulted me—tunnels that twisted through a jungle, telescoping in and out through the ropy vines. Grids of wallpaper patterns that fractured and re-formed around me. Colors infusing me through my pores, sluicing through my veins, lighting up my cells and organs. I turned in slow motion, sensing Jamie standing near me.

"Did Garnet put mushrooms in that tomato pie?" I asked him, the words feeling strange in my mouth.

"I don't think so," Jamie said. "Are you okay?"

I touched my face gingerly. "I feel a little . . . I don't know. Weird. You didn't drug me, did you?"

Jamie looked shocked. "Billie, no. God, no, I wouldn't do that. Are you sick? Do you want me to take you to Doc Belmont's office?"

I shook my head. "Peter wants a divorce," I said. My voice sounded like someone else's.

I could see there were a million questions he wanted to ask but wouldn't. Then his eyes took on a tender light. "Oh, Billie. I'm so sorry."

I shook my head. There was nothing to say.

"You know, I was jealous of him," Jamie said. "Of what y'all had. That night at Mayor Dixie's, by the fire, I remember watching y'all. The way he pulled you to him to dance, the way you responded, the way you moved together so perfectly. It was so easy. So familiar. Like you two had danced a million dances together. Like you had your own private choreography. I could feel it, here." His fist touched his chest. "Your connection. And my lack of one with anyone. I've been alone for a long time. Too long. But there's nothing to do about it. I'm not going to be with somebody I don't truly want."

"Well, it didn't mean anything in the end, did it? Peter doesn't want to talk to me. He wants to end our marriage."

He moved to me, so close I could smell him. "He's a fool. To leave you and Mere. Not to mention free lemon ricotta hotcakes whenever he wants."

I smiled wryly. "I never cook those at home."

"You would for me." His face lowered, angling toward mine. "Wouldn't you?"

I caught my breath and looked into Jamie's eyes. They were not just greenish-blue now, they were iridescent. He moved closer, laid his hand, gently, lightly, on my hip. He moved his hand up, over the curve of my hip, my waist, up my ribs. I lifted my arm, both arms, letting them cross lazily over my head, loving the feel of it. He used both hands now, following the curve of my arms, up, up, until he could grip my wrists.

How did I get here—in this life? How had everything gone to hell so quickly?

But God, it felt so good. He was touching me, but also someone who wasn't me. It was that other woman who had fucked up her life in such a few easy steps. He pivoted me against the wall, arms over my head. He held me with one hand now, the other moving back down, exploring the curve of my breast, my stomach, then between my legs.

I looked at him. Those iridescent eyes burned. I wondered what secrets they held.

"Can you consent?" he asked.

"Yes," said the other woman, the woman who was living another life. The woman who wasn't me.

"Let me make you feel better, Billie. Please. Just for a minute, let me make you feel the way you should."

I sighed, my eyes closed, some small part of me knowing it was a bad choice, the other part not caring. But I said yes anyway.

I woke at dawn in Peter's and my bed. The window was open, and a light breeze blew through the room. Jamie still slept beside me. God, we must've slept at least twelve hours, maybe more. Once we'd come back to the house, it seemed time had ceased to exist.

I pinched the bridge of my nose and squeezed my eyes shut, searching my memory for an anchor, something to center me. No weird, shape-shifting tunnels or garishly colored geometric shapes appeared. No colors and smells passing through my body like a screen door. Whatever weird high I'd had the previous evening had vanished.

Other things flashed in my brain. Jamie and I spending a good deal of time on the stairs, then moving the show to the bed. Everything that transpired there. As the night slowly replayed in my head, I was feeling the whiplash of regret.

I got up, pulled on the silk robe lying over the back of a chair, and went to the bathroom to pee and wash my hands. In the sink, the water spurted out an orange-red color. "Shit!" Startled, I jerked my hands back and watched as the water gradually went clear. Jesus. When I first saw the water, it looked like blood.

"Billie?"

I shut off the faucet and walked back into the room. Jamie was propped up on his elbow, smiling at me. The secret smile of a lover.

"Do you still feel it?" he asked.

"It's gone."

He shook his head slowly, deliberately. "I think it's this house. I think it might be mold."

I felt a stab of fear. "Mold?"

"You said Peter was sleeping all the time, right? And your cat was acting strange. Maybe it's something in the house. Some kind of contamination that's fucking up your brains or your nervous systems or something." He hesitated, like there was something else he was about to say.

"What?" I prodded.

He locked his gaze on me. "Move in with me. You and Mere."

I laughed in disbelief and sat on the edge of the bed. "You're kidding me."

He sat up. "I'm serious, Billie. Even if it's just until you can get it checked out and fixed. My cabin isn't anywhere as nice as this place, but it's big enough for the three of us. It's comfortable. You can stay as long as it takes to fix whatever's going on here. Or maybe by then, you'll decide you like it there."

I stared at him. Everything was happening so fast, I couldn't wrap my head around it. Peter walking out and Jamie walking in. I didn't know what to do. I was numb before. Now I was paralyzed as well.

"Hey," he whispered. "Come here."

I scooted closer to him, and he pushed my hair back. "I know you were not quite yourself last night." He eased over me, balancing on his forearms, and dropped a soft kiss on my lips. "I want us to be together because you choose it. Because it's what you want."

What I wanted was my husband. My husband who had left me. Who had left his daughter. Who wanted a divorce.

"Come here . . ."

I wrapped one leg around him, and he pressed into me. I let him in. I shut down the rational, reasonable part of my brain and looked into his eyes. I'd deal with the guilt later. Peter had done this. Peter had left me for no reason other than that he couldn't adjust to our new life. He'd left me alone, with our daughter, to explain to her. To lie to her. He'd betrayed everything we'd been working for. He'd broken all his promises. He'd broken my heart.

We shall meet but we shall miss him,
There will be one vacant chair . . .

I tried to shut out the song. To focus on the feel of Jamie's body—his broad smooth chest under my fingertips, the silky hair, his hard thighs. His lips. His hands. On this singular goal we were working toward together. The only goal worth reaching in this moment.

"Oh," I caught my breath, feeling the mounting pressure, the promise of pleasure to come. Oh God, it felt so good. And I needed to feel good.

Jamie shifted himself over me, his elbows on either side of my head. "I know it's too soon, Billie, but I want you to—" he started to say.

Stop talking. Please.

Just then, a snarling sound echoed through the house, followed by a high-pitched bark—an animal scream that sounded so primal that it made the hair on my arms stand straight up.

We flew apart. "What was that?" I whispered.

Jamie lifted his chin, straining to listen. "It sounded like—"

We heard it again, a high keening, that snarl, then a yelp of pain. I bolted up and away from Jamie, wrapping the robe around me again. He followed, hot on my heels. Half-dressed, we skidded out into the upstairs hallway. We heard thumps, bumps, more yelps and growls and followed them all the way downstairs.

It wasn't hard to locate the source—Ramsey and Ever in the conservatory, circling each other, fur bristled, lips curled, and fangs bared. Locked in mortal combat.

"Ramsey?" I shouted. "What are you doing here?" I looked over at Jamie. "He must've run away from the vet. Shit!"

The room was in shambles. Pots were overturned, potting

soil spilled across the tile floor, and all the plants Mere and I had bought uprooted. Ramsey lunged, Ever dodged, and a race ensued around the small fountain in the center of the room. After a couple of circuits, they returned to their corners, and the roles reversed, Ever attacking Ramsey now. A vicious choreography of thrusts and parries followed, one which threatened to develop into a full-blown fight to the death at any moment.

I shrieked. "Stop it, Ramsey! Get away from him!"

"Stay back," Jamie said, looking only slightly ridiculous shirtless and in his boxer briefs, waving his shirt over his head like a referee's flag.

Ever growled and inched toward Ramsey. He hissed back, the fur on his back making him look like some kind of feline stegosaurus. Ramsey leaped at Ever, hooking his claws into the dog's ruff, and she began to shake her head to get him off. I lunged at them, screaming, "Stop, Ramsey! Stop!" But there was no way I was going to be able to physically separate them. Ever was whimpering in pain and Ramsey continued to hiss like a demon.

Jamie appeared in the hallway, holding the garden hose in one hand, the other, keeping the length of it kinked to stop the flow of water. I watched in disbelief as he let go of the hose, releasing the full stream of water at the animals. "Cut it out, you motherfuckers!" he bellowed, aiming the spray directly at them.

Ramsey double-flipped off Ever, a perfect-10 Olympic gymnast move, and streaked out into the hallway, Jamie following and hose-herding him out the front door.

"Oh my God." I collapsed in relief then looked back at Ever, who had plunked her butt down on the wet carpet and was glaring at me, indignant, hurt, an expression of betrayal in her soft brown eyes. "Sorry, girl."

Jamie reappeared, soaked and breathless. "Your cat is a fucking monster."

"I know, I know." I started to pick up the overturned pots

and planters. Jamie brought back a broom from the kitchen and swept up the dirt and broken glass.

"How did he get back here? I mean, all the way from Dr. Undergrove's?" he asked.

"Maybe he ran away? But why didn't someone in the office call to let me know? It's past nine o'clock in the morning. Surely there can't be that many animals there that they haven't noticed. It's almost like—" I stopped.

Jamie stopped sweeping. "What?"

"I don't know." I threw up my hands. "Peter went to the doctor, weeks ago, but we still haven't heard back on the test results. And now my cat just mysteriously escapes from the vet? It's like no one wants us to find out what's going on in this house."

"To be fair, Peter was up to a lot behind your back. He might've heard from the doctor and just not told you."

"Yeah." I chewed at my thumbnail. "But now this Ramsey thing . . ."

"You really think Dr. Undergrove turned him out of the clinic on purpose?"

"Okay, just bear with me here. There's more that doesn't add up. When I asked to see the plat, to find out about the uncapped well that supposedly is on the property, it was missing. And then Mayor Dixie offered me another house."

"She did?"

"I think she knows this place is contaminated, and she doesn't want us suing her. I bet you anything she told Doc Belmont to hold off telling Peter that he had some kind of exposure to contamination. She may have even told Dr. Undergrove to get rid of Ramsey, too." I felt overwhelmingly weary all of a sudden.

Jamie looked serious. "I just think you should be careful who you talk to going forward. There's something going on, and I don't know who you can trust."

He had a point, but I didn't know how worried I was about

it at the moment. Something about the fight between Ever and Ramsey had jolted me awake. I couldn't focus on any environmental issue with the house or property—or Mayor Dixie's bizarre attempt at a cover-up—until I answered the questions burning away everything else out of my brain. Was this really the end of my marriage? Was I ready to accept Peter's request for a divorce?

I couldn't answer that, not unless I knew for sure what Peter and Alice had discussed on those tapes. In spite of what Jamie said, I was watching those videos. I had to.

Chapter 23

Jamie offered to stay, but I told him I needed some time to get my head together. He made me promise I'd check in with him later, and when his truck was at the end of our drive, I set the iPad up on the dining room table. If evidence of the reason Peter had left me was on this device, I had to face it on my own.

I watched every recorded video session Peter had made with Alice, and the evidence couldn't have been clearer. The woman was not having an affair with my husband. She was obsessed with one thing and one thing only, the subject of her every session with Peter: Wren Street.

Alice and Wren had been childhood friends, born and raised in Juliana just down the street from each other, and inseparable, at least until college. Alice had gone to the University of Georgia to study early childhood education, but Wren—a poet and artist—had gotten a painting scholarship to Pratt, the prestigious art school in Brooklyn.

At Pratt, Wren had fallen in with a group of wealthy kids from several prominent families. Unlike Wren, these new friends all had trust funds to bankroll their futures as artists, and after graduation planned to pursue a nomadic lifestyle with nothing to tie them down other than a bank account to deposit their monthly checks and a vague allegiance to a privileged, whitewashed version of Rastafarianism. They included Wren in their plans.

Unfortunately, in her junior year, Wren had gotten pregnant by a man she refused to name and had returned home to Juliana to have the baby. By then, she was heavily into drugs. Cocaine, pills, and weed, mostly. Lilah sent her to a variety of rehabs in Atlanta, but eventually the money ran out, and Wren still didn't have a foothold. Lilah threw her out of the house, keeping the baby. Wren's art school friends swooped in, ready to circle the wagon around their wayward cohort. *And to give her cash,* I thought. They all hunkered down together in the abandoned Dalzell-Davenport house.

It was the last file I opened that revealed what I was looking for. Alice was sitting in her sunny kitchen, wearing a Georgia Bulldogs T-shirt. Her hair was back in a ponytail. Dark circles shadowed her eyes. She and Peter exchanged pleasantries.

"So why do you think Wren didn't just leave Juliana?" Peter asked. "How do you think she talked all those rich kids from New York to come down here and join her? And why did they do it?"

"I assume she wanted to be near Temperance, even though Lilah wouldn't let her see her. But I think it was more than that. I ran into her once, at the Food Lion. I couldn't believe I was seeing her, but she wasn't the same. She was . . . different."

"Different, how?"

"Wren always loved Juliana. I mean, we all do. But when we talked, she seemed obsessed with it. She said she wanted to *redeem* the town." Alice made air quotes around the word. "She said that's why her friends had come down. To help her redeem Juliana."

"Did she explain what that meant to her?" Peter asked.

Alice nodded. "During the Civil War, General Sherman marched through Georgia. Juliana was just one of his many stopovers on his way to Atlanta. In every town he passed through, he burned any kind of industry he came upon that could be of any help to the southern army. He destroyed mills and railroads and coal mines."

This information jolted me. Of course! The picture I'd seen in George Davenport's box at Jamie's store—those soldiers *had* been sitting beneath an American flag. Jamie had it wrong. They were Union soldiers, not Confederates. Union soldiers who stopped in Juliana.

"So Sherman burned Juliana's mill?" Peter asked. I leaned forward.

She shook her head. "No. That's the thing. None of the three mills were burned. In fact, Wren said she'd discovered the mills weren't built back in 1832 like the people around here say. She said she found old books—history books—that proved they were built after the war."

George Davenport's history books, I thought.

"So then, Sherman just passed through town?" Peter asked.

"Not according to Wren. She was convinced that Sherman came here and killed people. The wives and children of the town's men who'd left to fight in the Confederate Army. Like a revenge thing. A war crime."

"She spent a lot of time out at the Dalzell-Davenport place," Alice went on. "Your house now. She said when she went out there, she could feel them. That she dreamed about them at night. A bunch of women and children, trapped somehow."

A chill ran up my spine.

Onscreen, Peter was quiet. I thought of his dream about the winged demon-horse. I wondered if there had been others. More realistic ones, he was thinking about.

"She said she heard them singing," Alice said.

My breath left my body in a whoosh. I felt faint.

"Singing?" Peter asked. His voice had a strange tightness to it that Alice probably hadn't picked up on, but I did. He was disturbed by what she was saying, too.

"Yes. The women and children Sherman killed. She dreamed about them singing." Her face had gone pale, and her voice had a tremor in it.

"How did he do it?" Peter asked in a low voice. "How did Wren think Sherman killed them?"

"She said he shut them up in an abandoned mine and left them there. They suffocated to death."

"A mine?" I shouted at the screen.

"A mine?" Peter asked at the same time in his calm therapist voice.

"A gold mine. Wren said there was a secret gold mine in Juliana that nobody knows about."

"Interesting."

Interesting didn't begin to describe it. I was leaning forward now, my hands out, like I could reach into the screen, grab Alice, and shake the next revelation out of her.

Alice fidgeted in discomfort. "I can't quit thinking about it—Wren up and moving to California. She didn't mention it during that conversation at the Food Lion. And as long as I've known her, she's always wanted to live in Juliana. She loved this town, and it really bothered her that there might be something bad that happened here."

"Not just something bad," Peter corrected. "Mass murder."

Alice nodded wordlessly. She looked ill.

"Did you guys stay in touch?" he asked. "After she moved?"

"She only texted Lilah a couple of times and me once. She basically just cut off communication with both of us because she said she needed space to rebuild her life. She doesn't even speak to Temperance. I don't know . . . I feel like I'm going crazy."

"Why?"

"Because I'm starting to believe that she didn't move to California. I think that someone"—she pressed fingers to her temples—"might've done something to her."

"What do you mean by that?" Peter asked.

"I mean, I think someone killed her, in Juliana, and then they texted all of us, pretending to be her in California."

Peter seemed intrigued. "Can you expound on that?"

"After I saw her that one time, but before she moved, I went over there once, to the Dalzell-Davenport house. To try to talk her into moving in with me."

"Tell me about that."

Alice sighed. "I just felt like her friends, those people she was hanging out with, weren't good for her. Those Pratt trustafarians were just so . . . out of touch with real life. Wren wasn't like them. She was so sweet, and she really valued people. The transformative power of art. She wasn't a taker. Anyway, when I saw her, I wanted her to come home with me for other reasons. She had become really . . . different."

"Different, how?"

"Jumpy. Irritable. She'd gotten really paranoid. All of them were. And they slept all the time—"

I straightened, my heart skittering inside my chest.

"They were all having the weird dreams. Hearing voices, like Wren. Wren said that as the women and children were dying in the mine, they sang this one hymn."

I went cold.

"What hymn?" Peter asked in a quiet voice.

"It's an old one, written around that time. It's called 'The Vacant Chair.'"

My eyes had gone unfocused, and I could feel my hands trembling. Peter didn't respond either. I wondered what he was thinking. He'd obviously downloaded the song because Alice mentioned it. Did he remember that I'd told him that song had been running through my head?

Alice continued. "Wren didn't want to move in with me. She said she wanted to make a podcast about the murders, what Sherman did. She was angry. She felt like it was something, like a sin, that affected Juliana. That there was a darkness here. She said she could feel it, because she was sensitive, an artist and an empath, and so could some of her trustafarian friends. She said she could feel that death ruled over Juliana."

My heart slammed against my ribs. I'd felt that. The night I was lost in the woods. But I'd chalked it up to the margaritas.

"But I think she meant it literally, too," Alice said. "She told me she had gotten a death threat. Somebody put a note in the Dalzell-Davenport house mailbox saying that if Wren kept trying to dig up history, she'd be the one dug up next, or something to that effect."

Everything stilled around me. Everything. The sun coming in through the old windows, the fine, white dust motes floating through the air, the chilled air shooting out through the vents.

Peter spoke. "Why do you think anyone would care so much about something that happened over a hundred and sixty years ago in this town that they would threaten Wren?"

Alice shook her head. "I don't know, but Wren took it seriously. She was scared. For herself, and for Temperance, and Lilah. And now I'm scared, too."

I paused the recording and sat back in my chair. A few things had become clear to me. Peter had been taping his sessions with Alice because she was sharing some potentially criminal information, and he was a mandatory reporter. He also knew he wasn't at his best, not by a long stretch, and there was a good chance he was going to miss some of the details by only taking notes.

He had been taking Alice's concerns seriously. So seriously, that he'd started looking into the uncapped well issue in greater detail. And then, at the party, he'd told Lilah that he thought the well story had been made up to keep us from exploring our property. But why would the old guard do that?

Was it because of the gold George Davenport had found?

Was the old guard afraid we were going to somehow find it and claim it as ours? If so, it made no sense. If they'd known about the gold when we bought the house, they'd never have let us move here. But they did let us buy the place, with the so-called dangerous well. Why? It felt like I was just steps away from putting the pieces together—making this all make sense—but I couldn't quite make the leap.

I closed the iPad and headed upstairs to George Davenport's room. His bookshelf held dozens of books, a handful about Georgia state history. Most were university press or self-published, authored by Georgians about niche parts of the state's history: the Trail of Tears, the land grab, the infamous, thieving Pony Club.

There were two books on the Georgia Gold Rush. I flipped through each, hoping Davenport had dog-eared a page, or underlined a paragraph that would guide me. Sure enough, I found a page marked with a small, pressed flower. A wild violet. I skimmed the page, my eyes stopping on one passage.

> *While the predominant method of mining in areas other than Dahlonega and Auraria were smaller operations that utilized placer mining, panning, and open-pit excavation, there was some tunneling. There was a smattering of unnamed mines established by the Cherokee people. In the area of present-day Acworth, the Allatoona Mine produced gold for at least four to five years. Several other mines are purported to have existed for short periods of time—one in particular was rumored to have produced a reasonable quantity of gold somewhere in the vicinity of Juliana, Georgia.*

I flipped through the rest of the book but didn't find any further mention of a gold mine in or around Juliana. But— along with his discovery of gold nuggets on his property and a dose of dementia—it had been enough to convince George

Davenport. Before he got sick, he was clearly on a mission to try to find the old mine and blow the entrance to high heaven. Wren had probably also found this passage.

My phone rang, jolting me out of my thoughts. I hit the speaker.

"Billie Hope." Dixie Minette's voice rang out, calling me as she always did by my first and last name in that southern twang. "I need to talk to you about Major, if you don't mind."

"Okay, sure."

"He's feeling poorly, and I think he should rest for a few days. I just wondered if you had someone else at the restaurant who could fill in for him."

I thought fast. "I'm sure the rest of the servers can take care of everything until he's back on his feet. Can I do anything to help?"

"No, don't you worry about that," she said in that exaggerated drawl that precluded any possibility of disagreement. "He just needs to rest. That's all. Thank you so much, darlin'." She hung up.

Darlin'. That was a first.

Chapter 24

The days that followed felt like a nightmare I couldn't wake up from.

I couldn't sleep. I had to force myself to eat. At the restaurant, I was an automaton, barely performing my tasks, zoned out when anyone tried to engage with me. All I could think about was getting Peter back down to Georgia so I could talk him out of a divorce, but he wouldn't answer my calls or texts. I had to save my marriage; I just had no idea how I was going to do it.

I told Mere that he was on a business trip. I hated lying to her, but the truth was difficult enough for me to understand; there was no way I was going to be able to adequately explain it to my six-year-old. She burst into tears when I broke the news, which made it all the more awful.

We were fully into the blazing hot, humidity-drenched Georgia summer. The trees had greened all the way out, the grass soft and lush and dotted with swaths of wildflowers I couldn't identify. Purples, whites, yellows—they painted the meadows outside of town, and I promised myself I'd learn their proper names one day. The garden Mere and I had planted was bursting with tomatoes, cucumbers, peppers, squash, and heirloom lettuces. Mere helped me weed and water and harvest in the twilight hours. One of those days, she said she wished she could squirt the hose right in Peter's face. I let it pass. Later, she walked over and stomped on one of the smaller lettuce plants until the stalk was broken and all the leaves lay shredded in the mud.

"Mere, stop!" I cried. "What are you doing?"

"That's Daddy and I smooshed him," she said petulantly.

I closed my eyes and took a breath. I couldn't cry. I had to hold it together if I was going to fix this. "That's not nice, Mere."

"I'm mad at Daddy, so I don't have to be nice," she snipped right back. I didn't correct her. She was going to have her feelings about all this, now and later. To be perfectly frank, I dreaded the later.

With Peter gone, I'd gotten laxer with her. I figured if Peter and I hadn't been able to locate the well, she wouldn't either, so I let her run free over the property, wild and barefoot, mud-spattered and sweaty. She loved it. Ramsey did, too. I called Dr. Undergrove's office and told them Ramsey must've somehow broken out and made his way to our house. The vet apologized profusely and asked if I wanted to bring the cat back, but I declined, saying I thought it would be fine. I still couldn't get over the idea that he might've let Ramsey go on purpose at Dixie's direction.

After about a week and a half of misery, something happened. One morning I woke up to discover that suddenly, inexplicably, I felt, if not great, certainly better.

I didn't know why, not precisely. I was sleeping again, soundly, with few dreams, which probably had something to do with it. And the weather was spectacular. The sky was almost always light blue and nearly cloudless. It got hot—up to the high eighties and then the low nineties—and I found the intense heat a balm, a strange, blanketing narcotic.

My body seemed to like it down here. My hair went wild,

frizzing and curling and expanding in the humidity, and I decided I liked it that way. My muscles uncoiled, and I felt a languidness I'd never experienced before. My skin glowed and I sweated without caring. I moved slower. I spoke slower. Whatever space I was in, it seemed I occupied fully.

One part of me, the part that was connected to Peter, to the idea of our family, was still in pain, but another side of me, the sensory side, was settling into a slower, lower gear. I couldn't explain it. I didn't want to. I just accepted the contradictory state of existence with a sort of grateful nod to my new hometown. In my grief, Juliana was consoling me.

So I would let her.

Mere and I started attending church. Juliana First Methodist, one of the four places of worship in town, had a minister who was an Initiative recipient recently relocated from Illinois. I assumed they knew about Peter, about Jamie and me, too, and were undoubtedly talking behind my back, Tilda Brennan in particular, but no one made me feel unwelcome or judged. As long as they left us in peace, Mere, specifically, I didn't care what they thought of me. The sermons made me feel calm and even occasionally hopeful. I would take what I could get.

I repeated my daily cycle: work at the restaurant, look after Mere, text Peter. He never answered any of my messages. I responded to the silence with paragraphs begging him to come home or blistering, angry diatribes. None of it made any difference. He was stonewalling me. At night, I found myself drifting into grim scenarios. What if this was fate at work—because we'd been meant to live here in Juliana, Mere and I, but not Peter? Maybe he'd had to leave so the two of us could truly be happy in Juliana. Was that even possible? Did fate work that way?

I saw Jamie Cleburne every day, but in my head, I put him on a shelf labeled DO NOT TOUCH. He hovered on the periphery of my consciousness, literally and figuratively, constantly there, always kind and attentive, never pushy. I tried not to notice him. I tried really hard. But I didn't know if I'd be able to say no if he made another move in my direction. I was tired. Tired and lonely, and pissed off.

When Peter had been gone for two weeks, I realized he wasn't the only one missing. Major Minette hadn't shown up to work for nearly the same amount of time. We made do, but at the end of the second week, I'd had enough. After Cam, Libby, and Susy cornered me after a particularly insane day, complaining about the impossibility of keeping up with serving, bartending, and bussing the tables, I decided it was time to pay old Major a visit. I untied my apron, grabbed my purse, and set out on foot in the oppressive heat for Minette Street.

Dixie met me at the door of her Pepto-pink Victorian, which surprised me. "Why, Billie Hope. Hello." She seemed less than pleasantly surprised to see me.

"Hi, Mayor Dixie," I said.

Her face took on a sympathetic expression. "How are you?"

"Can't complain," I said brightly. I was not about to discuss Peter with this woman; I'd rather jump off a cliff. "Is Major here? I wanted to check on him."

"Well, you know he's feeling poorly. Which is why I'm working from home."

"Two weeks is a long time to be sick, though, don't you think? Has he been to see Doc Belmont?"

"I think I know how to take care of my brother-in-law."

I straightened. "I'm not questioning that, Dixie." It was the first time I'd called her that, and she seemed to be okay with it. "I'm concerned about him. He's a valued employee at Billie's and we all miss him."

She seemed to wilt just a fraction.

"Dixie. Let me see him. Please?"

She shook her head. "I'm sorry. I'll have him back to work in a few days, all right?" She shut the door.

Okay, to hell with that. I wasn't going to let her put me off. I needed to know what was going on. I slipped around the side of the house. I knew Major lived upstairs in the old kitchen house I'd seen at the party. I glanced back at the main house but didn't see Dixie watching me from any of the windows.

Pushing the door of the kitchen house open, I walked into the dank, smokey-smelling space. On one wall was a huge fireplace festooned with old cooking implements. A hodgepodge of old appliances—stove, fridge, icemaker—were all lined up along the wall, and a scarred wooden farm table sat in the center of the room.

"Major?" I yelled up. "Hello? It's Billie Hope, come for a visit."

"Hey, Miss Billie," said a voice above me. "I'm here."

I spotted the stairs, narrow and steep. It was a wonder Major could get himself up and down them. "Can I come up?"

"Well, sure. Watch your step though."

I climbed the stairs to the second floor, awed at the space before me. The loft was spectacular. Wide open and light, with windows and expensive wood floors. The walls were decorated with taxidermied deer heads and ducks in midflight, as well as oil landscapes that looked old and expensive. There was a bed in one corner, a kitchen area in the other. On the opposite side were two chairs and a flat-screen TV affixed to the wall. Thick Persian rugs layered the wood floor.

And then there was the view. From Major's window you could see the town of Juliana, leafy trees and rooftops, and the horizon beyond. If you picked this place up and dropped it down in Manhattan, it would cost a million dollars.

Major was dressed in overalls and an old plaid shirt. He stood from the sofa where he'd been sitting and ambled toward me. "Hey, Miss Billie."

I gave him a hug. "Hey, Major. I just came to check on you."

"Dixie let you up here?"

"Actually, I sneaked back." I put my finger over my lips. "Don't tell."

"I won't." His eyes shifted from side to side. "I'm sorry I ain't made it back to work yet."

It made me smile, the country vernacular. "Are you still feeling bad?"

"I was just feeling nervous is all. Just a bit nervous." He returned to the long, low sofa and fidgeted with the tarnished gold-and-green ring he wore with pride. It said Class of 1932, I knew. His father's high school ring. Major had never gone past the tenth grade himself.

I sat at the other end of the sofa. "What's making you nervous, Major?"

He twisted the ring around his knobby finger.

"Is it something at Billie's? At the restaurant?" I leaned over and elbowed him gently. "Did you see a mouse in the kitchen?"

That got a smile out of him. "I ain't scared of mice. Get 'em all the time up here. Mice get in barns, and they get in palaces. They don't know the difference."

"Then what is it? Why did you quit coming to work?"

He sighed heavily. "I guess I don't want to see Jamie, is what it is."

"Jamie Cleburne? Why not?"

He shook his head, pressing his lips together. His eyes did that shifting thing again, and he fiddled with the ring.

I leaned forward. "Major, talk to me. You can tell me what's worrying you."

He looked at me and I saw his face was pale, his eyes full of fear. "I did something bad."

"What?"

His chin trembled. "I snuck and went fishing in his daddy's lake. Nobody's allowed on that lake, except Cleburnes. Jamie's daddy's real particular about that."

"Okay, but people sneak into places all the time, Major. It's called bending the rules. No one's going to be mad at you."

His eyes were fearful. "Yes, they will. Jamie will."

"Well, he won't know. What does Dixie say? Does she know what you did?"

He nodded. "She says I don't have a poker face. I can't hide nothing. If Jamie finds out I was fishing in that lake, they'll send me away. I was supposed to be in jail once, but Dixie got me out. Dixie talked to the sheriff and got me out. But they'll put me back in if they knew I was poaching."

Jail. Probably for that shoplifting habit Dixie had mentioned. I sent him a little smile, trying to lighten the mood. "So, what? She's just going to make you stay up here forever?"

He looked confused, desperate. "She said she might send me off to Atlanta, to live with her niece. I don't know her niece."

"Major, I promise, Dixie's not going to send you away and nobody's going to put you in jail."

"You don't know."

I hesitated. "What don't I know?"

His glance bounced around the spacious loft. I waited.

"I killed a boy," he finally said in a tremulous voice. "When I was just a boy. He was messing with my cat. Hurting her. So, I killed him with a knife."

I felt hot all over, my heart skittering a few beats. My God. I certainly hadn't expected that. I didn't know whether to bolt out of the room and down the steps or ask more questions, so I kept quiet.

"My daddy fixed it so I didn't go to jail. Minettes don't go to jail. But I don't know about now. Juliana's a different town with all you new folks. I don't know that the old guard can get up to what they used to."

The old guard. The Cleburnes, Dalzells, and Minettes.

"'Get up to what they used to'?" I repeated. "What do you mean?"

"The way it's been is the old guard takes care of everyone in Juliana. They make sure that people don't pay for much of anything. That everybody looks out for everybody else." He grinned a little lopsided grin. "You know, there ain't no property taxes around here. Not if you know the right people."

"No kidding," I said.

"The old guard picks the sheriff, too. Always been a Calhoun or a Childers. Calhoun or Childers, them boys like uniforms. That's why I didn't go to jail that one time."

I'd gone cold, chilled to the bone in Major's dim loft. "Wow."

"We're just like the royals over in England. That's what Dixie always says. Three families, just like Stuart, Hanover, and Windsor."

I thought about Dixie's party. Dixie up on her deck, whispering with Ox and Jamie. "Minette, Dalzell, and Cleburne," I said.

"Right. And just like those royals, we have to keep going. Marry and have children."

I blinked at him. "Is that why they came up with the Initiative? To get single people to come down here and marry into the three old guard families?"

"We have to keep up the bloodline. Being a Minette is a great responsibility. And they're not gonna be too happy with me."

"But you're allowed a mistake, Major. Trespassing is just a mistake."

He twisted his father's ring, shaking his head. He looked so afraid. I just couldn't understand it.

"Do you want me to talk to Dixie for you?"

He loomed over me and roared, "No! Don't talk to her! Don't you dare!"

I flinched and jumped up. "I'm so sorry, Major. I didn't mean to upset you. I won't talk to her. I won't tell her anything."

"And don't you go to the lake neither, you hear? I mean it." He was trembling.

"Okay, Major. I won't. I promise."

He backed away from me, turned to face the window. "Get on out of here," he said. "Go on. Get!"

I ran to the stairs, descending back down as quickly as I could. I slipped out of the kitchen and let myself out the gate through the side yard. I got in the Jeep and headed toward the Cleburne farm. Poor guy. Something in that lake had upset him, and he clearly didn't want me or Dixie to know about it.

Well, tough shit. I was going to find out what it was. I'd had just about enough of the mysteries of this town. And the way the old guard had decided they were the keepers of them.

I parked at the mill, in the gravel lot, and walked the mile and a half to the Cleburne farm, keeping close to the brush on the side of the road in case anyone drove past. At the black fence that bordered the farm, I could see the small lake, Mr. Cleburne's pride and joy, shimmering in the distance. I furtively checked in both directions, and seeing no cars, climbed the fence.

The farm was right out of a storybook with green fields bordered by neat hedges, pines, and huge old oak trees. The lake was the most pristine thing I'd ever seen. Not brown or murky—or rust red, like our creek—but crystal clear and green. Willows planted along the edge dipped delicate branches in the water. Clumps of purple lilies bloomed.

On the opposite side, far in the distance, I could see what must've been Jamie's childhood home, a stately white brick traditional with a row of soaring columns. I wondered where old Mr. Cleburne was now. Sitting on that porch in some ancient wicker settee, peering through binoculars, his shotgun trained on me?

To my right, a stand of pines rose up on a knoll beside the lake, and I headed toward them. I picked my way around the water's edge, toeing aside fallen branches and piles of leaves as I went. I rounded the shoreline, and a little mound of what appeared to be muddy sticks came into view, just a few yards ahead. I stopped and shaded my eyes against the glare of the setting sun.

A beaver dam probably, not that I'd ever seen one in real life, only replicated at the Museum of Natural History. As I approached the mound of mud and sticks, my steps slowed. I edged down to where the water lapped at the mossy bank, leaned closer, trying to make out the detail of the dam. I didn't know why, but for some reason, Major's fear had suddenly become mine. My heart was pounding, and I was taking in deep gulps of air like I couldn't get enough.

That's when I saw it.

A human arm, bobbing on the surface of the clear water.

I froze and stepped back. "Oh my God!"

I heaved, then vomited violently, directly into the water. My mind spun into a million different directions.

What . . .

Why . . .

The bile rose once more, and I vomited again, tears spilling down my cheeks. At last, my stomach emptied, I wiped my mouth and steadied myself. But I still couldn't move away. I was seeing stars, feeling like I may pass out. I backed away several feet.

This was what spooked Major, not that he went fishing without permission. And I had to do something. Pull myself together and take note of some real details so I could report it to the police. Covering my mouth in case anything else decided to come up, I forced myself to look again. To take my time and catalog what I saw as best I could.

An arm . . .

A leg . . .

The side of what could be a head . . .

What was left of a head, that is.

Behind my hand, I gagged again. The body was a bluish-purple and bloated with strange gases. It was barely even shaped like a body, impossible to tell if it was a man or woman, Black, brown, or white. There was no clothing left on it, not that I could tell, but something did catch my eye. Something at the end of the arm.

The hand, I told myself, even though this . . . gelatinous blob didn't resemble a hand. It looked more like a jellyfish. But there was something glinting on the surface of it. Something black.

I picked up a stick and waded into the water, drawing closer.

I reached out, holding my breath, threaded the stick through it, and lifted it off the body. It was a ring. One of those black rings men wore for wedding bands. Some men. I withdrew the ring from the stick and stared at it, not comprehending. Not understanding what I was seeing.

I turned the band so that the sun hit it and read the inscription.

To P from B, Forever.

I stared at it, reading it over and over. Trying to comprehend.

Forever, the ring said.

Forever, the promise.

But the promise was broken. Forever had just stopped, right there in that lake. Forever was gone, wasn't it, never to return? It had ended with my husband's body half submerged, caught in a beaver dam.

Peter, my husband, my love, the father of my daughter, was dead. Somehow, he'd fallen into Cleburne's lake and somehow . . . wound up wedged into a beaver dam. But no. No. That was impossible. You didn't just fall into a lake. Into a dam.

Someone had to put you there.

I opened my mouth—whether to scream or cry, I didn't know—but no sound came out. I was empty, standing at the precipice of the void, waiting for a push. It would only be a second, or maybe another, and something would give me that push and then I would tumble into it and begin falling, falling, endlessly falling, no bottom to ever reach.

My phone, tucked in the back pocket of my jeans, buzzed. In a trance, I gripped the ring, Peter's wedding band, in one hand, and with the other pulled the phone out. It was wet but clearly still working. A text had just come in. A text from Peter.

I'll be sending divorce paperwork soon, Billie, the message read. **One day we will talk but not yet. I'm not ready.**

2020
Juliana, Georgia

Madge Beatty sat in the circle of three girls on the floor of the dark bedroom. The bedroom was on the second floor of the abandoned house where they'd been staying. The girls' eyes were closed, hands crossed and clasped. A candle burned in the center of their circle, casting irregular shadows against their faces. All three had dreadlocks and wore clothes they'd scavenged from the Goodwill or Salvation Army. All three smelled like earth and sweat and smoke.

They chanted for the children and the women buried in the mine. They wailed and asked the dead to reveal themselves. To speak. To finally reveal the story of how they had been murdered. And then Wren started to sing, that same old hymn she was so obsessed with.

Madge was really getting sick of that fucking song. It never worked. Even after Wren supposedly found Davenport's directions to the gold mine, they hadn't been able to locate it, much less access it. And she was sick of hearing about the dreams Wren and Boo Dalzell kept having. Dreams of mythical creatures with wings and horns and blood-soaked talons. She had them, too—but she knew a drug-induced dream when she saw one.

The podcast idea had basically fizzled, the fun people had dipped, and Madge couldn't remember the last time she'd worked on her art. All she ever did was smoke weed and chant for the spirits. And listen to Wren sing that goddamn song.

We shall meet, but we shall miss him. There will be one vacant chair . . .

Madge scrambled up, ran out of the room, and down the stairs. She burst out the front door of the house and onto the weedy gravel drive, panting and pacing, happy to be out of that dark, stinking room. She was done with it all—the dreaming, the chanting, the singing. She and Wren were never going to get any real answers about this pathetic, sad little town. There was not going to be a hit podcast on HBO or Serial or whatever. The project was dead.

And now they were having to deal with this stupid virus. Even when she did get a minute away from this depressing haunted house, there was nowhere to go and nothing to do. Downtown Juliana had turned into a fucking ghost town, shops and restaurants closed, people cowering at home. And then the cherry on top of the shit sundae—Wren had gotten a death threat.

Hands on her hips, Madge walked in circles and sucked the cool country air into her lungs. She didn't feel great, to be honest. She hadn't been sleeping well, not since she'd come to Juliana. Her head hurt constantly, and now her throat felt scratchy, too. She massaged her temples. Maybe it didn't matter, whatever happened to those women and children all those years ago. Maybe there were just some mysteries that were meant to stay unsolved.

And frankly, she really was getting tired of living this way, pretending to be a nomad with no ties. She actually had a family. She had money. She could go back to New York, move right back into her loft in Brooklyn. Sleep on her massive, king-sized, pillow-top mattress and eat at whatever restaurant was still serving, even if it was outside between plastic dividers. She could call her old hairstylist to come over and shave her head, and then she could go down to Soho and buy a whole new wardrobe at Anine Bing or Rachel Comey or Marni. Fuck her art and fuck the sins of the past. She wanted a future.

She saw a man standing several yards away from her in the gravel drive in the center of a pale spill of moonlight. She froze. There was a truck parked behind him, a dog hanging out the open window. She hadn't even seen him drive up. He must've been here when she came outside.

"Jesus," Madge said. "You scared me."

"Sorry," he said, holding up his hands. "No harm intended."

She pointed at him. "Jamie, right? I know you. You own the antique shop. You're married to Emma."

She'd met Emma Cleburne at the Food Lion out on Route 140. Emma was from Washington, D.C. They'd bonded over the meager selection and dubious freshness of the produce section. They'd laughed about the accents around Juliana and everyone's obsession with grits. Emma had said she was a lawyer, Madge remembered.

"Was married," said Jamie Cleburne. "Emma left me a couple of weeks ago."

"Oh. Sorry."

"Thank you. That's very kind." He hesitated. "I was out taking a drive, to be honest. Clearing my head. I used to come out here all the time to think. Well, before you all moved in."

"Okay. Well. I better—" She had already turned back toward the house and started walking. For some reason, her heart was pounding, and she could tell that the man was following her. She looked over her shoulder. "I just want to go back to my friends," she said, breathless.

He was beside her now and took hold of her arm. "Wait."

She stopped, still breathing hard, and looked down at his hand. "Don't touch me."

"I'm sorry." He removed his hand.

She could've run, but she didn't. He was definitely the best-looking man in Juliana. And his wife had ditched him. He was distraught. She saw that now that he was close to her.

"Would you . . ." he asked. "Could I possibly convince you to take a ride with me?"

"What?"

Her eyes met his. He seemed completely disarming. Even nervous.

"Sorry. I'm so bad at this. Forgive me. It's just that you . . . I've seen you around with Wren and the Dalzell girls and . . ." *He seemed flustered.* "God, I'm really, really bad at this."

"At what?"

He looked into her eyes. "Asking a girl out."

"So, you didn't actually come out here to clear your head."

"No, not really."

She relaxed. Smiled at him. He really was cute.

"Look. I just wanted to introduce myself, that's all. Jamie. Jamie Cleburne." *He extended his hand.*

She held hers up and away, just out of reach.

"Oh, that's right. I keep forgetting," he said. "No shaking."

"Madge Beatty," she said.

"Madge." *He smiled at her, a warm smile. A pretty sexy smile, now that she thought about it. He lifted his chin to the house.* "Sorry we got off to a bad start. You all are trying to find out what happened in the gold mine, aren't you?"

Her eyes widened. "You know about that? I can't . . ." *She took a few steps closer to him.* "I didn't think anyone knew about it."

He nodded. "A few of us in town do, yes. The Minettes, the Dalzells, my family."

She narrowed her eyes. "Huh. That's interesting. The Dalzells I've met don't seem to know shit."

"Their father would've told them eventually, if they'd just been patient. We all learn in time. The story. I'll take you to the site, if you want. Tell you what actually happened."

"*You know how it happened?*" *She shook her head.* "*I can't believe it . . .*" *She thought for a moment.* "*I should go back and get Wren and Boo. They would really love to hear this.*"

"*No, please.*" *In the dark, Jamie's eyes were large and soft.* "*Just you and me first, okay? It was your ancestor, right, who was one of them? Who escaped and went up north?*"

She nodded. "*How do you know that?*"

"*Small town. People talk.*" *He took her hand, and this time she let him.* "*Let me show you where they all died, Madge. How the sacrifice was made. We'll show the others later.*"

"*I may be sick,*" *she said.* "*The virus. I may have it. I have a sore throat.*"

"*I don't care,*" *he said.* "*It can't hurt me. It can't hurt any of us in Juliana.*"

She only had a second to consider how strange a statement that was before he moved closer to her.

"*Come on,*" *he urged in a gentle voice.* "*Ever, my dog, can be our chaperone.*"

She looked over at the truck. The dog, a chocolate Lab, pricked up her ears. Maybe they had their podcast after all.

Chapter 25

Somehow, I managed to make my way out of the lake, back across the fields, and over the fence. The next thing I knew I was on the road. I looked around, feeling lost, unmoored, trying to ascertain where I was. I'd gone numb, my brain buzzing in my head, and I couldn't think straight. Waves of shock and grief and fear slammed me from every direction, but another part of my brain shouted at me through the storm.

Someone has Peter's phone. . . .

Probably the same person who did this. . . .

The person who killed him and stuffed him in a beaver dam on Mr. Cleburne's lake.

My heart rammed my chest. I tried to catch my breath but couldn't. Maybe Peter hadn't even meant to leave me in the first place. Maybe he'd just needed a break that morning, and someone had taken him. Maybe they had taken him and killed him that very first day. But why? Why would anyone do that to him? Peter was just a regular guy. An honest guy. He wasn't mixed up in any trouble. It made no sense.

I felt like screaming, but I was too busy gulping the air necessary to keep my legs moving. To keep me upright until I could get back to my car and think. *Make a plan, make a plan, make a plan.* A plan would give me purpose. A plan would keep me from falling apart. The next thing I knew I was back in the Jeep with no memory of how I'd gotten there. I was reeling, but I had to get control. I had to keep my wits about me. I should go now. Get Mere and run like hell.

But . . .

Make a plan, make a plan . . .

I forced my brain to slow down. Was running really the smartest move? They'd be watching me, whoever had done this. Watching for any hint that I knew about Peter. Dammit. Why had I taken off the Jeep's top back at home? All I wanted to do was shut myself inside it, away from the outside world, away from everything.

And then another wave of shock hit me.

The other remains. Found, right here at the mill, where I sat now, by Deputy Inman. Wren Street had been threatened, and supposedly she moved away to California. But she wasn't in California—something in me knew it now. Wren Street was dead, just like Peter. And after she'd been killed, the killer used her phone to text her family members, just like Peter.

Peter.

Peter . . .

Hands shaking, I clawed through my purse, looking for the card Deputy Inman had given me. I finally found it and dialed the number. It rang and rang, finally going to voicemail.

"Hi, Deputy Inman," I said, my voice trembling. "It's Billie Hope. We spoke a few weeks ago." I swallowed with difficulty. "I just wanted to call and tell you that I just . . . I did see something unusual . . ." I shut my mouth, suppressing the sob that crawled up my throat. ". . . and I wanted to let you know. Please call me as soon as you can."

I started the car, threw it into gear, and spun out of the lot, my tires kicking up a cloud of dust and spitting gravel. All I could think of was Mere. I needed her, needed to feel the solid, precious weight of my daughter filling my arms. But she was smart. She would pick up on my horror. I couldn't come in, guns blazing. I had to pull myself together.

I stomped the gas, hitting ninety, and as I flew down the deserted highway, the wind lashing my hair around me, I let out a scream. I screamed and screamed into the rushing wind, tears streaming down my face, pushing out the horror, pushing out the disbelief, my heart feeling like it had been lit with a fuse and had exploded right inside my chest.

And then, when there was nothing left inside me, I went quiet. It was in that blankness that my brain told me something. I needed a friend. Someone to talk to, someone I could trust. Someone who understood the way this town worked, the intricacies and habits of the old guard. Who might understand how Peter had inadvertently made himself a target.

I thought of my mother, but just as quickly discarded the idea. She was a million miles away in Maine, praying at vespers or weeding the vegetable patch with Edge or throwing money in Uncle Jimbo's collection plate. She had no way of getting down here. And I wasn't about to put her in the line of fire of these people. These dangerous people. I'd rather die.

Lilah was definitely my best friend here in Juliana, but Mere was still with her, and I couldn't risk Mere hearing about this. She might be in danger, too, as well as me. Not that I understood why. But I didn't have time for why right now. I had to do something.

A thought pierced through the fog in my brain. *Alice.* Alice Tilton knew Peter—maybe the only person in Juliana who did—and now that I'd watched all the tapes, I felt like I knew her as well. I was unsure about dragging someone else into this situation, but Alice was worried about Wren, too. Enough to turn to Peter. She could have some information that could help.

She was my best bet. My only bet. I would have to take a chance on trusting her. I called Lilah to make sure Mere hadn't worn out her welcome there. Lilah told me not to worry, she could keep Mere as long as I needed. I thanked her and headed to Alice's.

Alice lived in a small bungalow a few blocks away from the main ring of Victorian mansions that clustered around the square. The house was a sturdy little red brick with a deep, shaded porch. A welcome mat at the front door said ALL Y'ALL. I rang the bell realizing suddenly how terrible I must look—sopping wet from the waist down, hair wild, and eyes red from crying. But I couldn't worry about that. Peter's wedding band burned in my pocket.

"Billie." Alice stood in her doorway, face flushed, a questioning look in her eyes. She was dressed in a lavender yoga ensemble, her hair up. "What are you doing here? Are you okay?"

"Can I come in?"

She nodded, looking confused, then stepped aside, opening the door to me. I slipped in quickly, hoping no one had seen me. Wishful thinking, especially here in Juliana where everyone knew everyone else's business. Alice shut the door behind me.

"Are you alone?" I asked her.

Her eyes filled with alarm. "Yes. What's—"

"My husband is dead," I announced unceremoniously. "Peter is dead. I just found his body in the Cleburnes' lake."

Her mouth dropped open, and her face went white. "*What?*"

"I saw him. His body. I left him there." A sob escaped my throat. I couldn't believe the words coming out of my mouth. I couldn't believe I was upright.

"Oh, Billie. Oh no." She shook her head in confusion. "But what were you doing at the Cleburnes' lake?"

"I was—" I thought quickly, deciding not to include Major's part in the story. Not until I knew beyond a shadow of a doubt that I could trust Alice fully. "It's a long story. Peter and I have been having problems. He left me two weeks ago, but it just seemed like he was hitting the pause button, so we could both think and untangle some stuff."

She looked blindsided.

"Anyway, I was just looking around the area, at the lake, and I found him near the shore. He was wedged into a beaver dam. I don't know how long he's been dead. Could be the whole two weeks. His body was unrecognizable." I'd started crying again.

Alice was trembling. Her hand had gone to her mouth.

"I found this." I held up the black wedding band. "It's Peter's. The one I gave to him on our wedding day. There's an inscription inside."

She took the band, inspected it, then handed it back to me. She hugged me then, hard. I felt myself quaking in her arms, clinging to her.

She drew back. "I don't even know what to say—I can't believe it. I wondered what was going on when he cancelled our appointments. He just said he was traveling. Have you called the police?"

"Yes. I left a message with a deputy I know." I was shaking violently by now, and she made me sit. "But I wanted to tell you." I took a deep breath. "I know it was wrong, but I watched your sessions with Peter. I know about Wren and the trustafarians and the gold mine."

"Oh." Alice's face was frozen.

"I'm sorry. I didn't know what else to do."

"Let me fix you some tea."

She went to the kitchen and in a few minutes brought back a mug, but I found I couldn't touch it. I didn't think I could even swallow down the liquid. She sat beside me, her eyes blazing, and I told her about the remains they'd found at the mill. About Deputy Inman questioning me and Sheriff Childers taking the case from him.

"Honestly," I said, "I'm starting to believe they might be Wren Street's. The remains at the mill."

The truth dawned in Alice's eyes. "Oh my God. Oh my God. Yes. The death threat she got. You're right, Billie. You have to be. She's not in California. She's here. She's still here."

"And I think the same person who killed Peter probably killed Wren."

"Yes." She was thinking.

"But who? Who would do something like that? And why? Does it have something to do with the gold mine? With what she believed about General Sherman killing people in Juliana?"

"I don't know."

"The old guard would know," I said.

She gave me an odd look. "The old guard? Why would you say that?"

I felt a spike of frustration at her naivete. "Come on, Alice. Sheriff Childers shut down any sort of investigation. He was obviously trying to hide something from Deputy Inman and the rest of the town, probably because that's what the old guard told him to do. Those families run this town. Don't act like you don't know it."

"Just because they run things doesn't mean they'd *kill* someone. Are you kidding me? I mean, Mayor Dixie? Major or Toby? There's no way. It's laughable. And the Dalzell girls would never. Ox is too old, and James Cleburne is in a freaking wheelchair—"

"What about Jamie?" I interrupted.

She gaped at me. "Jamie kill Wren and Peter? No. No way. Why would he do such a thing?"

"You tell me." I leveled a look at her. "You were best friends with Wren, Peter was your therapist, and you used to date Jamie. You're the connection between all three."

Her eyes filled with disbelief. "Billie—"

"I'm not saying you're to blame, but I am saying you could be the key. You may know something and not even realize it."

"What about you?" She jumped up. "According to talk around

this place, you and Jamie have gotten a little too friendly. Maybe he killed Peter because he wants you for himself!"

"Fuck you," I snapped, and jumped up, too.

"Fuck you, too," she retorted.

We glared at each other from across her living room. One tension-thick minute passed, then another. I finally glanced over at her.

"Do you really think that's what happened?" I asked.

Alice heaved a sigh. "I don't know. No. I was just . . . I'm sorry, Billie. This is awful and I shouldn't have said that."

"There's more. Right after I found him, Peter texted me."

Fear flashed in her eyes. "What?"

"I received a text from his phone, telling me he wanted a divorce. While I was looking at his body." I held out my phone to her.

Her eyes dropped down to the phone, then back up to me. "No."

"Not only did someone kill him, they're pretending to be him in texts with me. They're buying time."

"For what?"

"So I don't get Mere and get the fuck out of this town." I jumped up again, started pacing. "I don't know how long I want to wait for this deputy to call me back. I think I can trust him, but the sheriff is another story. I'm taking a chance just being here with you."

"You can trust me, Billie. I swear."

I nodded. "I do know this . . . Whoever killed Peter is watching me. I need to leave, now."

"I think we just need to calm down and think," Alice said. "If Wren really was murdered and then Peter, and they're watching you now, that's all they're doing. If they wanted you dead, you'd already be dead, right?"

She had a point. I'd been alone plenty of times in the past two weeks. If Jamie was the killer, if the old guard wanted me dead, I wouldn't be standing here in Alice's living room. I'd be with Peter in the shallows of the lake. Or buried in a shallow grave like Wren.

"On the other hand," she said, "if you run, they'll know for sure you know about Peter, and who knows what they'll do. Right now, staying here in Juliana, you've got the advantage. They don't know you know."

She had a point. My brain raced. "Okay. Here's what I'm going to do. I'm going to get me and Mere ready to go and wait for Inman to call me back. Whatever he says, I'll do."

In the meantime, I could at least try to figure out what had happened to Peter, and why, without raising suspicion. I thought of Emmaline Dalzell, whom I'd seen in the kitchen at Eats.

"Did you talk to any of the Dalzell girls about your concerns for Wren? If all this has to do with her, maybe they could tell us something. They were friends with her."

Alice looked doubtful. "I went to school with Justine, the oldest, but we were never that close."

"And they're Dalzells."

She pursed her lips. "They are, but it's complicated. Ox protects his money like Rumpelstiltskin on his pile of gold. The girls barely speak to him. That's why they gravitated to Wren and her rich friends from New York, I think. The freedom they had—the way they could just throw away the expectations of their families and live the life they chose. I'm not sure they're in the old guard loop, is what I'm saying."

I moved to the door.

"Wait." Alice stepped toward me. "You're not going alone. I'm coming with you."

"Alice, I don't want you involved in this."

"I already am involved. They know you're here right now. You know it's true. They probably even know about me talking to Peter. So whatever happens to you is probably going to happen to me."

"I'm sorry."

"Forget it. But we should go."

I watched her as she started to gather her keys, phone, and purse; then she paused.

"One more thing . . ." She looked slightly uncomfortable.

"What?"

"You should probably text Peter back. Like you believe it's him. So they don't get suspicious."

I looked at her, stricken.

"I'm so sorry, Billie, but you really should, I think."

My eyes filled with tears. How could I do that? How could I text my husband like I believed he was still alive? It seemed impossible. "What do I say?"

She thought for a moment. "Just tell him whatever it is you never got to say."

I pulled out my phone, blinded by the tears. **I can't accept it's over between us, Peter,** I typed, fingers shaking. I looked up, breathless, feeling faint. Alice nodded encouragingly.

I focused on the screen. **I won't. We've been through too much. We have loved too fully and completely. You are my life.** I took a deep breath. **You are my everything. I'm begging you to call me.**

I handed the phone to Alice. She read the message, nodded, and hit send. We stood there for a minute, waiting for something to happen. For someone to reply. But no one did.

Chapter 26

Alice packed a bag and drove us over to nearby Acworth where we blitzed through the Dollar General, gathering snacks, drinks, and enough feminine toiletry supplies to last us a couple of months. Back at my house, I packed one bag for me and Mere, then secured the top back on the Jeep. Ramsey didn't come when I called so I left dishes of food and water on the back porch in case he ventured back home.

At the end of all that, Deputy Inman still hadn't called me back.

I drove us back into town, fighting the fear and grief roiling in my gut. We rolled past the courthouse, the hotel, and Billie's. Ox Dalzell was just coming out of the restaurant door, to-go coffee cup in hand. He caught my eye and raised the cup to me. My mouth went dry, but I nodded back at him and waved like I didn't have a care in the world. I gripped the wheel and gunned it in the direction of Lilah's.

When Mere scrambled into the passenger seat of the Jeep, she was ecstatic to see Alice. She took note of the Dollar General bags and Alice's duffel. "Is Ms. Tilton going on a trip with us?"

"I was thinking we might take a girls' trip, up north," I said. "To Maine, maybe."

Mere's eyes went round. "Where Grandma lives?"

"That's right. I thought it would be fun for Alice to come along. But not for sure. I mean, I have to work, and Alice still has to get ready for school to start. So we're not a hundred percent sure we're going, but we did think it sounded kind of fun, so we went shopping for supplies." I was babbling, I knew it, and shut my mouth before I said too much.

"It's Ms. Tilton, Mom," Mere corrected me.

"You can call me Alice if we go on the trip," Alice said to Mere. "How's that?"

"What about Ramsey?" Mere asked. "Is he coming with us?"

"He's fine," I said briskly. "At the vet." *Another lie I'm telling to my daughter. Add it to the list.*

"We need to make one quick stop, and I'm going to need you to stay in the Jeep when we get there, okay?"

"And then decide if we're going on a girls' trip or not?"

"That's right. Good girl."

Ox Dalzell's three daughters by his second, substantially younger wife, Nora, lived out at their mother's childhood home, a sprawling place on acreage just outside of town. When Nora Dalzell died, she left the girls the house, the only thing she owned independently of her husband. Ox had held up the issue in court. That's when the girls hooked up with Wren Street and her art school friends and moved to the Dalzell-Davenport house. Apparently, after Wren took off for California, the court awarded the girls the house and they moved in.

The house was on the opposite side of town from the Cleburne farm, which I was glad of. I maneuvered the Jeep down the long driveway that led to the house. It was a massive seventies-style ranch, all angles of stone and timber. I parked, told Mere to honk the horn if she saw somebody coming. "We won't be long."

Alice rang the doorbell. I could hear chiming inside, but there was no answer. I peered inside a long slender sidelight beside the door, taking note of the lacquered flagstone floors, popcorn ceilings, and groovy chandeliers. There was almost no furniture, rugs, draperies, or art hanging on the walls. Against a long wall of sliding glass doors that ran along the rear of the house, I could see a long sofa. One of those modern numbers that looked like a beanbag but probably cost five figures. There was a can of Diet Dr. Pepper on the floor beside the sofa.

"They're probably out back," Alice said. "Come on."

We walked around the side of the house, greeted with a view of something out of a 1970s movie set. A vast green lawn, shaded by enormous leafy trees. In the middle lay an aqua-blue kidney-shaped pool with a bright pink float that looked like a donut with sprinkles. Bright yellow plastic chaises and patio dining sets were scattered around. The cloying smell of weed filled the air.

Under the shade of a fringed umbrella sat three young women, dressed in a variety of sarongs and bikini tops or nothing at all. Two of them had long hair. The third sported dreads. All three were smoking.

Alice lifted her hand. "Hey, y'all."

"Alice!" screeched one of the girls with a top on. "My bitch!"

We headed toward them. When we got there, one of the girls with freckles and reddish-blond hair kissed Alice on the cheek. "My baby, baby bitch," she repeated. "Where you been, sweets? I haven't seen you in forever."

"Oh, you know, getting ready for school." Alice turned to me. "Y'all know Billie Hope, right? The one who runs the café? This is Justine . . ." She pointed to the one who'd kissed her. "Annaliese . . ." A girl with vine tattoos over nearly every inch of her body and wearing no top saluted me. "And Boo."

"Emmaline," said the girl in dreads, and I immediately recognized her from Garnet's catfish place. She had on a ratty T-shirt, knotted at her midriff, cutoff navy Dickies, and a scarf that looked like an honest-to-God, vintage Pucci holding up her locks. Her legs were propped up on the mesh plastic chair. They were bug bitten and scraped up. She offered me a perfunctory smile and then fixed her gaze on her joint.

"Baby's not Boo anymore," Justine said, and pouted. "She's Emmaline. Want a smoke?"

"No, thanks," I said. "I've got my daughter in the car."

"I wanted to ask y'all about Wren," Alice said. "Have any of you heard from her lately?" She hesitated. "Billie lives in the old Dalzell-Davenport house, and she found something of Wren's and wanted to send it to her."

Justine tapped her bitten fingernails on the glass table. Annaliese took a long drag off her joint. Emmaline/Boo said nothing.

"Wren ghosted us," Justine said wryly to Alice. "Just like she did you. She's in California, supposedly. I don't know where."

Alice sighed. "I still find it so weird that she just took off like that. Don't you?"

Justine shrugged. "I guess so, if it was anybody else, but this is Wren we're talking about, you know? The girl who moved into an old house so she could connect with the spirits. Who had dreams and visions." She addressed me. "That was when we were going through some legal stuff with our dad, and fighting over this house, so Wren invited us to hang out with her and her New York friends who had come down to help with the . . ." She trailed off.

"Podcast," Emmaline said to me. "We were going to do a podcast about General Sherman burying alive the families of Confederate soldiers in a gold mine."

"Whoa," I said.

"I know," she said. "Sick, right?"

"Sounds amazing," I said. "The podcast, I mean, not the burying alive thing."

Annaliese chimed in. "It was amazing, at first. There were these guys living in the house with us, these incredible musicians from New York. It was like this unbelievable jam session in the house every single night, with really good wine and everybody just vibing. The Fearz sisters came down from Maine. The big oil family. Some tech billionaire's son, I can't remember his name. And, of course, Wren's best friend from Pratt, too, the girl whose family owns like half of Canada—"

"Madge Beatty," Justine supplied.

"She was pretty cool," Anneliese said. "A sculptor. She and Wren met at school. She was the one who told Wren about the gold mine. Her ancestor had been trapped in there with the rest, but supposedly they escaped and ran to Canada."

"So this Madge Beatty had come down to help Wren with the podcast?" I prodded.

"And contacting the spirits of the dead," Annaliese said.

"Did it work?"

"Of course it didn't," Justine said. "Because that stuff is complete bullshit. Anyway, after a while it wasn't really our scene. Annaliese and I kind of gave up on Rasta. And then there was the whole no running water or electricity and the freaky séances thing—so me and Annaliese dipped." She cocked her head at her youngest sister. "Emmaline stayed, though."

I looked at Emmaline. She looked immensely uncomfortable.

"What happened then?" Alice asked.

Emmaline looked at her sisters.

"Tell them," Justine said.

Emmaline examined her thumbnail. "After Annaliese and Justine moved out, things went downhill. Wren was getting really tense about the whole gold mine situation. She was convinced George Davenport had found out the location of the entrance, and people in the town had gotten rid of him, like a conspiracy or whatever. She started calling his great-grandchildren down in Orlando, like, incessantly. Harassing them, basically, until they threatened to call the police and take out a restraining order against her. That's when most of the rest of the group moved out. The musicians, the Fearz girls, and the tech kid."

"Wow," I said.

Annaliese blew smoke sideways. "By then, Wren had run out of ideas. She'd already asked everybody in town about Sherman killing people. Nobody knew anything. They thought we'd made up the gold mine. They said it never existed."

"And Wren was driving Madge nuts, too. She finally ditched us one night without even telling anyone," Emmaline said.

That finger of dread was working its way up my spine. Madge left the group without so much as a goodbye?

"Have you guys heard from Madge since then?" I asked.

They all said no.

"We weren't as close to her as Wren was," Emmaline said. "I never exchanged numbers with her. I don't even think she owned a phone."

"Anyway, then Wren left," Justine said. "That's when we got our house back from Dad, and Emmaline came home."

I zeroed in on Emmaline. "You haven't heard from Wren since?"

She shook her head. I reached into my purse and pulled out George Davenport's Crown Royal bag.

"I found this in my house—the Dalzell-Davenport house— the other day." I poured the nuggets out on the glass table. Their eyes widened and all three leaned in as if magnetized by the metal.

"Holy shit—"

"—balls—"

Emmaline just stared in silence.

I spoke in a steady voice. "Madge and Wren were right about there being a gold mine in Juliana. I believe it's located on George Davenport's property where he found these gold nuggets. I also found a ledger hidden in his desk where he'd made a list of supplies to make an explosive device. I think he did find the entrance and was going to attempt to blow it open. But he couldn't because he got sick, and his family whisked him away to Florida. And then the town bought the house and acreage."

"Why?" Alice asked. "Why buy it and do nothing with it? A gold mine would be an incredible economic resource."

"Maybe because it was the site of a particularly gruesome war crime?" Annaliese took a deep drag on her joint. "The old guard are weird. They get really hung up on stuff making Juliana look bad. They like to keep that squeaky-clean image."

"I don't know," Alice said. "It seems a story like that, Sherman murdering a bunch of their citizens, wouldn't make the town look bad. It would only boost our visibility. You know—'come to Juliana and witness the site of a horrific result of our nation's greatest tribulation.' Juliana would be like Gettysburg or Andersonville. Bring in a lot of tourist dollars. Besides, it's not like anyone alive now was responsible for what happened there."

Justine leaned back in her chair. "Look, Alice. Wren got a death threat for asking questions. Whether or not the thing really happened"—she glanced at her sisters—"the three of us have decided it's not worth it to keep digging. The old guard is the old guard. Pissing them off is just not worth it."

"Do you think they'd follow through, though?" I asked abruptly. All three girls' eyes swiveled to me. "Do you think any of them are actually capable of killing someone to keep the gold mine murders a secret?"

Before anyone could answer, we heard a "Well, hey, hey, hey!" on the other side of the pool. I hastily swept the gold nuggets back into the bag and stuffed it in my purse, turning to see Ox Dalzell, his glasses glinting on his bald head, ambling toward us.

"Look at what we got here. What's happening, girls?"

Dressed in a dapper green glen plaid suit with a wide, pink tie, he looked like he'd just left a long, martini-filled lunch at the country club. At his appearance, his daughters all noticeably stiffened. Emmaline tucked her legs demurely beneath her chair. Annaliese drew up her sarong to cover her breasts and stubbed out her joint. Justine just stared balefully at him. I tried to look nonchalant.

"All my girls in one place," Ox said, hands on his hips. "How'd I ever get so lucky?"

"The patriarchy?" Justine said.

He didn't respond to that, instead turning to me and Alice. "Hey, girls. Taking a day off work?"

"Yessir," Alice said, automatically dropping into that southern way young women had around here of addressing men older than themselves, a tic that I had begun to detest.

"Ox, good to see you," I said, as if I hadn't just seen him outside of Billie's. He was following me, for sure. I hoped he hadn't seen the gold nuggets.

Ox turned to his daughters. "See, girls. These young ladies work for a living. They get up every day and go to a job and work all day until the job is done. And that's why they get paid."

"Actually, I pay myself," I said. "As well as everyone else on my staff. Also, Emmaline has a job. I saw her at Garnet's the other day."

Ox smirked at me. "Yeah, I heard Jamie Cleburne took you there for catfish po'boys." He turned to Emmaline. "You gonna open up a restaurant, Boo, like Mrs. Hope here? Takes a lot of elbow grease, my dear. Ain't that right, Mrs. Hope? But it's an honorable occupation for a woman. Y'all have a natural way in the kitchen. I mean, not my girls, but I'm pretty sure it's in most female DNA and they can learn. Maybe Billie here can teach you?"

Jesus, this guy. I shook my head at him, and he sent me a wink, like we were all in on the joke together.

"If you weren't already spoken for," he said, "I'd marry you myself."

"Dad," one of the girls said.

I sent him a flat smile and checked my phone. Still no call from the deputy. I was getting antsy. Beyond antsy.

He clapped his big, meaty hands together and surveyed his sullen daughters. "Listen up, girls. The judge finally ruled on my appeal, and I've got some news. The house is mine now and whatever's left inside that you didn't sell. You girls are gonna have to clear out, sorry to say. Get yourselves a new place. Get jobs maybe, like Alice and Billie here—"

Annaliese bolted up out of her chair, slamming the lighter on the table, and walked back into the house. Emmaline stared at her hands as they gripped her knees.

"That money is ours, Dad," Justine said. "This house is ours. Mom left it to us. *Us.* Her daughters."

"Or you could get yourself husbands like normal girls do," Ox went on like he hadn't heard her. "Quit smoking all that pot. Get married and have children and let your husbands take care of you." His voice had risen, his shiny scalp glistening and pink in the hot sun. "There are a couple of single fellas who've moved down for the Initiative. Justine, what about that fellow Jack? The one that's going to open up a Tex-Mex place?"

"Oh my God," muttered Justine.

Emmaline's hands moved from her knees to the edge of the table. She still didn't meet his eyes. "Dad, Mom wanted Annaliese to go to art school. She wanted Justine to travel—"

"You girls have a bigger calling than going to art school or traveling the goddamn globe!" Ox snapped. "You support Juliana. You stand for this town, no ifs, ands, or buts. You hear me? There is no other choice, not if you're a Dalzell. Dalzells pull their weight to keep our town in business."

Something on Justine's arm caught my eye. A delicate gold bracelet with two charms dangling off it, an *N* and a *J*. Her mother Nora's bracelet.

Suddenly the air was filled with the insistent sound of a honking horn. The Jeep's horn, I realized.

Mere . . .

"Excuse me." I took off, racing around the side of the house, skidding to a stop when the Jeep came into view. A tow truck was pulling out of the Dalzells' driveway, the Jeep's rear end lifted high in the air, attached to the truck's winch. Mere sat in the driver's seat, her eyes huge and panic filled. She was clinging to the steering wheel and pounding at the horn with all her might as the truck pulled the Jeep down the drive.

I ran toward the tow truck, screaming at the top of my lungs for the driver to stop. "Mere! Mere!"

I hit the window with the heels of my hands, but when I saw Mere going for the handle, I realized my mistake.

"No!" I yelled at her. "Don't open the door. Just stay there! Stay there!"

I ran alongside the tow truck, but it was gaining speed. Alice was right behind me now and we were both screaming. I charged ahead of her, circling around the front of the lumbering vehicle.

"Stop!" I screamed with everything in me and held out my hands. "*Stop!*"

Chapter 27

The truck driver jerked on the wheel and swerved just as Alice pushed me out of its path. Together we crashed onto the Dalzells' smooth lawn, arms and legs tangling. A few seconds later, the driver stomped around the front of the truck and surveyed us on the ground with a disgusted expression. "What the hell?"

I popped up, checking that Alice was unhurt and brushing grass and gravel off me. I jabbed a finger at him. "My little girl's in there! She's sitting in the Jeep, you *jackass*!"

He backed away from me, looking dubious but appropriately nervous. "I was told to take this vehicle back to Mr. Dalzell's house in town."

"Don't you know better than to tow an occupied car, you brainless motherfucker?!" I screamed, running to the Jeep. I opened the door and Mere fell into my arms. She was sobbing.

The man was shaking his head and muttering to himself as he headed back to the truck.

"Hey!" I yelled at him.

He ignored me and climbed back in the cab.

I pushed Mere toward Alice and charged toward the truck. "What are you doing? That's my car you're towing." Our get-away car. Which also happened to have all our bags in it.

"Actually, it's mine," Ox Dalzell said behind me. "The guy who sold it to you happens to be a friend—"

I rolled my eyes. *Shocker.*

"—and I bought the Jeep for him, but I still hold the title. Lloyd's got some problems, you know, and I didn't want him selling it when he got behind at the racetrack."

I shook my head. "That is absolutely incorrect. That vehicle belonged to Lloyd Childers. He's been driving it for years. Told me all these stories about off-roading with it. He said he was going to mail me the title when he could get it out of his bank's safety deposit . . ." I stopped.

"Not very savvy for a New Yorker, are you?" He eyed me sympathetically.

"Fuck you," I growled.

Ox blinked. "But just as nasty, I see. Look, Mrs. Hope, I'm sorry about the Jeep, but Lloyd's mother is a friend, and I promised her I'd look after him. I'll get your money back. And I'll write you a check if Lloyd's gambled it away. How's that?"

I looked over at Alice who was holding onto Mere. "We'll have to use your car." *And get more supplies,* I thought. We couldn't very well retrieve our go-bags with Ox standing here.

Alice sent me a pained expression. "My car's in the shop. The carburetor and some belt issues, I think. It wouldn't start this morning. They said we had to wait on a part."

Convenient. "I guess we walk back to my house."

"I'll have one of the girls give you a ride," Ox said, pleasant as anything. "I'd do it, but I've got some spring cleaning to do. Boo!" Ox bellowed at the house. "Boo!"

Emmaline stuck her head outside the door.

"Drive Mrs. Hope and them back to her house for me, won't you? Take the Benz. Mama's, not mine."

She disappeared, and the next minute a huge, champagne beige tank of a Mercedes rumbled up in a cloud of dust. I sat up front. Alice and Mere sat in the back. "Thanks," I said to Boo. She just shook her head as if to apologize for her father's behavior. I barely registered it. I was too busy kicking myself for not getting my daughter and me the hell out of this town when I had the chance.

It was going to be almost impossible now. The old guard had seen to that.

We were quiet on the way back to town. I propped an elbow on the rolled-down window and chewed on my thumbnail, thinking. In less than a few moments, everything had changed. We couldn't leave, and there was no telling where Isaac Inman had gotten off to.

So now the game—if that's what you could call it—hinged on me pretending I still believed Peter was alive and had simply left me. I had to play dumb and somehow figure out how I was going to sneak me, Mere, and Alice out of here without arousing too much suspicion.

We were at the square now, Emmaline's Mercedes rolling past Billie's. The place was jam-packed.

"You can pull around to the other side," I told her. "Drop us down the street."

She took a quick right at the courthouse and stopped.

"Out we go, baby," I said to Mere. "Alice and I just need to do a few things before we go back home." I leaned into Emmaline's window. "Thanks for the ride."

"Call me if you need anything else." She locked eyes with me. "Anything at all. I won't say a word to my father. Or to anybody else."

I hesitated, wondering if there was something she wanted to say, but she remained tight-lipped.

"Thanks," I said. "I appreciate your help."

As she drove away, I watched Mere skip over to a window box bursting with petunias and proceed to sniff them delicately. I turned to Alice. "I think the old guard getting rid of our cars says it all. They want us to stay in town."

Alice's brow creased. "We could go on foot."

I shook my head. "They'd definitely catch us. And honestly, Alice, I'm not okay with leaving Peter here with these monsters. It's not right. It's not fair to him." I scanned the square, the quaint, tidy buildings that had become a part of my daily routine. "This town was becoming our town, you know? Our *home*. They don't get to just take that away from us. I won't let them. I want to know what's going on. I have to."

"What are you suggesting?"

I met her gaze. "We expose them. We make them pay for what they did."

She looked slightly queasy.

My mind was finally working again, clicking through the facts I knew. "There is someone else we can talk to. Someone who might know why the people in this town are so freaked out about this gold mine. There was something I saw in Jamie's shop. . . ."

The old photograph in the stack of George Davenport's papers. The name he had likely scrawled in pencil on the back. I couldn't recall it, just that they were at UGA.

I glanced across the square. Jamie's truck was parked in one of the spaces on the street. How was I going to get another look at that photo without him knowing? My phone rang. The number was local, but not one I recognized.

"Mrs. Billie Hope?" The accent was thick, drawling, almost indecipherable.

"Yes?"

"This is Sheriff Frank Childers calling from the Bartow County

Sheriff's Department. Deputy Inman told me you called. He's working on another case, outside the county, so I wanted to follow up with you and discuss that information you wanted to share."

"Oh, okay." I signaled to Alice. *Sheriff*, I mouthed.

She shook her head in warning, and I nodded my assent. There was no chance in hell I was going to tell this guy anything about Peter.

"Yes, Sheriff Childers—" I said.

"Call me Frank."

"Okay, Frank, I don't know if it's any help or even if it means anything. It's just that I think there's some sort of contamination in my house. Like a pollutant or mold or something."

"Do tell."

"Yeah, it's weird. You know my husband has had issues with insomnia then sleeping all the time. Our cat has sort of gone wild. We've all had really strange nightmares."

"That does seem out of the ordinary. So why did you want to speak to Deputy Inman about it? Have you spoken to him about anything else in particular?"

"Oh no. No, I haven't. I've just seen him around the café. And I wanted to let Deputy Inman know about it . . . the contamination. Just in case like maybe . . ." I glanced at Alice who was listening, then over at Mere who was jumping on and off a low brick wall beside the shops. ". . . what happened to George Davenport doesn't happen to us."

"Mr. Davenport had a bad case of Alzheimer's, I believe."

"Sure. Yeah. Of course. I mean, if that's what the doctors say. But who knows, you know?"

"Mrs. Hope, I really don't think there's anything to be worried about. But if you'd like to look into buying a different house, I'm sure Mayor Dixie can help you with that."

"Thanks," I said. "Just trying to be a good citizen. And look out for our health. My family's health."

"Uh-huh. Well, I appreciate that. And I do appreciate you calling."

"Anytime." I hung up and glanced over at Jamie's shop. Thought about the photographs again. "Alice," I said. "I've got an idea."

Chapter 28

"Can we talk?"

I stood just inside the door of Cleburne Antiques, the small brass bell that hung over the door still tinkling behind me. There were no customers, just Jamie, bent over some papers behind the high counter. Mere darted into the jumble of dusty treasures to explore.

"Stay where I can see you," I called after her. I didn't need her stumbling upon Alice, who had entered through Billie's and would, at any minute now, be slipping through the door that connected the kitchen with Jamie's shop. I prayed George Davenport's box of papers and photographs were still in the same place in the shadowy corner far in the back.

Jamie looked surprised but genuinely glad to see me. He flashed his wide, gorgeous smile, and with absolutely no feelings whatsoever, I took note of the muscled, golden-haired forearms framed by rolled-up, rumpled, blue shirtsleeves. In an instant—the instant I'd found Peter's body in his father's lake—I'd lost all feeling I'd ever had for this man. All that was left was a burning shame and the deepest disgust I'd ever felt for a person.

Peter was gone. And I'd slept with this man, even as my husband's body had been decomposing in that beaver dam in his family's lake. There was not enough forgiveness in the world to cover a betrayal like that. I didn't even seek it. The only things I wanted now were revenge and survival. I was on autopilot, doing what I had to do to protect myself and my daughter.

"Of course. What about?" Jamie closed a folder of invoices and set it aside.

"About the thing you asked me the other day." I smiled, hoping I looked sufficiently coy. "Unless you're busy."

He straightened. Stood very still. "Sure. Okay. I was just going over some paperwork."

"We should be quiet." I looked over my shoulder. "Mere."

He nodded. "Understood."

I moved closer to the counter, feeling his eyes on me. Every nerve in my body felt taut. Every beat of my heart, every pulse of blood through my veins, felt like it might be visible to this man, but there was nothing I could do but just play the role as best I could and pray that he bought it.

"I wanted to tell you that while I appreciate your offer, and I do, I think it would be best if I found somebody else to stay with. Maybe Alice."

"Did she offer?"

"No, but I'm sure she'd say yes if I asked." I met his eyes, holding his gaze, playing hard to get. Pathetic, that a game this old could work, but it did. It was. I could see his frustration. His desire.

Was he the one who killed Peter? That secret I couldn't read in his eyes.

He hung his head for a second then looked back up. "Okay, look. I've got a confession. I already put in a call to an environmental testing and remediating company that can handle whatever's going on at your house. They're going out there today."

I stared at him. "I didn't ask you to do that."

He flushed. "I know, but I felt so bad that your whole family moved down here and bought that house, thinking it was this idyllic setup . . . and it turned out to be a nightmare. I talked to Mayor Dixie, too."

My mouth fell open.

"She said the city would pay for everything, no matter what they found." He hesitated. "You'll need to have it done anyway, if you decide to sell."

"I don't know. Peter may come back."

"Would you hate me if I said I hope he doesn't?"

I met his gaze, mentally calculating how much time had passed. I wondered how Alice was doing. If she'd found the box of pictures and the name . . . *Yes. Yes, Jamie, I would hate you. I do hate you. Because you know he's not coming back, don't you?*

"Even if he does come back, it still might be the best thing to sell the place." He hesitated. "But I do hope if you decide to do that, you'll find another house in Juliana. I would really like it if you stayed."

I felt a clean, sharp blade of anger slice through me and clenched my fists by my side. How dare he? How fucking dare he?

"I don't know what I'm going to do," I said. "Not yet. But in the meantime—"

"Come stay with me," he said in a rush.

I gave him a wry look. "I have a kid, Jamie. And a cat, who's kind of a terror, if you recall."

"The cabin is way bigger than Alice's house. Our farm is almost a thousand acres. The cat can roam forever if he wants."

"It's just that I don't want—"

"To be the center of gossip?" He lifted an eyebrow.

Peter's dead. His body is in your father's lake. Wedged into a beaver dam. I was trembling with anger. With pure rage. But I had to keep it together. I couldn't let him see.

"What would your father think?" I was grasping now, running out of excuses to put him off.

"Dad?" Jamie shifted, planted hands on his hips. "Oh. Well, he'll think he raised a good son who offered a woman and her daughter a place to stay while their poisonous home is being worked on."

I tilted my head, gritting my teeth so hard I thought I might crack a molar.

"And yeah, he'll take one look at you and know I've got ulterior motives."

I wanted to reach over the counter and grab him by the throat. Squeeze and squeeze until his face turned blue and he begged for mercy. Out of the corner of my eye, I saw Mere winding her way around the piles of furniture, toward the back of the shop. *Stop, Mere, stop. Hurry, Alice, hurry . . .*

Jamie folded his arms over his chest. "Billie, you have to know by now how I feel about you. How I've felt about you that first day I saw you standing in front of that space next door. I knew you were married. I respected it—"

I lifted an eyebrow. God, I was good at this game, wasn't I?

"Okay, I didn't respect it." He gave me a plaintive look. "I'm sincerely sorry for how things started with us, but I don't want that to disqualify me. It wasn't ideal, everything that happened, I know. And I know you're nowhere near over Peter. I just want you to give me a chance, Billie. Just a chance. That's all I'm asking for."

Revulsion filled me. There was no doubt in my mind, if he had killed Peter, I would make him pay, and preferably with his life. That fact was suddenly the clearest, plainest thing to me. It was the engine that would drive me from this moment forward. Along with my daughter's safety, the only other thing that mattered was bringing Jamie Cleburne down, in every way possible.

Mere appeared beside me, her hand slipping into mine. "A chance at what?"

"Tell you later, Mere, okay?" I squeezed her hand. She squeezed back, and I lifted my eyes to see Alice slipping like a ghost out of the gloom, weaving between the old pieces of furniture, toward the side door that led to Billie's. She nodded at me, and I stiffened reflexively.

"You okay?" Jamie asked.

I nodded vigorously. "I'm fine. Fine."

"Mama, where did Alice go?" Mere asked.

I gripped her hand tighter.

"Alice?" Jamie asked.

"We were hanging out earlier," I said.

"We're going on a girls' trip," Mere said.

"Really?" Jamie asked.

"Someday soon, if we needed to clear out of the house. We thought that sounded fun. Like, the beach or something," I said hastily.

"But that man took our car," Mere explained.

I waved my hand. "Long story. Turns out Lloyd Childers' Jeep had a lien on it. Who knew?"

Jamie laughed. "Sounds about right. So my place it is? I can come pick you up later on tonight."

"Sure. Okay."

He looked at Mere. "Hey, kiddo. Are you okay to stay at my house for a while, you and your mom and Ramsey, so the men can do some work at your house and make it safe?"

Mere frowned up at me. "What's wrong with our house?"

"The people are going to come check it out, to make sure it's safe, that's all." I glanced at him. "We need to go home first, find Ramsey, pack up enough clothes. That kind of thing."

"I can give you a ride home if you want," Jamie said.

I smiled at Mere. "I think we'll walk. It's a pretty day, right?"

Mere nodded. I could see she was confused. I needed to get her out of here, fast, before she started asking completely reasonable questions. "But thanks."

"Is Daddy coming to Jamie's house, too?" Mere asked me.

I swallowed down the lump that rose in my throat and tried to keep my voice level. "No. He's traveling, remember?"

She nodded. I avoided Jamie's eyes.

"I'll swing over around eight," he said.

"Sure. Sure, that'd be fine."

I smiled again to cover my boiling anger. It was a bitter pill to swallow, but if keeping my enemies close was the only way I could outsmart them, then down the hatch.

We met up with Alice around the corner.

"Did you find it? The photo?"

"Yes, and the name written on the back," she said under her breath as we hurried away from the square. "Dr. Sofia Argotte. UGA. A professor at Georgia, I'm guessing. I took a picture." She held up her phone.

"Text it to me, and I'll call her back at my house," I said, pulling Mere along.

"Mom, slow down!" she complained. "Where are we going now?"

"Baby, I'm so sorry we're running all around like this. But I just need you to hang tight with me for just a little bit longer."

"I don't want to go to Jamie's house."

"It'll just be for a little while." I turned to Alice. "Jamie called an environmental cleanup company to check out the house. We'll stay with him while they check everything out. I think if I go over there, I may learn something new. And hopefully, I can track down Deputy Inman. Mere and I are just going back to hopefully find Ramsey, and Jamie's coming back at eight. You should probably go back home."

Alice looked flummoxed. "What are you going to do if Inman doesn't call you back? Or if you find some kind of evidence that Jamie . . ." She didn't finish the sentence. She didn't have to.

I lowered my voice so Mere couldn't hear. "Then I know we're in deep shit, I'll steal somebody's car, and you and me and Mere will disappear."

She stopped me with a hand on my arm. "Do you feel safe at Jamie's?"

"Hell no, but I don't know how else to play this. Listen, Alice, we need to call this person, this professor, Sofia Argotte, to see if she has any information. Maybe a link between the past, the gold mine, and whatever Wren and George Davenport were onto. And what's going on in Juliana now. The more we know, the smarter we can fight."

Mere tugged on my hand. "Mama, I want to stay at our house. Just us and Ramsey." She'd settled into a full-blown funk, but who could blame her? She could sense the chaos. So much so that she longed for the pet she'd been afraid of.

Alice glanced furtively over her shoulder. "Would you feel better if I came with you? We can call the professor from your house."

"I think you should go home so they don't get suspicious. Just lock your doors. Windows, too. Don't go anywhere. Don't let anybody in."

She gave me a hug and peeled off in the opposite direction, and Mere and I forged on. It was a long trek—four miles and some change—and by the end of it, Mere was hot, dusty, and whining. I, on the other hand, was glad for the exercise. It was a distraction that almost kept my brain from repeatedly flashing to the image of Peter's body in Mr. Cleburne's lake. His black, bloated, shapeless body.

I could feel the weight of the wedding band in the pocket of my jeans. The very same wedding band I'd slipped on Peter's finger that day in Billie's in Alphabet City, with my mom and my staff and all our friends. *I'm stupid lucky,* he'd said in his vows, his gaze not wavering from mine. *I'll never know how I ended up with you.* I'd kissed him then, spontaneously, even before the minister had pronounced us husband and wife, and everybody had laughed.

Now tears rushed to my eyes, but I willed them away. Later, I'd have time to grieve. Later, I could fall apart. Right now, I had to keep going. For Mere.

When the house came into view, we saw Ramsey sitting on the front porch, eyes cool, tail curled neatly around his haunches, like some regal guardian of a Pharaoh's tomb. Mere ran toward him, and—praise be to the feline gods—he allowed her to scoop him up and cuddle him. Inside, I went to get Mere into a bath, then rustle up some kind of dinner.

I made a quick summer pasta with peas and pesto and a salad. We ate on the back porch, and when we were done, I told Mere to pack another bag and did the same. After that, I pulled up the picture Alice had texted and searched the name Sofia Argotte.

Professor of history at the University of Georgia, the bio read. *An expert in Civil War battles in Georgia and Sherman's historic march to Atlanta.*

There was only an email under her contact information, so I did a little more digging until I found a number. I dialed, but it went to voicemail. I left my name and number and a brief explanation of who I was—that I'd moved to George Davenport's property in Juliana and had reason to believe there was a gold mine on my property that was possibly connected to Sherman's march to the sea and some sort of wartime atrocity. I asked her to call me back and hung up, staring in the direction of the melting, orange sun.

The buried gold mine was just on the other side of that field at the base of the bluff. A mine and a tomb that held the remains of women and children murdered by Sherman. A story that the families who ran this town wanted to keep buried.

But there was more. There had to be.

A dove called somewhere out in the fields, the mourning sound long and low. The sound of loss and regret. I dropped my head in my hands and let out a whimper, and it was like a scab being ripped off a newly healed wound. The primal, guttering sobs that I'd been holding back for hours now, that I could only let out here in the privacy of this place demanded release. Still, Mere was in the house. I covered my mouth with my hand, but I couldn't stop the tears now, the low wails that joined the dove's, that poured out of me in a torrent. That felt like they would never stop.

But they did. At last, I was empty, squeezed dry of the pain, at least for the moment. I sat in silence, dazed, disoriented. I felt my scalp prickle, suddenly alert to the warmth of the setting sun. Was that the breeze rustling the overgrown camellias that lined the porch? Or maybe more moles, Ramsey's prey of choice.

I shivered, suddenly feeling as if I was no longer the only one out here. I could sense it, the presence of something else with me, something watching me. But unlike the eyes I'd felt on me for the past few hours—threatening, evil, bent on doing me harm—these felt different. These eyes felt somehow . . .

. . . *benevolent.*

Like they were on my side . . .

"Peter?" I whispered into the air.

Two short blasts of a car horn sounded in the stillness, and I jumped. Mere ran out onto the back porch, a canvas tote overflowing with toys and books. "Jamie's here!"

I downed the rest of my wine and headed out to meet him.

Chapter 29

In the lavender twilight, Jamie turned his truck down the asphalt drive that led to the Cleburne family farm. Even in the dark, the place would've been impossible to miss. Two stately brick gate pillars, freshly painted white, flanked the drive. A massive wrought-iron gate bearing a huge, scrolled letter C, parted to allow us entry.

Mere was all eyes as we rumbled down the dirt road. The property was immaculate, with green pastures, massive oak trees, and the view of the lake in the distance. I was barely aware of any of it. All I could see was Peter's corpse at the edge of the lake. He was there now, floating. Alone.

We reached a fork in the neat asphalt ribbon of road, and Jamie asked if we minded stopping by the main house to check on his father.

I glanced at Mere in the back seat. "Mere, we've got to go say hi to Mr. Cleburne. Can you stay in the car and hang onto Rams for me?"

"I don't want to wait in the car," she said, which was exactly what I expected her to say. The last time she'd done that, it hadn't gone so well. I sent Jamie an apologetic look.

"It's okay," Jamie said, looking in the rearview mirror. "You can bring Ramsey in. Dad loves cats. He loves all animals. He built this whole lake just because he likes fish so much."

Shit. I clenched my jaw, feeling dizzy, trying to settle my breathing. I was going to have to face the man, the patriarch of the Cleburne clan. I didn't know if I had it in me. I didn't know if I could stand there, making small talk, when I knew my husband lay dead not half a mile away on this man's property. This man, his possible murderer.

But that's exactly what I had to do.

Hold it together, Billie.

Just a little bit longer . . .

Jamie swung in front of the house, and I marveled again at the spacious white painted brick and soaring columns, the vast gravel court out front, like some kind of aristocratic country estate in England. I knew the house had been built by his great-grandfather back in the forties for the passel of kids he and his wife raised. Now only James Sr. and Jamie were left.

We got out and Jamie ushered us into the house. The foyer was a spacious room, light and filled with the expected oil paintings and an impressive array of taxidermied animal heads, many more than in Major's loft. There were several deer, a buffalo, some terrifying-looking birds, and a few African antelopes. I felt sick to my stomach. Mere, clutching Ramsey, gave me a wide-eyed look.

"Dad?" Jamie called.

"Back here," bellowed a surprisingly strong voice.

Jamie led us down the hall back to a large den. The room was paneled in expensive wood. There was a mix of antiques and modern pieces, all done in tasteful, southern traditional. Walls of bookshelves were lined with hardback novels by Grisham and Patterson and Thor. Three enormous TVs affixed to the wall played Bloomberg, ESPN, and the Outdoor Channel. A young woman dressed in nurse's scrubs whisked away a TV tray of dinner laid out on china, crystal, and silver that looked like it had barely been touched. In the center of the room, his father sat on a plush leather recliner. Mr. Cleburne struggled up from the recliner.

"Dad, no. Sit," Jamie said.

The old man didn't. He stood all the way up and then extended his hand to me with a twinkle and a grin that drooped slightly on one side. Immediately, I saw where Jamie had gotten his devastating charm and good looks. If Jamie was handsome, it was clear that James Cleburne Sr. had been utterly incandescent, movie-star good-looking, at least back in his day. Even now, at seventy-something and coming back from a stroke, he was still impressive. He knew it, too, the way he clasped my hand in both his and locked eyes with me.

"Billie Hope," he said in a warm, gravelly voice doused in honey. "I've been hearing about you from everybody in this town, including my son. I'm just sorry I haven't been in good enough health to make it to your new restaurant."

"Hopefully, you'll be able to one of these days. Just let me know and I'll save you the best table in the house."

"I'd love to see it." He released my hand. "And this must be Meredith. Hey there, little lady, how are you?"

"Pretty good," she said in her typical spare, New York girl way. "I have a cat."

"I see that. What do you call him?"

"Ramsey. He's named after another cat who belonged to the manager at my mother's other restaurant in New York. That was the original Ramsey."

"Hello, Ramsey, Junior. Pleasure to make your acquaintance," James Sr. said. "My son's a junior, too, so he knows the hardship of having another man's name."

He chuckled. Ramsey eyed him suspiciously.

"Can I offer y'all a drink? Wine, Billie? Lemonade for Mere-dith?"

"No, no, Dad." Jamie dropped his hands in his pockets. "We just dropped by to let you know—Billie here, and Mere, their house has some kind of contamination issue, so while they're getting it checked out, I told them they could stay at the cabin."

"Well, that's perfect. Would y'all like some dinner? I have a housekeeper who cooks all kinds of stuff I can't even eat. She makes something called profiteroles. You ever heard of that?"

Mere looked at me. Of course, she knew what profiteroles were—she was the daughter of a restauranteur. But I had a feeling he wanted the upper hand in this conversation, and I wasn't sure I was ready to challenge his alpha-male play, no matter how small. I gave him a noncommittal smile.

"We had dinner, thanks."

Jamie shifted his weight. He looked slightly nervous. "Well, we should mosey over to the cabin."

"Well, now wait a minute," James Sr. said. "I was just think-ing." He turned to Mere. "Can your mom hold Ramsey for you, my dear? Or better yet, let him go and see if he'd like to make himself at home here. Been a long time since we had a cat. Might be some mice around this place he'd like to chase."

Mere nodded, but her expression was tremulous. She re-leased Ramsey. He immediately darted across the room, piv-oted, and ran out the door.

"See that?" James said. "Just like I said. He's okay."

Mere watched him. I watched him, too, on edge. I couldn't tell what his game was. What he wanted from us.

"Would you do me a favor, darlin'?" he asked Mere.

"Okay," she said, and the vulnerability of her voice broke my heart. *Do. Not. Cry.* I picked a spot on the wall, an oil portrait of what appeared to be the Cleburne family in happier times. I stared at it with all the intensity I could muster.

"Run out to the hall," Cleburne continued. "There's a table out there and a box on top of it that's covered with shells. My late wife made that box. Jamie's mother. She found all those shells down at Sanibel Island, Florida, and glued them all on there. You ever been there, to Sanibel Island?"

Mere shook her head.

"Well, run on out there and open the box—it ain't locked. There's a bunch of stuff in there, but only one bracelet. Find that bracelet for me, will you?"

Mere stood, gravely. "Okay."

"Yessir," James Sr. corrected her, a sharp edge in his voice.

Mere froze and blinked at him.

"We say yes, ma'am, and yessir down here, young lady."

Jamie looked stricken.

"She's not—" I started to say.

James Sr. spoke over me. "You understand me?"

Mere nodded. "Yessir."

And then my daughter trotted out into the hall of the house. James Sr. turned to look at me and the air in the room stilled. I could feel my heart beating inside my chest. In his expression I detected a mix of triumph, amusement, but also warning. And it was that warning look that not only filled me with fear, but also sent a white-hot rage shooting through me. I started to tremble and gripped the side of the ottoman. James Sr. kept his eyes on me.

Don't fuck with me, they said.

But I was sending a message back, just as steady and cool as his.

You don't know me.

And that will be your downfall.

Mere ran back into the room holding out a delicate, gold bracelet.

James motioned her over. "Bring it here."

Mere dropped the bracelet in his hand. She glanced briefly at him. "Yessir."

He awarded her with a crinkly, warm smile, minus one side of his mouth. Slowly, deliberately, the man unclasped the bracelet and put it around Mere's wrist. He held up the small charm that dangled from it. "See that? It's a letter *J* and a letter *M*. You see that? The *J* stands for . . ." He raised his eyebrows at Mere.

"Juliana?" she said.

"That's right. Our Gentle Juliana. Now my wife's name was Margaret. We didn't have daughters, only a son, and so far, that boy"—he sent a pointed look in Jamie's direction—"hasn't had any daughter he could call Margaret or Molly or Mary. No *M* names, can you believe it? And then, you walk in here. *Meredith.*" He shot me a pleased grin. "Meredith who lives in Juliana. It's a perfect match. And it looks really nice on you."

"Oh, we couldn't—" I started to say.

He waved me off. "Nonsense. It's only twelve-carat. My wife had plenty of nicer stuff."

"Mere, say thank you to Mr. Cleburne."

"Thank you," she said. "I love it."

"You're welcome." James sat back, and the fine leather enveloped him. "How do you like Juliana, Meredith?"

"I like it a lot. It's very nice."

"Well, aren't you the sweetest? It is nice, but it's a lot more than that, you know."

I inhaled, bracing myself. I couldn't give myself away at this point. I had to let this man talk, no matter how much I distrusted him. No matter how much I despised him being within touching distance of my daughter. But I would not look away.

"Juliana is a very special place. You know it was a mill town originally."

A lie. How many more of these was this man going to subject us to?

"We sawed lumber in the 1800s, and then along about the time of the Great Depression, we figured out how to make sawdust into pressed logs. After that we made pulp for paper. The Minettes still run that one, the pulp mill. It's a ways out of town."

Mere nodded. I wondered what she was making of his words.

"Eight families started the town, Meredith. Eight families that came from places like South Carolina, Virginia, Pennsylvania, and New York, just like you. But there are three families that are the most important. The Minettes, the Dalzells, and our family, the Cleburnes."

She smiled, still unsure what the man was trying to tell her. My skin rose in goose bumps.

His expression darkened. "I want you to understand something about Juliana, Meredith. We love our town. We fight for it. Fight to keep it going, no matter what. The three families have always been here for each other, taking care of each other, and helping each other. Not one of us would ever let another one falter or lack for anything. We did this, not because we always got along—we didn't—but to maintain the strength of our town. Of our Gentle Juliana. And in return, she protects us from the world out there. She gives us shelter. She provides for us. But we have to do our part. We have to give her what she needs." He was staring at Mere now with an intense gleam in his eye. "Do you understand what I'm saying?"

Mere—only a child but already understanding that this man, this patriarch, held all the answers and her only job was to parrot his opinions—hesitated a fraction of a second before she nodded. I held my tongue, but I was still trembling with anger.

"We have to *love* Gentle Juliana," James said. "Love her

with our whole heart, and soul, and body." He stared at her expectantly. "So what do you say, little Meredith?"

She looked frozen. Confused.

"You say you love our town," he instructed.

"I love your town," Mere whispered.

"No, no. Say, 'I love Gentle Juliana.'"

She gulped. "I love Gentle Juliana."

"And then you give the charm a little kiss."

She stared at him.

"Go on."

She lifted her wrist and dropped a kiss on the bracelet. My heart was thumping so hard I felt breathless.

He seemed satisfied and turned to me. "Well, now. I hear you lost your car, Billie. You're welcome to borrow the Chevy pickup. It's a classic 1972, blue and white. I drove it for years, all over this farm, and it's still in mint condition."

I felt shaken by the sharp left turn of conversation. "Oh. Okay. Thank you."

We all stood.

"Mama, I don't know where Ramsey went." Mere's voice was a whisper. James Sr. had scared her, I could tell.

"Oh, it's fine," Jamie said. "He's free to roam around, as long as your mom doesn't mind."

"It's fine," I said through clenched teeth. "We'll find him later. Come on, Mere."

"One more thing," James said, behind us.

We turned.

"I'm having the guy down from University of Georgia, the aquatic biologist, to fine-tune some things in the lake. So you'll want to stay away from it, all of you. No swimming or canoeing or fishing. Especially you, little one." He tugged on Mere's shirt then his eyes met mine. He was still smiling, but beneath the warmth, there was a layer of ice.

I felt encased in ice as well.

This man—or his son—had definitely killed Peter. Now I had no doubt.

What I was going to do about it was the question. I had to come up with some kind of plan, and quickly. I was running out of time, I could feel it.

"Yessir," said Mere once again. She'd taken on a stiff, wooden appearance but slipped a hand in mine. I squeezed it reassuringly. She did not squeeze back.

Chapter 30

The cabin was made of logs, Swedish Cope-style, Jamie informed Mere and me, whatever that was. He said his father had built it back in the seventies to use as a fishing lodge. It was furnished with Cleburne hand-me-downs, he said, as well as a few antique pieces he had come across on his travels, with just enough tartan thrown in to let you know a man lived there. I forced a smile through the whole tour.

Jamie showed Mere to her room, cozy with an iron bed and antique washstand. Long muslin curtains, white and airy, lent a romantic feel. In spite of having to leave Ramsey behind at the main house, and the strange interaction with Jamie's father, she was ecstatic at the sight of her new room. She kept touching the monogrammed bracelet, too. It made my stomach twist with disgust and dread.

"Sorry about Dad," Jamie said, after he'd dropped my bag in my room. "He can get a little intense about Juliana. The old guard tends to lay it on a bit thick. But you've got to give them credit. They were the ones who chased off the automotive plant and came up with the Initiative."

I just nodded. I was too distracted by the possible plans to get Mere and me out of here that were running through my head. Should I try to sneak out and steal Mr. Cleburne's vintage truck? Email the local FBI office and wait around while they verified things with local law enforcement? I reviewed each idea, then discarded it. Juliana was like a tiny kingdom— an insulated, isolated bubble with its own aristocrats who had their own set of ironclad rules and threatened merciless punishment for anyone who dared break them. With the exception of Alice, they seemed to control most everyone around here, even the newcomers.

Was Deputy Inman part of it? My guess was no. That day he'd questioned me behind Billie's, he'd told me not to tell anyone he was looking into the remains found at the mill. And he wasn't from Juliana proper. Definitely not a part of the inner circle. Which was exactly why I wished he'd call me back.

Cooper Creek, I suddenly remembered. That's where he'd told me he was from. A little west of Juliana.

Jamie went to the kitchen to find a bottle of wine. I ran a bath for Mere and laid out her pajamas. My mind raced. In the bathroom connected to my room, I unpacked enough to make it appear I intended to stay. Then, from a side pocket of my bag, I pulled out the bottle of sleeping pills Doc Belmont had prescribed for Peter. When I came out, there was wine for two set on the coffee table in front of the sofa and a pair of candles burning. I could hear Jamie in the kitchen, running the faucet.

"Go ahead and start your wine," Jamie called. "I just need to clean up a bit in here."

"Thanks."

Mere appeared before me, wet hair and flushed, in her rainbow cloud pajamas. "Do I have to go to bed?"

I kissed her. "It's late, sweetie."

"Can I explore first?"

"Sure."

She proceeded to wiggle her way around the room, exploring, investigating, and peering into every nook and cranny of the cabin. I inhaled nervously and dropped my hand in my pocket, feeling the pill. I walked over to the glasses of wine. Hand shaking, I dropped it in one of the glasses and swirled the wine around. A lighter lay beside the candles and, on impulse, I grabbed it and dropped it into my pocket. I'd have use for it later on.

Then I peered at Jamie's glass of wine.

Shit. The pill wasn't dissolving. It was just sitting there at the bottom of the glass. I looked over my shoulder. Mere had climbed up on an old cushy armchair and was studying a painting of a horse. I dunked a finger into the wineglass, trying to stir the pill around. That worked to some degree. Bubbles were streaming up from the tablet, which might be worse than not dissolving at all, now that I thought about it.

Shit.

I picked up the other glass and swallowed a gulp, all the while swirling and swirling Jamie's glass. I walked around the woodsy, rustic room, studying the décor, swirling both glasses. Mere had climbed down from the chair and was galloping around the room like a pony. Still swirling the glass furiously, I stepped back into a small office, feigning interest at the framed certificates on the wall. University of Georgia, Emory. He'd gotten another degree there. An MD specializing in Family Medicine.

Jamie was a doctor?

"I was looking for this." He took the wineglass I'd been swirling out of my hands and took a small sip. He glanced around then kissed me swiftly.

"So you're *Dr.* Cleburne?"

"Oh yeah." He trailed his fingers down my arm. "That."

"Why didn't you tell me?"

"I didn't want to brag." He grinned. A lie. He hadn't wanted me asking all the obvious questions about the old guard.

"I don't get it," I said. "Why don't you practice?"

"Long story. We used to have another doctor in town, Bobby Minette. Dixie's husband. An ob/gyn. Unfortunately, he passed away at a young age. Doc Belmont's great. But he won't live forever, and they wanted a backup. Someone they could trust."

"Someone from the old guard."

He looked slightly embarrassed. "I know, I know. They're really set in their ways. Anyway, they sent me to med school, and while I'm cooling my heels at the antique shop, they make it worth the wait."

"How do they do that?"

He smiled. "It's a secret. You've got to pinky promise not to tell." He hooked his pinky through mine and my heart seemed to go still. I could barely breathe. "The council created a little trust fund for me. An incentive to keep my morale up, so to speak. They give me whatever I want, and one day, they know I'll return the favor."

I went cold all over. "And what is it that you want?" I asked. But I knew. Right there in that moment, I knew exactly what Jamie Cleburne wanted. Because the town council had made sure they got it for him.

They'd sent the email to me.

They'd made a house available that hadn't been.

They'd paved the way for Billie's to flourish . . .

. . . and they'd eliminated the one obstacle—Peter—who'd stood in the way of Jamie claiming his prize.

What Jamie wanted was me.

"Billie." His voice was husky. He moved closer and kissed me. He tasted warm and spicy with a hint of red wine. His hand, the one not holding the wine, moved from my arm to the curve of my lower back.

I pulled away. "Mere."

"Okay. Later." He sipped his wine, eyes burning into mine. I needed to slow him down with the wine. Jamie wasn't supposed to know he'd been drugged, just that he'd had a really fantastic night of sleep and not woken once. Him being a full-on medical doctor had definitely not been part of the plan.

I shuttled Mere off to bed, then joined Jamie in the living room where he had the Braves-Reds game on. He'd already topped off his wine. Frustratingly, not only was he still upright, he couldn't keep his hands off me. As I pretended to be engrossed in the TV, he kept rubbing my back and kissing my neck, and it was taking everything inside me not to scream and shake him off. I clenched my jaw and kept commenting on the game. And then, the obvious occurred to me. Short of straight-up anesthesia, the one-two punch of an Ambien and an orgasm would put him in possibly the deepest sleep a person could have.

I looped my arms over his shoulders and pulled him closer.

"Oh God, yes," he said, and pressed against me, body and face. It was like he couldn't believe he had me here, all to himself. Like I was his prize or something.

I tightened my arms around him. "Not too loud."

"My room," he whispered in my ear. He spun me and gently pushed me toward the opposite side of the kitchen. I spun back to him, grabbing the hand beneath my shirt with what I hoped passed for excitement, not the fury and disgust and fear I was truly feeling.

"Let me just make sure she's asleep. And I should shower."

He nuzzled me. "I can't wait."

"It's been a long day, Jamie. Please."

He softened. Lifted my chin and kissed me once more, this time tenderly. "Shower in my bathroom. I'll join you."

I pushed open Mere's door. She was asleep, thank God. If he would just fall asleep already, I wouldn't have to go through with this whole nightmarish plan. Time was ticking by. I couldn't just stay here in Mere's room. I needed to go back. If he was still awake, I was going to have to play this whole farce out to its bitter end.

I crept back through the house, quietly opened Jamie's door, and practically collapsed in relief. He was sprawled on his bed, shirt off, jeans still on, snoring away. In a flash, the relief was replaced with something else.

Rage. The kind of bone-shattering, teeth-grinding, blinding flood that wipes everything out of your mind other than the one pure, crystalline need to strike. I wanted to kill this man. I didn't care about the law or presumed innocence or any of that nonsense. I wanted Jamie Cleburne dead.

And then, I noticed it: a long-barreled shotgun, leaning in the corner of the room, on the other side of the nightstand, gleaming in the low light. As if in a trance, I walked around the bed and right up to it. I reached out and touched it, feeling the cold metal against my fingers.

I picked it up and placed the stock against my shoulder. Closed one eye and trained the sites on Jamie. I held the gun there, staring down the barrel, and saw myself pulling the trigger. I saw the blast, felt the kick of the gun. Pictured Jamie, exploding into a hundred pieces. His blood would spray every surface and I would watch that with nothing but satisfaction. My blood was singing. It felt like there was a chorus of angels around me in every corner of the room, holding my arms up, urging me on. Singing with heavenly voices a solemn dirge. A funeral song.

We will see him, but we will miss him.

There will be one vacant chair.

A rush of air escaped me, and my vision went black. I lowered the gun, returned it to the corner, heading for the door. Dizzy, I clawed at the frame, heaving, my mind racing.

Go, Billie.

Get your daughter and go.

I headed back to Mere's room. She was sleeping, arms flung over her head, the gold M and J bracelet still on her wrist. I gathered her limp, sleeping form into my arms.

The night was warm but bright from the moon. At exactly a quarter past eleven, Emmaline Dalzell met me on the asphalt road just beyond the white brick pillars in her mother's ancient Mercedes. I loaded Mere—still in her rainbow cloud pajamas and half-asleep—into the back seat and climbed into the front. I didn't bother with a seat belt. Nobody in Juliana was on the road at this hour and the Mercedes was, for all intents and purposes, a tank.

"Just drive for now," I told Emmaline. "I need to make a phone call." I opened a search for Cooper Creek, Georgia, on my phone. Hopefully Isaac Inman wasn't the early-to-bed type.

"Who are you looking for?"

I kept scrolling. "I'd rather not say."

"I swear I won't breathe a word and maybe I can help."

I only hesitated a fraction of a second. "Isaac Inman. He's a deputy in the sheriff's department."

"I know him." She kept her eyes on the road. "I played his sister in volleyball. You want his phone number?"

"Maybe not his. Someone in his family who might know how to get word to him without using his phone."

She glanced at me. "His grandmother. Eleanor Inman. She raised him. She lives over in Cooper Creek, on Franklin Road, I'm pretty sure."

I gave her a grateful look. "Thanks."

"She's been to your restaurant," Emmaline said. "Justine mentioned seeing her there once."

I got her point immediately: I could find Eleanor Inman on Billie's reservation app.

"I won't ask any more questions," she went on. "And I

promise, I won't say a word to anyone. I may be a Dalzell, but I'll never be one of them."

"Why?" I asked.

"Just something my mom told me a long time ago before she died. She said there was something wrong with this town, with the people, and my father knew about it, but he wouldn't tell her. Me and my sisters can't figure out what it is either. He doesn't trust us, not since we started hanging out with Wren and went to live in the Dalzell-Davenport house. Now he's just obsessed with making sure we get married and stay in Juliana and that we're always financially dependent on him. And he's dating one of those new Initiative women who moved here. She's a clothing designer apparently. Closer to our age than his. I swear, I think he's going to try to have another kid with her."

"I'm so sorry."

"What do you think they're up to? The old guard?" She looked afraid, so small and young. I wanted to comfort her. Unfortunately, I had more pressing matters to deal with.

"I'm not one hundred percent sure, but it does involve whatever happened in that gold mine back in 1864."

"You think it's something bad."

"I do."

"But what?"

"I don't know yet," I said. "But I'm going to find out."

From the back seat, I heard Mere issue a little sigh of sleep, just as I located Eleanor Inman's phone number on the reservation list.

"He's right here," said Isaac Inman's grandmother. "You want to talk to him?"

I wilted in relief. "Yes, please."

"Ms. Hope," came Inman's earnest, impossibly young voice. I had a brief, panicky moment of doubt. This guy was so young. How was he going to stand with me against a whole town?

"I'm so sorry to call this late, but you were asking me some questions a few weeks ago . . ."

"I remember."

"I gave you a call on the number you left me, but you never called back. You didn't, but Sheriff Childers did."

There was a moment of silence.

"Deputy?"

"That would be because I got fired a few days ago," he said. "Well, first I got taken off the case and sent off to work on some nonsense case over in Alabama, and then I got fired. I figured Childers didn't want me on the . . . particular case you and I discussed, and around here, when the powers that be decided you're gone, you're gone."

No shit.

We were almost to Alice's. I sunk lower in the wide seat. "Will you meet me at my house in an hour?" I asked him. "I'll tell you everything then."

"I'll be there. And Ms. Hope? Stay safe."

Chapter 31

At Alice's house, Mere hugged me so tightly I thought I would break. Alice gently extricated her from my grip.

"I swear I'll keep her safe," she whispered to me.

"Thank you. For everything."

Mere struggled away from Alice and wrapped her arms around my legs. "Mama," she wailed. "I want to stay with you."

I held her head, her tousled hair. "I know, baby. I know. I have to do some grown-up stuff, though, and I need you to stay with Alice while I do that." I leaned close to her ear, whispering fiercely into it. "Listen to me, Meredith Hope. I don't care what Mr. Cleburne said. You do *not* have to love this town. You love what you want to love, you hear me? It is your choice. Always your choice."

She nodded, sniffling. "I love you, Mama. That's my choice."

"I love you, too." I hugged her again, and Alice put a hand on her shoulder. I let her go, but when Alice shut the door, I felt like a huge fist had taken hold of my heart and ripped it out of my chest. I climbed back in Emmaline's Mercedes and clenched my fists as she wound through the streets off the square and headed toward my house.

I'd forgotten to leave on any lights, even on the porch, and the house looked menacing—a monster perched on the hill, wings folded, beady eyes following every movement of its intended prey. I stared up at it. There were secrets on this property. George Davenport had discovered some of them. So had Wren Street. Now it was my turn.

Emmaline told me to call her again if I needed a ride. "There's something else I haven't told you."

I stared at her.

"I know where the gold mine is. Like, the exact coordinates."

"What?"

She nodded briskly. "Wren figured it out and showed it to me before she left town."

A frisson of excitement set every hair on my body at attention. At the very same moment, a low rumble of thunder sounded in the distance. "Tell me."

"Climb down the bluff and head to the creek. There's this tree, an old oak with moss all over it. From there, use the compass on your phone. Sixty degrees northeast. The old entrance is covered with vines and stuff. But I'm pretty sure you would need some heavy machinery to dig through the embankment."

I nodded, thinking, then thanked her again and watched her drive away. I turned on my phone's flashlight and went around the back of the house to the shed. It was as dark as the house. Darker and definitely more foreboding. I'd been inside it a few times, to store extra bags of soil, fertilizer, and garden tools, but I'd never sifted through the junk heaped in various corners by George Davenport.

Thunder boomed, making me jump. I pulled the door open and shone my light around the bare-earthed space. It was a large wooden box in the back I was interested in, locked with a metal clasp. After a brief search, I spotted an old ax leaning against the wall, grabbed it, and went to work. The lock held surprisingly well, considering its age, but eventually I bashed it hard enough that it broke and fell away.

I lifted the lid and was rewarded with the sight of George Davenport's stash of explosive ingredients: pool shocker, ammonium nitrate, Drano, nail polish remover, cold packs. There were also matches, boxes and boxes of fireworks and nails. I surveyed them, wondering how the hell I was going to assemble this thing. I had no idea how to do something like that, and George certainly hadn't left me any set of instructions.

And then, in one corner of the box, tucked beneath a stack of neatly folded burlap bags, I spotted the solution to my predicament.

The nearly full moon illuminated the way, but the storm clouds were rolling in fast. I needed to hurry. At the edge of the bluff, I slid down on my rear end, holding a burlap bag carefully out in front of me. Finding the creek wasn't hard either, and in minutes, I'd located the oak tree. I turned this way and that, trying to find sixty degrees northeast, and once I had it locked, started walking at a deliberate pace. I hit the bluff at a particularly sharp rise, where the rocks formed an arch.

This had to be it. If it wasn't, I was shit out of luck. There was no time for second chances.

I lowered the bag to the ground and gently lifted out a trowel, then George Davenport's three small hand grenades, each wrapped in additional bags I'd found. I set to digging into the mass of vines and dirt of the embankment, and after about twenty minutes, I had three holes arranged in a triangle, each hole deep enough to wedge the grenades about an arm's length into the earth. I inhaled and exhaled, trembling. Was it like in the movies, where you pulled the pin ring and had a few seconds before the blast? I certainly hoped so because that was the extent of my experience with grenades. I hadn't had time to google. Sweat poured down my face and back, soaking my shirt.

Just do it, Billie. Do it.

There was no time to waste.

I drew in one last breath and held it, reaching into the first hole and pulling the pin. My heart ricocheted around in my chest, and hands shaking, I moved to the second hole when I pulled the next pin. At the third hole, the shaking was so bad that I could barely shove my hands in the hole. Sweat was blinding me, and I was quaking all over. With a cry of desperation, I pulled the final pin and stumbled back, falling, then picking myself up again and running away from the bluff. I splashed into the creek and up onto the other side, then crouched behind a fallen log. I held my breath. My heart continued to thunder.

Please, please, please . . .

Three successive booms shook the woods, instantly starting my ears to ringing and giving me a sharp, agonizing headache. I slumped against the log, panting in shock and relief, then broke into wild laughter. From my spot on the other side of the creek, it was too dark to tell if I'd adequately opened up the entrance, but still, certainly I'd done some damage. I unfolded my body. Strained to hear any sound over the ringing, but there was only silence.

Silence and the rumble of thunder. Or . . . or was that a car engine in the far-off distance?

Shit.

That was a car. Isaac Inman was already at the house. Had an hour already passed? It didn't seem possible. I waded across the creek then clambered back up the bluff, using vines to scale the steep incline. As I took off running across the field, hoping he wouldn't turn around and leave when he got there, the rain started to fall. I flew over the field, cutting around the back of the house as the car rumbled slowly up the drive. I peeked around the corner of the house, the rain pouring now, soaking me. Was it him? The car was idling, the headlights shining directly in my eyes, but it was hard to see. I threw up my hand to block the light and rain with a sinking feeling, realized I hadn't asked Inman what he drove.

"Mrs. Hope?" Isaac Inman's voice called through the rain. "Billie?"

I straightened, and for one moment I saw the dark figure of a man and he saw me. We both seemed to relax in relief.

I was about to call back to him, but before I could, a dark form flew at him, hurtling itself at Inman, tackling him to the ground. I cried out as the two figures rolled and struggled in the puddles, but I was frozen. I couldn't move. I also couldn't make out through the rain which was Inman, and which was the other person. It was just a tangled knot of bodies until suddenly it wasn't. The grappling stopped, both of them gone still, and then one of them cried out, a dull grunt of pain.

Everything slowed. The rain pounded. Another crack of thunder reverberated through the air. I saw the other man, the second one, struggle to his knees and raise his fist, which gripped a knife. Then I heard the unmistakable sound of that knife being thrust into Inman's body and the corresponding grunts, over and over again. The process was so quiet, so mundane. There was no accompanying soundtrack of shrieking violins or crashing cymbals like in a movie. Just the rain and rumble of thunder and my own pounding heart.

And then the dark form, the man who had wielded the knife, stood and slowly turned in my direction. I took one step backward. Then another.

"I can't see," said the man, and the porch lights on the house switched on.

Backlit by the harsh light, I saw the row of still, dark figures.

Five of them in all. Four standing, one sitting in a wheelchair. By their relaxed postures, it appeared they'd been there a while, watching everything that had just happened, waiting for this final moment of revelation. For the moment when all was made clear to me.

I couldn't see their faces, but I recognized their forms. Dixie and Major Minette. Toby Minette. Ox Dalzell and old James Cleburne. The old guard of Juliana, present and accounted for. I could feel their attention on me, rapt and yet somehow eerily cold. Dispassionately anticipating what was about to unfold. This was a show, it occurred to me in horrified disbelief. And I was the audience.

"Billie," said Jamie, standing by the still-running car and crumpled, motionless form of Isaac Inman. He was breathing hard, but he spoke in a gentle voice, as if I was a skittish horse. "Don't run."

His voice was like a starting pistol, springing me into action. I scooped up the burlap bag with the trowel, pivoted, and ran back the way I'd come, skidding around the side of the house, splashing through the mud and puddles. I could hear their feet clattering across the porch and down the steps. I could hear their shouts of "Come on!" and "Get her!" They were following me, at least the ones who could.

I sped up, heart slamming against my chest, heading through the downpour back to the bluff. A high-pitched noise keened in my ear, and it took me a few seconds to realize it was me, moaning. I shut my mouth and pushed my legs to move faster. I was younger than all of those assholes. I could outrun them. I just had to push harder.

I hit the edge of the bluff and without hesitation flung myself over the edge, landing about a third of the way down then sliding and tumbling through the mud, head over heels, the rest of the way. A rock stopped my momentum, one of the rocks the grenade blast must've dislodged. I could still hear their shouts through the storm, but no shadowy forms appeared along the bluff. Not yet. I scrambled up, grabbing the bag and headed for the hole in the earth that I'd just blown open.

For the gold mine.

Chapter 32

George Davenport's grenades had either been too old or not the kind made to do much damage, but the hole they'd made in the hillside was roughly the size of a drainage pipe. Not to be deterred, I jumped up and wiggled into it, pulling the burlap bag behind me, like some kind of precious talisman. It wasn't much, but if it came to it, I'd have no problem using the garden trowel to protect myself. But if they had knives, they surely had guns.

I was fucked.

I kept my head down and concentrated on breathing calmly and evenly as I inched farther into the side of the hill, deeper into the earth, clawing away more dirt. It wouldn't help to hyperventilate in here. I said a silent prayer that Emmaline had been right and the tunnel I'd blown open would lead me to the mine and not some dead end. This was a bad dream. Because it couldn't be real, could it? The hellish host of Juliana, standing together so calmly on my porch. Waiting there for me. It was something out of a nightmare. And my daughter was still out there.

Be okay, Mere, I thought. *I'm coming back for you.*

I'd gone maybe a dozen yards when I felt the dirt loosen, and I was able to dig with my hands and widen the narrow hole a bit more. I could crawl now, on my forearms first and then on all fours, and at last I tumbled out into the airy darkness, dropping to the floor with a thud. I caught my breath and righted myself. It was inky black in here, the dark, a thick, heavy, suffocating and solid thing. I closed my eyes to shut it out. To keep it from being more than it was. I could use my phone's light, but that would only last so long, and I needed to ration it. There was no predicting how long I'd be stuck in here.

I shivered, soaking wet, mud encrusted. I could hear the echo of drips in the cavern beyond, their percussive rhythm settling my heartbeat. Cautiously, I stood, reaching around me, but felt nothing—no walls, no ceiling. I needed to orient myself. I swiped down on my phone, hit the flashlight, and held it up.

I was in a tunnel, about ten feet tall by twenty feet wide, that had been hewn into the side of the earth. The walls and ceiling were solid rock, slimed over with water and rust stains and some sort of mysterious, phosphorescent green stuff. Heavy wood timbers braced the walls and ceilings. There was a set of iron tracks running along the floor of the tunnel.

The air was cool and damp. The narrow hole I'd crawled through was the only entry point. A few chunks of dirt and rock had fallen in from the explosion or from my entry, and I scooped up as much as I could and packed it back into the narrow hole. It wasn't exactly a deterrent, but it would have to do. I headed into the tunnel, deeper into the mine, breaking into a slow trot.

The ground was slippery, but I didn't dare slow down. If those ghouls were able to find the opening in the side of the bank, if one of them could crawl through the hole—or if they somehow managed to blow open a larger opening—I needed to be as far away as possible. Even if I was running directly toward a dead end.

I picked my way down a long set of rickety wooden steps, half of them rotted through, to a lower level, where I dropped from the last available plank to the hard rock floor below. Deeper and deeper down the tunnel I ran, stopping momentarily to peer into smaller offshoot tunnels, only to discover they only went a few yards before ending in massive walls of rock.

I was puffing now, out of breath and sweating. My bobbing light, trained ahead of me, seemed to have hit a different sort of wall. A darker surface, different from the brownish gray of the other rock. What was it? I was deep under the surface of the earth, could feel the weight of it above me. Here, under the earth's crust, I was a lost voice. A thin, wisp of nothing. Easily snuffed out and silenced forever.

Suddenly my foot hit something lying across the path, and I pitched forward, my phone flying into the dark. I grunted in pain but felt around, quickly recovering the phone and righting myself. The obstacle, a piece of equipment, like a long, thin, metal machine gun, appeared to be an old-fashioned drill. I crawled over it, peering ahead in the thin beam of light, and when I saw what I'd almost done, I let out a yelp of terror. Dozens of feet below me, in a huge cavern, shimmered a black pool of water. The light on my phone had been shining into empty space. Tripping over the drill had just prevented me from running straight off the edge of a cliff.

I scurried a safe distance away from the edge, my heart pounding, bile threatening to rise. I collapsed against the rock wall, gulping in deep breaths, then closed my eyes, straining to hear any indication that someone had followed me. Hearing nothing, I relaxed against the rock wall, trying to lower my heart rate. I needed to think. There had to be another way out. A tunnel I hadn't noticed before that branched off in a better direction.

Think, Billie . . .

I ran through all my options, none of which were good. And I was so tired, it suddenly occurred to me. Exhausted from the day I'd had, traumatized by the discovery of Peter, from seeing Isaac Inman so brutally, savagely stabbed . . .

A wave of lightheadedness hit me. Followed by a wave of despair.

Mere . . . Mom . . .

Was I ever going to see them again?

I was feeling so groggy now, my head lolling on my neck as heavy as a bowling ball. It was like the worst kind of high, the kind where you felt simultaneously wired and like you were floating through space. It was like that day with Jamie in my house. How disconnected I had felt from my body. From my will . . .

God, I was actually falling asleep.

I blinked hard a few times and pulled out my phone. There was no way I was going to have a signal down here. And yet, impossibly, one bar showed. I tried Alice first, but the call rolled to voicemail. I tried Mom then and waited for the beep after her outgoing message.

"Mom," I said, my voice breaking and echoing in the cavern. I hadn't even thought about what I was going to say, and now . . . now, I had to say it.

"Mom," I started again. "I'm . . . I'm in a bad spot, it turns out. I don't know what's going to happen, but I do know . . ." I took a deep breath. "I know I love you. That's it. I love you so much."

I hung up, then pillowed my head on my crossed arms, and then lay flat on the rocky floor of the cave. I was so goddamn tired. I would just rest for a few minutes. Just until I could think more clearly to make a plan . . .

I closed my eyes and slept.

* * *

I dreamed I was in the mine, but it was bright as a moonlit night, lit up with candles wedged into the cracks and crevices of the hard rock. The slick-wet walls glimmered with iridescent streaks of quartz, like permanent, continually flashing bolts of lightning, a subterranean cathedral.

I was on the lower level, but back at the foot of the wooden stairs. Faint music drifted through the cold, damp air, the plaintive cry of a faraway fiddle. I strained to hear the tune, but I couldn't make it out, so I walked down the tunnel, into the heart of the mine, following the same path I had before. I wasn't afraid. I only wanted to follow the sound of the music, to find who could be playing so beautifully, with so much heart-aching melancholy.

Besides the music and candles, there were other signs of life: drooping bouquets of wildflowers tied with ribbon and draped over nails in the timber braces, or over chisels stuck in the rock. There were not only shimmering streaks of quartz in the rock walls, now I saw gold there, too. Thick, rich veins of it running this way and that, crisscrossing the rocks in a fretwork of gilding.

The music grew louder. I could hear voices now, too. Simple, untrained voices, singing a song I recognized.

We shall meet but we shall miss him.
There will be one vacant chair.
We shall linger to caress him,
While we breathe our evening prayer.
When one year ago we gathered
Joy was in his mild blue eye,
Now the golden cord is severed,
And our hopes in ruin lie.

I came upon them in one of the safety tunnels—that's what they were called, I suddenly knew, built to provide the miners a place to hide when they blasted the rock—singing in quavering unison. Women and children huddled together, led in their song by a woman dressed in a long white dress. She was older, in her sixties, I guessed, and wore a wreath of gray braids around her head. Her eyes were not glittering jet, but a blue fire, and a silver cross hung from a chain around her neck. The woman from my dreams.

My mother, it occurred to me, with a jolt of recognition. And somehow at the same time, not my mother.

I was overcome with relief. Relief and joy and a surging of love. *Mom!* She'd come back to me. I wanted to run to her, to wrap my arms around her, but I knew I wasn't supposed to interrupt this solemn moment. I stood at the back of the tunnel watching the people, her people, sing the hymn. Another woman played the fiddle, a young boy the banjo. As the group sang, the old woman who was also my mother spoke to each of them, her lips close to their ears. Then they would step forward and put something in a crevice that ran like a seam down the length of the tunnel wall.

I pushed my way into the crowd, to get closer, to hear the words she was whispering to them. It was a hiss.

Never let them forget.

Never let them forget.

After she said those words, she turned her face toward me. Warmth filled me from head to toe. "How would you make them remember, Billie?" Her lined face, so familiar to me, and yet so unfamiliar, covered in a sheen of sweat, was so close to mine, I could feel her heat. Smell her rank breath. It was the smell of hunger, when a starved body had begun to eat away at itself.

"What have they taken from you?" she asked in her smoky cigarette voice. "Your heart? Your soul? The very hope that used to pulse within you and kept you going?"

I felt a tear slip down my cheek.

After the last item had been pushed into the crevice, the crowd of women and children shifted and turned, and now the old woman was leading them out of the safety tunnel and into the main one. I stood still, watching them file past, following her like sheep. They sang and she turned, bestowing a smile on them. She smiled sweetly over her shoulder at me, too, and beckoned me to follow. Soon we all arrived at the edge of the cliff, the one I'd nearly hurtled over.

"Join hands," my mother, the old woman, said in a solemn voice, and I felt hands on either side of me take mine.

I looked down. There was water below us, a huge pool of phosphorescent green water, but so far away.

"They will not prevail," my mother said. "We will martyr ourselves and bring the curse of our blood upon their heads." Her words echoed through the rock tunnels. The people lined up at the edge of the cliff swayed in the echo. I saw they had brought the old drill, dragged it to the edge, and kicked it over. It fell into the pool below with a thunderous splash. A cheer went up and they all clapped.

Suddenly my mother's face was next to mine. "Don't you see? That song we sing is not a hymn. It's a curse. A curse on all those who stand on the ground above our heads. They think they are above us. They think they are free, but they will not be. Because we pronounce a curse, here and now, in the bowels of the sacred earth, that they will never forget. Listen."

The women and children beside me were calling out curses in thin, quavering voices. Curses that would fall on the men who did this to them. On the town who turned its back on this evil.

A winged horse of war! one shouted.

A great eagle with horns, called out a small girl, *and talons for ripping flesh!*

A demon in every dog, cat, and horse! cried a boy.

Shaking hands and faulty minds!
Blood in the river, in the creeks, and the streams!

The voices overlapped now, rose like thunder in my ears. My mother's breath was warm on my neck. "You see? They curse their murderers. You can do it, too, Billie. You must do it. Make them pay for taking your family from you."

But I couldn't think of any curse to utter. I could see that she was disappointed in me. That I had failed her.

"Now jump," she said.

The gold and quartz walls glimmered in the candlelight. No one moved.

"Jump!" my mother roared, and I saw them leap. Heard the splash of bodies.

I turned to look at her. "I can't. I'm scared."

Her eyes bore into me. God, I missed her. I missed her so much.

"You can."

I shook my head.

"Of course you can, Billie. Don't you understand what you are?" she asked me in a fierce whisper.

A failure . . . a cheat . . . a worthless piece of shit . . .

"No, Billie. No." Her lips curled in a feline smile as she read my thoughts. "You're a goddamn Catawampus."

I felt one bone-rattling jerk, a push, and I was falling through the air. There was a rush of cold air and in the next instant, the shock of water closing over me. I let myself go, let the water take me, and the world burst open. It was a world of light and sound and vibration and possibility. I saw when the earth was formed, and the seams layered into the rock. I saw those seams—golds and whites and shimmering silvers—shooting off in all different directions, blasting through the rocks and dirt and mountains like they were nothing. Filling every crack, cooling, hardening into an impenetrable wall.

We were all seams of precious stone filling the cracks of the world. Hiding in the unforgiving rock. I saw the truth of myself, that my seam was nothing but a void of longing and desire and need. The longing for my mother, a mother who would never leave. A mother who would say, *You are gold to me.* A need to hear that I, Billie Hope—not so burnished, not so pure—belonged. Billie Hope was acceptable because she was *she.* I was me.

But I would have to be chiseled out first, I saw that. Even now I was being chiseled out by something horrible that had been conceived and born here in the center of the earth. Not a winged horse, but an old woman with gray braids and a silver cross who held an old-fashioned drill. The drill hammered the rock and me, because now I had become a part of the rock and the quartz and the gold. It was all dust, all raining into the rail cars waiting on the tracks below. I was the rubble. I would be smashed for the gold that lay inside me. And then people who were cannier than me would take that gold from me, profit from it, and I would be left alone on the floor of the stamping mill. The dust to be trampled underfoot for centuries to come.

I was dust. Only dust . . .

I woke, a scream trying to make its way out of my mouth but feeling a hand over my mouth, blocking it.

"Don't say a fucking word," hissed the voice that belonged to the hand. "Don't you make one goddamn, fucking sound."

I craned my neck, squinted hard, trying to see who it was, but I'd forgotten there was no light in this godforsaken tunnel. I couldn't see a thing.

"You're Billie Hope, right?" hissed the voice. A woman's voice.

I nodded, afraid to say anything more.

"If I take my hand away, you cannot scream, you hear me?"

I nodded again. The hand went away. I pushed myself up against the hard rock wall. "Who are you?"

The woman was feeling around in her pockets, looking for something, and then she found it. A small battery-operated lantern, which she switched on. The glow of it illuminated her face in harsh, nightmarish shadows, the way kids would stick a flashlight under their chin to scare their friends.

"I'm Wren. Wren Street. I hear you've been asking questions about me."

Chapter 33

I stared at the woman sitting before me, barely comprehending what I was seeing. Who I was seeing.

Wren Street.

In the flesh. Not dead, a pile of remains by the mill, but 100 percent alive.

Her eyes blazed and her lithe body was clad in dark leggings and a soaking wet oversized T-shirt that clung to her. She also didn't have the dreadlocks she used to have. Her hair was shorn in a buzz cut. She cocked her head with an expression of patient impatience. She looked a little like Finch and Falcon. Exactly like Temperance. I burst into wild cackling laughter.

"They think you're dead," I gasped. "They found your remains at the mill."

"The fuck are you talking about?" she asked, her voice sharp.

"Or maybe I just thought you were dead. I'm not thinking clearly."

She settled beside me, drawing up her knees and propping her arms on them. "It's just as well."

My head was still full of the disturbing nightmare I'd just had, and I was having a hard time accepting that I was truly awake. "They know I'm in here. They were following me."

"I know. It's fine, at least for now," Wren said. "I was hiding in the woods when you blew those grenades earlier, and after you left, I crawled in. I saw you crawl in later and run deeper into the mine. They were outside looking for you, but I'm pretty sure the rain slowed them down. They couldn't find your blast hole in the dark, and I heard them say they'd come back at dawn. And they made sure we can't leave. They left a lookout."

"Jamie," I said.

She nodded. "I texted Emmaline and told her to try to contact the next county's sheriff's department or the Georgia Bureau of Investigation. We should sit tight. Wait until daylight and one of the good guys shows up . . . hopefully before the bad guys do."

"How long have you been in town?" I asked. "How long have you been watching me?"

"A few weeks, on and off. I've been low-key staying with the Dalzell girls in their mother's house. They told me what was going on after you and Alice stopped by. I was just in the trunk of Emmaline's car when she dropped you off at your house."

I nodded slowly, trying to assemble the puzzle pieces.

"Emmaline said you found some gold nuggets," she said.

I shook my head. "I don't care about any gold. I was just trying to figure out why Mayor Dixie and the rest of the old guard didn't want us to find this mine. They killed a deputy who was coming to talk to me. They killed my husband, Peter."

"I know."

"They killed him because he was talking to Alice about you and your friends and what you were doing at the Dalzell-Davenport house." *And because Jamie wants me for himself.*

"I think those remains they found might be a friend of mine," Wren said.

I stared at her. "Who?"

"Someone I met in New York and who was living with us for a while at the Dalzell-Davenport house. But I want to hear your story first. I've been dying to contact you so we could talk, but me and the Dalzells . . . well, we weren't sure if we could trust you."

I wanted to laugh at that.

"You were having a dream, weren't you? Just now?"

I nodded. I still felt the shock and relief at seeing my mother, at being so close to her again. I peered down the shaft. The drill that I'd tripped over was gone.

Had I been walking in my sleep and thrown it over the ledge into the water like in my dream? Or had I just imagined it was there in the first place? Or . . .

. . . or had it never been there in the first place?

Jesus, I was really losing it.

"You know," Wren said, like she could read my mind. "It's because of the carbon monoxide."

I looked backed at her. "There's gas? Down here?"

She nodded. "They didn't properly seal it when they blew the entrance up back in 1864. There's been gas leaking from this hole for probably over a hundred and sixty years. Haven't you noticed how everybody's just a little off their rocker in Juliana? Nobody remembers anything, everybody's got the shakes. It's like Whoville on really good bud in that town. You and your husband probably had it worse because you were living right on top of it. It fucked me up when I lived there. I couldn't sleep. I had nightmares."

I thought of that hallucinatory afternoon with Jamie. The nightmares and bizarre visions. If Wren was right, my whole family had been breathing in poisonous gas for months. Mere.

Poor old Ramsey. For some reason, Peter had suffered the worst. His insomnia, his irritability, and then constant sleeping. It would be a tidy explanation for all of it, wouldn't it?

Except for the dream I just had. The curses I'd heard those poor, doomed women and children pronounce on their murderers before jumping to their deaths. Curses that matched up with the things we had all experienced in the past few months . . .

"I've seen you with Temperance," Wren said, jolting me from my thoughts. "I followed you and Mom to the school on open house day. Tell me about her."

My eyes reflexively filled, thinking of Mere, but I swallowed the tears back. "She's extraordinary. Really smart and sunny. Imaginative. She's my daughter Mere's best friend."

Wren's eyes looked shiny, and she wiped her nose. She looked like she wanted to say something but didn't, just glanced away, nodding.

"Why didn't you take her with you when you left before?" I asked. "Why did you leave her with Lilah?"

"I knew she would be safer with her than with me. My mom is a good person. She has no idea who these people really are, and she never will, if the old guard has their way. That's how they keep their power, by making sure everybody else stays in the dark." She laughed. "Quite literally, in one aspect."

"I don't understand."

"It's a long story, how this nightmare started."

"We've got till sunrise. Tell me."

Wren Street wasn't the average Juliana girl. She had excelled in painting in high school, and it wasn't long before she was being showered with scholarships, most notably from the prestigious Pratt Institute in Brooklyn, which she accepted. Wren missed Juliana, but she blossomed in New York, in and out of the classroom. She loved her classes. She loved the nightlife even more. She went to underground parties, funky, off-off

Broadway shows, avant-garde performance art pieces. She also was introduced to a wide range of drugs. At one of the many drug-fueled parties, she encountered a young woman named Madge Beatty. Just a few years older than Wren, Madge was from Toronto, a college dropout who moved to New York. Madge's parents were from Canada and happy enough to let Madge live off her Beatty family trust fund and create art.

Madge Beatty was everything Wren aspired to be. Worldly, sophisticated, and truly gifted. A trustafarian, the girl jokingly called herself, someone with plenty of money but who chose to live simply. Madge was a sculptor who worked in pine wood and gold leaf. She had a fire-hose work ethic and a manic desire for her art to leave a legacy. Wren was blown away with Madge's talent, and soon the two became close, moving into a broken-down Brooklyn warehouse that Madge had bought as a twenty-first birthday gift to herself.

Wren had asked about one of her sculptures, the figure of a girl, naked, lithe, an enigmatic expression on her wooden face as Madge had dripped molten gold over her. The gold spattered on the tarp below, and Wren thought it looked like a Klimt painting come to life. Madge said the piece represented her great-great-great-grandmother who'd worked in a gold mine down in Juliana, Georgia.

Wren was stunned. "You mean Juliana, where I'm from?" She'd never met anyone outside of the town who had any connection to the place. Everyone she knew from there stayed there.

Madge confessed the truth: she'd always been obsessed with the origins of her ancestor, how she'd come to work in the mine. When she'd found out that Wren was from Juliana, she'd befriended her, hoping Wren would help her discover more. She didn't want Wren to think badly of her. "I just couldn't believe that I was going to meet someone from that town," she said. "It seemed like . . . destiny."

Wren didn't think badly of Madge. To the contrary, she was intrigued. "But," she assured Madge, "there was never a gold mine in Juliana." She knew Juliana's history backward and forward.

Madge hadn't backed down. "Oh, there was. My ancestor worked in it until the town elders heard Sherman was coming on his way to Atlanta, so they herded all the workers, the women and children, inside and disguised the entrance. Sherman marched through, never realizing he was marching right past a gold mine."

Wren sat in stunned silence.

"They never got them out," Madge went on to tell her. "The town elders buried those women and children alive. They murdered all those defenseless people. Only my ancestor, who was twelve years old, got away. She ran all the way to Canada."

Madge explained to Wren that the miners and their families were the poor, working class. They didn't associate with the wealthier families in Juliana, the old guard. Each group had their own churches, schools—or lack thereof. They even lived in a completely separate part of town. It would've been easy enough for the town elders to convince everyone that Sherman had shipped off the women and children and that no one was to speak of the tragedy or the mine. When the men came back from the war, the town elders probably fed them the same bullshit, and as the years passed by, a lie became the truth.

Wren was enthralled and horrified by the story. She and Madge stayed up all night, discussing a new idea: move down to Juliana and investigate the century-old murder—maybe make a podcast about the incident. But then, a few weeks later, Wren discovered she was pregnant as a result of a casual dalliance, and their plans were put on hold.

Wren made the decision to keep the baby and returned home to Juliana. She had the vague but heroic goal of discovering the truth about what had happened in her hometown on her own, this new baby becoming a symbol of sorts of Juliana's fresh start. For a while, things went well, but then reality hit hard. Wren's addiction resurfaced with a vengeance, and when Temperance turned three, Lilah insisted Wren move out. Wren traveled for a few years, always returning to Juliana to see her daughter. When she did, she slept in the town square.

At the beginning of the pandemic, Wren was at a low point, financially and emotionally. Madge and her motley group of trustafarian friends, needing to flee New York, came down to Juliana to help Wren out. They all moved into the abandoned Dalzell-Davenport place, where Madge helped Wren wean herself off the pills and convinced her to return to their original mission from those college days—locating the site of the gold mine and blowing the whole story wide open. The podcast they were going to make would take the world by fire. It would be a reckoning with the past. An examination of the enduring theme of the way the privileged class view the working class as expendable. A transgressive, rebellious, beautiful work of art.

Since Wren had gotten nowhere asking questions in town, they would start their investigation by contacting the spirits of the dead women and children. The three Dalzell girls joined them, and a stream of eclectic guests rotated through the house. They bound everyone to secrecy and held séances. Some of the group experienced strange, hallucinatory experiences, which they attributed to psychic phenomena. When Wren found George Davenport's books and surmised they were living close to the mine, she was ecstatic. She found the spot where they thought the original entrance had been, written on a page in Davenport's ledger. They were so close to uncovering the story.

Then Wren received the death threat. Two of the Dalzell girls returned to their mother's place and then a few of the others bugged out as well. Even Madge was getting antsy, stir-crazy, and bored with the podcast idea. She left one night without even saying goodbye.

Wren, alone and scared, came to the terrible conclusion that she had to go, too. Temperance would be safe with Lilah, and when enough time had passed, and the furor had died down, Wren could send for her. Taking only Davenport's notation of where the mine was located with her—the ripped-out page from the ledger—she hitched rides out to California. Peter, using the phone number Alice gave him, had contacted her out there, explaining who he was and what he suspected about Juliana. She'd come back then, holing up at the Dalzell girls' house on the outskirts of town.

"Peter knew something was wrong with this place," Wren said to me now. "Very wrong. I think he believed I was the only person he could trust who would tell the truth."

"Why did you tell Alice Tilton that story about it being Sherman who'd murdered the women and children?"

"She's been my best friend since we were kids," Wren said. "I had to tell her something—what I was doing in the house— but I didn't know that I could totally trust her. She was dating Jamie Cleburne. If she married him, she'd become one of the old guard. Maybe she'd try to stop us from doing the podcast."

"Okay, that's what I still don't understand," I asked. "Why would the old guard go to such lengths to keep the truth from coming out? It's been over a hundred and sixty years. No one's alive who was involved."

"I don't understand it either."

"But they killed my husband and Deputy Inman and . . ." The realization hit me. "Madge. You think the remains at the mill that Inman found are Madge."

She nodded.

I held her gaze. "So old guard has murdered three people. But I don't believe it was to hide some piece of ancient history. I believe they did it because they're hiding something they've done recently."

"I agree. Something big," Wren said.

"Yeah," I said, feeling even worse than I did before. What could be bigger than three murders? I had no idea, but we were about to find out.

Just then, I felt a strange sensation. That of the earth rumbling beneath me, as if it was realigning itself. Swaying and sliding into a new formation. And then, a percussive wave hit us followed by a deafening explosion that rocked the walls around us, showering down rocks and dust on our heads.

Chapter 34

Wren jumped up when the shower of rubble subsided. "It's them. They've come back."

"Shit!" I scrambled up, then nearly fell again because I felt so weak. Was it really carbon monoxide, like Wren said? I did still feel out of it. Out of it and panicked out of my mind. Not a winning combination. "Do you think Emmaline got the police?"

"No idea, but from the sound of it, they've blown open the entrance, and we don't have time to find out." She was looking around. "This goddamn tunnel only goes in one direction. Come on, give me your hand. We've got to go!"

She hauled me up as another explosion rocked the tunnel.

"We have to go down. To the lower level," Wren said. "There's supposed to be a side tunnel, a way that leads to the surface. But if we can't find that, at least there might be a place to hide."

I thought for a minute, begging my brain to penetrate the fog that had wrapped itself around it. "They jumped."

Wren eyed me, doubtful.

"The women and children that were trapped here. That must've been how the one girl found her way out. We can do it, too. With rain and stuff, the water table should have risen in the past one hundred and sixty years, so the pool might be a lot deeper."

Now we heard the roar of some kind of heavy construction equipment, working back at the entrance.

"They've got a fucking Bobcat," Wren said in disbelief.

There was another tooth-rattling boom, and we sprang to life, running the few yards to the ledge that hung over the pool. Panting, we looked down. Now that I was seeing it again, I realized it had to be over a thirty-foot drop to the water. High enough that it made me dizzy. High enough that if the pool was too shallow, we'd be in a bad way.

The sound of faint voices rang out behind us—"Come on!" "Let's go!" "This way!"—and we exchanged terrified looks.

"There's no other way," I said.

"Agreed. But slide, don't jump," Wren said.

We scooted over the edge on our bellies, hung by our fingertips, then attempted a sort of combo repelling-slipping maneuver until we finally were close enough to the pool of dark water to drop safely into it.

I held my breath and hit the surface hard, going deep, deeper than I'd expected. The water was freezing, and for the few moments I was completely submerged, all my stunned brain could picture was the bones of all those women and children that lay at the bottom, just beneath me. When at last I broke the surface, I gasped in a combination of shock and fear and extreme cold and paddled furiously toward the dim light.

"Billie!"

My name echoed against the rock walls of the cavern. I looked around and saw Wren already on the other side, drenched, on a small outcropping of rock on the far edge of the pool. I swam toward her, and she hauled me out of the water up onto the rock. I was shivering but the freezing water had woken me up. My head felt clear, the fear reduced to a manageable level.

Wren peered into my face. "You okay?"

I nodded, breathing hard. "Do you see the way out, the passage—?"

"Hey!" came a voice, shouting from the top of the cliff down at us.

We lifted our gaze up the sheer rock wall, and I felt my heart go still. They were there, standing in one long formidable row, shining their lanterns down at us. The Minettes—Dixie, Major, and Toby—Ox Dalzell, and Jamie Cleburne.

"Gang's all here," muttered Wren. Except the wheelchair-bound James Sr. He was probably still posted back at my house, ready to sound the alarm call if he saw anyone heading toward the mine.

"Got yourself into a pickle, looks like." Ox, of course, sounding like he'd just happened upon us at a barbeque.

"Where's my daughter?" I yelled up at Jamie. "What have you done with her?"

Jamie gazed down at me, a mild expression on his face. "She's safe, Billie. Still at Alice's where you left her. We would never hurt her."

"You expect me to believe that?" I retorted. "You murdered Isaac Inman, an officer of the law. You murdered my husband and dumped his body in your lake!" I was seething, breathing fire.

"Pipe down, Billie," snapped Dixie Minette. "Your daughter's fine. And you have no right to judge us. We do what we have to do for Juliana. You should understand that by now. Juliana comes first."

Jamie put out an arm to silence her. "Billie, you don't understand what we have here in Juliana. It's not the kind of thing you could find where you're from. Up there, it's all about the individual. You look out for number one and make sure nobody infringes on your precious rights. But here, we take care of each other. We live, we bleed, we die for each other." His voice turned gentle. "That's why you came to us. Because you were looking for that same sense of belonging. You were *longing* for it."

"I never asked to be a part of your sick, twisted secret society!" I screamed at him. "I did not agree to the rules. And I never will. I want out, Dixie. Whatever I have to do, I want out today."

"It doesn't work that way, Billie," Dixie said smoothly. "You should know that by now. It may be too late for Miss Street there—she's proven she can't be trusted with Juliana's secrets— but you, Billie, you're different."

I didn't know what she was talking about. What made me so different?

"You have a chance to redeem yourself," she went on. "A chance to take part in Juliana's beautiful future. To become a part of one of the original founding families."

My expression hardened, but my legs felt weak. What was she saying?

"Billie. History is always two stories—the story they teach in the classroom, and the real one. You may think you know our story, the one about the gold mine and the women and children, but you truly know only a fraction of what really happened."

Major stepped forward, closer to the edge. His face was creased with concern. With the fire of a true believer's fever.

"Miss Billie," he said, his voice pleading," just listen to Dixie and Jamie. We love you so much. And we love Mere, too. What happened with Peter—" He hesitated, looking anguished. "Well, it's sad, but—"

"Hush, Major," Dixie snapped. "Billie doesn't need us to sugarcoat it. She's a big girl. We can tell her the truth."

I was trembling. *The truth.* It was going to be something horrible, something so ghastly, but there was no stopping it now. Everyone was looking at Jamie, and in the lantern light, his face looked skeletal and grim.

314 *Emily Carpenter*

"It was a divine accident," he said gravely. "The elders only understood the true power of what they'd done after the war was over. When the rest of the South was suffering through the abuses of Reconstruction, Juliana was doing just fine. Business was thriving, farms were producing bumper crops. The sawmill brought in business from all over the state and the citizens grew wealthy. Alfred Minette knew why. He'd tried to tell them before, but it was only then that the other elders truly believed. Those women and children, the ones they'd buried in the mine, they had been a sacrifice. An offering for the well-being of our town . . . made to the protector of our town. And she rewarded them."

"The protector of their town?" I asked incredulously.

"Juliana Minette." Jamie's voice was low and reverent. "Firstborn of Alfred Minette. Protector of our town. Angel who watches over us. Good Juliana. Gentle Juliana . . ."

"*Gentle, Gentle Juliana.*" The others repeated in a chilling monotone. Their voices overlapped each other and echoed through the walls over the cavern. I thought of the town grace. The way they all kissed their Juliana charms like subservient acolytes. A wave of horror convulsed me. Jamie had actually been telling the truth when he'd said these people worshipped Juliana.

They literally worshipped a dead girl.

"After that the founders faithfully taught their families about our patron," Jamie continued. "How she watched over them. How her benevolent wings kept them covered. How she brought the rainfall and the sun. How she brought forth the harvest and caused the life of this town to grow. Every generation of Minette, Dalzell, and Cleburne taught the one after it. That Juliana watched over us . . . but that, sometimes, a sacrifice was needed to prove our devotion."

"*I will freely sacrifice unto thee. I will praise thy name, O Lord, for it is good,*" Mayor Dixie said.

"You people are crazy," Wren said.

"You shut your mouth, you dumb bitch," Toby snapped.

Jamie sent a condescending smile in Wren's direction. "Any crazier than the person who prays that God will help him pick the right lottery numbers? Any crazier than the guy who gives up caffeine or beer for Lent and thinks that will help him sell more insurance policies at work?" He smirked. "You poor, oblivious child . . . you have no idea what our three families did for you. We *carried* you—year after year, generation after generation. We took responsibility for your well-being, and we bore that burden so *you* could sleep at night. So you could live your carefree lives and build your wealth and grow your families."

"How many people did you kill?" Wren shouted at him. "I want a number."

He shrugged. "It's not relevant. And it's none of your business."

"George Davenport?" Wren asked.

"He drove himself crazy," he said. "We didn't have to do a thing."

"What about Emma, your wife?" I asked.

"She's alive and well," Jamie said mildly. "But I'm assuming you're referring to the remains at the mill. That's our Canadian interloper, I'm afraid. Madge Beatty."

Wren let out a muffled cry.

"As you know, the virus was a challenge, and the town was struggling. Ms. Beatty was asking a lot of questions she shouldn't have been. Like you, Wren."

"So you murdered her," Wren said.

"We call it an offering," he corrected in a matter-of-fact voice.

"Well, it didn't work, did it?" Wren spat. "Your offering. You still had to do the Initiative. You still had to bribe people to come live in your precious, pathetic town."

The group shared amused looks, and Jamie laughed. "We

didn't start the Initiative to help Juliana." He focused on me now, his face gone still and soft. "Juliana's original three families were in danger of dying out. Toby here was single. Ox was, too, and didn't think he could trust his daughters with the truth. And my wife had moved back to D.C. We started the Initiative to ensure the old guard would endure."

They all turned to look at me.

I swallowed, my throat cracked and dry, as the horrific truth hit me. "You targeted me," I said in a voice I didn't recognize.

Jamie nodded. "I had never forgotten seeing you years before in New York. The way you were with the customers. With the staff. You were so beautiful. So capable. Such a *leader*. I knew you were the one for me, Billie. The one meant to help carry on the Cleburne name."

I was trembling now, uncontrollably. I wanted to scream, but the scream was locked inside me.

"It wasn't ideal," he went on, "you already being married, but I couldn't deny how I felt. I took it to the council"—he sent the others an appreciative look—"and they were kind enough to give their blessing and allow you and Peter to buy the Dalzell-Davenport house. When we actually met that day outside the old general store . . ." He seemed to search for the right words. ". . . you were so perfect. Everything I'd dreamed of. And you felt it, too, I could tell. You wanted me just as much as I wanted you."

I shook my head. It was all I could do.

I was the reason Peter was dead.

It was my fault.

"It felt like destiny when you and Peter started to have problems. And then when I saw him the morning he left you, getting a coffee in the bakery, he blamed me. He almost took a swing at me, if you can believe it. The therapist turned out to be a tough guy." Jamie chuckled. "It was so easy, Billie, to follow him to the outskirts of town. To run his car off the road, take care of him then hide the body. A quick text from his phone to you, and it was done."

I was shaking now, sobbing. "So . . . what, Jamie? You were just going to make me—make Peter's daughter—think that he had gone back to New York and didn't ever want to see us again? You were going let us suffer like that? You were going to let a *child* suffer like that?"

"You didn't love him the way you should've, Billie. I think you would've accepted that he was gone. You would've let him go."

"I would've never accepted it!" I screamed.

Jamie looked consternated. "Oh, Billie, no. Please don't cry. I swear to you, everything's going to work out. I'm going to give you the life you've always wanted. You'll have the love and loyalty and support of a community. You and Mere will finally have a family."

I wiped my tears away. "I had a family."

"You didn't love Peter, Billie. You told me you didn't know him anymore."

"That didn't mean I didn't want him anymore!" I screamed, my throat raw. "It didn't mean I wanted him dead!"

Mayor Dixie stepped forward. "Billie, calm down. You have a choice to make here. Accept Jamie's offer of marriage—"

I made a sound, something between a scoff and a sob.

"—or we'll deal with you. You have to understand, Billie—" She drew herself up. "Juliana Minette was not just a girl. She is the spirit of this town. She *is* this town. And this town is us. Don't you see what I'm trying to tell you? We are all intertwined. It's the divine mystery, a beautiful gift. A gift you're being offered—"

"Okay, I'm going to need you to shut the fuck up," Wren barked, at the same time pulling a gun, sleek and black, out of the waistband of her leggings. She pointed it at Mayor Dixie.

"You all just want power, plain and simple," Wren said.

"And you are so deluded that you think *killing* people brings you some kind of good luck? You should all be put away!"

"You believe that gun gives you power, don't you?" Dixie asked.

"Yeah, I do."

"But it doesn't," Dixie said. "Power is so much bigger than a weapon you hold in your hand. We know that because we have found real power. Power that's not of this earth. That's not contained. *For the weapons of our warfare are not of the flesh but have divine power to destroy strongholds—*"

"Let us go, Dixie," Wren interrupted. "Or I start pulling this trigger."

But would it even work? She'd just been in the water.

"We will not," Mayor Dixie said simply. "We cannot. You've set yourself against us and therefore against Juliana. She sees and she knows."

Wren lifted the gun and fired it. A deafening crack rang out in the contained, airless space. Instinctively, I hit the ground. So did the figures standing on the cliff above us. Apparently, the gun worked just fine.

"Wren, no!" I shouted.

But she ignored me and, moving down the row, kept taking expert shots at each figure like they were ducks at a carnival booth firing range. I was screaming at her to stop, frozen between wanting to tackle her and thinking I should not be standing here witnessing cold-blooded murder. In seconds, the ledge was empty, save for two dark forms, Mayor Dixie and Ox, who lay crumpled on the ground. Toby, Jamie, and Major were nowhere to be seen.

Wren lowered the gun. "Follow me," she said in a voice like ice.

I didn't move. My legs felt like water. "Jesus, Wren. Where did you get a gun?"

"This is Georgia. Easier than getting French fries at a drive-thru." She stuck the gun in her waistband. "Billie, I need you to focus. We've got to go."

"How?" I felt dazed. Lost.

"Madge said there was a passage around here somewhere. Remember? It's how her ancestor got out. We need to find it. You with me?"

I inhaled. It was a long shot, but we didn't have a choice. Any second, Jamie and Toby, both of them young and strong enough to give chase, would be heading down the same way we had. Not only that, they had eyes on Mere and access to her, too, if that's what they wanted. I'd unwittingly given these people my daughter. All Wren and I had was Madge's hand-me-down family tale.

I glanced up at the cliff's edge. All the townspeople had vanished. Either shot or holed somewhere formulating a new plan. We had no choice but to go deeper into the mine and try to find the way out. I had to find Mere. That was all that mattered. That was what I lived for.

"I'm with you," I said.

Chapter 35

There was only one way for us to go, one crooked passageway leading from the edge of the pool into the darkness, and that was the path we took. Like some crazed gazelle, Wren scrambled over the rocks and leaped over a stream that trickled at our feet. I tried my best to keep up, but it was so dark. How could we possibly find the way out? Wren had never actually been inside the mine until now, and she'd only heard stories passed down through the generations of someone else's family about a possible way out. And stories that old never told the whole truth, did they?

That's what Dixie had said.

And still I couldn't fathom it, the story she'd told us.

Could a town really murder dozens of women and children—*offer* them to a little girl who'd died long before—and think that act brought them blessings and wealth and immunity from the world's ills? Could a group of educated, reasonably sane people actually believe that the dead girl, Juliana, actually had the power to determine whether they succeeded as a town or failed? It was like these people were stuck in a time warp and were practicing a form of ancient paganism.

Their very own twisted religion.

Suddenly, I saw a dim white oval before me. Wren's face. "Billie," she hissed. "Can you see me?"

"Yes."

"Grab my shirt."

Holding onto her shirt, I followed her through the shifting wet, black shadows that reflected light off the wet rock walls. She switched her phone light on, and I saw we were standing in a small opening, almost like a room. The cavern wall opposite us was split by a wide crack that stretched from top to bottom. The crack was narrow, maybe too narrow for an actual human body, which made me wonder if any person, even a small girl, had traveled through it successfully.

"Seriously?" I asked.

"Seriously." She took hold of my shoulder and turned me sideways, then pushed me into the crack. Another boom shook the cavern. I jumped, wedging myself deeper into the crevice. Why were they setting off more explosives? In the tight space, I could just barely turn my head, and when I did, I saw Wren had not followed me, but had stayed behind in the small cavern-room.

It took me a second to understand what I was seeing. She was crouched against a rock, her head thrown back, mouth wide open. The light of her phone showed a dark stain spreading over her thigh at an alarming rate, and she was wincing in pain. I couldn't see anything behind her. The explosion had actually been gunfire. Someone had shot her.

I wiggled back through the crevice to her and grabbed her wrist, pulling her. "Stand up. Wren! We have to keep going."

"Billie . . ." a voice called softly from the darkness. It was a warning. A promise. "Don't make me do it."

Jamie. I couldn't see him on the other side of the rock, in the shadows of the cavern, but I knew it was him.

I held Wren's shivering body against me. "Go ahead," I said

to the darkness. "But I hope you don't hit me instead. I'm your *intended*, right?"

Jamie said nothing, but there were no more gunshots, so I sprang to action, pulling Wren back into the passageway behind me. She whimpered, but I didn't stop. I inhaled a lungful of what might be the last breath of fresh air I enjoyed for a long time and, grasping Wren's arm, pulled us deeper into the crevice.

We moved forward along the narrow wedge of pitch black for what felt like an eternity. All I could hear was my beating heart and my breath, slow and steady, my feet doing their awkward side shuffle through the passageway, and Wren gasping behind me. There was no way Jamie could fit into this crack, but he may not have to follow us. Not if this hit a dead end. He'd just have to wait.

But the narrow path didn't end. Soon the crevice widened a few inches, and my boots began to make sucking, squelching sounds. Hope spiked when moments later, water sloshed over our feet. The next thing I knew we were ankle-, then shin-deep in dark, muddy water. The path widened and dead-ended into a small circular opening. On every side, the rock wall gently sloped up. A good sign. A really good sign.

"Wait here," I told Wren.

I looked up and, seeing light, scrambled up in a bear crawl toward it, pulling myself up on the small niches carved into the stone for my hands and feet. I went as fast as I could, my head alternately swimming and throbbing in pain. The gas was getting to me. I wanted to sleep so badly. To slide down the wall and land in a heap at the bottom and close my eyes and just sleep . . .

I heaved myself up, and at the top of the wall, tumbled over a ridge and onto level ground. A dirt floor. Dirt and the fresh smell of oxygen. Did oxygen have a smell? Maybe it was something else. Plants, trees, grass. The surface.

I pulled Wren up and we continued forward. It was lighter now, although I couldn't see the source. We were in a hallway, or at least something that looked a lot more like a hallway than a tunnel in a cave. The walls were stone and mortar, the ceiling held up by a fretwork of wooden beams. Elation surged inside me, and I was about to break into a run when I pulled up short. The way was blocked with boards that had been nailed on the other side.

I backed up a few steps and then launched a well-aimed kick at the boards. The center one shot out, flipping into the space on the other side, and I yelped in exhausted triumph. The next two took a bit more effort, but eventually they gave way, and I ducked through. Now I was in an honest-to-God basement with a set of stairs leading up to a door.

The basement of the Dalzell-Davenport house.

I breathed something between a prayer of thanks and a message to Mere to wait for me.

"We did it." Wren was beside me, but she didn't look good. She wasn't going to be upright for long from the looks of it.

I took her arm as gently as I could. "We have to get you to the hospital."

"No, no, no. You go. Find your daughter. I need to stay under the radar." She tapped out a text on her phone. To Emmaline, I guessed.

"Okay, but promise me you'll stay in touch."

"I will."

I hesitated.

"Billie. Go."

I hated to leave her, but the drive to find Mere overcame everything. I touched her arm, then headed up the stairs. In the dark hall, I stood for a second, just breathing in the scent of my house. I pulled out my phone and started to dial Alice. It was time to get the hell out of this place.

"Billie."

I dropped the phone. Major Minette stood with Mere, still in her rainbow cloud pajamas, her hair sticking up on one side from being slept on. She was barefoot, and I felt irrationally angry that no one had bothered to find her shoes. Major reached back and flipped on the lights, and I squinted in the harsh light. Mere squinted, too, and blinked in confusion and fear.

"Mere, baby." I picked up my phone, ran to her, and folded her in my arms.

"Mama, they woke me up." Her voice was froggy, so innocent and helpless, and her little body radiated heat. I held her tightly.

"Billie," Major said. "They want to see you."

I stared at him, not comprehending. "Where's Alice?"

"She's fine. She's at her house."

But the old guard knew I'd gone to Alice's house, that she'd gone with me to the Dalzell sisters' place. They probably knew she had been talking to Peter about Wren and the town's secrets. I was under no delusion that they would forgive such crimes.

"Major, you've got to tell me the truth. Is Alice okay?"

He said nothing. I couldn't tell if he didn't want to say anything in front of Mere or if he was being cagey for another reason.

"Major, did you let her go—?"

"I've got a car," he interrupted me. "I'm supposed to take you to them."

"Major, no. You don't have to do this. Any of this. You're my friend."

He looked at me, his expression full of regret. "I didn't do it. The . . . thing you saw at the lake. I swear."

I glanced at Mere. "Not here. Not now."

He nodded, understanding. "You have to give me your phone."

I handed it over to him and scooped up Mere. "Okay, baby. A few more errands tonight and then we can go to sleep."

I followed him out. The rain had stopped, and the air smelled washed clean. Sure enough, Dixie Minette's long white Cadillac was idling in the driveway—right next to Isaac Inman's car. Isaac Inman was nowhere to be seen. I covered Mere's eyes anyway and slid in the back seat. I was shaking.

But I wasn't ready to give up. Major might've let Alice slip away; there was still that possibility. And Wren was still out there, too. Injured, yes, but free. This wasn't over yet. I just couldn't let them win. I refused.

Major put the car in gear. "Buckle up, ladies."

We rolled past the shuttered shops, the empty sidewalks of the town square. The sky had a gray wash to it now, and there was a single, insistent bird trilling its morning song. Major circled the courthouse and took Minette Street, passing the bronze statue of little Juliana Minette. Her face held an expression of innocence and tenderness as she reached for the butterfly, just out of her reach. How many times had I walked or driven past it? Hundreds? Thousands? And not once had I ever dreamed the real reason the statue had been erected. Or that when Jamie Cleburne, and the other members of the old guard, saw this statue, they saw a dark goddess who demanded human sacrifice to curry her favor.

At the Baptist church, Major wheeled the Cadillac into the parking lot. "Come on, now." He opened Mere's door and helped her out. I scrambled out to follow. Major had Mere by the hand and was hurrying her into the church. My pulse had sped up, panic enveloping me. Were they going to kill us here? Because I'd refused their offer of Jamie as my new husband?

Major led us through a back door and into the white

columned, stained glass sanctuary. The air was cool, the space hushed. He had an arm around Mere, holding her close to him. She was fully awake now, eyes huge and lip trembling.

"Mama—"

I held out reassuring hands but Major held her fast so she couldn't run to me.

"It's okay, Mere," I said. "Don't worry. I'm with you."

Major nodded. "That's right, Meredith. You're okay and so is your mama. We're just going to wait until everybody gets here and then we'll all have a nice talk."

"Where's Daddy?" she asked me. She knew something was wrong. She knew we were in trouble.

"We're going to sit in here," I said, "in this church and wait for some help. And then we can talk about Daddy."

"Oh, no," she said in a small voice.

I held up a finger. "No, Mere, no. Don't cry. We're totally fine, I promise. I need you to be really brave and strong for me right now." I looked at Major, murder in my eyes. "Let her stand with me."

"She can lie down on that pew. And I'll sit right beside her." He pulled her over to the first pew, pulled off his suit jacket, and folded it for her. "Looka-there, honey. You can lay your head on my jacket just like it's a pillow." He said it like *pilla*. I wanted to scream, to fly at him and claw his eyes out.

Mere lay down, her head on Major's jacket. Major sat at her feet. He patted her leg and with his other hand, pulled a large, bone-handled knife from his trouser pocket. He gently unfolded it, the blade, toothed and gleaming, snicking neatly out. I was shaking with fear and fury and pure adrenaline. Hate coursed through me and the feeling that if I wanted to, I could kill this man with my bare hands.

He placed the knife beside him on the pew so Mere couldn't see it, but I could. "You oughta lay down, too, Billie," he commented after a few moments had passed. "They're going to be a while at the hospital. Wren Street ain't the best shot, but she did do some damage."

Mere's eyes found mine. I put my finger over my lips to telegraph to her to stay quiet. She did.

"Lay down, Billie," Major repeated. "Get some sleep. You have a big day ahead of you."

I looked up, my eyes landing on the large stained-glass window looming behind the altar. It depicted a large cross looming over the infant Jesus in the manger. The manger was flanked by three figures: Mary, Joseph, and a little girl with long brown curls, a closed-lipped smile, and a butterfly resting on her shoulder.

Chapter 36

I woke to the sun streaming into the church, splashing jewel-toned colors all over the pristine white walls. My clothes still felt damp. I sat up and looked around. Mere slept on her pew, but Major was gone, along with my phone. She and I were alone in the sanctuary. Just us, Jesus, and Juliana Minette.

At the back of the sanctuary, the double doors flew open, and the old guard swept down the aisle like some regal retinue—Mayor Dixie, her arm in a sling, Major, Toby, and finally Jamie, pushing his father, James Sr., in a wheelchair. Ox Dalzell was the only one missing. They arranged themselves at the front of the altar, and Mayor Dixie stepped forward.

"Major, sit with the girl," she commanded. Major obeyed. Mere startled awake, looking confused and scared, but Major shushed her. I wanted to go to her, to take her in my arms, but I knew from the looks on the old guard's faces they weren't going to permit it.

"Billie," said Mayor Dixie. "You've caused quite a bit of trouble, you and Wren."

I said nothing, just stared at her.

"Where is she, by the way?" Dixie asked.

"I don't know. I left her in the basement of my house."

"You know, Billie, we don't like to rush to judgment here in Juliana. We believe the best way to solve a problem is through a deliberate, measured approach. Our forefathers were always very circumspect about"—her eyes slid to Mere—"the many difficult decisions that had to be made. You may think it was a cruelty, what they did, but it was a necessity. Freedom doesn't come without a sacrifice."

You make me sick, my eyes said to Dixie. *You all do.*

Mayor Dixie smiled tightly in response. "Ox is wounded but he'll live. No small thing to gun down a founding member of this town, though. It's unwise to defy Juliana."

Mere shot me a startled look. "Mama."

I put out a hand. "I'll explain everything in a little bit, baby. Let the grown-ups talk first, okay?"

Dixie continued. "At any rate, I hope we can come to some sort of understanding, Billie. We don't want to lose you. You've come to mean so much to this community. Become such an integral part of all of that. Because of that and other reasons"— now her eyes flitted to Jamie—"we are unwilling to consider letting you go. I know it's difficult after everything that's happened—"

I clenched my jaw, glared at her. *Don't you say Peter's name. Don't you dare.*

"—but this town needs you," she went on. "And you need it. You need *us*, Billie. I know that you understand this."

I did understand it. I needed them because they held the key to my daughter's safety. They had killed my husband. They had killed Madge Beatty, Isaac Inman, and God knew who else—all in an effort to keep Juliana pristine and protected. So now they had to be desperate to keep me here . . . for Jamie. Desperate to make sure I was on board.

Desperate . . .

The word reverberated through my head.

Desperate people didn't think clearly. They didn't cover all their bases. They missed things. They left their vulnerabilities open, their greatest pride, their deepest longings unprotected. . . .

"Okay," I said. "I'll stay."

Dixie looked taken aback, and I had to admit, it gave me a little jolt of pleasure.

"We'll stay, and I'll keep the restaurant going. But you've got to do something for me."

Dixie straightened, somewhat affronted.

"I want financial compensation . . . for what you took from us. Specifically, I would like a stake."

Dixie's mouth opened. "A stake? In what?"

"The town. I want the town to deed the building where Billie's is located to me as well as the rest of the block. I want the old gold mine. All of it, in my name and Mere's, in perpetuity."

"But the mine . . . it could still be—"

"Producing? That's what I'm banking on. After I get the . . . contents of that pool inside the mine properly relocated, I plan to look into reopening it."

Her expression hardened. "It's too much."

"Is it? I'll be operating what's probably going to end up being a destination restaurant, maybe the best in all of the Southeast. Think what that'll do for Juliana. It'll be a gold mine, in addition to the actual, literal gold mine that could possibly bring in all sorts of new business."

Dixie's nostrils flared. "And you'll roll a portion of the profits back into Juliana?"

"Of course."

"And you'll stay?"

"I'll stay."

James Sr. spoke. "You'll have to make a pledge to have more children."

I turned my stony gaze to him. "For Gentle Juliana?" I didn't try to disguise the sarcasm in my voice.

James Sr. nodded. "That's right, Billie. For the town and for *her*. And you must promise they'll stay here, too. Marry and raise families of their own."

I held up a hand, feeling Mere's eyes burning through me. My daughter was smart. She knew something was wrong, just not the details of what that wrong was. "We'll discuss the details later. Do we have a deal?"

"Fine," Dixie snapped.

"We have a deal," James Sr. said.

Jamie beamed triumphantly.

"And I'd like my phone back," I added.

Dixie looked annoyed, but she gave Jamie a nod. He handed me my phone. It was dead, but I wrapped my hands around it, feeling instantly better now that it was back in my possession. Had Mom called? The history professor from UGA?

I stood. "Mere, come to me."

She trotted over to me, pressing her body against my hip. I draped a hand over her shoulder and addressed Dixie. "I want all the pertinent documents at my house tomorrow morning no later than ten A.M. Now I'm taking my daughter home."

Back at our house, the Jeep was sitting where Isaac Inman's car had been. It was gleaming in the morning sun, washed and waxed, and apparently now free of any liens. The first of the perks for agreeing to marry into the old guard. Jamie said nothing as he watched Mere and I climb out of the cab of his truck, and I was glad. I didn't know if I could've kept up this game with him, even to protect Mere. The urge to attack him, to kill him with my bare hands, was practically choking me.

Inside, I ran a bath for Mere and assured her Ramsey, who was nowhere in sight, would be home soon. I could tell she was full of questions about everything that had happened in the church but was too scared to ask.

"I'll explain everything soon," I promised her. "For now, wash your hair and have a good, long soak in the bubbles. I'm going to go make us some breakfast."

I checked the basement, but there was no sign of Wren. I came back upstairs, and I threw open windows and stuffed towels around the basement door. We were still in danger of contamination, but I figured with the main entrance of the mine now blown open, and some of the gas leaking out that way, we'd be okay for now. There wasn't much in the fridge, so I made Mere a peanut butter and jelly sandwich, sliced a carrot, and poured us both glasses of apple juice. I found a can of mixed nuts and a wedge of gouda and went to check on her progress.

After setting her up in my bed with a Disney movie and my *Joy of Cooking*, I showered, dressed in leggings and one of Peter's old sweatshirts, then went back downstairs. I needed a plan. Some way to get me and Mere out of this—and to bring the old guard to its knees. But my mind was a blank.

Peter's iPad was still on the piano, dead. I found the charger and plugged it in. When the device glowed its welcome screen, I scanned his files, the ones Edge had helped me to transfer over from Peter's work laptop. Patient after patient file was arranged in neat rows, including Alice Tilton's file and the clients he'd brought with him from his New York practice. My heart squeezed painfully in my chest. Oh, Peter. He'd been so neat and methodical, my husband. That's what he valued above all—a calm, measured approach to life. He believed everyone deserved the chance to heal from their traumas in peace. How unfair, that his last weeks had been an actual living nightmare.

That I'd allowed such evil into our lives.

A wave of grief crashed over me and for a minute, tears poured out of me. I clamped a hand over my mouth so Mere wouldn't hear the sobs rising in my throat. I couldn't breathe. How was I going to do this? How was I going to take care of my daughter and get us out of here? And then I saw it, something I hadn't noticed before back on that drunken and distraught night—another folder on the iPad screen.

It was labeled *BILLIE*.

I smeared away my tears, and I stared at it. Had it been there before? It had to have been. I just hadn't noticed it in my maniacal focus on hacking into Alice's file. I double-clicked on the folder, and it opened. Inside were several files and their names set my heart thumping and my throat dry.

Emma Jackson.

Minette Gold Mine.

And then another file that read simply *For You.*

Chapter 37

The Emma Jackson file was first.

Like Alice's files, Jackson's were all video recordings. Emma was a strikingly attractive woman with funky angular green eyeglass frames, bright pink lipstick, and brown hair she wore in a long braid over her shoulder. The session was recorded, like Alice's had been, but this was clearly no therapy session. It was more like an interview. She told the whole story of how she met and married Jamie Cleburne, but how when she moved down to Juliana, things had gotten off to a rocky start.

She thought it was sweet at first, Jamie's unwavering devotion to his father. In fact, all the younger people in town seemed to defer to the older generation in a way that was really refreshing. But then it started to feel off to her. No one traveled unless they had to for work; everybody seemed perfectly content, even preferred to hang out in Juliana all year round.

Emma had brought her dog with her from D.C., a scrappy little Jack Russell who, wild with his newfound freedom in the country took to breaking out of his electric fence enclosure and running all over the town. One day, he was picked up on the road next to the Dalzell-Davenport property. He was a filthy, matted, snarling mass and had attacked the man who rescued him—almost like the poor thing had a case of rabies—and they'd had to put the dog down. It had pushed Emma over the edge and started the unraveling of her and Jamie's marriage.

"That town is fucked up," Emma told Peter. "The founding families don't pay for anything; they barter. They do deals with each other for everything. I don't even think any of them pay property taxes. The county commissioner may not be one of the three main families, but he's one of the originals. And if you're a Tilton or a St. John or a Childers, Calhoun, Street . . . you do whatever the old guard tells you to do.

"But it's more than that. My dog was sick. Like he was possessed or something. It's like they're all possessed. Or obsessed. There's something in the air. Or the water. Literally, I think."

Then Emma Jackson had taken off her glasses and leaning forward, had pointed at the camera. "I'm telling you, you and your wife should get out of there, Dr. Hope. I don't know what it is but there's something really bad going on in that town."

I clicked through the other files. The Minette Gold Mine one was basically a collection of archived papers and old newspaper entries about the 1832 Georgia land lottery in which Alfred Minette had been awarded forty acres, part of it right where the Dalzell-Davenport house stood now. Peter had obviously been piecing the mystery together long before I was, connecting dots in his typical calm, well-thought-out, methodical way.

I clicked on the last document, the video file labeled *For You.* Peter, my husband, the man I'd loved for almost thirteen years, appeared before me in his office, kicked back in his creaky old office chair. He wore a wrinkled white button-down and jeans. Brown hair tousled, tortoiseshell glasses, and freckled skin. The sight of him sent a lightning bolt of sharp, searing pain through my entire body. I touched the screen, as if somehow I could touch him.

Onscreen Peter cleared his throat. "Hi, Billie, it's me.

Obviously. There's a lot I have to say, so you should probably grab a paper and pen. You're going to want to take notes.

"I've been doing some research," Peter said, looking directly into the camera. Directly at me. "That's all I've been doing, as I'm sure you've noticed. You can always sense when we're disconnected, Billie. When I'm not fully present. I may be the therapist, but you've always been more in tune in that area."

I swallowed back the threatening tears.

"I've called every history expert I could find," Peter went on. "And they all say the same thing. There was no official record of a gold mine in Juliana, Georgia. There's a public record that Alfred Minette won a lottery for forty acres, on which he established the town of Juliana, but the official story is that he never found any gold. He built a mill."

Peter went on to tell me he'd come to believe that there was no well, uncapped or otherwise, on the property. It had all been a ruse to keep us from finding the gold mine. Alice Tilton had confirmed its existence. Also, his sleeplessness, our nightmares, and Ramsey's odd behavior pointed to poisoning from leakage from the mine. He suspected Doc Belmont of purposefully misplacing his labs. And he worried we were being watched. He had somehow managed to track down Wren Street and they'd compared stories. Compared nightmares.

Something was terribly wrong in Juliana, he said, and we were at the very center of it.

He leaned toward the screen, his expression serious. "I'm worried I've made myself—that I've made all of us a target. If you're watching this . . . I'm guessing something has happened to me. If that's the case, I need you to listen to me carefully."

I sat very still.

His voice lowered to a growl. "Run, Billie. Take Mere and get the hell out of this place. These families have killed people, and I have no doubt they'll do it again. There's no use trying to prove it or trying to hold them accountable. Murder is a state crime, not a federal one, and from everything I've found, local and state law enforcement takes orders from the three families as well. I wouldn't be surprised if the State Attorney General is a fucking St. John or Calhoun."

He was right about that.

"Just get out, Billie—get yourself and Mere to someplace safe and start a new life. And one more thing . . ." He hesitated and I did, too, waiting for him to speak.

Just say it, Peter. Tell me it's my fault.

"I don't blame you for moving us here," he said, as if in reply to what I'd just thought. Like we were still connected by a cord that hadn't been broken, even by my betrayal. Even by his death. My throat felt tight, my eyes burned with tears.

"I don't blame you for any of it. Sometimes you do what you do to survive. To live. I know after you lost your restaurant, you lost your mom, that moving away from New York was what you had to do. It was a cruelty, what happened to you, and I didn't see how much it hurt you. I didn't see how much you were suffering and keeping it inside.

"I've been a bad husband, Billie. I've failed you and Mere, and I'm ashamed of how badly I've handled all this. I'm sorry. I'm so sorry for everything, and I just wanted to tell you . . . I *love* you, Billie. So fucking much." His voice broke. "I will always love you—you and Mere—I will always love our life more than anything. Don't ever forget that. Don't ever believe anything different."

I let the tears go and, as if somehow it would get me closer to Peter, pressed my hands onto the iPad screen.

I cleaned the kitchen, then absently sifted through the pile of mail stacked on the counter. I hadn't gone through it in weeks, and it was in danger of creating an avalanche. As I was sorting, one caught my eye—a bill from the Bartow County Tax Commissioner.

Shit. I'd totally forgotten about our county property tax.

I opened the envelope and eyed the balance due amount. It was almost three thousand dollars—an amount I'd known was coming due on the house and twelve acres we'd gotten for a song but hadn't thought of in weeks. And then I noticed the return address. Bartow County's Tax Commissioner, someone named Lemmy Street. One of Lilah's many cousins, no doubt.

Emma Jackson's words echoed in my brain. *I don't even think any of them pay property taxes.* And then Major's: *You know there ain't no property taxes around here. Not if you know the right people.* Then Peter's: *Murder is a state crime, not a federal one. . . .*

And suddenly I had it. Our way out of Juliana.

Chapter 38

The following week, Ramsey, filthy, fiery-eyed, and apparently full of hard-won, worldly wisdom, came waltzing back home.

It was a lucky break that I even saw him. The old guard had insisted Mere and I go back to Jamie's cabin—to keep me from running, the unspoken reason—and there was rarely a moment we were left alone. I had finally convinced Jamie to let me drop by the house to pick up some of Mere's school clothes, and when I saw Ramsey's scrawny body perched by the door, it felt like a good omen.

Something I was in dire need of.

By then, everything was in order, my plan ready to execute. Well, actually mine and Wren's plan. After I'd left her, she'd managed to slip out of Juliana and gotten herself down to Atlanta where a friend got her medical help. While she was recuperating from a nasty bullet hole in her right thigh, we'd stayed in contact on a messaging app. I'd finally heard from the professor at Georgia, too, about the gold mine's existence and rumored grisly past, the last puzzle piece and confirmation that this nightmare was real.

Alice Tilton had disappeared, maybe thanks to Major, but I had no way of knowing. No one in town seemed to think it was out of the ordinary, and her class, including Mere and Temperance, were assigned to other teachers. I hoped she was safe. I also hoped she knew how much her courage and friendship meant to me.

At the Dalzell-Davenport house, I put Ramsey in my Jeep and drove him and the box of Mere's clothes back to Jamie's cabin. I had agreed to marry Jamie in late September. A wedding at the Cleburne farm, beside the lake where my husband's body had been stashed. Where it still was, for all I knew. Jamie had seemed thrilled at the prospect. I assumed he thought it was romantic.

I had asked Jamie to allow me to sleep in my own room while I tried to figure out what to tell Mere. I said it was the least he could do, give me the time I needed, and he agreed. With Mere, I had been sticking with the Peter-still-being-away-on-business story, but it had begun to feel like she could see right through the lie. When I told her we couldn't call him because "he's just super busy, babe," she'd just stare at me with a terrifyingly cold look in her eye. Jamie, on the other hand, watched me in an entirely different way, like I was a piece of meat, and he was a starving man.

"I only want you to be with me because you want it," he said the night we moved into his cabin, after he'd helped me unpacked my things in the guest room next to Mere's. He pressed an agonizingly long kiss to my forehead as we stood at the foot of the bed. "When it happens, it's going to be so good."

I sent him a coy smile, perfectly calibrated to make him think I was just as tempted as he was. And then my phone whistled. An alert from Wren. I froze, my heart banging in my chest.

"Somebody texting you?" he asked.

I put a hand on his arm. "Scheduling app for the restaurant. Cam sends me an alert when we're short on staff."

He put his hand over mine, trapping it against him. "I like it when you touch me."

It took every ounce of strength in me not to snatch my hand away. "Soon, Jamie. I promise." His eyes shone with sexual excitement as I moved to the door of my bedroom. "Good night," I whispered and shut the door.

My hand trembling, I locked the door, then checked my phone.

Good news. Got a call with lawyer set up for tomorrow at noon.

I typed my reply. **Perfect. Talk then.**

I switched off the notifications on the app, sat on the bed, and let out a long, shaky breath.

Things were humming along at Billie's. We were doing bigger numbers than ever, and with the exception of Major, the rest of the staff showed up every day and worked like normal. Then again, as far as they were concerned, everything was normal. The dirty business of Juliana was a purely underground operation run by its three elite families. The average citizen was blithely unaware.

Our regulars continued to stop in—Agnes Childers, Max St. John, Ray and Darlene Calhoun, and of course, Lilah. Even Ox Dalzell returned, now out of the hospital and using a cane, as a result of the supposed self-inflicted gunshot wound to his femur that he sustained while cleaning his pistol. He was occasionally accompanied by his strangely mute, obedient daughters, all of whom pretended they didn't know me.

There was a brief mention of Isaac Inman's murder on the local Atlanta news—it was believed he'd been stabbed to death by some meth addict who was passing through the area—but the investigation had apparently hit a dead end. It was surreal. Living in this bubble of a town where real crimes—murders, even—weren't reported or investigated. They were just buried. Like Peter, in James Cleburne's lake.

Thanks to the Initiative, new families continued to move to Juliana every day. They showed up in my restaurant, eyes bright and hopes high, naively thinking they'd found paradise in the charming little town of Juliana. But those dreams would be dashed if my plan didn't succeed. It was this thought that drove me the hardest. It was the thing that kept me up at night. That haunted me more than anything.

If I didn't stop the old guard, someone else was going to die.

It was a bright Sunday morning in mid-August, the day before school was to start. The cloudless sky promised the day would be hot as hell. From eight to ten, business was constant but slow. As soon as the churches let out, though—around twelve-thirty—I knew we were going to be slammed.

I had almost the entire staff working that day. Even Mere was sitting at the bar, coloring. I was flitting from the kitchen to the bar to the tables, barely able to keep my nervous hands steady. I ended up rolling silverware in an unobtrusive corner behind the barista station. The robotic action was soothing, not to mention allowed me a view out the window so I could see who was coming up the sidewalk before they reached the door.

By eleven, there was an hour wait, people milling around on the sidewalks and congregating around the benches Mayor Dixie had finally, reluctantly, installed across the street on the square. One by one, I watched as the regulars trickled in and Finch sat them at their preferred post-church brunch tables. Ox Dalzell and his daughters at table thirteen. Agnes Childers and one of her many nieces at fourteen. Lilah and Temperance Street sat at sixteen, and Dixie, Major, and Toby Minette, along with Ronnie Coleman, at my four-top, twenty-one. The Calhouns, who always preferred the bar, were already ensconced there, working their way through a pitcher of mimosas. Jamie and his dad were at our largest table in the back corner, joined by Doc Belmont St. John and Max, his grandson.

Right around the time the Bloody Marys, mimosas, and bellinis were flowing, I slipped into the kitchen. Falcon and his team were jamming at their stations, a well-oiled piece of machinery that sent a twinge of melancholy through me. When the dust settled from what I'd set in motion, I might have to completely start over. It was a damn shame. But I'd started over before. And if there was one thing moving to Juliana had taught me, I'd do anything for my daughter. Starting from scratch was nothing.

Back out in the front of house, the servers were huddled around the barista station.

"Weird vibe today," I heard one of them say in a low voice.

"Super weird," came the answer. "Not a fan."

"Okay, guys," I clasped my hands under my chin and gave them an energetic smile. "Let's get these plates moving."

Through the window, I checked the square across the street. One gentleman in particular stood out, fully dressed as he was in a dark suit, tie, and aviator sunglasses. Unlike all the other people milling around waiting for their names to be called, he wasn't scrolling his phone or chatting. He was sitting very still, watching the entrance of the restaurant. Beside him sat a young woman, also in a dark pantsuit, also in sunglasses. I noticed around the corner two sheriff's vehicles had pulled up. It was time.

Tossing a furtive glance over at the tables, I pushed through the front door and stepped out into the sunshine. The window boxes that lined the restaurant were bursting with lush, cherry-red geraniums. I picked a handful and went back inside. I walked slowly through the restaurant, from table to table—the Dalzells, Childers, Streets, Minettes, and finally the Cleburnes—dropping a single geranium into each empty vase. As I did, each of them sent me indulgent smiles.

Yeah, we're one big, happy family, aren't we? Flowers for everyone.

As I dropped the last bloom in the vase next to Darlene

Calhoun's water glass, the man and woman in the dark suits who'd been waiting outside entered the restaurant. They were trailed by Sheriff Childers, who was looking fairly green around the gills, as well as three deputies. They lined up beside me, allowing me the one courtesy I'd requested—the chance to address my customers directly.

"Can I have your attention, everybody?" I said, trying to ignore the way sweat had sprung out along my hairline and was now pouring down my back. I waved Mere over, and she slipped off her stool and walked to my side, taking my hand. I squeezed it tight.

The restaurant stilled as each face at every table turned toward me.

I willed my voice not to shake. "I apologize for interrupting your brunch, but we have some special guests here today. Cherokee District Attorney Clint Evans and Assistant DA Dorinda Lopez. They are criminal prosecutors for Bartow and Gordon Counties."

A murmur rippled through the restaurant.

"They have some business to attend to here today—"

The door swung open again, revealing Wren Street. Pale, but upright, her black hair grown out just enough so it covered her head like a cap. She wore a tie-dyed maxi skirt and a T-shirt with the Mona Lisa on it and leaned on a cane. There was a discernible rustle as everyone turned toward the front of the restaurant, and then the room fell silent. From behind me I heard a shriek, then Lilah rushed past me. She took her daughter in her arms, weeping and smothering her with kisses right before Temperance hit them like she'd been shot out of a cannon.

"Mama!" the little girl cried and clung to Wren.

No one else in the place uttered a word. I found Jamie's face at the back of the restaurant. He looked momentarily thrown; then his face settled into a grimace, like he had some kind of pain in his gut.

I turned to the Street family, still tangled in an awkward embrace. "Lilah, why don't you have Wren join you at your table?" I grinned at Wren. "Diet Dr. Pepper?"

Wren nodded. "Thanks."

Lilah, barely able to contain herself, somehow got Wren and Temperance back to their table.

I turned to the crowd. "As I was saying, if you all will just sit tight and let our special guests do their thing, when they're finished, dessert is on the house."

One of the deputies stepped up to table twenty-one, where Mayor Dixie and her brother-in-law sat, and announced in a loud, clear voice, "Mayor Dixie Minette? Toby Minette?"

All over the room jaws dropped, as a shock wave of incredulity mixed with alarm rippled through the air. The atmosphere crackled with electricity. I felt like my whole body was on fire. Like I could run up a mountain or rip out the bolted-down bar with my bare hands.

Mayor Dixie stood, her face a study of shock, confusion, and fury. Toby followed suit. Major and Ronnie Coleman along with everyone else in the place watched in bewilderment.

"Mayor Dixie Minette," the deputy said in a monotone voice. "Toby Minette. Put your hands behind your back."

Dixie didn't move. Neither did Toby. They both glared at Sheriff Childers.

The man in the suit, District Attorney Clint Evans, addressed Mayor Dixie. "Mrs. Minette, you are under arrest under Georgia Code Title 48, Chapter 1-6 'Unlawful filing of false documents; omissions; tax evasion—'"

"What?" Dixie snapped, mortally offended. "I don't know what that is." She addressed the sheriff. "Frank, an explanation, if you please?"

"Allow me," I stepped closer. "Title 48, Mayor Dixie, is what they charge you with when you've bribed a government official, in this case a county tax commissioner, to waive your property taxes for the last, oh, three decades."

Out of the corner of my eye, I saw Jamie rise slowly from his seat.

ADA Dorinda Lopez turned to the restaurant and announced in an authoritative voice, "We request that anyone with a red geranium on their table stay seated at this time."

Jamie sat back down with a thunk, his eyes murderously fastened on me.

"Just about everyone here today who owns a home in Juliana has been ducking their property taxes for decades," I announced to the stunned room as the two Federal agents and the deputies continued their business, going from table to table, cuffing people, and marching them out the door to a waiting van. "Dodging upward of a million dollars. The families you trusted to lead you, to keep Juliana safe and healthy and thriving, shirked their duty to pay what they rightfully owed—letting the rest of you shoulder the lion's share of the county's budget. The crime is a misdemeanor but can result in up to twelve months in jail, fines, and restitution, which I'm guessing may wipe many of them out financially since they've been doing this for decades."

DA Evans turned to Sheriff Childers who was standing just behind him. "You're next, sir."

Childers' face went slack, his eyes hard as flint. "You put those cuffs on me, son, and I'll wallop you," he said and, hitching his pants, marched out of the restaurant, one of the deputies trotting after him.

All around me, I could hear the sound of the other two deputies reading the charges and the subsequent soft *chink* of the handcuffs. Ox Dalzell limped out, fully cuffed, leaving his daughters sitting in stunned silence at their table, then Ray and Darlene Calhoun. Even old Agnes Childers went, leaving her bewildered niece. As they marched Lilah Street past us, I stopped her.

"I'm so sorry, Lilah. I asked them not to include you."

She regarded me with eyes full of love. Full of pain. "You gave me back my daughter. This"—she glanced down at the cuffs—"this was my mistake."

They led her out, and Mere took my hand and huddled closer to me. I saw, at the back of the restaurant, that Jamie was finally up, offering his wrists to the deputy standing before him. As he was led past me, he stopped and turned to face me. His chin jutted in haughty defiance, his eyes cold and dead. He appraised me, slowly, with loathing. But if I could've breathed fire like a medieval dragon and reduced him to ashes in return, I would have.

"You're a liar," he said.

"We do what we have to."

His upper lip curled, and I could've sworn he bared his teeth at me.

But I wasn't going to let him go that easily. "But if you want the truth, here it is. This is just the tip of the iceberg for you, Jamie. The beginning of your nightmare. The Feds are looking at you and your father, the Minettes, and Ox for felony murder, federal tax evasion, bribery, kidnapping, wire fraud, witness intimidation, witness tampering, obstruction of justice, and every kind of fraud wrapped up in your Initiative program. There's lots more to come for you."

He shook his head and looked away from me, a smile twisting his lips.

"You tried to destroy my family," I said, "but you failed, and now I'm taking everything you hold dear. Your shop, your home. Your *town*. It's mine now. Mine." I turned to my daughter. I was shaking with fury and relief . . . and who knows, maybe the carbon monoxide that was still pouring out of the Minette gold mine. "Mere?"

Without me saying a word, she knew what I wanted and ripped the gold bracelet off her wrist, holding it out to Jamie.

He ignored it, and she dropped it on the ground. I told her to go back to the bar.

"She won't forget," he growled at me, a glint of unbridled insanity in his eyes. "You've angered her, and she won't let you get away with it."

The sheer fanatic zeal in his eyes sent a cold chill through me. *She.* He meant Juliana Minette. He truly believed in a dead girl, who protected this town from beyond the grave with her magical powers. It was so hard to wrap my head around. I was staring right in the face of pure, unhinged lunacy.

The deputy gave him a push and then they were all gone, leaving only a smattering of customers and the staff behind, looking shell-shocked. Falcon and the rest of the back of the house had come out and were staring at the now mostly empty tables, all of them still bearing their single, red geranium.

I turned once more to address the people left. "I have a new thing I whipped up that I'd love for y'all to try," I said. "It's peaches and fresh mint and crème fraiche. Not sure what I'm going to call it, but for now, we're going to go with 'Just Desserts.'"

Someone whistled, long and low. Somebody else let out a wry chuckle. As I walked back toward the kitchen, my heart still beating fast, my mouth dry as dust, everyone started to clap.

Chapter 39

As interim mayor of Juliana—appointed by the remaining members of the town council after Dixie's arrest—my first official action was the removal of the bronze statue of Juliana Minette from the town square.

The event took place on a clear September morning. As the entire town gathered around, a giant crane ripped the thing off the marble pedestal, lifted and swung it around, and lowered it onto a flatbed truck. It would be hauled off to a recycling company to be melted down for scrap. The monument pedestal, a big square block of red marble that sat in the center of the fountain, was destined for the county dump. There had been a vote held whether to replace the monument with some other one, but with a resounding no, Juliana decided that the town would have no monument. We would look only to ourselves. Believe only in the strength of our commitment to one another.

Worship was for imaginary gods.

Love was for neighbors.

I also presided over the auction of all the properties in Juliana that had become available when a majority of its citizens were thrown in the slammer. Dixie Minette's Pepto-pink Victorian went to the Slaters, a family of six from Arizona. Ox Dalzell's green Italianate was sold to a couple from Texas, Rafe and Miguel, who opened a bed-and-breakfast. The Cleburne farm was sold to a Braves outfielder, an avid hunter and fisher, who planned to retire there. I held Alice Tilton's house back, just in case she decided to return. I would understand if she didn't come back. I fully believe the old guard wanted Major to kill her because she knew too much. All I know is if Alice doesn't come back to Juliana, I think I'm going to turn her house into a bookstore. Every town needs a bookstore.

I moved out of the Dalzell-Davenport house and am working with a mining company out of California to investigate the gas leak and restart operations. I purchased fifty acres north of town and designed—along with an architect, an incredibly talented woman who moved here from San Francisco—a simple, modern farmhouse with a wraparound porch and a pool in the back. It's a place where I can experiment with foraging wild plants to use in new recipes. Where Mere and Ramsey—and Jamie's dog Ever, who's come to live with us—can ramble as far and wide as they want.

Mom and Edge have been down to visit a few times. I think they're dating or married or common-law. They do seem to be losing interest in The Gathering and have met with a real estate agent down here. I'd love to have them here, to start strengthening those family bonds I thought had snapped so easily during the pandemic. To see Mom, sitting at one of Billie's tables, waiting to share a plate of French toast with me. Ready to talk about anything and everything. We'll see.

Telling Mere about Peter was the worst of the aftermath by far. Without a doubt, the worst thing I've ever had to do in my life. I found her a therapist, a young woman who moved down from New Jersey. She and I visit Peter's grave every day, out near Acworth, about a half an hour's drive from our new home.

I used to apologize to him every day, until I realized I was wasting my time. Peter doesn't need my apologies. He knew everything, even before I did, and tried to put it all together for me. He was my guardian angel. After a while, I quit apologizing and started bringing sea salt dark chocolate squares. Every time I go, I leave one on his headstone.

In late winter, the entire Minette family—Dixie, Major, and Toby—as well as Ox Dalzell and James Cleburne Sr. were convicted on a laundry list of federal charges and sent to a variety of high-security penitentiaries around the country. The so-called "offerings"—coldblooded murders—had apparently been going on for decades, and there were remains to be recovered, mostly from the mill property, which they'd basically turned into a graveyard. There were families to be contacted as well, missing persons cases to be closed, and finally news to be announced to the citizens of Juliana. It was a grueling process, this macabre accounting for all the sins of the past, but I refused to skim over the facts. For Juliana to heal, its citizens had to face the truth.

I was drinking my morning coffee on my newly constructed back porch when I read the news that Jamie Cleburne was charged with three murders—Peter, Madge Beatty, and Isaac Inman's—and was given multiple concurrent life sentences. I promptly vomited into a pile of sand that the bricklayers had dumped. I wiped my mouth, then shoveled out the offending lump and carried it over to the dumpster. For me, that was the end of Jamie.

I haven't seen Alice Tilton since that night. I don't know where she went, and so far, she hasn't reached out. I wish I could see her, if only to thank her for how she helped me and Mere, but I understand why she stays away. I wish her well. I miss her.

I fully expect most of Juliana's families to return to town after they've served their brief tax evasion sentences, and I plan to welcome them back. Like Lilah Street, they weren't aware of the horrific things the old guard was involved in, so I cannot lay blame on them. But I do think they bear some responsibility. Their need to turn a blind eye to anything that looked remotely amiss created the right conditions for the old guard to wreak their havoc. The people of Juliana so desperately needed for their lives to go on as usual, to remain untouched by darkness or any trouble, that they failed to hold those who were leading them accountable. They let the power of their leaders go unchecked and paid the ultimate price. They won't make that mistake again.

As for the old guard, I will never be able to explain how otherwise reasonable, educated men and women could be persuaded to believe that a child, dead for nearly two hundred years, held the power of health, wealth, and success in her hands. But we humans are frail, superstitious things. We long for something to fasten our hope on. Something unshakable to keep us tethered to the ground. And I guess it's not the craziest thing a group of people has ever chosen to believe in.

And I include myself.

Down in the mine, the few items that the murdered women and children tucked into the rock crevices were salvaged and sent to Professor Argotte at the university for cataloging and archiving. They included scraps of lace, ribbons, and buttons. Wisps of hair. Scraps of paper with names written on them. The names of the dead, demanding to be remembered.

The results came back from the lab, and while there was a bit of carbon monoxide seepage in the mine, I was informed the levels were low. *Negligible* was the word. Not enough, they said, to cause the hand tremors the citizens of Juliana suffered. To turn a cat wild or a creek, rusty red.

So, yes, I suppose I'm as superstitious as anyone else. In the end, I can't deny what I experienced. I saw those women and children. I heard their music and the curses they pronounced. It may defy logic, but I believe they were real. They were the voices of the dead calling through time and space for justice.

And we gave it to them. We gave all of those souls justice.

It was a difficult decision, whether to stay in Juliana or leave, but Mere and I made it together. "Juliana's our town now," she said when I asked her one morning if she missed New York. "Don't you think, Mom?"

I did. For better or worse, Juliana did feel like our town. And with the old guard gone, the town felt like a ship without a rudder. I knew I wasn't obligated to be captain of that ship, but I couldn't deny its pull. After everything we'd been through, I couldn't just walk off into the sunset. I wanted to stay and see the town recover and thrive. For my family and for every person who loved this place.

Gentle Juliana, My Forever Home.

So now it's become my life's mission to protect this little town in Georgia. To keep Juliana safe and healthy, free and fair, for me and my daughter and anyone else who comes seeking shelter and a place to rest from the turmoil of life. If they come, when they come, they will find Juliana's arms flung wide with welcome. They will find a family. They will find home.

ACKNOWLEGMENTS

In the summer of 2021, hemmed in by the four walls of my house and grappling for a new direction in my writing career, I asked a friend if she had a job for me at her restaurant, a local breakfast-brunch-lunch eatery that had recently reopened after the lockdown. She said yes, as a matter of fact, she could use a host. In spite of my having zero experience in the service industry, I started a part-time job there.

The experience was a challenge but also a complete godsend. Working with the delightful group of young people employed at Fellows Café in Roswell, Georgia, gave me the psychological second wind I was desperately in need of. The surprising twist? I ended up making friends I will cherish for life. Some of their names (and those of their cat's—thanks, Nick) are sprinkled throughout this book.

When I first came up with the idea for *Gothictown*, Billie was not a restaurant owner. But working at my new job, I quickly realized it was the right business for her. I was seeing firsthand what a number the pandemic did on these establishments and how they truly unite the members of a community, so it was a perfect fit for the character. I owe a huge thanks to Christina and Tony DeVictor for giving me the opportunity, showing me the ropes, and letting me cry some. They run a magical establishment. Billie's is similar to Fellows in a lot of ways but, in the interest of narrative brevity, I glossed over the amount of hard work it actually takes to run a café. Any mistakes I made are purely mine.

Thanks also to my terrific, tirelessly positive agent, Samantha Fabien, Gabrielle Greenstein, and the rest of Root Literary; Becca Rodriguez; and Beth Moore. Elizabeth Trout, you are every writer's dream editor. Thanks also to the whole team at Kensington: Steve Zacharius, Adam Zacharius, Jackie Dinas,

Lynn Cully, Susanna Grüninger, Lauren Jernigan, Alexandra Nicolajsen, Vida Engstrand. Megan Beatie, you're a force!

Thank you to Camille Pagán for the new mindset, to Catherine McKenzie for advocating on my behalf, and to Shannon Kirk for believing. Early readers Manda Turetsky, Kimberly Brock, and Kimberly Belle have been a continual support. The Low-Tier Girlies, a gift. Thanks to my dad and to my writer sis, Katy, for her encouragement and support.

Rick, Noah, Madi, Alex, Haley, and Everett—I love y'all!

AUTHOR'S NOTE

As I was creating the fictional history of Juliana for this story, I drew from my own town's real history, which has haunted me since I first learned about it. Roswell, Georgia, was founded in the 1830s by a man named Roswell King. He built two cotton mills on the banks of Vickery Creek, a branch of the Chattahoochee River. Roswell is now a suburb of Atlanta, but it still retains its historical flavor in the form of a quaint square, King's lavish house, and the remains of one of his mills where people hold weddings and corporate events.

During the Civil War, Roswell distinguished itself among the many unlucky towns targeted by General William T. Sherman in his infamous March to the Sea, for being a possible spot for his troops to cross the Chattahoochee River. The first to scout the town with his four thousand cavalry unit, Brigadier General Kenner Garrard discovered in Roswell an excellent crossing point on the river at the aptly and still currently named "Shallowford."

He also discovered the town's cotton and wool mills (three by this point). In the absence of men who were all away fighting, the mills were operated by women and children: churning out sheeting, tent cloth, rope, and uniform cloth. In a failed ruse to claim neutrality, the mills were operating under the banner of a French flag, but Garrard wasn't fooled. Nor was Sherman. The general ordered his man to burn the mills and hang the superintendent. To arrest and charge the millworkers with treason. "The women will howl," Sherman wrote in his letter to the brigadier general, and the approximately four hundred women and children were then marched to nearby Marietta and shipped via train to Kentucky and Indiana.

Historians (most amateur hobbyists) have discovered what they believe happened to a handful of these women and children. Some died of disease and malnutrition, others found work at mills up in Indiana, some remarried and started new families. A few were tracked down by their husbands, who returned home after the war, and brought back to Georgia. Many were never found.

To be clear, there is no denying the Confederacy was a treasonous, criminal entity, rebelling against the union in an effort to maintain the institution of slavery, so it is a tricky proposition to feel sympathy for its citizens. Whether or not these particular women were pro- or anti-successionists (and data suggests there were very few citizens of the South who were against succession), ripping them and their children from their homes, making refugees of them, was not the humanitarian choice. However, knowing these families were on the wrong side of history doesn't lessen the pain and heartbreak these women endured.

Stories allow us to wrestle with our darker desires so we can access our humanity in real life. I let my ghosts get their revenge, but I know real life is more complicated than that. I have a small hope that, along with being a good time, this book is a path to that humanity.

GOTHICTOWN

Emily Carpenter

ABOUT THIS GUIDE

The suggested questions are included to enhance
your group's reading of Emily Carpenter's *Gothictown*

Discussion Questions

1. At the opening of the book, Billie has lost her restaurant and her mother. Discuss the impact of these losses and how they set her up to fall for Juliana, Georgia's charms.

2. Both Billie and Peter, while essentially good people, are deeply flawed and engage in questionable behavior in the book. How do their mistakes and the resulting shame and regret leave them vulnerable to the forces of evil in Juliana?

3. In addition to being a required element of appeasing Juliana, the "offerings" always benefit the old guard in some tangible way. Do you think the old guard are true believers or do they just like being able to get away with murder? Why do you think it was so easy for the old guard to get away with murders through the years? What does this say about how certain people are valued in society?

4. Juliana doesn't have a bookstore. Why do you think the author included that detail? What do you think that says about a town?

5. The Southern Gothic genre deals with the sins of the past in the American South and typically includes eccentric characters, derelict settings, sinister or ghostly events, as well as crime and violence. What elements of the book would you say fit this genre?

6. Have you ever wanted to start completely over in a new town, new life, and new job? What is the universal allure in that idea?

7. How are the concepts of belonging and family explored in this book?

8. The women and children who died in the mine seem to have ghostly presences that demand justice. Do you believe in paranormal beings? Or that the living have the ability to communicate with the dead?

9. Do you agree with Billie's decision to stay in Juliana and act as its mayor rather than leave? Would you have done that? What do you think would happen to Billie and Meredith in a sequel?

10. Who would you cast as Billie, Peter, and Jamie in a TV show or movie?